THE ETERNAL ROSE

Books by Gail Dayton

The Rose Trilogy
The Compass Rose
The Barbed Rose
The Eternal Rose

Other Books
Her Convenient Millionaire
Hide-and-Sheikh

THE ETERNAL ROSE

Gail Dayton

JUNO

THE ETERNAL ROSE

ISBN-13: 978-0-8095-7165-9
ISBN-10: 0-8095-7165-X
Library of Congress Control Number: 2007928882

Juno Books
Rockville, MD
www.juno-books.com

info@juno-books.com

To Jared in the U.S. Army;
his brother, Chad, in the U.S. Navy;
and their sister, Lindi, in the U.S. Air Force.
Thanks guys, and take care of yourselves.

Also a big, BIG "thank you" to
Catie in Ireland and Sarah in College Station
for pitching this book to Juno for me.
I scarcely had to lift a finger. You're the best.

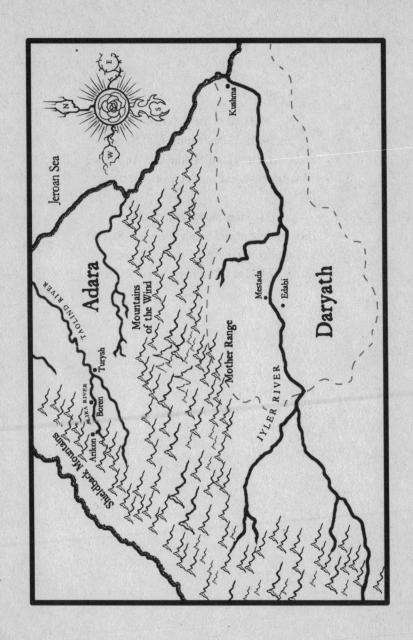

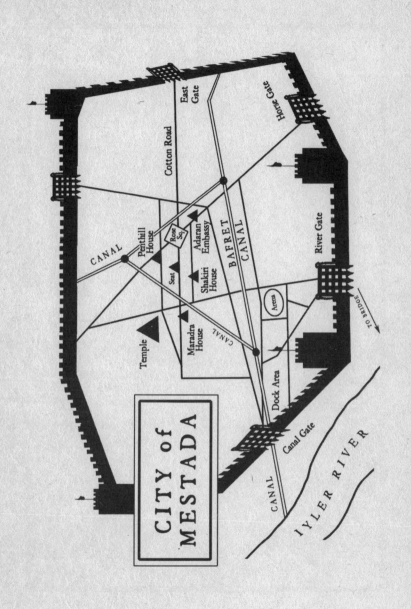

CITY of MESTADA

East Gate

Horse Gate

Cotton Road

Penthill House

Rose Sq.

Adaran Embassy

CANAL

Seat

Shakiri House

BAFRET CANAL

River Gate

Arena

Temple

Maradra House

CANAL

Dock Area

Canal Gate

TO BRIDGE

CANAL

IYLER RIVER

Chapter One

The air tasted wrong.

Not like yestereve's fish course lingering beyond its welcome, nor like the stinks of backed-up palace plumbing. Nothing so simple, so ordinary, could taste so wrong. She hesitated, breaking the rhythm of her stride to sample the air more carefully, and her entourage stumbled into confusion around her.

"What is it, my Reinine?" one of them asked.

After six years, she had finally got past the urge to look around to find whom the courtiers addressed, had finally grasped the idea they were talking to *her*. To Kallista Varyl, Godstruck Naitan of the One, Ruler of all Adara from the Devil's Neck and the Jeroan Sea in the north to the Mountains of the Wind in the south, from Dostu prinsipality far to the east to Emtai in the west. *She* was Kallista Reinine.

She still didn't *feel* like a Reinine, but she'd become fairly adept at pretending. And after six years the court had mostly stopped saying things like "but Serysta Reinine always—" or "a Reinine must never—" They had learned that Kallista Reinine had her own way of doing things.

"Kallista?"

Her name, the touch on her elbow, brought her out of her thoughts. She looked up at the chief of her security and answered the question in his eyes by spinning a tendril of magic from him. His mouth quirked in the tiniest of smiles and he moved a step closer, motioning her other bodyguards into tighter formation with a sweep of his eyes and a turn of his head. Torchay Omvir had been her bodyguard for more years than she liked to remember and one of the first of her iliasti, her temple-bound mates. He was also father to her eldest child.

"Trouble, my Reinine?" Leyja Byrek rested a hand on the hilt of her sword, eyes scouring the palace around them for enemies. Sunlight pooled just under the tall windows that lined one side of the corridor in Summerglen Palace here in the heart of the capital city, making the white marble floor almost too bright to look at.

The last of Kallista's godmarked, magic-linked mates, Leyja had been bodyguard and ilias to the Reinine who had come before. Tall and freckled, with hair a lighter red than Torchay's near-crimson mane, she could have passed for his kinswoman. But Torchay hailed from the Devil's Neck prinsipality of Korbin while Leyja's home was in the coastal swamps of Kimishen prinsipality, near the port of Kishkim.

"Maybe trouble. Maybe not." Kallista gave as much of an answer as she knew. She swept a hand forward. "Let's move on. I grow impatient for my luncheon."

She spilled magic gently into the air, sending it to search out the tastes and find the wrongness. Her midday meal was waiting, her favorite time of day when all the sycophants and hangers-on were dismissed, and her family gathered. All ten members of their ilian, plus the nine children.

The noise tended toward deafening, the manners non-existent—and that was without considering the children. But the whole family was together.

Her councilors hated it, begrudging any of the time between the chimes of the countless clocks spent on anything besides Adara's affairs—and hence their own—especially at midday. But Kallista was adamant. She was ilias and parent before she was Reinine. She could delegate many of the Reinine's duties. She would not delegate her role as parent to her children.

A flicker of motion ahead caught her attention. Had the magic found something?

She checked, found her spell burbling merrily along, poking into corners, sweeping up desiccated husks of expired spells cast by various naitani in the palace, including herself. Torchay's shout explained what she'd seen.

"*Girls!*" His roar could surely be heard halfway across the city of Arikon. "Stop right there."

Two small bodies froze in midstep where they'd been scurrying along, hugging the corridor wall leading to the family dining room.

Kallista's twins hunched their shoulders in anticipation of the scold about to come thundering down on them.

Torchay strode forward, catching each girl by the arm to lead them farther from the company of courtiers. Kallista turned and inclined her head at the entourage. "I leave you here, prinsipi, friends."

Someone protested. Someone *always* protested. Kallista gave them the narrow-eyed glare she'd been working on for the last six or so years. Apparently she didn't have it yet perfected, because the protests didn't stop until Leyja glared at them. Her troop escort remained to make sure the courtiers actually stayed where they'd been left, while Kallista stretched her steps to catch up with Torchay and the little girls.

"You know better than comin' off alone into the palace, do you no'?" His north mountains accent thick with the strength of his emotion, Torchay was barely getting into his scold.

Kallista folded her arms and scowled to hide her trembling reaction to the thought of what might have happened to her precious daughters, even here in the Reinine's palace tucked into the heart of Adara's capital city.

Six-year-old Lorynda gazed up at her father, waiting patiently for him to be done with his lecture. Her night-dark baby hair had fallen out and come back in auburn waves by her second birthday. Already she was taller than her fraternal twin Rozite, fidgeting next to her. Rozite's hair had bleached yellow-white in the summer sun, like her father's, but now that fall had arrived, it would be darkening again over the winter.

Kallista took pity on her. "Do you have anything to say for yourselves, girls?"

Rozite's eyes flashed to hers in relief. "We wouldn't have gone, Mami, we wouldn't, but we can't find Omri."

Kallista eased her alarm with the reminder that her son's favorite game was hide-and-seek. With a flick of her eyes, she summoned Leyja to organize the search for their wild child. Omri was three, almost four, with an insatiable curiosity and an uncanny ability to move from one place to another with the speed of his mother's native lightning magic and the silence of nothing Kallista knew.

"Search the whole palace," she murmured, "but keep it as quiet as possible. I don't want anyone taking advantage."

"*No.*" Leyja's expression was grim. She had always taken her bodyguard duties as seriously as Torchay took his, but when it came to protecting their children, she became a fire-breathing guardian that no one dared cross. None of the children were of her body, but it seemed to make no difference to Leyja.

Keldrey Borr arrived out of breath from the family quarters to fall on the twins with another scold. As both ilias and bodyguard, he supervised security for the family quarters.

"Wait, Kel." Kallista put a hand out. "Omri's missing."

"I know. I got the whole staff scouring quarters for the little devil."

"But—" She gave her daughters a stern look. "Why were you looking for him *here*, girls? What makes you think he's not at home?"

Lorynda bit her lip. Rozite stared at her shuffling feet. Finally, Lorynda spoke. "We were playing hide-and-seek with him because he wanted to come find you, Mami. Or Papi Obed. He didn't want to wait for lunch."

"He wanted lunch early," Rozite said. "So we were playing with him so he would wait."

"But what if he came to hide in the lunch room?" Lorynda was biting her lip again.

Keldrey gave them a little shake. "Why didn't you come tell me?"

"Omri's our *brother*," Rozite blurted out. "We didn't—"

"We didn't want him to get in trouble," Lorynda finished for her twin.

"Well, now it's all three of you in trouble." Keldrey gave them another gentle shake as he spoke to Kallista. "I'll look after these two. You go find that little imp."

Kallista glanced over her shoulder at the courtiers still standing half a corridor behind them, blocked by the guards from advancing, eagerly watching everything she said and did. Resentment swelled in a relentless internal tide. She'd never wanted to be Reinine, never asked for it. She wanted to live her own life with her family, without everyone gawking at her, gossiping about her, wanting things from her.

She should never have agreed to move the family luncheon from her private quarters to a state dining room. Just because it required a good fifteen ticks to walk from the audience chamber and workrooms to the family's quarters and another fifteen to walk back was no reason to bring the children out of that secure environment. The sleeves of her red overrobe billowing around her, she waved her bodyguards on. She needed to be away from those grasping busybodies before she throttled one of them. And she needed to find her son.

Torchay led the way, slightly to her right, with Leyja on her left and the third bodyguard—the new one whose name she could never remember and who was too, too young—at her back. Since the rebellion that had ended in the assassination of the Reinine before her, Kallista always had at least three bodyguards on duty. It had been several years since they'd proved necessary, but she still had them.

Leyja whirled, sword half-drawn, at the sound of boots running up behind them, then slid it back into the scabbard. Kallista already knew through the magic linking her to her godmarked iliasti that Omri's father approached. She turned, walked backward a few steps till Obed reached them.

"Have you found him?" He caught Kallista up in a quick, fierce hug and kiss.

"The twins think he's in the dining room." She walked faster as Obed fell in on her right side. Obed im-Shakiri might act as the family's man of business and trade like any merchant, but his sword-skills were the equal of the best bodyguards.

"I swear, even I was not this bad as a child." Obed shook his head. "I did get into a great deal of trouble, yes, but not *this* much."

Torchay grinned over his shoulder at them while he strode down the corridor. "The two of you are a dangerous combination."

Before Kallista had time for retort, the magic screamed.

Danger. Inside the palace. Kallista froze motionless, her body unable to move while her mind scrabbled to read what the magic told her.

"Oh dear heaven, *the dining room*." She burst past Torchay at a dead run.

Please, Goddess, Omri wasn't in there with it.

Torchay and Obed overtook her, running ahead. Leyja and the new guard kept pace with Kallista. She opened her senses to the dining room, searching as they reached it. The men grasped the handles to open the doors, their motion as simultaneous and synchronized as ever.

"Don't!" she screamed, snatching at their magic to stop them, in case fear for their son overrode her order.

"Why?" Obed shuddered with the need for action.

Her little twist of magic had found the wrongness, the danger, but it hadn't been able to name it. Now she could.

"It's a murder knot." She fought to control the pounding of her terrified heart. "West magic. Assassin's magic."

"Goddess, will they never leave us alone?" Obed's cry echoed her own heart's plea.

"For a group that claims to hate West magic, the Barbs certainly seem to have no problem with usin' it." Torchay sounded as bitter as she felt. "Why won't they just die?"

"Because we didn't get all the demons." Kallista had broken the back of the Barb-led rebellion six years ago by destroying the demons who'd driven it. All but one. She'd been hunting it ever since, but it had eluded all her magic-driven skill. And she didn't have time now for guilt or regrets.

"Is Omri in there with it?" Leyja asked. "What will it do if he is? What is a murder knot? I've never heard of such a thing."

Kallista called up every bit of rumor and fact she'd ever heard about the deadly magic. "They're part magic, part poison bomb and can be spelled to seek out a single person, or to eliminate every living thing in a given space. The magic empowers the seeker part of it and adds to the deadliness of the poison. They key off motion."

"Oh, sweet Goddess." Obed's hand tightened on hers in a crushing grip. She hadn't noticed taking it. "Is Omri in there with that thing?"

"I don't know. They can also be constructed to track magic. If I look, the magic could draw the knot to him. If he's there."

"So what do we do?" Torchay's twin Heldring-forged short swords were in his hands, a sure sign of his agitation.

Kallista had to think. Panic wouldn't save her son. She drew on the magic her godmarked iliasti carried within themselves, magic only she could use. The hot rush of power calmed her.

"Omri likes to hide," she said. "He's good at it, at being quiet and still, so if he is in the dining room, he's probably safe."

At the "probably," Leyja moaned, a tiny fragment of sound. Torchay set his hand on her shoulder and squeezed, taking comfort as much as giving it.

Kallista bit her lip, looking past them back down the corridor as the rest of their godmarked arrived from quarters. Each of the eight carried magic with distinctive qualities. As the Godstruck and only naitan among them, Kallista could shape their magic, weaving the different and necessary qualities into a whole strong enough to destroy demons. If she and her iliasti could do that, then surely they could save their child.

Kallista drew hard on her iliasti's magic, till she felt near to floating away with it. Over the past several years, she hadn't needed to use this much at one time, and using it now stretched her, challenged her.

"Stay here," she said. "One of you—Obed, come with me to grab Omri and get him away while I deal with the murder spell."

"I'll be comin' too," Torchay said. "In case there's somethin' else waitin' for you."

She nodded, not surprised. After sixteen years at her side, Torchay was as much a part of her as her magic. She divided the magic she'd called; some to find Omri and protect him, some for shielding the boy's rescuers, and the rest to deal with the murderspell and its poison.

"Ready?" Kallista met Torchay's eyes, then Obed's, deliberately not looking at the others. She knew what she would see—the same worry and need to act that she felt. But she would not risk any more of them. She took a deep breath, nodded, and the two men opened the dining room doors.

They blew into the room, slamming the heavy doors shut behind them as the knots—*two of them*—shot through the air, one from either side of the long, column-lined room, bright with light from the windows behind the columns. They resembled little balls or knotted buttons, just smaller than a walnut, and they glowed a faint poisonous yellow.

"Don't move!" Kallista fumbled a little, getting magic around both knots and pulling it tight. *Damn it*, she should not be this out of practice. She'd been focusing her magic too much on farseeing and truthsaying rather than more physical types of magic like holding or moving objects. She was ready to do two things at once, but one of them had been meant to find Omri.

Torchay and Obed stood frozen on either side of her, waiting for her signal while she organized her magic, siphoning off another bit from them to search out the boy. A giggle echoed around the empty room.

"Omri, stay there, son." Obed called out. "*Hide*. Hide well."

A third poison-bearing knot flashed toward them from the decoration at the top of a column. It must have been hidden there, waiting for some trigger to send it into action. Torchay knocked it away with the flat of his right-hand sword. Kallista looped magic around it, snatching it to a mid-air stop.

"Find me, Papi!" Omri's voice came from the far end of the room.

Obed looked at Kallista, the terror in his eyes mirroring what she felt. What if there were more murder knots? Already she struggled to hold three of them against their magic-spelled need to reach the necessary proximity and burst into a puff of poison. She should have never let her magic practice slide, no matter how peaceful Adara had seemed.

"*Go*," she said through lips as still as she could make them "Get him out of here." She spun out a bit of magic to make sure. "He's inside the sideboard holding the cakes. There's a door to the kitchens just beyond."

"Yes."

"Don't let the knots touch you and don't let them get too close. Use your sword. Hit them to me. I'll catch them."

"Be careful."

"I will. Take care of Omri."

Obed nodded once, slowly. Kallista felt his love for her and their child flood the magic-born connection between them and sent her own love back the same way. She tightened her grip on the deathspells and spread magic to trap any others.

"Papi!" Omri called, making her heart jump and pound. "Come find me."

In a swirl of black robes, Obed sprinted the length of the room. He knocked aside a fourth knot with his Heldring saber. Kallista captured it, beginning to feel a faint quiver at the strain. She followed, the imprisoned knots bobbing around her like rebellious dogs on leads. Torchay mirrored her, at her side as always. She didn't follow too closely, but close enough that Torchay could help Obed if needed.

The sideboard door opened and Omri fell half out of it, bracing his hands against the floor, his ink-black hair all in his eyes. "Here I am, Papi," Omri announced to the world.

"No!" Obed bellowed, leaping across the remaining distance.

A fifth poisonous ball flashed into action. Kallista screamed. Torchay shouted. He leaped forward, swinging wildly at the tiny, glowing button. Obed scooped up the child, his billowing robes seeming to distract the spell. Torchay slapped the knot to the ground with a sword and stepped on it to hold it there as Obed slammed out the kitchen door with Omri in his arms.

"Have you got this one, K'lista?" Torchay shifted his weight. "I think it's trying to burrow through my boot."

"Get off it then." Kallista took hold with her magic and at the same time, reached out to seize a sixth knot before it could leave its flower arrangement hiding place. Was that all of them?

She bound the spells into a mid-air bunch, save for the one Torchay had crushed, which seemed to have lost its aerial ability, and sent the magic to scour the room clean. She found one more murder knot tucked into the frame above the servants' door where Obed had exited. Seven spells. The number of misfortune.

Kallista let curses fall from her mouth as she fought to control the deathspells. Only the seventh gave her no trouble. The "seeker" part of its spell hadn't yet been triggered. But it felt as evil as the rest of them. The knots made her skin crawl with an ugly, blighted, invisible *something* that oozed off them like stink off old fish, creating a miasma of awfulness around them.

"Even after all the legends I've seen come to life, I thought these things might not be real." Torchay stood glaring at the hovering, quivering knots, body balanced and ready, short swords in his hands. "I should have known better."

"North Academy has records. We studied weapons like this, even though supposedly no one had proper magic to make them, not in a hundred years or so. We knew they were real." Kallista put her gloved hands into the fetid atmosphere and gathered up the little balls, hoping it would be easier to use her magic to keep them from bursting open if she held them in her hands. It still took both magic and physical strength to keep them prisoned.

"Let me help." His lower sword back in its sheath, Torchay had a hand out to take some of the knots. His bare hand.

"No!" She didn't want him near the evil things. "You're not gloved. This poison can soak through the skin's surface. You can't risk it." Kallista still wore gloves in public, like the soldier naitan she'd been.

Military magic was considered too deadly to risk getting loose among the populace. Any covering over the hands stopped magic, save for that under the most exquisite control. But gloves hadn't stopped Kallista's ability to throw lightning, the magic she'd been born with. They had even less effect on the Godstruck magic she'd wielded for the past six years. Still, they made people more comfortable around her, so she wore them.

"Well then, smash the things and be done with it." Torchay's left-hand sword was in his hand again.

"I'm trying." She pried at the deathspell's protections. They were sealed tight, like oysters in their shells. How could she immobilize the things without bursting them and releasing the poison contained within? She drew more magic, and then more, finally shaping it into a great fist and squeezing until the knots were crushed flat.

Carefully, she pulled her gloves off, turning one inside the other to contain the terrible stuff. The awfulness seemed to cling, but she didn't dare try to *shake* it off. Who knew what it was or where it would fly? She rolled her gloves into one of the napkins laid ready on the table.

"No luncheon in here today." She led the way to the doors where the rest of their family waited. "Have the kitchens send everything to our quarters."

"Yes, my Reinine." Torchay held the door for her.

She sighed and shifted her shoulders as the Reinine's robe of responsibility settled its weight back into place. Her captain's ribbons, even the major's gold ribbons she'd worn for a short time, hadn't weighed nearly so much. Not so much that she'd minded Torchay calling her "Major." Being called "Reinine" by her mates was different.

The crowd outside the dining room was larger than they'd left it. Obed had made his way around to join the rest of the ilian with Omri clinging to his neck, excited and frightened by all the attention. All of their troop of bodyguards had arrived, along with a squadron of regular soldiers. Her administrator, the High Steward, hovered in the background.

"General, Steward—" Kallista held out the napkin-wrapped bundle. "Get a dispatch bag to hold this. It's the remnants of seven deathspell murder knots."

"*Seven,*" whispered around the antechamber from a dozen throats.

"I want our best people on it. Gweric first, then whoever else we have." Kallista named the eyeless Tibran youth she'd brought back from their first demon-hunting quest. Grown man now, he was their oldest West naitan, the best of any at sniffing out demon-taint. She shifted her shoulders against the odd discomfort she felt. "Anything that can be learned about who made it, where and how, I want to know. And find out how they got it into that room, if you would be so kind."

"Yes, my Reinine." The general bowed low as she held open the hurriedly located leather bag for Kallista to drop her wrapped gloves inside.

"Tell them to be careful. The poison is as much magic as *chemical.*" She used the new word created by those studying the physical properties and interactions of all sorts of strange things from ground rock to salt to—she didn't know what. One of her first projects after becoming Reinine had been to open academies for such studies. The Tibrans had once invaded with non-magical cannons and gunpowder. Adara needed to know more than merely magic.

"Now." Kallista held her arms out to her iliasti and embraced the first one to reach her. "I am *starving.* Lunch. In quarters."

"But, Majesty, it's already half of noon." The head of her council quivered in protest. "We are meeting delegates from the far south at first chime after."

"Postpone the meeting. I am having lunch with my family."

"But, my Reinine—"

Kallista ignored the protests. She ignored the hovering sense of impending catastrophe as well, the bad taste lingering in her mouth, tucking it into the back of her mind to deal with later. The murder spells changed everything.

But the children were waiting.

Chapter Two

Lunch was noisier and more chaotic than usual, and Kallista delighted in every ear-numbing moment. At least with a ten-strong ilian, they had plenty of adults to deal with nine small children. Their family had blossomed, despite the challenges. Because she'd agreed to be Reinine when they selected her six years ago, Kallista couldn't do anything about some of those challenges. But the rest of them would end. Starting today.

Kallista managed to hold her temper until the children were gone, back to the Temple school or the nursery rooms. The moment the door closed and the ilian was alone again, Kallista burst from her chair. She fought her way out of the red robe of her office and threw it across the room.

"No more!" she cried. "I have had enough!"

"Enough of what?" Torchay asked.

At the same time, Viyelle said, "I don't think you can resign."

"I don't want—I thought they'd finally given up." Kallista couldn't hold still, her restlessness carrying her to the far end of the somewhat battered family dining room and back as she paced. "It's been, what? A year since the last assassination attempt? And then they were caught before they got out of Boren. The generals tell me how hard they've been working to dig out the last of the rebels and destroy the Barinirab heresy."

"They haven't lied." Viyelle Torvyll had grown up at court, daughter of the prinsep of Shaluine, a prinsipality on the central plains. She acted as liaison to the interlocking intrigues of Adara's courtiers as well as keeping an eye on the bureaucracy, serving as Kallista's chief of staff without the official title. "You know how many rebel strongholds have been rooted out, how far they have traced the secret membership. You presided over most of their trials yourself as truthsayer."

"The Order of the Barbed Rose has been virtually eliminated." Joh Suteny had once been a low-level member of the ancient order. Deceived and betrayed by the Master Barb, he now personally oversaw its dismantling, as well as assisting Obed in the family business.

"It's not enough." Kallista paced the room, destroying the hairstyle created by her dresser that morning, running her hands through it over and over again, her temper on edge. "This has to stop. Bad enough they keep trying to kill *me*, but our children—They could have killed Omri today. *My son.*"

Torchay caught her as she stalked by, tried to hold her, comfort her, but she was in no mood to be comforted. She didn't understand the mood, but there it was. She fought free of him.

Obed touched her shoulder, his expression haunted beneath the swirling script of the tattoos on his cheeks. Kallista paused, unable to ignore him. "*Our* son," she whispered.

Her hands began to shake, the first crack in the wall she had built inside herself this morning so she could deal with the death magic sent against them. The tears she hated, the ones that had been frozen behind her aching eyes, sheeted down her cheeks. Obed gathered her into his arms, holding on tight enough to keep her from shaking apart.

The rest of their ilian crowded close, embracing, touching, sharing the fear and relief. Kallista could feel it through the links of magic that bound them. She *reached* for the magic, weaving it between them. Often the magic brought a rush of almost sexual pleasure, but today it was comforting. Reassuring. She stretched and found Keldrey, bound as ilias but the only one of them not godmarked, and managed to weave him in too, a little. The strangeness eased.

Finally, her shuddering slowed, and stopped. Kallista dried her face on Obed's robe and her own sleeve, and she let the magic slip gently through her disembodied fingers and home into their separate bodies. Her ilian moved apart, allowing her to emerge from their center.

She began once more to pace. "This has to stop."

"You said that already." Stone, the first of her godmarked to find her back when it had all begun, a Warrior in the invading army from Tibre across the sea, leaned a hip against the table and folded his arms. "Any suggestions as to what we might do that we aren't doing already?"

"Yes." Kallista combed her fingers through her hair. Pulling out the rest of the pins, she began to braid it. It was too long for a proper military queue, as it hadn't been cut since her selection, but that could be remedied later. "It's time I remembered who I really am. Who *we* are together."

Leyja shook her head. "How can you be anything but what you are? The Reinine of all Adara. Godstruck by the One."

"That's the problem right there." Kallista let Torchay take over the braiding of her hair. He was better at it to begin with and he hadn't let himself get out of practice. "I have been Reinine first and Godstruck second. But I was Godstruck before I ever became Reinine. *That* needs to be first.

"We were marked to deal with demons, and there is still one out there. As long as it exists, Adara will not be safe, not for our children or anyone else's.

"But I have let peace trap me. I've let it fool me into listening to these prinsipi and councilors, bureaucrats and rulemakers. I've been lulled into thinking the danger was past. That I didn't have to worry about war and demons and could concentrate on trade regulations and grazing permissions. I let myself get caught in the endless, niggling, petty, bickering *politics* of being Reinine, and I have forgotten my true purpose. We are *godmarked*."

"How can you say you have forgotten?" Obed protested. "Every day, you spread your magic and search for this demon. Every night, even while you sleep, you search in your dreaming."

Kallista sighed, touched his hand. "But don't you see? After so long, hunting every day—I let it become rote." She put a sing-song foolishness into her voice. "Morning. Time to get out of bed. Stretch. Yawn. Scratch my head. Oh yes—time to send out the magic to find demons. There you go little magic, hunt away." She frowned.

"I stopped *expecting* to find it. I stopped—I think I stopped *wanting* to find it."

No one spoke, though she could tell they wanted to. Torchay glared at her down the length of his hooked nose. Fox glared too. Another Tibran Warrior, Stone's battle partner since childhood, he'd lost his sight and very nearly his life when the One's magic had marked him—had marked them all—back at the beginning.

That day seven years ago, on the walls of Ukiny, when the magic had poured into Kallista, a red, raised mark had appeared on the nape of her neck and on the others marked that day. Kallista's mark was the shape of the complete compass rose, the symbol of the One. The rest were marked with the rose alone, the symbol appearing at the time of their marking.

Blindness had cost Fox his caste, made him into less than nothing until he'd run away, driven to find Kallista. She had used the magic to give him an odd sense that let him *know* where things were around him, but he couldn't see them. The lack of sight made his glare no less effective.

"Don't you understand?" Kallista stopped to clear her throat of the guilty tears threatening to choke her. "Despite all the . . . complications of becoming Reinine and the hard years when we rode across Adara putting down the rebellion, it was good. We were together and we were happy. *I* was, anyway."

"We all were." Aisse didn't often speak in these meetings—she tended to focus on running the family—but when she did speak, she had the knack of saying what everyone felt.

Aisse was as Tibran as Stone and Fox, but as a woman, she'd been outside the Tibran caste system, abused by it—until she'd escaped when brought to Adara to serve the vast invasion army. She'd attached herself to Kallista, first as a servant, then as one of the four original members of their ilian. She hadn't been godmarked until later.

Kallista took a deep breath, accepting the truth. "And then, when things quieted enough, I had Omri, and when the magic came back after he was born . . . Happiness—*peace*—had seduced me. I still hunted the demon, but I was only going through the form of hunting. That ends today."

Kallista straightened the red military-styled tunic she wore beneath the discarded robe. Once she had worn blue for the direction of her

North magic lightning, but since the mark, her magic came from all four cardinal points of the compass. The prelates gathered for her selection as Reinine had decided that red was the appropriate color for a Godstruck naitan. Every Compass Rose symbol, representing the One's gifts of magic, held a red rose at its center.

"What does that mean, exactly?" Torchay looked wary.

"It means that I am going to leave the politics to the politicians. I have people I trust in the important places. *We* are going to find that damned demon and destroy it."

Stone cheered, grabbing up his nearest ilias—Keldrey—and attempting to dance him around the room. Being next thing to a rock, Keldrey didn't dance far, and his startled, disgruntled expression made Kallista laugh.

"What are you so happy about?" their oldest ilias demanded, sending Stone skidding with a shove.

"If we're going after demons, there's bound to be head-bashing involved. I haven't bashed nearly enough heads lately." Stone picked himself up off the sofa where he'd landed, grinning happily at them all.

"You go out with the patrols nearly every weekend night to bash heads." Fox said.

"You're there with me, often as not." Stone grinned at him.

"How—" Torchay raised his voice to be heard over the others. "How do you mean to do it? What else can you do? You already search for the demon every day."

"I'll search harder. Farther. Pay more attention to the magic as it searches." Kallista rolled her shoulders, still aching in indefinable places from today's unaccustomed magic use. "And we're going to practice the magic more, push the edges of what we can do. I haven't been using it like I should, like I can. I've been using the easy bits, and all those spellknots—I'm tired. More than I should be. Like I've used a different set of muscles that are out of practice."

In the last years—since Omri's birth—she'd used less strenuous forms of the godmarked magic most often. Truthsaying, almost constantly. She had to know if the courtiers and diplomats were speaking truth—although often *their* truth and her truth were not the same. And she regularly set aside time to preside over court trials and appeals to the Reinine's justice.

She used farseeing magic every time she sent out the seeker-spell after the demon, adding it so she could *see* on the off chance the spell found something. Her fore-seeing magic tended to use her rather than the other way round. Several times in the past six years there had been warning of hurricanes hitting the north and east coasts, and of floods along the Taolind and Tunassa Rivers. When the disasters were particularly bad, she would ride out to join the rescue and rebuilding efforts, often using her healing magic on those who could benefit.

But this other magic, the defensive magic and the demon-destroying magic—she had not used it in too long. Granted, it was difficult to practice destroying demons when she could not *find* one, but there had to be ways of building up those particular "muscles." It was past time she learned them.

A knock sounded at the door and Keldrey excused himself to answer it. High Steward Edyne stood behind it.

"I know I'm late," Kallista said. "I'll get there when I do."

"I think you should come now, my Reinine." Edyne stepped just through the doorway, into the edge of the room. "I think you will want to."

Kallista raised an eyebrow as the high steward handed a small something to Keldrey to be brought to her. Edyne was one of those few who helped protect Kallista's precious private time, not one of those who chipped away at it. If Edyne thought Kallista would want to do something or know something, she was usually right.

Keldrey glanced down at the object in his hand, then up at Kallista as he walked toward her, his face perfectly blank. Her nerves, already unsettled, jumped. It was that important? Keldrey had been a bodyguard so long, he had that expressionless no-face perfected. But he didn't use it among themselves any more unless he wanted to hide some strong emotion. Which was in itself a betrayal of that emotion.

Unable to wait, Kallista moved to meet him, hand out for the thing he carried. He put it in her hand—small, flat, oval—and stepped back, holding her gaze with the flecked amber-green of his own. Disturbed, Kallista looked away, looked down, and saw a small portrait.

The size of her palm, framed in a simple gold ring, the painting showed a child of about five or six years old. A boy, she thought. His hair curled around her face, sunkissed gold over brown. Blue eyes shone from warm golden-ivory skin. Rozite had the same skin tone—not quite Tibran gold, not Adaran pale, but a beautiful blend of the two. Kallista's heart stopped, then began to pound double-time.

"Who is this? Who sent it?" Her eyes flicked up, sought and found Stone, then Fox. They were at her side in an instant, staring down at the portrait.

"It was brought by one who traveled with this afternoon's delegation," Edyne said from her place near the door. "I am told there are messages."

Obed came to stand with Kallista as Stone took the portrait from her, gazing at it with greedy eyes. The delegation was from Obed's homeland far to the south. It was one reason Kallista hadn't minded putting them off. Southroners, particularly these, tended to be difficult.

"Messages from my cousin?" Obed asked.

Stone handed the portrait to Torchay who studied it with similar care before passing it to Aisse.

"I believe so," the high steward said, "though they were not specific."

"Could it be possible?" Stone voiced the question Kallista feared to ask.

She took a deep breath and let it out, then closed her hand around his. "Let us go and find out."

"I have put the messenger in your privy chamber." Edyne Steward held the door as Kallista swept through it, trailed by her entire ilian.

Kallista strode through the palace at a brisk clip, faster than usual, because her discarded robe wasn't tangling her up or weighing her down. Courtiers who tried to catch her in the corridors and slip in a request while she crossed the distance to the waiting messenger found themselves hard put to keep up. Those who managed could scarcely contrive to gasp out two words together.

Which suited Kallista fine. She had to get some control over her whirling thoughts before this meeting. The demon was not the only thing for which she searched every night. In truth, their ilian was not ten-strong, but eleven.

The demon Khoriseth had escaped destruction by riding the body of one of their iliasti. At the end of the battle that had seen the death of Serysta Reinine, the demon had possessed their ilias and driven her out of the palace, out of the city, perhaps out of Adara altogether. They had not seen her since.

Merinda Kyndir was a midwife-healer who had come to them to assist with the birth of Kallista's twins. She had stayed to help with the babies, and to help Aisse when the time came for her first child to be born a few months later. When the Barbs' rebellion broke open during the wait, Merinda had accepted a temporary bond as ilias under the countrified *durissas* rites. Intended for times of crisis, a *durissas* bond only lasted until the crisis was over, unless everyone agreed to exchange it for temple vows. Or a child came into the equation.

Kallista still didn't know whether Merinda had done it deliberately—Kallista had been afraid of her own reaction if the answer was yes. But during the journey north to take a pregnant Aisse and the infant twins to safety with Torchay's family, Merinda had seduced both Stone and Fox, and become pregnant. The dangers of the journey had changed her mind about wanting to join the ilian, but because of her child, she let Kallista talk her into making temple vows. Merinda had been only three months along when the demon stole her away.

For six years, Kallista and her ilian had been searching for any sign of Merinda or her child. Soldiers and couriers rode the depth and breadth of Adara, inquiring after a pregnant brown-haired healer. And then, as time went on, about a healer with a baby, a toddler, a child.

Obed's merchant traders went nowhere without searching, asking. Diplomats in embassies throughout the world made roundabout investigations. And never had there come any credible news. Not even of bodies found in some lost and lonely place. It was as if Merinda and her child had vanished into nothingness. With the demon.

It had to be more than mere coincidence, this news arriving today at the same time as the murder knot attack—the first assassination attempt in years to penetrate Arikon, much less the palace grounds. Kallista could see the hand of the One working to bring things together.

"My Reinine, my Reinine—" The courtier gasping beside her sounded as if she had been repeating the words for quite some time. "About the mines in the upper Heldring—"

New veins of metal—iron and tin, mostly—had been found not long ago, and the squabbling over who got to exploit them gave Kallista more headaches than the rest of it all put together.

"See the High Steward," she said as she reached her workroom antechamber. "Make an appointment."

"But, my Reinine, the miners are demandi—" The voice was cut off when the heavy workroom doors swung firmly shut.

The messenger standing in the center of the cluttered chamber was no one Kallista had seen before, a young woman barely into adulthood standing slim and tall and proud. Exotically beautiful with black hair and eyes and an arched nose that resembled Obed's, she seemed startled when so many crowded into the room. She stared, her eyes flicking from one to the other of them, as if she was not sure whom she would address. Then she saw Obed and her upper lip curled in a tiny sneer.

"Cousin." She inclined her head in such a minuscule bow, she might as well not have bowed at all. She extended a hand in a languid gesture to hover palm down, fingers gracefully curved as if awaiting some obeisance.

Obed eased forward until he stood beside Kallista. "You name me cousin, but I do not know you."

The young woman flushed deep red beneath her dark skin, and her eyes glittered with anger. Her outstretched hand curled into a fist as she drew it back. "I am Thalassa il-Shakiri, daughter to Bekaara who is daughter to Shakiri Shathina, Head of our Line."

Obed inclined his head scarcely more than she had. "I greet you, Thalassa, granddaughter to my aunt. You speak our language well."

The flush remained as words poured from her mouth in a liquid flow, the language of Daryath, apparently assuming the others didn't speak it. She was wrong. Mostly. They didn't speak it well. But she didn't need to know that.

"Cousin." Obed refused to follow her into Daryathi. "You should have learned sometime in your education that it is rude to speak in a language the others present might not understand. However, I can see you were overcome with delight at meeting a new kinsman for the first time. Or the first time in a very long time. I seem to recall an infant in Bekaara's arms when I came from the skola for the visit."

Thalassa's pretty face was marred by her scowl. Kallista thought about intervening—they did not need to make her their enemy, not with her news untold—but this was Obed's kin, Obed's culture. He would know best how to deal with her.

"Besides, Daryath is no longer my home." He went on in the same gentle voice. "You know that when a man is chosen as mate, he joins the Line of his wife. Her home becomes his. Let me make you known to my mate."

This was the tricky part. Most of the nations south of the Mountains of the Wind did not have iliani. In Adara, any family based on fewer than four individuals bound in temple vows was considered crippled, half-formed. Up to twelve persons in any combination could make up an ilian, though outside the temple families, iliani tended to be smaller, usually four to six.

But in the Southron countries, any marriage of more than two persons, one male and one female, was considered an immoral abomination. It was the chief thing that made dealing with them difficult. Primarily because Southroners—*these* Southroners especially—saw themselves as the center of civilization and therefore *right* while everyone else was *wrong*.

Kallista generally handled it by introducing only one of her iliasti as her mate, just to keep from ruffling the waters. She didn't deny any of her others, but she didn't push the truth in any faces. Though she did have trouble keeping track of just who she'd introduced as mate to which diplomat. That was what she had a High Steward for.

Obed turned to her and Kallista took his hand, let him draw her closer. "This is Kallista Varyl, Chosen and Marked of the One, Reinine and Ruler of all Adara. My mate."

Thalassa's eyes went wide. She bent low in one of the straight-legged bows of Obed's people and stayed there. "Your Majesty." Her voice shook, just a little.

Finally. The preliminaries were done and they could get down to business.

"Rise please, little cousin." Kallista had learned long ago that politeness would get one further toward what one wanted than other methods. If it didn't work, then the stick could be brought out, but honey first. "I am told you have messages?"

The girl's eyes slid to the small crowd of people behind Kallista and Obed. "They are private messages, Your Majesty. Concerning a matter your husband communicated to my mother several years ago."

Kallista's heart threatened to pound its way out of her chest. Could it be real news, after so long? "These are my Godmarked, bound to me in service to the One. The child we seek belongs to one of them."

"Oh?" Suspicion floated across Thalassa's face. She would have to learn to school her expression better if she hoped to succeed in diplomacy. Or trade, for that matter. Her mother Bekaara was a trader, the one who'd set Obed up in his business. "I thought the child was yours."

Kallista let herself smile. "How could it be, if I am searching for both the mother and the child? But, bound as we are by the marking of the One, the child of any is the child of all." Nothing but the truth and nothing to disturb strange Southron sensibilities. She hoped.

"Then whose child is it?"

What did it matter whose child it was? Ready to bring out the stick, Kallista startled when Stone pushed forward.

"The boy is mine." Stone's eyes held a silent plea when he looked at Kallista.

"His eyes are blue." He quieted his voice, but Kallista feared not enough to keep the Southron woman from hearing. "All three of Fox's get have brown eyes, but this boy's eyes are blue. Like Rozite's. Like mine. And he looks like Rozite." He turned the portrait up in Kallista's hand so she could see it, as if she had not already burned the image into her memory. "See? Around the eyes and the jaw. His mouth is softer and his nose isn't so thin or straight as hers, but you can see it."

Rozite was the only child in the ilian of Stone's siring. Not for lack of trying. He filled the beds of all the women in their ilian, though most nights he slept on the other side of Viyelle from Joh. Aisse, who had been barren when she joined the ilian, liked babies. She had given four to the ilian so far. Viyelle had given two. And when the children were born and their bloodlines read, none of them had been sired by Stone.

Kallista would not have thought that Stone, being a Tibran raised in their caste system before the destruction wrought by the demon Tchyrizel had shattered it, would care whether he had children of his own blood and seed. But apparently he did. And the portrait did look a bit like Rozite, made boyish.

"So?" Kallista looked up at Obed's cousin, away from the portrait, trying to stifle her hope for fear of disappointment. "Who is this?"

"He is a servant." Thalassa watched their faces as she spoke. Kallista hoped they didn't show anything they did not want the Southron woman to know, though what that could be, she wasn't sure.

Thalassa kept talking. "He and his mother appeared, working as bound servants in the House of the Habadra Line some half a year before this caravan departed Daryath. She is a healer, as our cousin informed us, and the boy looks as you see him there."

Kallista glanced up at Obed. She had no guess as to how long it would take for a caravan to reach Arikon.

"About ten weeks," he murmured, as if reading her mind. "Ninety days."

"Have you any other messages, Thalassa Cousin?" Kallista tried to contain her impatience.

"Only that my grandmother, your aunt, adds her personal invitation to the invitation of the en-Kameral to come to Daryath. It is time our families became better acquainted."

Instead of a single ruler, Daryath was governed by the en-Kameral, a group made up of representatives from the Hundred Lines, the elite families of Daryath. They were from various cities and sectors of the countryside, certain segments of society, and intended to represent them. For instance, the Shakiri Line were primarily merchants and traders.

Obed was able to tell her little more. Not only was he male in that very matriarchal society, but he'd been sent away from Daryathi society and shut up in that skola of his to become a dedicat champion—whatever that was. He still hadn't explained it to her satisfaction.

He didn't know the nuances of Daryathi power or government. But from all Kallista had been able to gather in her encounters with Daryathi delegations and the little Obed had told her, the Lines mostly represented themselves. Meetings of the en-Kameral were more chaotic than the meeting of the selectors in Adara.

Of course, the selectors only met perhaps once every ten to twenty years, and there were only fifty-seven of them—the prinsep and the head prelate from each of the twenty-seven prinsipalities plus the head prelates from the cities of Arikon, Turysh and Ukiny. And when they did meet, they only had one task: to select the next Reinine after the death of the previous one. Although Kallista's selection had taken only a few hours, hers was the exception. Virtually every other time in the past, the selectors had taken weeks to decide.

Daryath had one hundred Kameri, and they met daily to decide every aspect of the governance of their state. From Kallista's short experience, they decided very little, and half the time they changed their next decision back to the way it had been before. One thing they seemed to be set on, however. They wanted Kallista to make a state visit to their country.

Adara had restricted trade with Daryath since early in Serysta's reign. Traders were advised not to leave the coastal trade cities to enter the interior. The desert land bordered by mountains could be deadly to those unfamiliar with its natural hazards. The religious fanaticism of the inhabitants could be just as dangerous. Most traders heeded the warnings because the coastal trade was profitable enough, but those who did not—few of them returned. Daryath wanted the visit to open trade again.

Until now, Kallista had always declined to leave Adara. In the early days of her rule—and didn't the sound of that *still* make her uncomfortable—the last remnants of the rebellion had needed crushing. Then the Barbs had proved as stubborn and elusive as they had been through the long centuries their heresy had persisted. And Kallista had feared putting herself out of reach of news of their missing ilias and child. Now, however—

"Thank you, Cousin. We will consider it. Perhaps this year, we will come." She shifted into the role of cordial host. "Have our people treated you well? Your chambers are comfortable?"

"Yes, Your Majesty, most delightful." Thalassa gave a small bow-of-gratitude. "I have everything I could need or desire."

"Excellent. You will dine with us at the high table tonight, of course. And come to us tomorrow after lunch, to meet our—" Kallista stumbled over her words. She really shouldn't say "children" before this disapproving Southroner, cousin or no. Obed had only given her one child. "Our son. We will have pastries and cha, and time to hear news of family."

Thalassa's face almost unbent, almost found a genuine smile, but didn't quite. "I look forward to it, Your Majesty."

She departed and Kallista had a moment of space to catch her breath. She turned to the others, but before she could open her mouth to speak, Joh did.

"I'll get the packing started and speak to the generals about the escort." He'd been a lieutenant in the Adaran infantry, and was an organizational genius.

Kallista frowned at him. "What escort?"

"We are not going to Daryath without a troop escort," Torchay said. "A big one."

"Did I say we were going to Daryath?"

"Didn't have to." Fox winked a sightless eye at her. "You're not the only one who can pick things up through the links. Not after this long. Our sense of you may be dim, but it's definite."

"I'll get the children organized," Aisse said. "Keldrey and I." After four children in seven years, her figure had softened, but her fierce mother-tiger attitude was still the same, as was her short-cropped gold-blond hair.

"You're not takin' them to Daryath." Keldrey's outburst wasn't quite question, nor exactly protest, but something in between.

"I'm not leaving them here," Kallista returned. "You weren't with us till after, the last time we separated. I swore then we'd never split up like that again, and we won't."

"You didn't have me then. I'm not marked. I can stay here, keep 'em safe, and not mess up the magic."

"And what if, while we're gone, the demon comes here?" Kallista didn't want to think about it, but she had to. "No one here can protect against demons but us. If they're with us, we can keep them safe."

"Even if we're riding into a nest of demons?" Leyja sounded as skeptical as Keldrey.

"Even if," Torchay said. "We're better off together."

"*Are* we riding into a nest of demons?" Stone asked.

Kallista took a deep breath. "I don't know. I haven't dreamed any. Gweric hasn't seen signs of them either. But the demon departed here riding Merinda. It could have left her, but what if it didn't? This is the first hint of either demon *or* Merinda we've had in six years. It could be coincidence that we get this news the day I make up my mind to take the battle to the demons, but somehow, I don't think so."

"Where did the murder knots come from?" Torchay looked at Obed. "Could they have been brought here, across the mountains?"

Obed inclined his head, acknowledging the possibility. "Daryathi politics are often deadly. I have not heard, myself, of such a thing, but my own involvement in politics tended to be both less frequent and more . . . direct."

"So." Kallista surveyed her iliasti, catching the gaze of each one, as well as sifting through the feelings the links gave her. "We are agreed? We go to Daryath to see whether this is our ilias and our child, and whether the demon is still with them."

Not all of them nodded, but they all agreed.

"When do we go?" Joh asked, his eyes already far away, seeing what lay inside his head as he calculated lists of supplies and personnel. He snagged a quill from the nearest worktable and a scrap of parchment, his waist-length queue sliding forward over his shoulder as he stretched to reach it.

"Within the week, if possible."

"Let's say on Firstday next. Quickest route south that's possible." Joh made his first note to himself.

Kallista clapped Torchay on the shoulder. "Come, bodyguard. Let's go break the good news to the Daryathi delegation."

Chapter Three

Sun beat down on the caravan jingling along the dusty road. Leyja tucked the cloth that veiled her face against the fine gritty dust more securely beneath the wide-brimmed hat she wore to protect from the fierce rays of the sun. Her skin, like that of their other northern iliasti, burned red in mere moments under this Southron sun, even as summer waned.

But the Tibrans and even Joh and Viyelle turned brown after the burnt skin flaked away. Only Leyja and Torchay with their red hair, and oddly, Kallista, though her hair was nearly as dark as Obed's, continued to burn without ever tanning. The need for protection was a nuisance, but at least Leyja could easily shed the loose robes she wore against the sun if she needed to fight.

She sent her gaze sweeping across the family group again, counting children. Leyja considered it a gift of the One that they had traveled so far and not lost any. The journey down the Alira River to the wide Taolind at Turysh and on along the great river to the sea had been marked by enough "accidental" plunges into the water and forbidden explorations ashore that Kallista had been forced to cobble together a sort of magical leash to use on the wild creatures.

It allowed her to pinpoint the location of each child with only a moment's thought, kept them from straying more than ten paces from their bodyguard or nursemaid, and set up an alarm if any tumbled into danger. During the sea voyage along the eastern coast from Ukiny to Kushma in Daryath, it had alerted them when Omri had goaded his same-age sedil, River, Aisse and Fox's son, into the rigging ten paces *above* his bodyguard. That was merely the most alarming incident.

After that, Kallista had tightened her warding and the adults had heightened their guarding.

The rest of the voyage had been—relatively—peaceful, as had the journey by horseback along the Iyler, the great river of the south. This time of year, in fall, the river was too low for even the local lightweight reed boats once they left the coast.

The size of their caravan had kept bandit attacks away, though sneak thieves had been tempted by its richness. The regular troops had been kept busy guarding the wealth. The bodyguards' duties had been lighter. Leyja's own rest had remained undisturbed during the entire journey. But that did not alter her vigilance, especially now, as they neared the Daryathi capital city of Mestada and the end of the journey.

Leyja was a bodyguard. First and foremost, she protected those in her charge, with her life if necessary. She had done it well when it had been mere duty, but now, when she did it for love— She shook herself all over, like a horse shaking away flies, banishing the fear that any harm would come to these.

Many Adaran women joined the army as a way out of poverty, a way to succeed and advance and live well, if not wealthy. Few of them joined the ranks of the bodyguards because the training was difficult and the life was risky. That was why Leyja had done it. To prove that she could.

She'd been too tall and too thin in her girlhood, and book learning had been difficult for her. The only thing she had was determination. Because she refused to give up when things got hard and because eventually, her body filled out and learned to do what she demanded of it, Leyja had become a bodyguard. She had moved up rapidly, becoming bodyguard to the Reinine herself.

At that moment, when the Reinine had held out her hand in greeting and smiled, Leyja fell in love. She had loved Serysta Reinine with a pure and silent love for a double hand of years. The day that love blossomed, when Leyja had learned not only did Serysta love her in return, but that she wanted her in the same way she wanted Keldrey and the others was the day Leyja learned what joy truly was.

And the day Serysta Reinine died in her arms was the day Leyja learned about pain. It was also the day Leyja was marked by the One and she learned the consolation and comfort of God. Gradually the numbness and grief wore away and Leyja woke to realize she loved again.

It wasn't the same wild emotion, with the ecstatic highs, bottomless lows and desperate passion, because Leyja wasn't the same. Those she loved were different also—save for Keldrey and she'd always felt as much amused exasperation as affection for him. This love didn't burn. It warmed. It healed. Even the passion she'd found with Aisse comforted rather than consumed.

Perhaps it was because the object of Leyja's passion and the object of her devotion were not the same. Leyja loved Kallista in a different fashion than she loved Aisse. Kallista was Reinine. She was naitan.

She could forge the metal of their magic into any tool that was needed, from shield to healer's needle to sword. Then she could take that magic and twine it around and through the marked ones without even touching—though it was better when they did touch—and make them scream with the pleasure of it.

And then there were the children.

Leyja's gaze passed over the children again, always moving, registering everything as she scanned their surroundings. The grain fields were stubbled dun after harvest. Other fields looked to be covered with rows of dead, brown, snow-filled brush. Harvest-ready cotton, according to Keldrey, who'd grown up in the warm southern plains of Adara.

Between road and river, the fields held sway, even as they neared the city. To their right, away from the muddy river banks, the cottages and homes of farmers and small villagers gave way to large sandstone-and-granite estates. The workers in the fields were servants now rather than owners of the land.

The sand-colored walls of Mestada loomed before them. The Daryathi government, abetted by the diplomats Kallista had had to bring along, wanted them to camp outside the city walls overnight so they could enter the city in a grand processional parade. Kallista had refused.

She would parade twice around the city tomorrow if they liked, on her way to meet with the en-Kameral, but tonight would be spent in the comfort of the Adaran embassy. Or rather, the mansion next to the embassy that had been hurriedly purchased and added to embassy property in preparation for the Reinine's visit. The previous embassy would never have held all the people she brought with her—the troops and bureaucrats, diplomats and bodyguards, not to mention the Reinine's entire family.

The primary reason for Kallista's refusal, the one she hadn't shared with the Daryathi, was that she did not want the children exposed to public scrutiny. No one could miss a caravan the size of this one. Everyone would know who entered the city. But with their faces veiled against the pervasive, invasive dust that coated everyone—ruler, soldier and servant alike—it would be more difficult for an enemy to mark who was who. And tomorrow, during the processional—only once around the city—the children would stay safely tucked inside their quarters.

Leyja spurred her mount, riding alongside the Reinine's duty bodyguard—Jondi, today—to be first behind the troops through the gate. It was dark and cool in the deep, long shadow beneath the thick city wall, and smelled of sand. Once inside, the troops kept marching, following their Daryathi escort to the embassy. Leyja and Jondi stopped just inside the gate to watch for threats as the Reinine and her family came through.

The three oldest girls—Kallista's twins and Aisse's Niona, born during the rebellion—perked up as they entered the city. The younger children were waking with the noise, save for year-old Lissta, sleeping in Aisse's arms. Nothing short of a gunpowder explosion would wake her once she slept, and sometimes Leyja wondered if that would. Sired by Keldrey, Lissta felt more truly Leyja's than any of Aisse's four.

Leyja was smiling, her gaze moving on to the massed bureaucrats coming through the gate behind the family, when an anomaly registered in her mind. Something was different about the children. Was it something *wrong*?

She scanned back over them, urging her horse forward, alongside. There. Rozite had a necklace dangling halfway down her sturdy child's body, a large, faceted red globe pendant on a heavy gold chain. It might have been glass, but it wasn't.

Leyja had been present when the infant Rozite had latched onto the walnut-sized ruby as a toy. Serysta Reinine had insisted she keep it. Lorynda had a matching sapphire and Niona an emerald. Serysta had always been fair. But the other girls weren't wearing their necklaces.

With a sigh, Leyja pushed her horse though the troop escort. "Rozite Varyl Reinelle."

The girl jumped at the sound of her full name and title. Guilt flashed across her face before it vanished under false innocence. "What, Mami Leyja?"

"What have you been told about wearing that necklace anywhere but in quarters?"

Rozite hid her face behind a too-long fringe of sun-bleached hair. "I don't know," she tried, before giving up the attempt under her Fifth Mother's stern gaze. "Not to wear it."

"So where should it be?"

"In the luggage." Rozite's shoulders moved dramatically up and down as she drew breath. "But Mami Leyja, the luggage is all packed up on the mules. I can't put it there."

Leyja held her hand out to Rozite. Who looked at it, then looked up at Leyja as if asking why she was doing such a thing and what she expected Rozite to do with her hand.

Leyja crooked her fingers, beckoning. "Give it to me, Rozite. You knew you weren't supposed to wear it, and you did it anyway. Now it's mine."

Rozite clutched the big stone to her. "Not *forever.*"

"For now. We'll decide how long some other time." Leyja beckoned again. "Give it here, Rozite. Now."

"I don't want to. I'm the Reinelle. I should wear necklaces."

"*Now,* Rozite." Leyja reached to take it off her and finally, reluctantly, the child pulled the chain over her head and laid it in Leyja's hand.

"You're *a* Reinelle, not *the* Reinelle," Leyja said as she tucked the necklace into a thigh pocket. "You have eight sedili who are all Reinelles just like you. You're special because you're Rozite Varyl. Not because of who your birth mother is. You don't need a necklace to make people notice you."

Rozite didn't look particularly comforted by Leyja's lecture. "But I *like* it. It's pretty."

"It is. And you can wear it again in quarters when you can remember that *that* is the place to wear it."

"When we get there?"

Leyja hid her smile at Rozite's attempt to avoid penalty. "I don't think so. Your parents will discuss it and we will let you know."

"Why do we have to have *ten* parents to be mean to us?" Rozite's lower lip shoved forward in a pout.

"You think just four would be any nicer?" Leyja made a mock-fierce face and got a smile from the girl. "We'll get there soon. Try to act like a Reinelle until we do."

"Yes, Mami Leyja." The agreement came out on a heavy, put-upon sigh, but it was agreement.

Leyja eased her way back out to the edges of the caravan, wondering just how far they were going to have to travel through the city to get to the expanded Adaran embassy. A long way, most like. The government house, where the en-Kameral met, was at the heart of the city, like the Reinine's palace in Arikon. But the Seat, as the building was called, was not also a residence. The homes of the Hundred Lines were arrayed around the Seat of Government, with the various governmental offices and the embassies interspersed among them. To reach their destination, the Reinine's caravan would have to traverse half of Mestada. Leyja didn't know how far that was

The streets were narrow, forcing the caravan to stretch out, riding no more than two abreast along much of the way. Occasionally, a low stone bridge would take them across one of the canals that interlaced the city, exposing them for a moment to the open. Leyja didn't like it, nor did any of the other bodyguards. She could tell by the way they sat their mounts, the way their hands rested near their weapons. At least they were relatively safe from attack from above. Most of the streets were shaded by awnings stretching from one side to the other.

Even where the streets widened into a sudden square with a well or trickling fountain for the locals to obtain water, poles held up the awnings to provide shade from the sun—and hide them from anyone lurking on the flat roofs or the upper floors of the buildings. Most of the buildings in this sector of the city rose no more than two stories, and many were only one. Though, ahead in the city center, Leyja could see a few tall, sharp towers punctuating the skyline.

As they passed through a market square that seemed to be devoted primarily to flowers and fruits, someone bumped against her horse. Leyja would have thought nothing of it—the square was crowded with shoppers—but afterward, her balance had changed, just a bit. The necklace was gone from her pocket.

Instantly, she went beyond alert to that bodyguard state of awareness, cataloguing every person in the square by level of threat. Was this the beginning of an attack on her family, or merely theft? People stared at their passing, but with curiosity, not malice. Mostly, they went about their business.

There. The youth walking away toward the fountain, adjusting his clothing as he went. Slightly better than rags, they were not the sort of clothes one fussed over.

"Stop!" Leyja cried, using one of the words she remembered from Obed's language lessons. "Thief!" she shouted in Adaran. She pointed at the boy—man—his age didn't matter—and set her horse after him.

"Stop him." She ordered a pair of foot soldiers out of ranks to circle round and intercept him as she took the more direct route straight through the crowd.

The thief looked back over his shoulder at her, showing wide, startlingly blue eyes above the cloth that wrapped his face and hair. Then he ran.

He was fast and slippery, sliding through the crowds like an eel through water. He left the soldiers—unaccustomed to the heat—behind easily. Leyja, mounted, was harder to shake. He climbed to rooftops. She followed from below. He ducked into buildings and she found her way round to the exit. He wove through a warren of narrow streets and narrower alleys, doubling back until she was utterly lost, and still she followed.

Until finally her horse clattered into a tiny square with a well in the center and no sign whatsoever of the thief. He wasn't on any of the rooftops, hadn't gone down any of the streets. He had simply vanished.

She hadn't heard a splash, but she rode over to the well anyway and peered into its depths. Nothing. She screamed out her frustration to the sky.

"That necklace was my daughter's," she shouted then, hoping he might still be close enough to hear. "Do you steal from children?" Probably he did and was glad to. It was easier.

The thief would speak only Daryathi and she'd shouted in Adaran. It would do no good, but still she added an appeal. "Let me redeem it. Come to the Adaran embassy and I will pay you what it's worth. You won't get half that from anyone else."

Leyja scanned rooftops, doorways, windows, looking for any sign of a response, but they remained empty and silent. "Adara!" she shouted. "Leyja." She pointed at herself. "Ask for Leyja."

She waited another long moment, but finally had to give up. Now she looked around her for some indication of the way back to her ilian. A faint tug at her magic came from—mostly west, but a little north. Kallista was showing her the way home. Leyja found a street leading west and followed it.

Inside the well, far enough below the level of the street to be hidden in shadow, a niche had been painstakingly dug out of the well's side and lined with stones pried up from the paving. The niche had been enlarged over the years, made taller, wider, deeper, but still the thief barely fit inside it. He had grown as his hole had.

He held his breath, or rather breathed as quietly and smoothly as he could. After that chase, running across most of Mestada, not to mention all the climbing, jumping and ducking, it was breathe or die. Though if the choice was between not breathing, fainting from lack of air and falling to the water some fifty paces below to drown, or being dragged out of the well by his hair and skewered by that warrior queen . . .

He rather thought he'd prefer the skewering, if it came from such a magnificent specimen of female. Not that he lacked female companionship when he wanted it. When he could pay for it. But the females of his general acquaintance tended to be soft and somewhat squishy, women who wheedled, who used tears and seduction to get what they wanted instead of chasing him halfway across Mestada, then offering straightforward bargain.

It wasn't the bargain that intrigued him. It was quite literally the words that Leyja the warrior queen had shouted. Words in a language he hadn't heard in fifteen years, a language that reminded him of who he'd been. Who he truly was.

Padrey. That had been his name once. Before.

He was a thief now, one whose head would be parted from his body if he was caught. He was a very good thief, which was why his head was still attached at the ripe old age of twenty-six or thereabouts. But once, he might have become something else.

Padrey reached inside his shirt and pulled out the gaudy trinket he'd stolen, carefully, lest he drop it in the water just past his left elbow. The well was low this time of year, but still deeper than he cared to dive through after the thing. The chain weighed more than he'd expected. Could it truly be gold? Could the stone be more than glass?

He'd stolen it on a whim, just to prove he could. The vast caravan with its huge guard escort had been too tempting to ignore. But a stone this size—he'd seen the glint of red before he'd hidden it in his shirt. He didn't dare hold it out in the well's drop to try to catch a ray of sun. No sunlight reached inside the well this time of day anyway, and there was a chance someone might see the jewel. In fact, if he did not exit his hidey-hole soon, he would have to stay till full dark, after everyone had drawn their water for the evening.

Padrey tucked the necklace inside the box he kept in his hiding place. The box had been his reason for digging out this niche, back in the beginning, a place to hide the coins he saved to purchase his freedom—before he understood that he would never be allowed to do such a thing, that any time he neared the amount, the price would go up. And so he had freed himself from his slavery, after a fashion.

A thief's life was only marginally better than a slave's in terms of food, shelter, or housing, but one advantage it did have. It was his own.

Padrey closed the lid on his new treasure. If the necklace was indeed gold, and the stone a garnet or even—wonder of wonders—a ruby, the warrior woman was right. No one he knew would give him full value. But before he presented himself at the Adaran embassy, hand out to trade, he wanted to know more about these people. Who were they? What were they doing here? Could he perhaps gain more from them than mere money?

Idiot. When had money ever been *mere?* What else was there of value? Nothing. He'd learned that lesson well. The things he remembered could be nothing more than child's illusion. He was a child no longer. He knew how to see through illusion. So he would watch and learn and decide how to best use what he saw.

He listened another moment more, hearing only silence in the afternoon's heat. Finally he unfolded a leg from its knee-to-ear position and the arm that had been wrapped around it, reaching out of his niche for the carefully concealed hand- and footholds. Tonight he would find the Adaran embassy. He tried to squelch the tingle of excitement, but he couldn't quite eliminate the lingering whisper of *home.*

Kallista strode into the extensive family quarters set aside for the Reinine, playing the best "majestic" she could summon at this moment. She was tired. More than she should be, she thought. She waited, then waited a bit more while a whole army of servants carried in luggage. She would have wondered how much luggage nineteen people could require, but she knew. Mountains of it.

Especially when one of them was ruler of half a continent and required to wear ridiculously ostentatious clothing for a hideously enormous number of occasions. Kallista hid her shudder. She understood the need to impress, but she could only go so far. And she could only wait so long.

When the servants stopped bringing in more bundles and trunks from the courtyard and began opening them to remove the contents, Kallista decided she had waited long enough. "Out!"

She clapped her hands to get their attention, then waved them to the doors. "That's enough unpacking. Go find food. Arrange for baths. Go away from here."

"There are gardens." The head of the nursery servants, gestured toward an enclosed courtyard beyond gauze-draped doorway openings. "The children can run."

"Take them. Go." Kallista ruffled River's hair as he rushed by. "Make noise. Have fun. When the food arrives, we'll come out and join you. No, Keldrey. Stay, please."

The children flowed away. The servants departed. Bodyguards disposed themselves at entrances and windows and courtyard walls. When she was at last as alone with her ilian as she was ever allowed to be, Kallista stretched.

"I don't remember aching like this the last time we traveled in caravan." She groaned as Obed dug his fingers into her aching shoulders. She had felt . . . *off* since they'd left Arikon. Not bad, exactly, just *wrong* somehow. It had to be the worry. What else could it be?

"We were younger then, love." Torchay winked at her. "We've reached forty. It changes things."

"Speak for yourself." Stone sent a cushion flying across the room at the red-haired man, who caught it and sent it flying back. "Some of us haven't reached thirty yet."

"Stop reminding me," Keldrey grumbled. "Some of us are older than all of you." He and Leyja were nearing the half-century mark.

Kallista shivered, suddenly cold, though the air was scarcely cooler inside these thick walls than out under the sun. Now that they had arrived, the reality of the pretense they would be forced to live in this place was sinking in. As long as they'd been on the road from the coast, it had been almost a game, something they played at during the journey. But now, here, a slip could result in the collapse of all their plans.

"Torchay—" she began.

"Where *is* Leyja?" Fox asked. "I heard the noise, but I was too far back to tell what happened, except for people running in all directions."

"Here." Leyja walked in, hatless and coated with dust—more than the rest of them who had taken the chance to shake off the worst of it.

"Where'd you go?" Keldrey demanded. Kallista let him, willing to put off the awful discussion a little longer.

"Thief chasing." Leyja found the water carafe on the low central table, poured and drank. She told them of Rozite's disobedience and her own adventure in a few succinct words.

"So where did you stash this thief?" Stone peered around the room, as if suspecting her of hiding him in a corner.

Leyja scowled, slamming her cup down hard enough to dent the thin metal. "He got away."

Everyone stared, shocked. No one escaped Leyja, unless they were very, very good indeed.

Kallista sighed. "I suppose we should see about getting a copy of the necklace made. Rozite will be impossible if she never gets the thing back."

"See if he brings it for ransom first." Leyja collapsed onto the nearest divan, sprawled out in weariness. "I offered."

"You think he understood?" Stone collapsed next to her.

Leyja shrugged. "At least, since it's been confiscated, I'll have time to find it before I have to tell Rozite I got her necklace stolen."

"Rozite got her own necklace stolen by wearing it when she was told not to." Kallista perched on the edge of a round upholstered stool. "But you're right. It's been taken up. She doesn't have to know it's missing. Not yet."

She sighed. The diversion was over. "While we have a moment to ourselves—" She tried to sound casual, but knew she failed miserably when every head turned toward her, every body tensed, drifted closer. They all sat, as if awaiting some news too awful to receive standing.

"We have to be careful," she said. "You *know* how things are here, without iliani."

"We know. *Believe me,* we know." Stone made a face, eliciting a few chuckles. "I don't like sleeping alone. And I especially don't like doing without—"

At Kallista's upraised hand, he broke off, changed direction. "Without other things," he finished.

"We're alone in this room, but how alone are we?" She indicated the room with its pierced stone tracery and wall hangings that servants were meant to lurk behind. "We brought as many servants with us as we could, as we needed for the journey, but more were hired locally. Every one of those local servants is a Daryathi spy—perhaps not bearing tales to the en-Kameral, but to their neighbors, their local prelate. Tales about the scandalous behavior of wicked Adarans. We need to be careful. More than we are used to being. More than we have been."

"Goddess." Torchay swore a few more choice oaths. "It was me, wasn't it? I did it. I said—I called you—I'm sorry, Kallista. I didn't think—" That one word, one endearment—*love*—at the wrong time could ruin everything.

"No, you didn't think—" Obed stopped when Kallista touched his arm.

She spoke for his ear alone. "It's going to be hard enough. Don't make it worse."

Obed put on that perfect blank-face he did so well, hiding his emotions, but he subsided. Kallista couldn't read anything through the link either. Having grown up in Daryath, Obed had struggled with jealousy from the beginning. Jealousy that tended to focus on Torchay because of the years the bodyguard had spent at her side before ever the godmarked magic struck. Would it become a problem again?

She looked up at Torchay. She wanted to hold him, tell him his mistake didn't matter, that he could call her "love" all he wanted. But it did matter, and he couldn't call her that or any other sweet name, couldn't touch her even in passing because if he did, she would be touching him back, and more. She sent as much love down the link to him as she could.

"We have to remember *at every moment* that things are different here. We might be able to share quarters because we are bound as godmarked, but here, we cannot all be married together." She kept her voice quiet, reinforced the sense of what she said through the links. She couldn't speak through the links, save to Joh when she was seeing through his eyes, or when the others were dreaming together with her, but she could send a sort of knowledge. "Here, we are *paired*."

And the pairing made things awkward. Over the past years as the ilian settled in to their ordinary life, they had formed smaller groupings within the whole. Sometimes they changed around or all ten of them came together, but generally, Kallista slept between Obed and Torchay, Viyelle with Stone and Joh, and Aisse, Fox, Keldrey and Leyja all together. But threes and fours were as frowned upon in Daryath as tens.

"Obed is my only mate here," Kallista said. "And Torchay is my bodyguard only, not ilias. Viyelle and Joh, Aisse and Fox, Leyja and Keldrey. You know this. We worked this out together. If we are going to pry our people out of the hands of the Habadra Line, we are going to have to play their games—"

"Do not think of them as games," Obed interrupted. He spoke quietly, his voice fervent. "The attitude here against iliani, against more than two in a marriage is so strong that people have been killed. Traders who are incautious have been slaughtered in the countryside, and even here in Mestada. As members of the Adaran diplomatic mission, we are exempt from Daryathi law, but *not* from Daryathi prejudice. As servants to the Habadra, Merinda and her child *are* under Daryathi law until their status is changed. They could refuse to return them to wicked blasphemers. Or worse. We dare not risk them."

Kallista took up her warning again. "Do *not* forget who you're paired with. Especially you, Stone. Since you claim Sky as your son, that means Merinda is your mate."

They had no idea what Merinda had named the boy, nor whether he was Stone's child in truth or another of Fox's, but they couldn't keep calling him "the boy." Stone, with consultation from Fox, had named him Sky.

"It is *hard*, I know, and not what we are used to. I miss you, all of you, more than I can say, even though you are right here with me, because I must watch my words and my actions." The catch in her voice stopped her for a moment, "The One willing, we will have our ilias and our son back with us soon. Once that is done, it won't matter so much what gossip the local servants spread. Then, if there is a demon here to destroy, we will do that, and we can go back home. But until then—*be careful.*"

Kallista watched Torchay until he looked up and met her gaze. The sadness in his eyes at their separation tempted her to throw aside every caution she'd just spoken. Except—they still had their lost ones to consider—Merinda, and their son.

Chapter Four

The food arrived, and the meal in the shade of the vines and flowering trees with the children clamoring around did much to restore the mood. Baths immediately following did more.

The enormous sunken stone pools, similar to the smaller ones in the lower levels of Summerglen palace in Arikon, were obviously meant for more than one person. Once the children were clean in a massive orgy of splashing and dunking, their parents bathed in pairs, in an attempt to reinforce Kallista's reminder.

Obed waded into the steaming water and turned, too late to watch Kallista get in as he'd hoped to do. She slid all the way under, her hair floating out in a dark swirl, hiding her. Finally, just as he was about to worry, she came up, air bursting from her lungs as she dragged in fresh.

"I was beginning to wonder if I ought to pull you out." He moved in behind her to press a kiss on her nape, hungry for the feel of her skin against his. The journey upriver had been devoid of opportunity and he'd missed her.

Kallista eased away. "I think the dirt has gone an inch deep into my skin." She picked up the soap, its scent carrying him back to his childhood with its fears and anxieties. But she turned to rub the soap over his chest, her fingers moving over his skin, so it was all right again. She was touching him. He didn't mind washing first, especially if she wanted to wash him.

"Perhaps the dust is an inch-deep coating on the outside." Obed captured her hands and chuckled at her expression as he rubbed his chest against the softness of her breasts, sharing the soap. "I like washing this way."

Kallista's chuckle sounded strained, as if it caught in her throat. "I'm too dirty to get clean this way. Turn around."

Rather than wait for him, Kallista turned him, washing his back and body with brisk efficiency. Obed wanted more, but at least she washed him. Touched him. She did love him. He was sure of it. She washed his shoulder-length hair, letting him lean his head against her breasts. And she let him wash her without rushing, allowing him to take his time. Somewhat. He could sense her impatience, so didn't linger as long as he would have liked. Others were waiting their turn.

They were out of the bathing pool, drying themselves with vast lengths of cotton toweling, when Obed opened his towel and wrapped Kallista in it with him. She shivered, softened as he pressed his damp-hot body to her damp-cool one and touched his lips to that spot just under her ear. Goddess, he wanted her. But when he brushed his kiss over her mouth, she flinched away.

Obed broke from her, whirling, his temper sending his towel flying in a flat, fluttering arc to land crumpled against the wall. "Goddess, Kallista, what now?"

"I just— I can't, Obed."

"Why in hell not?" He spun to face her, clenching his fists against the urge to lash out, break something. There was nothing here to break, "I am your mate. Your husband. I've missed you on this journey, Kallista. I need you. Can't you see how much?"

"Stop it!" Her voice snapped with anger, but her eyes flicked to his screaming erection, making it shout at him all the louder. "Just stop it. I don't need this now. You're *not* my husband. You're *ilias*. So is Torchay. And Stone. And while they're— If they don't— If we— I just *can't*, Obed. It doesn't feel right." Her anger faded into confusion and distress.

Obed had his own anger and distress. He propped hands on hips. Kallista's eyes flicked toward him again, then turned stubbornly away.

He fought the growl wanting out of his throat. "If they do not get sex, then I don't either? Is that what you're saying?"

Kallista's head tilted, as if she thought it over. "More me than you," she said after a moment. "That *I* don't. But I suppose—yes, that's right."

Need swelled to desperate levels. He had to change her mind. "They don't mind the magic sex."

She shook her head. "It's not the same. You're right about that." She clutched her towel to her, as if she feared he might attack her.

The way he felt, he just might. How could he persuade her? "Taking a lover who is not your mate is a common practice in Daryath." He struggled to keep his voice quiet, to keep her from sensing how much he needed her. "So common, it is expected. No one will be surprised that Torchay is your lover. In fact, many will believe it, no matter how strongly we might deny it."

"Then—" she frowned "—why all the fuss about the evils of iliani if they are doing the same thing?"

"Because they can pretend." He clamped his mouth shut to keep from saying anything else. Would this work? Would it get her under him? Or on top of him? He didn't care what position, as long as he got inside her.

"What are they pretending?"

Obed didn't want to say, but silence was as much a lie as untrue words. "That they are true to their mate, that the lover is nothing to them. The lover is a secret hidden away in the dark. But everyone knows."

"That sounds—" Kallista shuddered, as if shaking away his words. "Awful. Shameful. Doesn't it shame both lover *and* mate?"

He shrugged, then tilted his head in an acknowledging nod. He remembered the whispers in Shakiri House when he was a child, how they would stop and start again whenever his aunt's "special friend" would walk by. It was one reason he'd turned down all the invitations during his dedicat days. He'd held out for marriage. And look what he'd got.

"Oh no." Kallista shook her head hard enough to send water flying. "No. I couldn't do that to you. Or to Torchay, or Stone. None of you. You mean that much to me."

That was something, anyway. Not much, but something. The conversation had dissipated the urgency of his need, his arousal fading. Kallista tossed him the loose Daryathi trousers he'd taken to wearing again, before hurriedly pulling on her tunic.

He couldn't help his disgusted huff of breath as he put them on. "We had better conclude our business in Daryath soon."

She laughed. "You mean you don't want a nice long visit with your loving family?"

He gave a derisive snort. "My family makes yours look like Powlás and the Three." He named the legendary first ilian formed thousands of years ago by the first Godstruck naitan, famed for their love, harmony and angelic children. He'd met Kallista's parents, heard their quarrels. But they were merely . . . awkward. Cold and belligerent at the same time. They didn't murder each other, or control each other with that threat.

He pulled his overrobe on over trousers and bare chest, leaving exposed the tattoos near his shoulders and around his navel. It gave him back a bit of the confidence Kallista had taken away, to show his tattoos. Very few sported as many as he had earned. "Come. The others will be wanting their baths."

"There's only Leyja and Keldrey left, I think." Kallista shoved her feet into lightweight slippers and pulled her tunic hem down over her trousers.

"Two more who won't be getting any sex till we leave here," Obed muttered.

Kallista playfully punched his arm. "You think the others are?"

"Joh, maybe not, but Fox? Oh yes. Aisse doesn't have your qualms, and Fox isn't one to pass up any opportunity." Obed held the door for her to pass into the hallway.

That same evening, a message arrived from Obed's cousin Bekaara. She had contacted the Head of Habadra Line where the servants worked, those who might be Merinda and Sky, and asked about buying out their contracts. Between veiled insults, the Habadra had stated she would negotiate only with the Adaran who claimed kinship to her servants. Apparently Habadra Line had a long-standing rivalry with Shakiri Line. Not the best news.

Other news was better. The child and his mother were apparently well, or had been when they were last seen, before the inquiry from Bekaara.

"We knew it wouldn't be easy, going into this," Viyelle said from the sofa after the messenger had gone.

Kallista sprawled beside her, suddenly exhausted. The endless day was catching up with her. "At least the Habadra is willing to negotiate."

"With *me*." Stone sank onto the edge of one of the wide, round upholstered stools. "I think I'm going to need lessons in tradecraft. I've never paid any attention to the business."

"You have the first, most important requirement, I think, Stone." Kallista sent a touch down her link with him. "You are determined to win."

"But you cannot let the Habadra know." Obed paced as he offered his advice.

"How can she not know?" Stone asked. "I'll be negotiating for my *son*. My child."

"Sons are not important in Daryath. When they marry, they leave the Line of their birth to add their talents and seed to that of another Line. Their only importance is as . . ." Obed paused in his pacing to hunt words. "As trade goods. To seal alliances—or contracts—between Lines. Most Heads of Lines pay no attention to their sons and grandsons until they are old enough to send for training. Then they are sent away till their training is complete, so they are not present to be noticed."

"If that is the case," Viyelle spoke over Obed's quiet response. "Maybe one of the women should do the negotiating."

"The message said the Habadra would deal only with Stone," Kallista said. "With Merinda's mate. Sky's father."

"More than that." Obed stopped beside Stone's round couch. "The method for redeeming a bondservant is written down in the Law. Someone who is kin must offer the redemption price. The Habadra's message demands a particular kinsman—the father and mate. But we would have to send Stone anyway, because we have no other of Merinda's kin with us."

"Right." Stone sighed. "Are you sure I can't just bash somebody over the head and grab them?"

Kallista couldn't help laughing. She loved the way Stone could always make her laugh. She loved Stone. "That's always an option, if the other doesn't work. But since it could make things a little tricky getting back home to Arikon, let's try negotiations and bribery first."

She leaned her head against Viyelle's shoulder, needing the physical touch. Even the Daryathi accepted close friendship. "Think of it as a battle. A duel between the two of you. That's how I get through all that diplomatic and bureaucratic sparring. It *is* a battle. Just not with swords."

"Too bad. I'm *much* better at head bashing." Stone pushed himself to his feet. "I'm off to my lonely bed. May as well sleep, since there's nothing else going to be happening in it."

"Best dress tomorrow," Kallista reminded them, as the group dispersed. "We have to sparkle. Blind everyone with our shine. Tomorrow's the big day for impressing Daryath." She sent a surge of affection through the links, spreading it through the web she'd created between their nine so all could sense the love from each of the others.

At the fourth chime after dawn, give or take several ticks, the entire official Adaran contingent gathered in the embassy's entry courtyard. The escort troop was resplendent in gleaming metal helmets with horsetail plumes above long sleeveless gray jackets with double rows of brass buttons marching up the front. Kallista had to admit the new uniform design looked impressive.

The hordes of diplomats and bureaucrats all wore their best multi-colored court dress, most decorated with gold or silver embroidery. Kallista and her ilian outshone them all.

All of them glittered with precious stones and gilt embroidery in various shades of red. Kallista's clothing differed only in degree. Some of the cloth still showed through the decoration on her iliasti's garments.

They had decided to bring only the godmarked into official notice. Keldrey's sole assignment on this visit would be the safety of the children who would remain in the embassy. Kallista envied him, getting to stay behind. So did Stone. He believed the pomp and ceremony got in the way of reclaiming their son, and told them all so. Often. But since the Habadra had not yet contacted them, they might as well do the diplomacy show.

When the party was arranged to Torchay's satisfaction, Kallista signaled the guard at the gate. It swung open and the state visit of Adara's Reinine to Daryath officially began.

They paraded six abreast down broad avenues and over silent, swift-flowing canals back to the gate where they'd entered, then circled half the city before reaching the widest paved thoroughfare Kallista had ever seen. Even the avenue-parks around the palace complex in Arikon were not this broad. It arrowed straight through Mestada to the building where the en-Kameral met, the Seat of Government.

Crowds lined both sides of the road, cheering wildly. The copper coins scattered by the Daryathi escort at the head and tail of the procession brought on the adulation. Kallista would rather have simply marched through town, but apparently this was the Daryathi custom and one neglected it at risk. So she smiled and waved and wished to be out of her stiff, heavy garment.

Finally, they reached the Seat. Built of local white limestone, it glowed in the bright Southron sun. Broad steps led up to a colonnade shading a deep porch three stories high. Above the columns, a vast, reddish dome rose even higher.

Impressed despite herself, Kallista dismounted, along with most of her escort. As she climbed the stairs, the troops gradually dropped behind, lining the stairs with protection, until she led the way to the group waiting at the top.

There were five of them. Beyond the columns, in the shade, so many others stood crowded so close that Kallista thought they would have been at the steps to greet them if they could.

The five women dressed in identical fashion, in white hooded robes over brightly colored, ankle-length dresses. The robes were embroidered in colors that matched the dress beneath. Each wore a broad pectoral collar of heavy gold in elaborate, jewelled designs—the badge of office for the Head of a Line.

One of them, tall, with a sleek coil of snow white hair above black brows and an unmistakable air of power, stepped forward and bowed in the austere Daryathi way with her arms down by her sides. The other four followed suit from where they stood.

Kallista put her right leg forward, brought her hand up in a hopefully graceful flourish, and gave them the most elegant bow she could manage, her ilian matching her.

When Kallista rose, the white-haired woman spoke. "I greet you, Kallista Reinine, Ruler over all Adara and Chosen of the One. I bid you welcome to the Seat of the en-Kameral. I greet you Kallista Varyl, wife of my sister's son. I bid you welcome in the name of my Line."

"I greet you, Shakiri Shathina." Kallista responded as she had been endlessly coached on the journey by her foreign ministry and by Obed. "And I thank you for this welcome to Daryath. I greet you, sister of my husband's mother, and I thank you for the gift of your Line."

Everyone bowed again. Then Shakiri Shathina introduced those standing with her. These five women served as what was loosely translated as the executive council. They had the power to make decisions in an emergency, when there was no time for matters to be brought for debate to the whole of the en-Kameral. They also supervised the bureaucracies that managed the day-to-day running of Daryath. Their decisions were then approved by the entire en-Kameral. If they were not approved, the council members were turned out of office and new ones chosen.

Kallista paid close attention to the names since her high steward had not come on this journey to remember them for her. Three she did not recognize, but the fourth—a dark-haired woman of perhaps fifty with a stern, square face and a pectoral collar adorned with amethysts and cranes—proved to be Habadra Khori.

Chapter Five

The Habadra held Kallista's gaze as they mutually acknowledged the introduction. Kallista smiled, doing her best to seem inoffensive and perhaps slightly stupid. Negotiations often went better if the other side thought her easy to fool.

"Let me make known to you the Godmarked of Adara." Kallista beckoned her iliasti forward. She couldn't rush through the introductions, but she wanted to. The sun was heating up as it rose higher, and if it got too much hotter, she would melt like so much ice and slither right out of the heavy court-tunic.

Finally Leyja, the last of them marked, had given and received bows and they were escorted through the rows of Kameri waiting on the porch into the cool of the stone-walled building. The year was winding down, but autumn had not yet found Daryath.

Kallista and Obed were seated in high-backed chairs just below the dais where the five-member council sat. The rest of the godmarked were given chairs hurriedly set up in the open floor space before the dais. She leaned toward Obed to mutter, "Why do I get the feeling they don't quite know how to deal with the Godmarked?"

His smile flashed before he could hide it. "Probably because they do not. I am certain my aunt believes it no more than an honorific."

When all the Kameri had filed in, they took their seats in a simultaneous rumble of noise, and the speeches began. They were good speeches, as speeches go. If one could get past the fact they were given alternately in Daryathi and Adaran, each sentence coming first in one language, then the other.

Kallista had never been fond of speeches, especially when she had to give them herself. Unfortunately, the Daryathi en-Kameral seemed determined to give each Head of the Hundred Lines the chance to have her say.

For the first few speeches, Kallista entertained herself by translating the Daryathi sentences using what she'd learned from Obed over the years, and comparing them with the official translation. She did quite well, which pleased her. But after five or six speeches, even that entertainment lost its value. The vast chamber, filled with well over one hundred bodies, grew warm. Kallista began to have trouble keeping her eyes open.

She propped her elbow on her chair's padded arm, propped her chin on her fist, and hoped that when the inevitable moment came and she fell too soundly asleep to catch herself, she would not fall onto her head and totally humiliate all of Adara. She was a soldier, for heaven's sake. Not a connoisseur of oratory.

"*Majesty*. My Reinine." The harsh whisper had Kallista jerking awake.

She straightened in her chair and wiped her damp knuckles on the seat cushion, slanting her eyes this way and that to see if anyone had noticed. Torchay had, by his half-smothered smile. He always did, curse him. Stone and Fox likely had, the way they were whispering together and snickering. No one else. She hoped.

She cleared her throat. "Yes, Ambassador?"

The woman who'd awakened her was Namida Chand, Adara's Ambassador to Daryath. "My Reinine, the speeches will go on until you indicate you have heard enough. They do not wish to disturb you if you are listening to what they wish to tell you."

"Might have been nice if somebody had told me this," Kallista muttered. Her backside was as flat as the chair she'd been sitting in, cushion or no.

"Apologies, my Reinine."

"What do I do to let them know 'enough'?"

"You stand."

"That's a simple thing. Thank you, Namida Aila." Kallista braced her hands on the arms of the chair and heaved her flattened backside out of it.

Immediately, the Head of Line speaking at the lectern fell silent. She stepped to one side, bowed, and the entire en-Kameral rose to their feet.

With the executive council leading the way, everyone filed out of the meeting chamber and through the building to a lovely shaded courtyard where the splash of fountains cooled the air and tables laden with food waited to be piled on plates and eaten. Too bad Kallista hadn't known about the standing-up-to-end-speeches thing far, far sooner.

Obed and Torchay took turn about at eating so that one of them was always hands-free to guard while Kallista chatted with the various Kameri who presented themselves before her. All the chatting made it difficult to eat much of the excellent food. Having to watch every word against a slip of the tongue made it nearly impossible. She could eat back at the embassy afterward.

But the woman she most wanted to talk with never came close. Now and again, Kallista could see the Head of Habadra Line across the courtyard. Occasionally, Habadra Khori would meet Kallista's gaze, always without smiling but without challenge either. Whenever Kallista tried to work her way through the crowd to the place where the Habadra stood, a half-dozen Kameri, mostly of the lesser Lines, would appear and request introduction.

With Namida Ambassador at her elbow, Kallista couldn't be rude and shove past them, though she wanted to, badly. Especially when she realized the interruptions were orchestrated by Shakiri Shathina. Kallista was beginning to dislike Obed's aunt. Still, it was early days yet. Time enough for rudeness and head-bashing later. The reception couldn't last forever.

Padrey edged nearer the front of the crowd, pulling his hood forward to shade his face. It was more a guard against notice than protection from the sun, but it served as both. His hair tended to bleach in the sun like cheap cloth, acquiring streaks of gold no respectable Daryathi would ever sport, and his skin would never brown dark as theirs. Even tanned, he would burn. No wonder he'd become a thief. Night was more comfortable for his northern hide. Which was why he'd missed this morning's parade. He'd been busy till late, and overslept.

Adara, the warrior-queen Leyja had said. These were the visiting Adarans. Padrey wanted another look at them, to see whether he actually wished to deal. He would try to spot this Leyja in the ranks for whatever he could learn.

The double row of champions marched by, faces impassive under their varied tattoos as they tossed handfuls of coppers into the crowd. Padrey snatched a few from the air, but let the rest scatter on the street for the children and the desperate to gather. He'd had a good night. And he still had the necklace.

Behind the champions, Adaran soldiers rode on compact, heavy-muscled horses. The soldiers wore gray, sleeveless jackets with squared-off tails that came down over their thighs and buttoned up the front in a flash of brass buttons. Their hair, all colors from white blond to sable brown and even shades of red, was tied back into short, braided queues. The sight of them brought a stab of homesickness so strong that Padrey almost staggered. He should have been one of them. Too old now.

More soldiers rode behind the men in gray, these dressed in black trimmed with bands of red at the neck and hem. Padrey shivered a little when he saw them. These weren't mere soldiers. They were more. More deadly for certain.

Some of those in black wore more elaborate uniforms, decorated with gold braid and jewels. There, *she* had to be Adara's Reinine—the one in the center, in the scarlet tunic stiff with crimson and gold and glittering stones. More braid and jewels twisted up the crimson trousers to her knees.

She wore her darkest brown hair in a military queue like the soldiers, though its greater length, well below her shoulders, and the hair that had escaped around her face softened the look. High cheekbones and a slim straight nose gave her an aristocratic appearance, while the square jaw indicated strength. The wide generous mouth— Someone spoke to her and she smiled, transforming an austere, handsome face into beautiful.

Then she turned and seemed to look straight into Padrey's eyes, the smile lingering on her face. A word chimed through his mind, as if someone had spoken it directly into his thoughts. *Freedom.*

His whole body shuddered with the echoing reverberation. He gasped. Then he gasped again.

The woman by the Reinine's side, tall and terrible in her elaborately decorated black uniform was the woman who had chased him through half of Mestada. Leyja.

Padrey tugged at the sleeve of the person next to him. "Who are they? The ones in black and red?"

The person he'd accosted shrugged him off, but someone else answered. "The personal bodyguards of the Reinine."

"Even the ones with all the decoration? All the braid and such? Are they just higher ranked?"

"Those are in her household."

"Don't be stupid." Someone else, a woman, spoke up. "They're her lovers."

"You're both wrong," came a third, self-important voice. Everyone shut up and listened. This speaker wore the tattoos and belt badge of an en-Kameral champion. He stood at the edge of the street, holding back the crowd. He would know. "They are the Godmarked of Adara."

"What does that mean?" Padrey had never heard of the title, though admittedly he'd been a child when he lived in Adara.

"I'm not sure," the champion said. "I couldn't hear much, but from the way everyone acted, especially their Reinine, they're very important government officials. Very, *very* high up. Personal friends of the Reinine."

"See? Her lovers," the sour-voiced woman said.

"They are not." The man sounded as if he disagreed with her often. Likely her husband.

Padrey paid them no attention as he eased away. The people he'd come to see had passed. He had no need of the coppers coming at the end of the procession. He needed to think.

Dear Goddess, Leyja was one of these *Godmarked*. In the highest circles of Adaran government. Judging by the trim on her clothing, she certainly would be able to pay a nice ransom indeed for the necklace. She could also lose him in a dungeon so deep he'd never find his way out again.

Padrey rubbed his palm over his chest, trying to ease the hollow ache there. That word still resonated somewhere inside him, like the lingering vibration of a bell. Could he actually have it—freedom? Could he find it there? With the Reinine?

He shook himself. What was he thinking? He *already* had it. He had freed himself. Oh all right, he was a thief. He lived in an attic that leaked during the rains and roasted him in the dry. He skulked and lurked, trying to avoid notice, because if anyone noticed, he was dead.

But he did what he pleased—after a fashion. He was beholden to no one—if you didn't count Falon One-Eye who collected the protection money. Though the only protection he provided was from himself. Nor could you count his landlord. Or the owner of the Drunken Weevil. Or— All right, Padrey wasn't beholden to any more people than the average ordinary non-escaped-slave person. He was free. Mostly.

Padrey slowed his walking and looked around. Where in seven hells was he? He would sure as morning be dead if he didn't pay better attention to where he was going and who was around him. He turned, hunting landmarks—the dome of the Seat or the temple spires—and almost fell over someone.

"Sorry." Padrey set him back on his feet, resisting the urge to pat him down for treasures. "Wasn't looking. Didn't mean—" He broke off when he got a good look at the young man.

He had no eyes. The man wasn't just blind, he had no eyes. Someone, sometime had brutally removed them, barely leaving enough behind to be sewn shut over the empty sockets. Padrey shuddered in horror and sympathy. Why didn't the man wear a scarf or—or *something* over his scars?

He was a foreigner, obviously. No Daryathi would let such a cripple run about in the streets of Mestada. Beside that, his hair was bright gold, the yellow of the sun, and his skin was a light golden brown. And he wasn't alone.

"*Naitan,* are you all right?" The words were Adaran, spoken by a soldier—a *bodyguard* in unrelieved black—who rushed up to the eyeless man. "I am sorry, I got too far ahead. Is this man accosting you?" The bodyguard turned suspicious eyes on Padrey.

"No, no." The—the *naitan* laughed. He actually laughed. "I am fine, Kerry. Neither of us was watching where he was going—"

"B-but you *can't.*" Padrey didn't realize the words he blurted out were Adaran until he'd spoken them.

The naitan turned his uncanny no-eyes on Padrey, still smiling. "You speak Adaran. *Excellent*. And it's true. I can't see you" He made a regretful face. "I'm afraid you haven't any magic for me to see."

"'Sall right. I knew that." Padrey shrugged.

"You're Adaran?" The bodyguard's wary stance didn't soften. He was older than his charge by a dozen or so years, his hair streaked with silver. "What are you doing in Daryath?"

"Parents were merchants. They died. I . . . got stuck here." Why was he telling them truth? Had the world gone crazy? Had he?

"Even better," the young naitan said. "That means you know your way around. We're lost."

"We're not lost," Kerry the bodyguard muttered. "We just have to retrace our steps, find where we went off."

"We're lost," the naitan repeated. He held his hand out to Padrey. "I'm Gweric, by the way."

"Padrey." Now he was giving his true name? Bemused, he took Gweric's hand and shook it.

"So, Padrey, how do we get to the Adaran embassy?"

The bodyguard grabbed a fold of Gweric's tunic and dragged him a few steps away. He didn't bother to soften his voice overmuch as he spoke. "We can't trust him. He could lead us straight into ambush. To a thieves' den. *Anywhere*."

"We *can* trust him—"

Padrey had to work harder to hear Gweric's reply.

"Because there is a hole where he stands."

What? Padrey looked around himself, trying to figure out what the man meant by that bizarre statement.

"Kerry, there is demonshadow and demonstink all over this whole, hell-kissed city." Gweric's voice, his stance, his whole being was matter-of-fact, as if the existence of demons was established fact rather than religious superstition.

"It clings to people here, wafts through them. But it goes *around* Padrey. If it touches him, it doesn't stay. It doesn't like the taste of him. And anyone the demonshadow doesn't like, I do. We could be trying to find our way back to the embassy until we died of old age. He'll show us the way."

Padrey was suddenly glad he hadn't lifted the naitan's purse, even if it would have been dead easy to steal from a blind, crazy man. No one had trusted him since—well, since his parents died. It made him feel strange. He looked up again, hunting the landmarks he'd forgotten to find. *There.*

The temple spires speared into the white-hot sky, their onion-shaped domes blazing with color and pattern in the afternoon sun. And there was the dome of the Seat, beyond and to the left. So the Adaran embassy would be . . .

"Padrey? *Can* you show us the way?"

The thief looked at the young naitan, then at the bodyguard, for once not evading any gaze. "Follow me."

Back at the embassy after the reception's end, Kallista beckoned her ambassador into the family gathering room and sent a servant to collect Keldrey. She wanted the entire ilian present for the ambassador's debriefing. Kallista was the last to return from changing out of the elaborate court dress. Of course her clothing was the most elaborate. She felt more tired and irritable than she thought she should. But then, court functions could do that to to a person.

"Excellent. Food." Kallista clapped her hands together and rubbed them before she fell on the meal Aisse had ordered. "All right, Namida Ambassador, begin. How bad was it?"

"You did well, overall, though by failing to partake of the feast prepared for you, the insult is great. You implied that you feared poison. That you do not trust them."

"I don't." Kallista beckoned the ambassador into a chair at the table beside her, the ilian filling in the rest of the places. "Is poison likely?"

"It is a common weapon of assassination, yes." Namida sat primly on the edge of the gilt chair. "But not likely at such a large gathering. And you should not trust them, but you should *appear* that you do. You should have eaten what they offered."

"I did, a bit." Kallista made a face. "My iliasti ate the food. My nerves were on edge. I was afraid it might not agree with me. I didn't want to sick up on the flowers."

"Er—no, that likely would not have been beneficial." Namida seemed flustered by Kallista's easy manner. "And it will have been noticed that your—that the Godmarked did partake."

Namida had been accompanied to Daryath by the three other members of her ilian. Its small size and two-and-two orientation allowed them to avoid unwanted notice, but they were still obviously careful not to even use the words.

The ambassador changed the subject. "Your patience in the assembly room and the number of speeches you heard will go far in making up for any missteps."

"Good. What else?"

Namida produced a sheaf of parchment cards, made beautiful with the flowing Daryathi calligraphy sprawled across them. "I received these invitations this afternoon, on your behalf."

"At the reception?" Kallista spread them across the table, appalled. Almost as many had been delivered to the embassy before she'd arrived in Mestada.

"Yes, my Reinine. You are already committed to Shakiri House tomorrow evening, with your Godmarked, and to each of the other councilors on successive evenings. They are the most important. If you like, I will consult with your chief of staff regarding the rest."

"Viyelle—" Kallista looked down the table and got the prinsipella's nod.

"I'll meet with you first thing tomorrow," Viyelle said. "Ninth chime."

Namida stood, bowed and made her way out.

Kallista waited for the door to shut solidly behind her before looking up at her ilian. "So? What did you learn?"

"The rivalry between Habadra and Shakiri has escalated in the past year," Viyelle said. "It's gone beyond who can throw the best party to duels in the streets. And it's spilling over into other Lines. They're beginning to take sides. There are still quite a few neutrals, but I gather that they're beginning to have trouble maintaining their neutrality."

"How did you learn all that at a party?" Stone demanded.

"I listen. I ask questions. People talk."

"I listened. I was listening to you ask questions," Stone said. "All I learned was that these women have a fascination with blond hair."

"Red hair too." Torchay shifted. "And they like to pinch."

"I talked to the Habadra," Aisse said. "Fox and I."

"And?" Kallista leaned forward, as did Stone.

"She was curious. She wanted to know which was Merinda's husband, and seemed very interested when we pointed Stone out."

"When she realized I was blind," Fox said, "she pretended I wasn't there." They had decided to conceal Fox's magical *knowing* sense, to let him play blind man until the moment came when they could gain advantage by revealing it.

"The flawed are hidden away," Obed said. "The blind and the lamed, the simple-minded."

"All of that fits you, Fox," Stone said. Fox merely clouted him again. Everyone else ignored him. They'd learned by now that Stone used the jokes and teasing to ease his worries.

"That way," Obed went on, "the rest of Daryath can pretend they do not exist. Things *appear* to be perfect."

Obed paused, and blinked as if struck by a thought. "In Daryath," he said slowly, "appearance is more important than truth. What a thing *is* does not matter so much as what a thing can be made to *seem*. They give voice to the ideals, but in reality, they do as they please, as long as they *seem* to be obeying the Law. Even the ambassador has said so, just now. Do not trust, but seem to trust."

"Which makes me wonder about demons," Joh said. "Much of the Barbs' philosophy involved seeming to be one thing in order to conceal the truth."

"Fox?" Kallista looked down the table at her blind Tibran.

His bright gold curls were pulled back into a tight queue falling between his shoulder blades. It would take years before it reached the length of Joh's glossy, waist-length braid, but he seemed determined to grow it that long.

"I didn't see anyone who looked wrong in that way," Fox said. "But I can't tell if anyone is demon-ridden *now*. Only if they have been in the past."

"So if the demon is here, it's not changing horses—so to speak." Kallista drummed her fingers on the table.

"Do you have any doubt that it's here?" Joh asked.

"Actually, no. I agree with you, Joh. Too much here *feels* like demons." She snagged another meat bun off the tray. "Speaking of which, is Gweric still out?"

"He's just come in," Leyja said from near the door. "Do you want to see him?"

"Yes. Send for more drinks. He'll be thirsty."

Gweric entered the large airy room, his bodyguard joining the others at the room's perimeter. Gweric's hair—blond like the rest of the Tibrans—stood on end, sticking out in all directions due to the sweat that matted it. He collapsed onto the chair Namida Ambassador had abandoned. He drained the cup of water Kallista handed him, poured another, drank it and poured a third cup of fruit-flavored liquid to sip at.

"Saints, it's hot out there." He blew out a gusting breath.

"You should have come back sooner," Viyelle scolded.

Before Viyelle had been marked and married into the ilian, she and Gweric had had a brief "fling." After some adjustment—Gweric had been more upset over not being marked by the One than losing a lover—they had settled into a sedili sort of relationship, with Viyelle as the overprotective older sedil.

"I meant to," Gweric was saying. "But I didn't realize how far I'd walked or how far it was to get back." He stole a bun off Kallista's tray and bit in.

Kallista slid the tray closer to him. "What did you find?"

Gweric's magic involved sight. An odd thing since his eyes had been taken by the demon-ruled Tibran Rulers when they'd made him one of their Witch Hounds, a magic-user forced to use his magic to spy out others with forbidden magic gifts. Without his eyes, all Gweric could see was magic, demons and—sometimes—the future. His bodyguard had a small gift of magic, of striking true with weapons, which enabled him to serve as Gweric's guide when necessary, since the young man could see him.

"There is demon taint all across the city," Gweric said. Everyone sat up straight at this news. "The shadows and stink are everywhere."

"Is it stronger in any quarter than another?" Kallista asked. "Can you track it to its source?"

Gweric shook his head. "Not where I was today. It's too pervasive. Still, I barely covered a tenth of the city. If that much. Maybe it'll be different in another quadrant. *You* might be able to track it, but—I just don't know. There's so much of it."

"Damn." Kallista rubbed her hand across her mouth, trying to think.

"Kallista. Reinine." Gweric's use of her title had Kallista's head jerking up. Her attention arrowed in.

"I think there is more than one of them," he said.

Chapter Six

Kallista stifled her oath. "How many?"

"I don't know," Gweric said. "More than one."

"Seven?" Joh asked.

Seven demons had stirred up the rebellion that had ended with Kallista being selected as Reinine.

"I don't know," Gweric repeated. "There is enough demonshadow for seven. Or perhaps just one or two very powerful, very evil demons. I can't tell more than that."

"One or two *more*," Kallista said to clarify. "More than Khoriseth."

Gweric nodded. He shoved the tray of buns away. "Suddenly I'm not hungry."

"I'll send the magic out tonight," Kallista decided. "At the regular time, so it—so *they* don't suspect anything out of the ordinary. I hope. I'll see if I can count them."

The door leading to the nursery opened and Niona peeped through, a mischievous grin on her face. Kallista grinned back and gestured her in. "Looks like quiet time is over," she said. "Playtime now. Magic practice after dinner."

Children flowed into the room, every one of them finding a lap. Only Stone somehow sat alone, too far around the table for the impatient little ones to reach. Kallista met his eyes over Viyelle and Joh's little Sharra in her lap, and her heart nearly broke at his wistful smile. Then Rozite gave up her attempts to wheedle Leyja in favor of pouncing on her Papi, and his attention turned to his daughter.

The One willing, they would have their lost son home soon.

Night fell quickly in Daryath, a blanket of darkness floating gently down over the city to offer respite from the fierce sun. Kallista sent everyone off in their designated pairs not long after dinner because she wanted to practice calling magic at a distance and to practice the dark veil. She'd even insisted that Torchay, Obed and Leyja retreat to other rooms, though she had to accept Keldrey's presence beside her army-assigned bodyguards when they all threw fits about her being insufficiently guarded.

The demon-destroying magic came to her hand as easily as if they had all been standing next to her. But once she had called it, she didn't quite know what to do with it, given that they didn't know where or how many the demons were. So there she stood, in the middle of the embassy's private garden courtyard with her hands full of magic and nowhere to send it.

She certainly didn't want to kill anything but demons with it, not even grass, as she'd once done while practicing on the Adaran plains. Daryath didn't have enough vegetation to be able to spare any. Nor did she want to put anyone to sleep, which the dark magic could also do. She needed everyone alert and aware.

In addition to all the other considerations, Kallista did not want to alert the demons to her intent, if they did not already fear that she had come to destroy them. She twisted the magic into multi-flavored strands and amused herself by braiding and weaving it into pretty designs while she tried to think what to do with it. She'd tried once to use the magic to *teach*, but in the confusion of the Barbs' rebellion, had no way to discover whether it worked as intended. She could put the magic back, but that defeated the purpose, didn't it?

Shouts in the street came over the walls of the courtyard.

"What is that?" Kallista found Keldrey in the shadows.

He passed a hand signal to a guard near the gate who trotted off, returning a few moments later. The young soldier snapped to attention. "Fighting, my Reinine. In the street outside. The captain stationed with the embassy says it's likely duels between competing Lines. Might be a few Sameric clerics as well. They don't like Adarans on principle, the captain says."

"Thank you." Kallista smiled and the soldier blushed. Goddess, they got younger every year. She sent him back to his post.

But his report gave her an idea. "Peace," she whispered to the magic. "Calm. Good sense."

She willed those things into the magic and drew a bit more of Stone's joy to add . . . because. A little calm good sense would benefit everyone, even those standing watch. Could she do this? She'd never tried it before, had no idea what might happen. Surely nothing bad, not with peace and good sense willed into it. She gave the magic a metaphysical kiss and threw her hands wide, setting it free.

It burst in all directions at once, no dark veil this, though it carried the same power. The Godstruck magic was pure magic, its purpose willed into it by the naitan who called it. It glowed, a pearlescent shine of all colors and none. And as it flashed from her, so quickly it seemed a trick of the moonlight, *through* the walls and into the streets, the shouting faded and then ceased.

A long moment after the magic passed them by, the guards around the walls protecting the embassy let out a breath, or perhaps took one in, a sort of gasping sigh. Keldrey blinked at her, as if dazed.

"Are you all right?" Kallista reached him in three paces, took his arm.

Keldrey put his other arm around her, bringing her into a close, casual-seeming embrace. "Better than all right." He shook his head. "I feel . . . blessed. Like the One just stooped down and gave me a kiss. The magic?"

Now Kallista blinked. She hadn't known the magic could do such a thing. "It must have been. Why didn't I feel it?"

"Maybe because that's what you feel every time you call it?" Keldrey gave her a brief, tight squeeze, but didn't let go.

Kallista slid her arm around his solid, stocky body, wishing she could give him a kiss of her own. She had come to love this rough and steady man, and she didn't like pretending otherwise. And she felt even more guilty for failing to practice the magic over the past years, to experiment with what it might do. To use it as she could have. As she should have. She could have—blessed—all of Adara with the good things of the One.

And given Keldrey a taste of what the godmarked had.

She stretched up and pressed a kiss to his temple, catching the barest stubbled edge of his shaved head. "I miss you."

Keldrey chuckled and moved aside. "Yeah. Me too. You done tonight?"

"For now, I suppose." Kallista let him go, trying not to show the reluctance she felt.

"The little ones'll be wanting their kisses and stories."

Kallista smiled. "Trust you to remind me of what's important."

"We're all important." He grinned and winked. "But right now, it's their turn."

When the younger set were finally quieted—the magic seemed to have energized rather than calmed them—Kallista was as ready for sleep as they were. It had been a long day. But she had yet to send her magic out hunting demons.

Yawning, she headed back toward the courtyard with Obed and Torchay trailing behind her. At the wide doorway leading out, she paused and caught hold of the gauzy, breeze-blown draperies. Someone already occupied the courtyard.

"What's wrong?" Torchay stepped up beside her, nostrils flaring as if he sniffed for trouble.

"Nothing. Stone." Kallista touched Torchay's hand, caught Obed's eye. "Wait here. Please."

Torchay nodded, acquiesced. Obed frowned, opened his mouth as if to speak, then nodded without speaking. Kallista smiled and squeezed his hand in apology, though she didn't know what she apologized for, and went out into the flower-scented night.

Stone stood, one foot propped on the fountain's basin, breaking bits of twig into tinier bits and tossing them into the water. Kallista put her arms around him from behind and leaned her head on his shoulder. He wasn't much taller than she, so it was a comfortable fit.

"Should you be doing that?" He laid a hand over hers where she'd clasped them at his waist, tossing the rest of his twigs away all at once in a faint patter on the paving.

"Probably not, but I don't care. It's dark." She kissed the rose-mark on the nape of his neck beneath the soft gold hair he kept cropped when he remembered to do it. Just now, it curled almost to his collar.

His laugh was bitter. "We're standing in the light of a full moon. Not so very dark at all, with Daryathi servants around to see us." Stone peeled himself out of her embrace.

He kept his hold on her hands, as if afraid of what she might do with them, and turned to face her, gazing solemnly down at her. "I don't want to care either," he said. "But we have to. I want my son back. We can't give them any excuse."

"We all want him." Kallista led him by the hand to a wood-and-iron bench that sat beneath a delicate, multi-trunked tree exploding with hot pink flower clusters. They had no scent to mingle with the honeysuckle, their color dimmed in the night. As she sat with him, crinkled petals drifted down to settle in their hair. "Are you so sure he's *your* son?" She had to say it.

"Does it matter?" Stone brushed the petals off his head.

"I don't know. Does it?" She hid their joined hands in the shadows between them, reluctant to let him go.

"No. Even if he's another one of Fox's, I want him back." He looked up then, the blue of his eyes somehow visible in the moonlight, and held her gaze. "But he *is* mine, Kallista. There's some connection, some . . . *thing*. The same connection I feel with Rozite. I don't love her any more or less than the others, but that connection is there. And we have to get him back. Whatever it takes. Whatever we have to do. We have to have our son."

A shiver traveled down Kallista's spine and she tightened her grip on his hand. This connection he spoke of was what a prelate naitan read to determine a child's sire within the ilian for the temple records. They spoke of reading bloodlines, but it was magic they read. The connection was weak, difficult to detect, and at the same time one of the most powerful magics in the universe because it was virtually impossible to break. A child's cry for his parents, a parent's need to protect. If Stone felt it this strongly, Sky's situation couldn't be good.

"We will get him back, Stone. I promise you."

"Whatever it takes." He stared hard into her eyes, his face more serious than she had ever seen it.

"Yes," she said. "Whatever we have to do."

"No matter what," he insisted.

"Yes, Stone." Goddess, could she reassure him enough? She needed to hold him. "No matter what. I swear it."

He held her gaze another moment, then nodded, once. "Good."

Stone swallowed hard, sudden longing in his eyes, thrumming through the link, a need simply to be held, a need for the comfort of human warmth and contact.

Kallista reached for him and he twisted away, stumbling to his feet. "We don't dare," he rasped out, and fled.

An instant behind him, Kallista followed. At the doorway, Torchay met her gaze, then turned and loped after Stone. Kallista fell into Obed's arms. She *hated* this, but Stone was right. They didn't dare.

Obed held her tight, pressing kisses to her hair, then he swept her into his arms and strode with her into the Reinine's sleeping room. When he would have set her on the bed, Kallista clung, her arms twining around his neck.

He followed her onto the bed, stretching out beside her, hand resting on her stomach. He nuzzled her ear, his tongue licking out to tease. "You said you did not want this."

"I changed my mind." Kallista looked inside herself, where the links with her godmarked lived, and lifted out the two that tasted of Torchay and of Stone—sweet and rich, powerful and joyous. She wrapped them around herself and called magic, sharing it with Obed. She turned her head, spoke with her lips brushing his. "But we won't be alone in it."

"I do not care." Obed rose to his knees, dragging off the tunic that concealed his body tattoos.

Kallista sent the magic flowing back down the links. Torchay and Stone were together. The room was designated for Stone and Merinda, but for now, Torchay shared it. None of them liked sleeping alone any more. Stone groaned as the magic shivered through him, and collapsed onto the bed. Torchay shuddered, sitting on the opposite edge when his knees gave way.

Playing the magic as six years of practice had taught her, Kallista stripped off her clothes and pressed herself against Obed's bare, sleek skin, sharing the sensations among the four of them. She brushed kisses across Obed's cheeks, feathered them along his eyes and down his nose, cherishing Stone with Obed's body. He was beautiful. He was beloved, whether she touched him with hands of flesh or of magic.

She reached the tattoo around Obed's navel and her tongue licked out to trace the flowing script. Someone cried out—the rough tenor was Torchay's, but it held some of Obed's dark richness, so perhaps he cried out too. She moved lower, slid her mouth over him, drawing the feel of it through Obed's link and sending it to the others. Stone's arm flew out, reaching for support, connection. Torchay caught it and they held on, gripping forearms as they writhed, fully clothed, on the bed.

Kallista had played long enough. She rose to her knees, took Obed inside her and sent the magic spinning between them. Almost, it felt as if they were all in the same room together, loving her, letting her love them. The sex was incredible, but the love—ah, *that* was the glorious thing. She poured her love for them down the links and received it back in return as the magic built the pleasure higher and higher still.

"*Enough.*" Obed's body bowed upward, spilled into her. His climax exploded the magic, sent it blasting through all of them. Kallista held on, screamed as the magic wrung them dry, left them drained and satiated with delight before she let the last dregs slip away, back into its various homes.

She collapsed on top of Obed, her face mashed into his neck because she hadn't the strength to move. Obed lay suspiciously still, his hands flat on the mattress beside him rather than stroking her as he usually did afterward. Goddess, what now? Didn't she already have enough emotional debris to clean up?

Kallista carefully stifled her impatience. It wouldn't help. "Obed?" She slid off him, to the side, keeping her leg over his in case he thought about running. He hadn't done it in a long time, but coming to Daryath seemed to have unsettled him.

He huffed a breath out through his nose. "You made love to *them*, using *my* body."

"Yes, I did. I'd have used their bodies if I could have, but I couldn't. Not here. I made love to you too. And you said you didn't care."

"Would you have touched me at all if you had not wanted them?" The look in his eyes accused her. "Did you even want me?"

"Of course I did. I always want you. Always. You know that." She moved his arm out to make a place for herself inside it, snuggling close. Touch always made him feel better, especially skin-to-skin. Her too.

He seemed reluctant to bring his arm up around her to hold her, but he did. As if he couldn't help himself and didn't like that he couldn't. "But I don't. How can I know such a thing when you turn me aside?"

"When did I—? Oh." She had. Just last night. *Saints.* Men and their fragile sense of self. "It wasn't that I didn't want you, Obed. I did. I just— It was— *This place . . .* " She trailed off, confused, not sure she could explain it to him. A lot of things confused her lately, as if her thoughts were stolen away before she had time to think them.

A long moment later, Obed sighed and rolled to face her, his dark eyes solemn. "You are right. *This place.* It has me falling back into old habits. Old *bad* habits. I have no need for jealousy."

Because Obed had grown up in Daryath where pairs were the rule, he'd had difficulty adjusting to life in an ilian. Especially after the twins were born and their bloodlines followed to different fathers. It had led to backlash—a dangerous collapse of half-formed magic—when his jealousy had cut his magic off from Kallista's call.

The situation had been resolved with the help of a set of gold arm bands that locked together, allowing Obed to give up his rigid control. Backlash had never been a problem again. Obed had learned to share Kallista with the other members of the ilian, but he still could not manage to share himself. In six years, he had not made love to any of the others.

Obed looked ruefully at the metal cuffs he still wore, mostly because they both enjoyed the games that could be played with them. "I may yet need these."

"Or maybe it's the demons, rather than the place." Kallista realized what she'd forgotten. "I haven't yet sent out the magic to hunt them. Gweric said there's demonshadow everywhere."

"Do you have enough magic left to you?"

She smiled. "No matter how much magic I use, there is always more. The gifts of the One have no limits. The strength of the naitan who uses them is the only boundary. And I feel wonderful." She stretched, leaning into Obed for a kiss, then drew magic, *reaching* for more from each of her other links.

In the distance, she caught a faint, amused sense of *Again?* from Torchay that faded quickly as she wove the magic first into a spell that would scrub the embassy clean of any demon taint and protect it against further intrusion. She had to strengthen it twice with more magic before it could eliminate the last of the stains, then fed even more into the protections.

"The demon has to know that we know it's here," Kallista said when she was done. "After all that." She sat cross-legged in the center of the bed, Obed curled around her.

"All of—your hunting?" He traced a finger down her naked spine.

Kallista shook her head. "I cleaned it out of the embassy—all the demonshadow—and warded the place against more coming in. Maybe I shouldn't send the hunter magic out."

"If it knows that we know it is here," he said, "why not send the magic? What harm can it do? You hunt for demons every night. If suddenly you stop, would that not cause more notice?"

"Hmm. You're right. If it expects . . . But what if it does something to Sky? Or Merinda?"

"Would it not do this something anyway? Even if you do not hunt it?"

Kallista blinked at him. "Right. You're absolutely right. Were you always this smart and just never let on?"

He smiled and bowed, a difficult thing to do while reclining on one elbow. "Association with you has made me smarter."

"Flatterer. I know better. It's just that by comparison with me, you're brilliant." She called more magic to shut him up. The brief, quick rush of pleasure usually did. Braiding in the separate strands, she shaped the magic to hunt and to count, to scent any different flavors of demon that might be in the city. Then she sent it out, leaving a thin strand connected to bring it home again.

A yawn caught her, stretching her jaw until it ached. Obed eased her down into the bed, cradled her against him. "Sleep," he said. "Today was a long day. Tomorrow could be longer."

Sometime in the night, the magic returned, whimpering with frustration. In her dreaming, the wrinkled scent hound that represented the spell conveyed its confusion and unhappiness. So much demonshadow overlaid the city of Mestada, it was impossible to trail it to its source. And it all stank the same. Kallista scratched the long floppy ears and sent it home, than stalked the multi-colored misty dreamscape alone, searching. She also found nothing but stains and shadow.

Kallista took the next morning to communicate through farspeakers with Arikon, to maintain contact with what was happening in the government at home. High Steward Edyne had the Steward's Privy Seal so business could be conducted, but there were still decisions Edyne did not want to make herself. Kallista could do her own farspeaking, but she preferred not to, except in emergency. People tended to panic when they heard the Reinine of all Adara speaking in their heads. Besides, farspeakers made excellent secretaries.

She had just finished the most pressing of the business—everyone was still squabbling over those new mines north of Heldring—when Torchay approached and bent to murmur in her ear.

"Messenger," he said. "From Habadra."

Kallista stood, with dignity and aplomb rather than leaping from the chair fast enough to knock it over the way she wanted. "That will be all for now, Taylin." She dismissed the secretary-farspeaker. "Have Fenetta stand ready in Arikon at the same time tomorrow. I may not need her, but I'll let you know tomorrow."

The young farspeaker bowed and began gathering paperwork as Kallista led the way to the formal reception room where the messenger would be waiting.

Kallista hadn't been in this room before. Quietly impressive, it had the wide Daryathi floor-to-ceiling doors open to the courtyard breezes—a different courtyard from that off the family quarters. It was decorated in Adaran fashion with inlaid stone mosaics on the floor and columns along the walls.

A young man, his black hair caught back in an unbraided queue, stood at attention in the center of the room. Bare-chested beneath a leather harness, he wore a purple kilt embroidered with white cranes from waist to knees held in place by a wide belt from which two empty scabbards hung, both of these on his left side. Sandals laced up to his knees.

Kallista had seen a good number of similarly dressed young men at the en-Kameral yesterday, and had assumed they served the same purpose Torchay and her other bodyguards did. But here this one was, serving as messenger.

He straightened from his bow. Tattooed face, unmarked hands, Kallista noted. In fact, he had no tattoos anywhere but his face. With most of him on display, it was easy to see. Champion then, but not dedicat. Obed had explained that only dedicats carried the body tattoos, and the more tattoos a champion bore, the higher he had developed his skills before leaving his skola. Was this why Obed was so modest now? Because he'd worn so few clothes before, to let the tattoos show?

She inclined her head in recognition of the man's bow. "You have a message for me?"

The young champion bowed again. "Honor to the Reinine of all Adara."

He paused as Stone entered the chamber, followed by Namida Ambassador, then bowed to each of them in turn.

"Habadra Khori bids me say these words to you," he went on when all the bowing was done. "Habadra Khori will meet with the husband of her servant this night at the first bell after sundown, to discuss terms. As a sign of her high esteem for the Reinine and of her eagerness to treat with you in an open and honorable fashion, the Habadra has sent this one—" Here the young man bowed again, lower than before. "—as a gift to the Line of the Reinine to serve as pleases her."

Chapter Seven

When he finished speaking, the messenger—*gift?*—widened his stance and clasped his hands behind his back in what would be Adaran parade rest, while Kallista tried with all her might not to goggle at him. She beckoned Namida closer and whispered to Torchay, "I think we need Obed on this one. Send someone—"

Torchay was already signaling one of the other men in bodyguard's red-trimmed blacks. With Stone here, Torchay would allow her secondary guard to play errand boy.

"Tonight is the party at Shakiri House," Namida said, her voice too quiet to carry far. "The Godmarked are invited with yourself, my Reinine."

"I'm sure that's why the Habadra has made her invitation for tonight." Goddess, Kallista hated politics.

"I'm going," Stone said, his jaw set stubbornly. "To meet this Habadra woman."

"Yes," Kallista agreed. "But not alone. Viyelle, and whoever else wants to go."

"That'd likely be all of us, but we can't all go," Torchay said with a wry smile. "Fox will want to. Take him."

"And Joh," Kallista said. "Between him and Viyelle, you'll have all the negotiating skills you might want."

"But Shakiri—" Namida Ambassador spoke up.

"Will have to make do with the Reinine, the official Reinas and three Godmarked." Kallista looked up as Obed strode in, his black robe billowing behind him.

"You have need of me, my Reinine?" Obed's Adaran-style bow still creaked at the edges, but not badly enough for any but another Adaran to notice.

"Yes, love." Kallista touched his cheek, feeling as if she played to a crowd. She did, though the crowd held only one member. "The Habadra has gifted us with this young champion. What in seven hells am I supposed to do with him? How big an insult would it be to send him back?"

Namida blanched.

"Big enough to make an enemy of Habadra for generations to come," Obed said. "I am told this is what began the enmity between Shakiri and Habadra. The Shakiri sent back a gift of the Habadra. It was a breeding bull, not a man, but it was the same principle."

"I was afraid of that." Kallista propped her hands on her hips and studied her new retainer. He pretended not to notice, staring straight ahead at nothing at all.

"And, my Reinine," Namida Ambassador spoke up. "You must send a gift of equal value with your response to the message."

"Well, I am certainly not sending her one of my bodyguards." Kallista's voice rose with her temper until anyone in the courtyard outside could hear. "*Or* one of our troopers."

"No, my Reinine. Of course not." Namida bowed as low as the young champion had, though with more style.

Kallista blew out a breath. "So what *can* we send? Ironwork?" Adaran ironwork was prized worldwide. "A horse?"

Obed nodded slowly. "A horse would do. One of the stallions bred from the drover-Korbin-Southron cross, perhaps . . ." He addressed the messenger. "Are you Habadra-tha or –sa?"

The young man flushed, gathered himself and bowed again. "This one is Habadra-sa, Reinas."

"So." Obed turned back to Kallista. "Not a stallion. A mare. A stallion is much more valuable than this champion. A mare, because she can only produce one foal a year, is only a little more costly. That would show generosity, but not recklessness or desperation."

"A horse is more valuable than a man?" Kallista muted her disapproval, but oh, she liked this place less and less.

"Horses are more fragile and not so easily replaced. And he is only -*sa*." Obed must have seen Kallista's confusion, for he continued. "There is -*tha*, -*sa* and -*ti*. They are the families associated with a line. Habadra-*tha* would be the families who have served as trusted retainers since the line began. Habadra-*sa*—like this one—are the families that associated with the line after its formation, but for many generations. Habadra-*ti* would be those who have no names of their own. The servants who bind themselves to serve a line in payment of debt, who will again have no names when the year of the jubilee comes and they are freed. Merinda and her child are Habadra-ti."

"Oh." Kallista tried to absorb the knowledge. They were ranks—tha, sa and ti, in descending order. Surely she could remember that.

"Since we're keeping him," Torchay said. "What do you suppose we ought to do with him?"

Kallista opened her mouth, but had no idea what to say. "I don't know," she said finally. "I'll let you and Keldrey sort that out. Obed, you choose the horse. And we'll need a messenger to take it, I suppose."

"The embassy has messengers, my Reinine," Namida said. "Might I suggest a troop escort as well? To discourage thieves?"

"Fine, fine." Kallista walked up to her new champion. "What's your name, son?"

He flushed crimson and bowed once more. "This one is called by any name you choose to give me—" He paused before he spoke again, almost choking on the words. "My Reinine."

This was going to work *so* well. He obviously was not happy at being given away like—like a puppy who'd grown too big.

"Do you accept this gift from the Habadra?" The champion held his upper body at a slight angle, a half-bow, his eyes—his whole face cast down.

Kallista sighed. "Yes. I accept this gift from Habadra Khori to the Varyl Line." She didn't want to insult anyone before they had their family members out of the Habadra's power.

The champion finished his bow, then bent and unlaced his sandals. Kallista decided it must be part of some gifting ceremony when he removed them and wrapped them neatly together. He took off his belt, but set his empty scabbards in a separate pile. The leather harness came off next. She didn't get worried until he unwrapped his short purple kilt and folded it on top of all the leather. Surely he would retain at least his smallclothes, the lightweight short-legged breeches he wore beneath the kilt. But no, those came off too.

Obed stopped her when she would have protested, murmuring in her ear. "It signals his change of allegiance from Habadra Line to yours. He comes to you with only himself and his skills, embodied in his swords. He leaves behind everything Habadra, including his name, and becomes Varyl-sa."

Kallista blinked at her new champion, who picked up his scabbards and held them in one hand as he returned to attention. He was certainly a fine-looking young man. She was still blinking when she turned to look at her iliasti.

Torchay choked back laughter. "If you could see your face . . . I've never seen you so flummoxed."

"Yes, well—" Kallista's voice cracked.

Namida cleared her throat. "He certainly is . . . flummox-worthy."

"Yes, he is." Kallista took another peek. "Torchay, find him some clothes. And a place. Namida, you and Stone work out the message for the Habadra. Obed, don't you have a horse to select?"

They began to scatter, to fulfill her orders. Before he could escape, Kallista punched her dark ilias in the arm. "Why didn't you *warn* me?"

"Warn you what?" Obed gave her a puzzled look as he rubbed his practically-imaginary sore spot.

"About this gift thing." She punched him again. "What he was going to do."

Obed shrugged. "It is a change-of-allegiance thing, not a gift thing, and I did not warn you because I did not know it was necessary."

"Did you ever—?"

"No. Not until I left the skola. I was im-Shakiri, of the direct line, who never change allegiance until they wed. And I was dedicat as well as champion."

"And just what *is* a dedicat?" This time, she was determined to get answers out of him.

"Many things." Obed smiled. "Set apart from the world, from other champions to focus on what would be demanded of us. Champions go out into the world to serve where they are needed—as bodyguards, to keep order—in many ways. Dedicats . . . do not."

"So what do they do?"

Obed bowed, still smiling. "I would tell you, but it is a very long telling, and I am commanded to choose a horse."

Kallista growled and he laughed. "Truly," he said. "I will tell you. But it will take time, and time is not a luxury we have just now."

Reluctantly, Kallista let it go. "Fine. Go pick out the right horse. But I have your promise. You *will* tell me."

"I will." He blew her a kiss and strode from the room, his robe blowing with the window draperies as he passed through.

Kallista found herself alone with two of her young military bodyguards. As she left the reception chamber, Leyja came jogging up to join them with a smile, a nod and a murmured "My Reinine."

Ah, the joys and burdens of rule.

The Shakiri party began just at sundown, before Stone was expected at Habadra House. Kallista didn't like leaving him, even with the others, but she had to trust him to handle things. Stone only seemed irresponsible. He knew what was important and fulfilled all his duties, though he might joke while he did. He had acted as sole protector of the most vulnerable members of their family during the early days of the Barbs' rebellion and kept them all safe and whole. He could certainly do this.

Still, Kallista's attention was not fully on the people before her when she dismounted from her gaudily decorated horse outside Shakiri House a few streets from the embassy. Namida Ambassador had suggested sedan chairs as more befitting the Reinine's dignity. Kallista had refrained from retorting that being carried about in a lacquered chair by six strong men as if she were too feeble to carry herself would be positively *destructive* of the Reinine's dignity. She said only that she was Reinine *and* soldier, and that she would ride.

Fortunately, there was more fabric than decoration to tonight's party dress—white, trimmed with red and gold—so she could move with a bit more ease. The trousers beneath the long side-slit tunic were trimmed only at the ankle and she wore no overrobe at all.

Obed, dressed in matching white, red and gold, took her arm and escorted her into the House of the Line to which he had been born. Torchay stalked at her opposite elbow in his military dress red-trimmed blacks, the brown-and-gold stag of his home prinsipality reduced to a badge on the left shoulder of the new button-front uniform tunic. Behind them followed Aisse and Leyja in their party-going finery, Leyja's blacks matching Torchay's save for her silver-shell prinsipality badge. Aisse wore red, white and gold, but in her dress, the red dominated.

They strolled through the entrance courtyard filled with temporarily erected statuary, fountains and exotic blooming plants. Servants stood on either side, holding torches in a living arch of light. Stone filigree separated the public and private sections of the courtyard. Invited guests stepped to either side and bowed as Kallista and the Godmarked entered, creating an aisle to the double doors flung wide in invitation.

There, Shakiri Shathina waited, her white hair coiled atop her head like a crown, interlaced with a gold chain that reinforced the crown look. She wore an ankle-length dress of six or seven delicate layers shading from deep blue-purple to a blue so pale it was almost white, each layer shorter so that the last fell just below her hips. The dress was cinched at her waist with a heavy gold belt that matched the elaborate pectoral collar inlaid with sapphire-mosaic lotus blossoms. The whole of it looked incredibly heavy, despite the lightness of her dress.

Kallista was grateful that the Reinine's primary symbols of office were the seldom-worn crown, safely back home in Arikon, and the seal hanging from her belt, mingling anonymously with her military honors.

She waited, a small, polite smile on her face, for the Shakiri to bow. Kallista had spent all of her adult life in the military. She knew rank and its value, and by any measurement, even if she was married to one of the im-Shakiri, Kallista held the higher rank. Kallista was sole ruler of the entire Adaran nation while Shakiri Shathina shared a seat on the Daryathi executive council with four others. And Kallista was Godstruck.

So she waited, smiling, for the Shakiri to recognize that fact. As the moment stretched, Kallista calculated her response should the Shakiri offer the insult of failing to bow. Turn and walk out, she supposed. Had anyone ever denied this woman anything? Had anyone ever defied her inside the walls of her own House? Finally, with a sour grimace, Shakiri Shathina jerked into motion, executing a grudging, barely polite bow.

Kallista let her smile show real pleasure—she was grateful Shathina had enough sense to avoid a diplomatic incident—and returned the bow in elaborate Adaran style. "Thank you for your courtesy, Shakiri," she said, taking the woman's hand in both of hers. "You remember these of the godmarked?"

She beckoned her iliasti forward. Obed scowled, but Kallista ignored it. Perhaps it was a breach of etiquette not to introduce him first as husband, but Shathina knew him already. She could greet him first.

"Are there not more of these godmarked in your court?" Shathina freeed her hand from Obed's double-handed clasp. "Where are they?"

"A matter concerning their children." Kallista answered Shathina's intrusive query—one the older woman doubtless already knew the answer to—with a polite evasion that had the benefit of being truth, if not all of it.

"Oh? I hope it is not serious." Shathina kept her attention on Kallista as she exchanged perfunctory greetings with Torchay, Aisse and Leyja.

"I fear that it is." Kallista hoped she was conveying the message that she would tolerate no interference in the matter. "I am most concerned."

"Then, if it please the One, I hope everything turns out as you wish." Shathina's smile went no deeper than the tint coloring her lips

Kallista returned her own grim smile. "I am sure it will."

The Shakiri's smile went stiff, and she turned away, toward a woman standing literally in the Shakiri's shadow. An echo of Shakiri Shathina, the woman was some thirty years younger. She wore a lighter gold chain through coils of dark hair beginning to show a lacing of silver, and a smaller gold collar. Her dress matched the Shakiri's, except the layers shaded with the deepest color on top. She had the same austere, handsome features as the Shakiri, but this woman seemed somehow more . . . alive.

"My daughter, Bekaara." Shathina flipped a hand her way. "I understand you have had dealings."

Obed almost grinned as he caught the hands his cousin held out to him.

"I see you have landed in thick cotton," Bekaara said as she pulled him in for an embrace.

"More than ever I expected. All thanks to you for your care and instruction." He drew her toward Kallista. "Bekaara taught me all I know of trade and of honor."

Shakiri Shathina made a noise that sounded suspiciously like a snort, but since she said nothing, Kallista ignored her.

"Cousin," Obed held Bekaara's hand in one of his and took Kallista's in the other, drawing them together. "This is my Kallista." He didn't hesitate, as he might have if he'd been choosing between 'wife' and 'ilias.' "My beloved. Chosen and marked by the very hand of the One. As are we all."

He reached toward the others, bringing them closer. "My chosen brother and sisters, my fellow godmarked. There are four others, but they are—" Obed glanced over his shoulder at his aunt, who had moved away, apparently to give instructions to servants. "They are dealing with the Habadra."

"Will it make trouble for you? Helping us deal with Shakiri's enemy?" Kallista clasped Bekaara's hand now, in greeting and more.

She shrugged. "I will endure it. I am my mother's only daughter."

"But you have a daughter," Obed said.

"Shakiri Shathina has not yet succeeded in turning her completely against me. I am safe enough for now." Bekaara smiled and waved her hands as if shooing away biting insects, or evil biting thoughts. "Enough about that. I want to know what you mean when you say 'Godmarked.' Do you mean literally marked? As Obed is marked?" She gestured at the tattoos on his face.

He laughed. "No, cousin. These symbols were made by men as signs of devotion and achievement. The One made Her own mark upon us." He brushed Aisse's short-cropped hair aside. The small woman didn't have to bend to allow Bekaara to see the rose-shaped mark on the back of her neck. "We all bear this sign."

"My mark is different," Kallista said. "A rose like that with the addition of the One's compass points. Because I am the naitan and given the ability to use the magic poured into my godmarked by the One."

"It is magic?" Bekaara breathed the words.

"Yes." Kallista frowned. "Do you not have naitani and magic in Daryath? I had not heard that you have lost these gifts."

"There is magic," Bekaara said. "But it is not so common as in Adara. It is rare and precious. Even those who have the homely South magics are taken into the temple to serve there with their blessed sisters, where they are safe and protected."

Baking bread that would keep for a year seemed an odd service for a temple to need. "Where is the temple?" Kallista asked. She hadn't seen any building that resembled the four-petaled temples of Adara, with their high central sanctuaries.

"Beside the Seat. Didn't you see it when you rode in yesterday?" Bekaara led them deeper into the broad reception room as servants passed carrying trays of drinks.

Kallista selected one at random and called a thread of magic to test it. It was safe to drink. She checked all the food and drink and found nothing suspicious.

"The walled building." Obed sipped at his wine. "The one with the painted scenes—"

"Oh yes. All those pictures of people burning in fires and impaled on stakes and—" Kallista shuddered. It seemed awfully gruesome for a place of worship, but different people emphasized different aspects of the One. In Daryath, the face of Judgment seemed pre-eminent. "That was the temple? But—where do people go in to worship?"

Bekaara frowned now. "Worship is in the plaza outside the walls, under the One's own sky and sun."

Kallista thought about that a minute, then nodded. "Hmm. I suppose it doesn't get as cold here as at home in Adara, so— What about the healers?"

"Why would healers be in the temples?" Bekaara asked. "The people are in the city."

"Even those with healing magic?" Kallista tried to piece things together.

"There is such a magic?" Bekaara sounded stunned.

They were getting nowhere answering questions with more questions, but Kallista didn't know enough to do more than guess. "So—no one goes into the temple—"

"Of course not. Who would carry our petitions to the One if no one entered?"

Kallista thought it was easier to carry her own petitions to the One herself, but she wouldn't say that. Not until she knew Bekaara better. "So who does go into the temples?"

Bekaara's confusion showed. "There is only one temple. The clerics and the prelates live on the temple grounds and the prelates go into the temple itself to plead on our behalf with the One."

"What about the naitani? Those with magic?"

"They are prelates, of course. Is it not so in Adara? Are you not yourself a prelate?"

Kallista scratched her head and exchanged a glance with Obed and the others. How to explain this? "Now," she said. "Now that I am Reinine, I am a prelate. Technically. Officially. But before I was selected, I was a soldier. My parents were both prelates of Riverside Temple in—"

"*What?*" Bekaara's shock resonated through the room.

Kallista reviewed what she had said. No, no mention of iliani. What could have—?

"Adara has many temples," Obed was saying very quickly. "There are six in Arikon alone, five in Turysh, three in Ukiny. Every village has its own temple. And remember, Adara has many, many naitani. They are almost commonplace. You traveled there in your youth. You remember. You told me of the wonders you saw."

"I remember." Bekaara nodded. "I had forgotten, but I remember now that prelates in Adara marry."

"That's right." Kallista smiled at Obed to thank him for his rescue. "Do they not marry in Daryath?"

"It is not *forbidden,*" Bekaara said. "But I have not heard of such a thing in many, many years. Of course, we hear very little of what goes on behind the temple walls. Only the clerics come out. The prelates stay within."

"But what about the schools?" In Adara, children were educated in the schools held in the south wing of every temple. "Where are they?"

"Each Line educates its own children," Bekaara said. "Boys and girls together until they are twelve, when the boys are sent away to the skolas and academies."

"Interesting." Kallista wanted to know more, but her ambassador was making frowny faces at her. She couldn't let one person, no matter how congenial, monopolize all her time. "We will have to meet again soon to discuss this more."

"My time is at your disposal." Bekaara bowed. "You have only to send word."

Kallista returned the bow and with a sigh, bent her attention to the difficult task of mingling with the other party guests. She wondered how Stone was faring, but it was too early to check. They wouldn't have left yet for Habadra House. Only a few more chimes to endure before she could escape.

Chapter Eight

Darkness deepened. Dressed in finery equal to that of Kallista and her fellow party-goers, Stone paced in the embassy courtyard, climbing the steps into the entry hall every few rounds to check the time on the table clock there. He would not be late, not for this.

"You can't make the clock move faster by looking at it," Viyelle said from the courtyard bench where she sat beside Joh.

"Why not? I should be able to. What use is this magic we carry if we can't do anything with it?" He reached for his hair and stopped himself in time. It would not help him to go looking like a madman with his hair sticking on end. It had taken him half a chime and half a jar of hair cream to make it lie down.

"Not even Kallista can make time move faster." Fox leaned against a column between courtyard and entry.

"We can leave soon," Joh said. "It will take a little time to walk the distance. The captain will let us know when the escort is assembled."

"I don't know why we need an escort anyway," Stone grumbled. He collapsed onto the bench where Viyelle patted it.

"So we look important." She looped her arm through his and Stone took a moment to lean his head on hers, seizing the warmth she offered.

"Why couldn't Sky have been yours?" he grumbled. He'd have liked to have a child with Viyelle. Or Aisse. Another child to tie him closer to them. Another living, laughing expression of the way he felt about these people, these women. The Tibran caste system he'd grown up in separated men from women, and boys from their mothers at an early age—the twins' age. He much preferred the Adaran way of mixing everyone together. And he loved having a family, one that loved him back. He'd have to try again for a child, try harder, when Sky was home with them.

"He *is* mine." Viyelle squeezed his arm and Stone moved away, rising from the bench, afraid she might do more, might betray her feelings somehow.

Be honest. He was afraid the closeness might cause him to betray his own feelings. Tibran Warrior Caste weren't supposed to have feelings, but Stone hadn't been Tibran for many years now. He was Adaran. Ilias. Godmarked.

Since they had reached Daryath, Stone had been set off by himself, alone, separated from the others by local custom and by worry. Would they get their son back? Was he safe? Did he have enough to eat? A dry place to sleep?

Torchay had shared Stone's tent, and in the city, shared his room, but Stone had still felt set apart, separate. Kallista's magic last night had changed that, some.

Now, Stone stood in the courtyard and looked at them. At Joh, who most usually shared Viyelle's bed with him, who had become a second *brodir*. What was it about these quiet thinkers that made them such good friends? Though Fox wasn't so quiet with his thinking. Stone and Fox had been side by side since they were boys and would stand together the rest of their lives. But now they had Joh and Torchay and Obed and Keldrey and their women to stand with.

Viyelle. Stone filled his eyes with her familiar face, her smooth caramel brown hair grown longer now for a queue, like most of the others. She wore it loose tonight and it blew in the breeze across the dark wings of her eyebrows, over the mixed green-brown of her eyes. Stone had learned about love in Adara. Tibran Warriors didn't know what it was—women there were treated like pets one could have sex with, though it might have changed since the demon there had been destroyed. But Stone knew.

He loved these people and they loved him. He felt it, *knew* it every time Kallista called magic. They would not give up until they had his son safe within the family. They believed he could succeed. So he would. He couldn't let them down.

Fox turned his head away as if listening. Stone could hear nothing, but Fox turned back. "The escort is ready."

Viyelle caught Stone's arm before he could bound up the broad steps into the building and pulled him into a tight hug. "You'll do fine. You'll get them back for us."

Them. Yes, he was negotiating for Merinda too. Sky would need his mother. Stone hugged Viyelle, kissed the spot on her right temple— never the left—that always made her shiver. "Yes."

Joh extended a hand and when Stone clasped his wrist, Joh used it to haul him in for another embrace. "Luck."

Stone tugged Joh's queue because he couldn't force out more words, and went to give Fox a back-pounding hug.

"Enough," Fox said, turning Stone round and shoving him toward the door. "I'm going to be black and bruised where you pounded me. My next hugs are reserved for Sky."

Yes.

Habadra House sat almost atop the Seat of Government, a good fifteen-tick journey away. The soldier escort lit the way with torches, pushing aside groups of already drunken revelers. Patrols of face-tattooed champions gave sullen way, sending prickles of warning down Stone's neck.

Trouble waited here. It only required the proper match to send it raging out of control. He'd seen it, been one of those ruthlessly quelling the riots, when he'd been part of Tibre's conquering army. He'd felt the trouble build until it burst, unable to predict when or where it would begin, only knowing that it would. Mestada's night had the same feel.

The gong-like city bell had just sent its booming sound shuddering out over the night when Stone stopped before the iron-barred gate in the high, white stone walls surrounding Habadra House. When the sound faded, Stone rapped at the bars of the gate with the stick hanging there from a braided purple cord for that purpose.

"Stone Varyl vo'Tsekrish," he said to the gatekeeper when she appeared. "Godmarked of Adara. I am invited here with my—with these other of the godmarked to meet with the Habadra Khori on a matter of family and business."

The gatekeeper frowned. "Only you were invited. I am not authorized to allow these others within."

Stone gave his iliasti a "what now?" look. He did not want to go in alone, but he would not leave without meeting the Habadra.

"We will wait," Viyelle said. "Might we wait in the public courtyard, Aila?" She used the Adaran form of polite address.

The gatekeeper pondered the request for a long moment. "The god-marked may enter the courtyard. I may not permit armed champions of another Line within this gate without authorization from the Habadra."

"That means the troop escort stays in the street," Fox murmured.

"I know that," Stone snapped. He knew Fox was teasing, pretending he needed the explanation, but Stone's patience and his sense of humor had both abandoned him. He bowed to the gatekeeper, not low, and waited for the gate to open.

"Be polite." Joh spoke quickly and quietly as they entered the courtyard together. "Don't commit to anything. Don't blink, no matter how outrageous her demands. Don't say yes or no to anything. Remember it's a battle. But not with swords."

"Right." Stone took a deep breath, tugged his elaborately decorated tunic—red for the warrior he was and for the godmarked magic—into place, and stepped through the simple wooden gate into the private section of the Habadra House front courtyard.

Another servant, this one male, waited to escort Stone into the house. The heavy carved doors opened onto a wide entrance hall. In the precise center of the room, a delicate stand of Adaran ironwork held an exuberant mass of flowers nearly overflowing the pale vase that attempted to contain them. They perfumed the air as Stone followed the servant through the candlelit room and out into the courtyard beyond.

The sound of water trickling from one of the ever-present fountains covered the footsteps of the woman who approached, holding her hands out in greeting. Confused, Stone took her hands and bowed awkwardly over them.

This was indeed the woman who had been introduced yesterday at the en-Kameral as Habadra Khori. He recognized her square-jawed face and sharp, high-bridged nose. But rather than the heavy pectoral collar of yesterday, she wore a narrow chain with an amethyst pendant carved into a crane over her simple white muslin dress. Stone felt incredibly overdressed.

"Welcome to my home, Stone im-Varyl." The Habadra tugged him down to kiss him on each cheek.

He thought about correcting her, but decided against it. If she thought of him as a son of Kallista's Varyl Line, maybe she would give him what he wanted all the sooner. The Tibrans in Kallista's ilian had all adopted her family name, since they'd had none of their own. "I am honored to be here, Habadra."

Stone bowed again, managing to free his hands for a proper Adaran-style bow with flourishes. Obed had drilled him on forms of address and etiquette. The main thing that had stuck with him was: "When in doubt, bow."

"Come. Sit." Habadra Khori reclaimed his hand and led him to a cozy seating area beneath the spreading branches of an oak that had dropped its acorns to crunch underfoot. "May I offer you refreshment?"

"Thank you." *Take what was offered.* He sat on the cushioned bench and scooted into the metal arm when the Habadra sat close beside him. Too close.

Stone managed not to jump or squawk when she set her hand on his thigh and slid it round to the inside where she squeezed.

"I find many things refreshing, don't you?" the Habadra purred.

Stone cleared his throat. Obed's instructions had not included protocol for handling something like this. Gently, in hopes of avoiding offense, Stone picked her hand up from his leg and held it in both of his, mostly to keep her from putting it back. He floundered for a way out. How would Fox do it? Or Joh? What would they say? "Habadra Khori, I am—flattered."

Would holding her hand like this make her think he was interested? Stone eased himself from the bench and gave her back her hand, stepping a safe distance away—he hoped. "But I am married. I keep my vows, honored Habadra."

She made a face, a pout better suited to a younger woman. "Your wife is my servant. I can order her to divorce you."

Goddess. Was the woman mad? "That would not change my vows, Aila, only hers." He smiled, hoping he had not ruined things already. If it came right down to it, he supposed he could do sex with this woman if that was the price to free his son and the boy's mother. But he would really rather not.

The Habadra sighed. "Yes, well—I had to try. You're an attractive man, as I am sure you know. Pity that you're an honorable one as well."

She stood and clapped her hands sharply. "I suppose you'll be wanting to see your wife."

"Yes, please, and my son." Stone bowed again.

"All in due time, my dear." The Habadra's smile made him ease another step back.

A female servant entered, wearing only the same sort of knee-length kilt as the messenger-champion the Habadra had given Kallista that morning. This one was plain white. The woman was thin, her ribs almost showing beneath dry, dull skin. Her naked breasts sagged and swayed as she strained to carry a heavy tray laden with decanters, glasses and covered platters. Lines of struggle marked her face, spread from the corners of her sunken eyes. Despite the drastic changes, he knew her. "Merinda."

Kallista was right. No matter her faults, Merinda did not deserve this. Stone strode across the courtyard, took the tray from her and slid it onto the waiting table. He tipped her face up, brushed back the hair that had escaped from its leather binding. "Merinda?"

He dropped his voice to softer than a whisper, quieter than the murmur of the fountain. *"Ilias."*

She heard him, he knew, for she blinked, but she would not look at him. She kept her eyes cast down, her face impassive.

Stone wished for one of Obed's overrobes or—he could take off his own tunic and give it to Merinda, give her something to cover her nakedness. But would that play into the Habadra's hands? Give up some advantage he needed?

"I take it then that this *is* your wife?" The Habadra's voice was dry, all its previous seductive purr gone.

Stone turned away from Merinda. It wasn't easy, but he faced the Habadra Khori. "Yes," he said. "This is Merinda. My wife. What has happened to her?"

The Habadra shrugged. "Life. Service."

Stone fought to control his temper. He didn't often lose it, but when he did, it sometimes frightened even him. "And my son? Is he in a similar state?"

Again the Habadra shrugged. "I doubt it. Those who come to service young do not struggle so against it."

Stone took a deep breath, intended to calm him, but it didn't help much. "And what is the redemption price?"

Her gaze sharpened. "I would be within the Law to demand that you take the place of your wife and child in my service, in exchange for their freedom."

"But you will not." Stone was as hard, as unmovable as his name. "I am Godmarked of Adara. I serve no one but the One who has marked me with His own hand. This is my wife. Her child is my child. I will pay what is owed, but I will not pay more."

"Ah." Habadra Khori gestured at the wine and pastries. "Then let us refresh ourselves and see whether we can come to terms."

Stone inclined his head in that slight, oh-so-superior way Obed had, and took the glass of rich, red wine she offered. "The redemption price for a man-child of such tender years should be no more than five Adaran krona."

The Habadra sipped her wine and shook her finger at him. "Now Godmarked, you know we must begin with the mother before we can come to the child. She is a healer. A—what is it your people call them? A *naitan*. She is worth a great deal to my Line."

"How much?" Stone tasted his drink, intent on keeping a clear head. It was good wine, not too strong, so he drank again, his nerves making him thirsty. He took a pastry to fill his stomach with something more than wine.

The battle had begun, the opening salvos were fired. It would be long, bloody and hard-fought, but in the end, he would win. He had no other choice.

Kallista accepted a plate of food from Torchay. "Do these Daryathi never sit to eat?" she muttered to the room at large.

"Rarely, at gatherings of this sort," Namida Ambassador murmured back. "More business can be done when one is free to move about."

"We're going to have chairs—lots and lots of chairs. And benches, when we host 'gatherings of this sort' at the embassy." Kallista took a bite of one of the little flaky, rolled pastry tubes. This one was filled with delicately flavored fish and crisp vegetables. Daryathi food was proving a delicious adventure. She never knew what she might bite into next, and so far, everything tasted wonderful. But her knees were beginning to ache and her feet had gone numb a chime or so past.

She took a sip of the wine Torchay held for her, thanking him with a private smile. He wouldn't let her set her glass on one of the delicate mosaic tables scattered throughout the house for the purpose. Anyone would have access to it.

"How do you suppose Stone's mission is going?" Kallista spoke quietly, for Torchay's ears only as she handed him her glass again, daring to voice the thought uppermost in her mind.

"Why don't you tell me?" He raised an eyebrow, reinforcing his question.

"I can't see through his eyes like I can Joh's, and I looked earlier. Joh's outside the house with Viyelle and Fox. I don't like you playing servant like this."

"I'm not playing servant. I'm playing bodyguard. You should be used to it by now." He drank from her glass. Not servant behavior, since he drank after her rather than before. He couldn't claim to be checking it for poison. The blatantly insubordinate behavior made her feel better.

So did what she could pick up of Stone through the link. Despite an undercurrent of worry, he was focused intently on a task. Kallista could sense his determination, but little more. She smiled at Torchay. "Things are going fine. I think they're bargaining. He's not worried—not any more than he has been."

He picked up a fresh glass of wine from a passing server and handed it to her. "Check it," he ordered.

She rolled her eyes, but she bled off a tendril of magic yet again to check the wine for poisons. "Clean. Like all the rest of it. I checked it *all*, remember?"

"Then—" He held up the glass he'd been drinking from for a toast. "To Stone's success."

Kallista touched her new glass to his and drank. "To bringing them all safely home."

"What are we celebrating?" Obed's smile touched only his lips as he joined them. Women kept drawing him away to flirt, as fascinated by his tattoos as Kallista had been, though all but the marks on his face and hands were hidden. Kallista might have been jealous, but she could sense a flare of jealousy through Obed's link over her moment with Torchay, that was more than enough for everyone.

"Nothing yet." She smiled at him, sending a surge of reassurance down his link. "Only the hope of success. Things seem to be going well enough."

With a last touch of Torchay's hand as she handed him her empty glass and a quick glance into the blue of his eyes before he lowered them, Kallista looped her arm through Obed's and turned him toward more of his aunt's allies and guests.

"And if all those women keep flirting with you so blatantly," she said, "I may decide to lock you up safe at home the way Bekaara tells me husbands were once kept."

Instead of laughing as she hoped he would, Obed looked at her with haunted eyes. "Would you? Do you care that much?"

"Obed." Kallista halted in the middle of the noisy, crowded party. She set her plate aside so she could take both his hands. "I care more than that. *I love you*. I love you enough to trust you. To trust that you love me. Can you love *me* that much?"

His eyes flicked to all the people around them, now staring at the little domestic drama in their midst. Kallista didn't care. She probably would in the morning, but right now, she needed to know.

"Yes, of course. It's not—" He gazed at her, that lost look beginning to fade.

Kallista staggered, *wrongness* chiming through her like the sound of Mestada's booming bells.

"What is it?" Torchay caught her arm, the dishes he held crashing to the floor as he dropped them to catch her. Obed let go her hands to support her other side.

The links. Frantic, Kallista sorted through them, fumbling as she hunted the sense of *wrong*, the growing pain—*Stone.*

She must have said his name aloud. Torchay barked out orders, gathering their iliasti from across the room, summoning their escort. Kallista scooped up magic and threw it down her link to Stone. He was hurt . . . Sick . . . *Poisoned.*

Kallista sensed Torchay and Obed stagger as they bore her along when she drew hard on their magic. She'd practiced the healing magic, hadn't let it slide like she had so much of the other, and once she'd healed Fox at a greater distance. Or kept him from dying so his body could heal on its own. Surely she could keep Stone alive now.

She poured magic into him, trying to see where the poison was killing him. There—his heart slowed. She fought the poison back, working frantically everywhere at once. The awful stuff seemed to have already spread everywhere. Vaguely, she heard shouting, people rushing about, asking foolish questions. Stone's heart beat slower, his lungs struggled to fill with breath. *No.* She would not lose him.

Kallista called even more magic, the demon-destroying magic, shaping it this time for life. If she could shape it for peace, she could shape it for life. She named it, filling it with all her love, all the whole ilian's love for their Stone, and *pushed* it down the link.

It touched him, began driving back the poison, purging it from the blood that had spread it through his body. Stone's love for all of them surged back. Kallista shared it out, knowing they all needed this. He was healing. *He would live.*

And the link snapped.

The magic broke. The love ended.

Nothing was there in the place inside her where Stone lived but . . . nothing. Emptiness. *Loss.*

Kallista screamed.

Chapter Nine

The sound of her scream sliced through Torchay like a demon's terrible, fleshless talons. She screamed Stone's name, over and over again. The horses finally came from wherever the Shakiri's servants had taken them.

"Mount," Torchay ordered Obed, who seemed only slightly less shocky than Kallista. Torchay had to pull Kallista from Obed's grip to allow the other man to mount.

"Take her." Torchay gave up the precious burden into Obed's arms so Torchay could keep them both safe.

"What is happening?" Namida Ambassador asked for the fiftieth time. "I have to explain—Shakiri Shathina is outraged—Is the Reinine ill? Is she poisoned?"

"Not poison," Torchay said, then had to correct himself. He hadn't learned much in the few moments Kallista had linked them all together, but what he had managed to sort out from the confused jumble of impressions was not good. Was so bad it seared his soul.

"Kallista's not poisoned," he said. "Not here. No one here. Our ili— Godmarked. Stone was attacked. At Habadra House—maybe. I don't know. Don't know all of it, but whatever it is, it's bad."

"Wait—how do you know?" Namida clutched at Torchay as he mounted. "What do I say?"

"It's *magic*." Torchay held his horse on a tight rein, his agitation communicating to the animal and setting it to circling. "We are godmarked. Linked. She *knows*, Ambassador. She herself is not harmed, but nothing can happen to any of us without her knowing."

"*Reinas*," the captain of the guard was shouting. "Bodyguard, where do we go?" Everyone was finally mounted.

"The embassy," Obed said.

"*No*." Torchay knew better. Kallista would not want to go to ground, not when one of hers was in danger. They couldn't hold her there if they tried. "We ride to Habadra House."

The captain looked to Obed, then to Leyja for confirmation. After a brief exchange of glances, they all nodded. The captain saluted and led the way clattering down the street.

Chaos reigned outside Habadra House. Part of the troop escort that had accompanied their other four stood beating on the gate, shouting for admittance, while the rest of them stacked benches and other appropriated materials in a pile to climb over the walls. Inside the gate, in the public courtyard, Joh held off a handful of servants with his sword in one hand while he held a half-naked woman with the other arm round her neck. The woman was streaked with blood, her once-white kilt soaked in it, dripping scarlet onto the white pavement.

Kallista screamed again, her voice raw and hoarse with pain. Torchay felt the draw of magic and wished he knew how to give it without her having to call.

"Down!" she cried and he threw himself against his horse's neck for what shelter it might give.

The iron-barred gate exploded into powder. Adaran troops leaped to their feet and poured through into the courtyard. Kallista, apparently in control of herself and her magic again, ordered Obed after them. Torchay went after her, as always.

Soldiers took possession of the woman Joh had captured. They warded off the Habadra servants, herding them unharmed into a corner. Kallista threw herself from the horse into Joh's arms, nearly slicing herself in half on the sword he held. Torchay swallowed his shout and dismounted.

"Where?" Kallista had blood on her hands from somewhere, from Joh, who'd got it from the woman. She smeared it on Joh's face when she touched him.

"Inside." Joh covered her hand with his bloodier one, pressing it to his cheek. "It's bad. Worse than you can imagine. But I know I can't tell you not to go. Follow the blood."

He looked up then, met Torchay's eyes, flicked to Obed and came back before letting Kallista go. Horror shivered cold fingers through Torchay, settling in a jagged icy shard in the middle of his gut. *Goddess, how bad was it?*

The door to the inner courtyard stood open, as did the door to the house itself, a thick trail of blood leading the way. Kallista's steps slowed from their first rush, as if she feared what she would find at the trail's end.

Or as if she knew already and didn't want to see it.

Torchay moved ahead, taking point against any danger that might lie ahead, leaving Obed and Leyja to deal with that which might come creeping up from behind. He did not want to see either, but he had to be there, had to be ready for Kallista when she did.

The bloody trail was smeared across the polished floor by the footsteps that had run through it, slipped in it. It led through the broad entrance hall into the courtyard beyond, lush with greenery and fountains. Torchay drew both his swords as he entered, damning himself as an idiot for not doing it sooner.

The crunch of his footsteps on gravel brought Fox's head up, but not his sword. His *knowing* would have told him who approached.

"Don't let her come." Fox's voice sounded broken. Candlelight gleamed off the bright gold of his hair.

"You think I could stop her?" Torchay tried to see through the flickering shadows. "Is it safe? Anyone coming?"

"No one close enough yet to matter." Fox flipped his sword hilt in his hand, turning the double-edged, magic-forged blade over. He did it again and again, almost spinning the grip in his hand. He obviously wanted to kill, but had no target in view.

Torchay glanced over his shoulder. Obed was with Kallista, holding her up, talking non-stop in her ear. He wouldn't change her mind, but he might slow her down. Torchay took a deep breath, then wished he hadn't because the sharp coppery smell of blood permeated everything, overpowering even the flowers' perfume with its terrible scent.

He walked forward along the path, until he stood next to Fox twirling his sword. There, on the white limestone paving, lay two bodies. The Habadra Khori lay crumpled near a table and chair. The table held a tray filled with refreshments and a wine glass tipped on its side. Red wine spilled across the table and dripped onto the hem of the Habadra's white dress, staining her feet scarlet.

Blood pooled, deep and still spreading, around Stone's sprawled body. Viyelle knelt in the midst of it, holding on to his head, despair and horror in every line of her bowed body. She looked up at Torchay, tears flowing unchecked down her face, as they flowed down Fox's, down Torchay's.

"I can't make it stay," she said. "When I let go, his head rolls. It won't stay."

Oh Goddess. Torchay dropped to his knees—they wouldn't hold him. The blood splashed a little when he fell in it.

"Don't let her come!"

Fox's shout had to mean Kallista had entered the courtyard. Torchay struggled to collect himself, to rise, to get out of his ilias's spilled blood, but he couldn't. Oh, Goddess, *Stone.*

If he was so shattered by this, what would happen when Kallista saw?

The thud of many running feet and Fox's lack of reaction told Torchay their own troops took command of the courtyard. He had to get control of himself, had to think what to do next. He tried again to stand, and lost his balance, put his hand down to catch himself—into Stone's cooling blood.

Torchay threw himself aside to retch in the bushes. Then Joh was there, helping him up, handing him his swords. Aisse, Kallista and Leyja knelt with Viyelle, the four women embracing as they wept for their lost lover and friend, and suddenly, Torchay was glad he had fallen.

They all had, even Obed just now struggling to his feet, all of them stained with the blood of their ilias.

"Keldrey," Torchay said. "He should be here."

"He's been sent for." Joh gripped Torchay's arm, though his legs would support him now. Torchay turned his hand so he could grip Joh's wrist in return. If it weren't for the continuing likelihood of danger, he would hold on to more than just arms. Their ilias was dead. Slaughtered.

"Someone comes," Fox said. "Many of them. Strangers."

"Stay sharp," the escort captain called out. "But stay calm. This isn't our house."

The warning was apt, because the new arrivals erupted into the courtyard with a rattle of weapons, their tattooed faces stark and eerie in the torchlight. Behind them a woman ran barefoot, her hair falling loose down her back over her simple lavender dress. Perhaps ten years younger than Kallista, she had the same square jaw as the Habadra.

Torchay slid one of his swords into the upper scabbard on his back so that he held only one instead of two in the same hand. This could get bad quickly.

"What is happening here? How dare you invade this House with armed men!" The woman burst through her troop of champions to confront the men standing in the path—Torchay, Joh, Fox.

"You wish to know what is happening?" Kallista's voice rang out and they parted to let her through. Torchay let go Joh's arm and stepped up close behind her, into his place.

"Murder," Kallista said. "Murder has happened here, and that is why I dare. I am Kallista Reinine, Godstruck of Adara. Who are you?"

Torchay touched the small of her back. He could sometimes calm her that way, when her temper was on the edge.

The woman drew herself up as straight and proud as Kallista. "I am Chani, heir to Habadra. Who is murdered?"

Kallista shuddered. Then she bowed, deeply, in the Daryathi way. "I share your grief. May the One hold you in her hands through this time." She stepped back, to the side of the path, Torchay wheeling with her in a sort of military maneuver. Fox and Joh stepped aside, revealing the whole grisly tableau to the Habadra heir—the new Head of Habadra Line.

With a keening cry, Habadra Chani ran forward, splashing through Stone's blood, and fell to her knees. She bowed over her mother's body, her hands hovering as if afraid to touch.

Obed eased past Fox and Joh to stand on Kallista's other side, causing the Habadra champions to raise their weapons, which had the Adaran troops rattling theirs. The Adaran muskets had a much greater chance of harming someone by accident than did the Habadran swords, and Torchay tensed.

"Stand down!" Kallista called half a moment before Torchay would have. "We have all lost someone here."

"This is my *mother*," Habadra Chani cried. "How can your loss compare with mine?"

Kallista went rigid with anger and Torchay opened his hand, pressing it flat on her back. Obed's hand bumped his, as he did the same, and Torchay pulled back. He was not ilias here, not lover. Only bodyguard.

Kallista ground her retort in her teeth, averting disaster. "It serves no purpose to compare grief."

"He is im-Varyl," Obed said, as if that would explain it. And perhaps it did, for the Habadra subsided.

A man near the murdered Habadra's age pushed his way through the soldiers. He staggered when he saw the bodies, but recovered with a quiet, anguished dignity. He walked to the new Head of Line and bowed. "Habadra Chani."

She turned her grief-stricken face up to him. "Father. How can she be gone?"

He shook his head, unable to answer. Then he lifted the lifeless body of his wife and carried it from the courtyard. The new Habadra struggled to her feet, wiping her face with a hand. "Who has done this evil deed?" She glared at Kallista.

"My Godmarked was here alone with your mother. They are both dead, but it was my il—my Godmarked who was mutilated. In *your* House. Perhaps—"

Joh stepped forward, cleared his throat. "There is a woman. She was caught running—"

"Where?" Habadra Chani interrupted him, striding forward with hate in her eyes.

"Here." The Adaran guard captain stepped out from her place near the door. She kept the lines of retreat open. Torchay nodded approval.

The captain dragged with her the blood-soaked woman Joh had captured. One of the Habadra champions made as if to take possession of her, but the captain's glare and the steel in her other hand stopped him, as did Joh's advance. He and Fox took custody of the woman, bringing her the rest of the way to the secluded patio where Stone's body still lay horribly exposed.

Torchay reached behind Kallista to get Obed's attention. He'd worn one of the loose Daryathi-style overrobes tonight. Torchay gestured for him to remove it and cover Stone's body. Obed nodded, but when he moved to lay the elaborately adorned robe over him, Kallista said "No, don't. Don't cover him yet."

Obed did so anyway, for once in perfect accord with Torchay. She didn't need to see that awful sight any longer. None of them did.

There was an ominous stillness in Kallista, and Torchay looked for its cause. She stared at the woman held by Fox and Joh. Torchay frowned. The half-naked servant looked vaguely familiar. Could it be—? But *why?*

"A servant?" The Habadra spat out the word. Then she also looked more closely at the woman. "This is the servant your people wanted to redeem."

"Yes." Kallista confirmed it. The woman was Merinda.

God in heaven, what had happened to her? She looked older than Leyja, though she was years younger than Kallista, near Viyelle's thirty-four.

"She is *your* people. Your people did this, killed my mother, slaughtered her own husband."

"But we have not seen her in six years," Kallista retorted. "She has been in *your* hands. She is so changed I almost did not know her. What have you done to her that would drive her to such an act? And are you even certain that she did it?"

"Look at her!" Chani waved her hand along Merinda's blood-smeared body.

"Look at *me.*" Kallista spread her hands, showing the blood on her clothing where she had touched Stone, held him. "Blood alone is not evidence enough. I am naitan. Truthsayer. Question her. Let me use my magic to see what the truth is."

The Habadra's eyes narrowed with suspicion. "How do I know what *you* say is the truth?"

"Don't you have naitani? Send for one. She can read my truth."

Torchay had listened to Bekaara talk about Daryathi magic. He didn't know whether their naitani would leave the temple, and from the way the Habadra snarled, she didn't believe they would.

"We can try the truth in Daryathi fashion," Chani said.

What was Daryathi fashion? Torchay didn't know. Obed obviously did, for he had gone utterly still in that way that meant someone could die in the next moment. Not good.

"She is ours," Kallista said. "We have her. We will try the truth in Adaran fashion. If your naitan will not come, I will set a spell so that you can hear the truth yourself, so that you will know as she speaks it whether it is truth or lie."

Could she do that? Torchay had never heard of such a thing, although he'd seen Kallista do too many things no one had ever done. But she didn't have Stone. The one time the ilian been separated before, she'd said the lack of Stone's magic had made the remaining magic difficult to shape. Would it be so again?

Habadra Chani still frowned, still bristled with hate and grief, but she nodded. Once.

Torchay braced himself against the pull of magic so that it would not distract him from duty. Over the past years, he'd got better at not being distracted. He could feel the odd buzz that told him Kallista was working magic. The buzz had changed when the mark of the One had struck her, but Torchay had been able to tell when she used magic long before then.

He blinked. He'd never been able to *see* it before, however. Not like this. An odd white glow, like a mist but filled with light rather than hiding it, spread across the center of the courtyard just above the heads of the people in it. Torchay blinked again, but the mist was still there. Everyone else seemed to see it too, so he relaxed. It was Kallista's spell.

She stood close enough to him that he could feel her trembling. Was the magic so great a strain? Torchay laid his hand on her back again, offering what support he could. She said his magic held power. Perhaps by touching, she could access it easier. He shifted his touch to her bare hand and she closed it around his, a sense of gratitude coming through their link.

"The magic will tell lie from truth." Kallista indicated the mist overhead. "No matter who is speaking. If any of us fails to speak the truth, the magic will show us."

With another narrow-eyed glare, Chani spoke. "Shakiri Shathina is my dearest friend."

The mist roiled and turned a dark, ugly yellow-brown.

"Shakiri Shathina is my aunt." Obed said, and watched while the mist cleared to pure white again. Then he added, "But I do not love her." The mist stayed white.

"Satisfied?" Kallista raised an eyebrow at the Habadra who nodded grudgingly. "Then we will begin on the edges and work our way through to the center of the truth. Joh. What did you see?"

Caught off guard, Joh cleared his throat, then fell into a parade-rest position, hands clasped behind his back. "My Reinine." He inclined his head in a little bow, then stared straight ahead at nothing as he spoke.

"I came here with my—wife, Viyelle Prinsipella Torvyll, to assist Stone Varyl vo'Tsekrish in redeeming his wife and child. Fox Varyl vo'Tsekrish, Stone's *brodir,* also came."

The mist floated peacefully overhead, maintaining its clean color as Joh explained where everyone had been.

"We waited twenty, perhaps thirty ticks. It could have been less. Time passes slowly when waiting. And we felt—it was—" He stopped, looking helplessly at Kallista. "You pulled magic. We all felt it. You were worried and I think—it seemed your worry was for Stone. We stood, but didn't know what to do.

"You were still calling magic and—your worry faded. I sensed— Stone. For just a moment. Then he was gone, completely gone. And you screamed. I could hear your scream."

"What kind of nonsense is this?" Habadra Chani's voice oozed scorn. "Even I know the Reinine Kallista was at Shakiri House. How could—?"

"It is truth." Kallista pointed at the pearl-white mist. "Do you know magic? Know anything of its working? Do not dismiss a thing simply because you don't understand it."

"How do I know the magic is working for him? Maybe you set it for only the Daryathi born."

"Joh. Tell us a lie."

"When you screamed, I stayed in the courtyard with Fox and Viyelle."

Immediately, the mist darkened to a muddy purple.

"Interesting." Kallista cocked her head as she studied the magic. "Joh, change your lie."

"I stayed in the courtyard," he said. "Fox and Viyelle ran inside."

The mist, which had cleared to white again during Kallista's words, went grayish-lavender.

"So, partial truth, but not all of it." Kallista let go of Torchay and propped her hands on her hips as she stared up at her truth-mist. As long as she looked up, she didn't have to see the blood, didn't have to think about—

She took a deep, shuddering breath, wrapping invisible arms around the links to her remaining mates and held them tight as she drew in tiny driblets of magic to maintain the mist. She had to hold herself together. Later, she would have time for grief.

A commotion sounded across the courtyard, voices raised in argument and Adaran curses. Keldrey was here. The smile didn't reach Kallista's face, but it settled round her aching heart.

"Let him through," she called. "He is one of ours."

Keldrey pushed himself past the Habadra champions and came to join them. Unlike their iliasti, he did not fall, but then he had been warned. He knew what he would see. He went heavily to a knee, laid a gentle hand on Obed's robe where it was pulled over Stone's head, then moved to stand beside Leyja.

Kallista had to look away, at Joh still standing at parade rest, still staring off at nothing, a pair of fresh tears making new tracks through the blood Kallista had smeared on his face. *Magic.* Think about the magic.

"Tell another lie, Joh," she said. "Another sort of lie. Like the one the Habadra told."

He considered for a moment, his throat working as if he had to swallow down grief before he could push the words out. "I do not care what has happened."

Instantly, the mist seemed to shudder as it flashed to such a dark, ugly brown as to be almost black.

"Oh, that is such a lie." Kallista hugged her links tight, clinging for comfort as she stared hard at the mist, fighting her own tears. She could see shades of pustulent yellow deep within the darkness. It was the same color as the Habadra's lie, but much deeper, much farther from the truth.

"So, the magic has different colors for different sorts of lies," she said. "And different shades for different levels of truth. If it is a partial truth, the color is closer to white."

The truth-mist turned a pale, delicate pink, and Kallista felt bizarrely like laughing. "That is almost correct, but not quite, or so the magic says."

She turned to Habadra Chani. "Shall we go on?"

"I do not see why we do not just execute the woman and have done with it," the other woman said sullenly.

"Because I want to know the truth. Joh." Kallista looked at him again, at his well-loved face, austere beneath the smooth line of his pulled-back hair. "Who ran into the house?"

"We all did."

The mist cleared to white.

"We had to break down the inner gate. A servant tried to stop us. Fox stopped him—nothing broken, just a headache. We ran into the house and fanned out to search. Viyelle found him. Them. She went into the courtyard. She screamed. We came."

Joh paused, cleared his throat, struggled to regain his composure. "We found Stone's body, but his head was missing." He choked on the words, on his pain.

Viyelle edged closer, her hand brushed his and Joh grabbed a fierce hold.

"I saw someone moving," he finally went on, voice steadier. "Someone sneaking from the courtyard, going back into the reception hall. I gave chase. Viyelle came with me. We caught her in the courtyard, the public one. She had—" He coughed. "She had Stone's head. Viyelle took it—brought it back. Servants came. I held them off. I had Merinda. I couldn't—"

Kallista swiped her face dry with both hands. "That was when we arrived."

"Yes."

Even the Habadra looked shaken at Joh's story. Kallista took the hand Obed offered, leaned back into Torchay's hand at her back. *Later,* she reminded herself. She wiped her eyes again.

"Is that how it happened?" Kallista looked at Fox and Viyelle.

"Yes," they said in unison. Viyelle shuddered, swayed toward Joh and he put an arm around her.

Kallista turned her attention to the woman Fox held prisoner. "Merinda."

The half-naked slave twitched, but did not lift her eyes.

"Merinda, look at me." Kallista put all the authority she could summon into her voice.

Slowly, Merinda looked up and met her eyes. Kallista recoiled at the madness in the depths of the other woman's green gaze. What had caused it? The demon that had driven her from Arikon and their ilian, or the enslavement here in Mestada?

Chapter Ten

"Who are you?" Kallista asked. "What is your name?"

"I am Merinda Kyndir," she said in a hollow, echoing voice. "Here, they have named me Hieran. It means midwife." She spoke in an odd mix of Daryathi and Adaran, switching back and forth.

"What did you do today? This evening." Kallista narrowed her question. She did not want a recitation of Merinda's every move since dawn.

"I was told my husband had come to redeem me and the boy. I was given a tray of refreshments for the Habadra and her guest. I—"

"Who gave you the tray?" Kallista interrupted.

"The House steward. Zyan-sa."

"Did you do anything to the refreshments after the steward gave them to you?"

"Yes." Merinda said nothing more. Slave training, to answer only the question asked? Self-preservation? Or something else?

"What did you do?"

"I put poison in the wine."

Habadra Chani hissed at the words. She snatched a knife from her nearest champion and lunged at Merinda, but Keldrey was there first, blocking her.

He gently removed the knife from her grasp and handed her back to her people. "Wait till the Reinine is done."

"What is there yet to know? She poisoned my mother." The Habadra threw off the hands restraining her, but stayed where she was.

"Where did you get the poison? Did someone give it to you?" Kallista asked. The new Habadra would want to know that.

"I made it. In my workroom." Merinda's voice was flat, perfectly emotionless. Utterly unlike the woman she once was.

"For the One's sake, why?"

"In case I needed it to protect myself."

"Why did you think you needed protection? Who were you protecting yourself from?"

"Him." Merinda pointed at Stone's body beneath its ornate covering. She looked at Habadra Chani then. "I am sorry your mother died. She was not a bad master."

"You killed my mother just to be sure of killing your husband?" Chani seemed unable to take it in.

Merinda's face changed, went suddenly feral, frightening. "He is not my husband!"

The Habadra swung toward Kallista. "Then he had no right to attempt to redeem—"

Kallista held up a hand to stop Chani's bluster. "Merinda, is Stone the father of your child?"

"No," she said, sullen.

The mist turned a dark maroon.

"That is a lie, Merinda." Kallista made fists to keep from striking the woman. "Is Stone the father of your child?"

"Maybe. He might be. Or it might be—" The mist faded to a rusty brick-red and Merinda trailed to a stop as it refused to lighten further.

"The truth, Merinda. You have East magic. You can read bloodlines. *Is Stone the father of your child?*"

"Yes." All emotion had vanished again from Merinda, back to the flat tones, expressionless features.

Kallista took a moment to find a safe wording for the next question. "Did you participate in a legal ceremony that married you to Stone Varyl?"

"Yes."

Kallista hid a sigh of relief. Merinda had gone back to her limited answers. If Kallista asked her questions carefully, surely the other woman wouldn't add that she had been married to eight others at the same time.

"Why did the mist stay white when she said he was not her husband?" Habadra Chani demanded.

Merinda said nothing. The Habadra hadn't asked the question of her.

"Why do you say he's not your husband?" Kallista had to clear her throat and rephrase what she couldn't say, not yet. That Stone was dead. "Because you are now a widow?"

"I divorced him," Merinda said.

"When?" Kallista had sent people to check temple records all across Adara, with no result.

"When I left Arikon."

"Did you have the divorce recorded in a temple?"

"No."

"So you were never actually, *legally* divorced."

Merinda shrugged without speaking.

"But you *considered* yourself divorced." Kallista wanted to get everything straight so she and the Habadra could understand the magic's reaction to Merinda's answers.

"Yes," the blood-soaked woman said.

"Even though you never went through any legalities or filed any documents."

"Yes."

The mist stayed white.

"Then why did you have to kill him?" Somehow, Kallista managed to keep the howl out of her voice.

Once more, the flat, emotionless Merinda cracked open and the wild, feral Merinda burst forth. "Because he wanted me back. He came to get me, to take me back. Nothing bad ever happened to me before I met you, before I caught his child. But after, nothing good ever happened to me again. You *cursed me*. If he hadn't got me pregnant, I'd be free of you."

Fox gave Merinda a little shake and her raving shut off abruptly.

This time, Chani's glance at Kallista was almost sympathetic. Almost. "But why," Chani asked, "did you have to—mutilate his body? After you had poisoned them?"

"So he would stay dead." Merinda said it as if the Habadra were stupid for not knowing.

"*She—*" Merinda pointed accusation at Kallista. "She was bringing him back. I could see it. He was moving again, coming awake. But he was still on the ground, weak. Powerless. So I took his sword—it didn't want me to hold it. It didn't like me. But I took it anyway, and I killed him again."

"Oh Goddess," Kallista moaned. She couldn't help it. It hurt too much.

"Is this true?" Chani demanded, all sympathy gone. "Were you healing him? *Could you have healed my mother?*"

"I don't know."

The mist curdled, parts of it going gray-blue shadow, other parts staying white. Chani's scowl darkened with it.

"I mean—yes. I was healing Stone. I think—it's possible I had healed him. But about your mother—I don't know."

The mist cleared to white as Kallista went on. "I think perhaps I could have healed your mother, if I had known she was poisoned too. And if I had been closer. I could not have healed her without touching her, and I don't think I could have reached Habadra House in time. Once a person dies, there is nothing I can do. Their soul has gone to the One and will not want to come back again from that place." She had learned this much through painful experience.

"Then how did you know this Stone was dying? How could you heal him from Shakiri House?"

Kallista didn't really want to explain, but given the situation, she didn't think she could avoid it. "I am Godstruck. Stone was godmarked. This is not a mere title. It is not a rank or official duty. It is *magic,* given from the hand of the One. We—I and my Godmarked—are bound closer than husband and wife by this magic."

The Habadra looked confused now, as well as angry and suspicious. Kallista sighed. What were these Daryathi thinking, to lock their naitani away in a temple?

"Most naitani," she said, "magic users, draw their magic from the air, from the *direction* of their magic. I was born with North magic, with lightning." Kallista called a spark of lightning to her fingertip. "It comes to me out of the North, from the cold, clean, earth-air-water power found there."

She flicked her finger and sent the spark to crackle with a tiny, staticky shock against the Habadra's shoulder.

"The Godstruck magic is more. It is shared out from the One to the Godmarked." Kallista cast an eye to the mist. Pale pink again. She had some of the facts right, but not all of them. "I am guessing, and you can see that my guesses are not entirely correct. I call the magic from the Godmarked to use for the One's purposes, and when I am done, it goes back inside them.

"Because of this magical binding between us, I know where my Godmarked are at all times and I know their welfare. I know when they are injured or dying. And I am able to heal them."

The Habadra's expression changed very little, becoming more sullen and suspicious, if that was possible. She obviously did not follow much of the explanation, and didn't seem to believe what she did understand. "Are you satisfied with the truth you have heard?" she asked. "Is this 'trial' over?"

Kallista considered. If this was all the trial Merinda would get—and it appeared that it would be—they ought to at least attempt to follow the proper forms. "Is there anyone who will speak for the accused, Merinda Kyndir?"

She looked from one to the other of her iliasti. Most of them looked away, unable to meet her gaze. Leyja glared her anger back in defiance.

"I will," Fox said, startling everyone. "I will speak for the wife of my *brodir*, the mother of his son."

"His murderer," Habadra Chani said in a harsh whisper.

Keldrey took possession of the prisoner so Fox could speak unhindered.

"When Merinda left us," Fox said, "a demon had possession of her. I cannot see, but I can tell when a person has been demon-ridden, after the demon has left her, or him. The longer the demon stays, the more . . . *twisted* their presence becomes. As time passes without the demon, they begin to recover.

"The demon left Merinda some time ago—I don't know how long ago that was. But it rode her for a long, long time. Maybe most of the time since she left us. For years. She is so twisted, I . . . Demon-driven madness has done this thing."

"*Demons.*" The Habadra's voice dripped with scorn. "Do you expect me to believe—"

"Demons are as real as magic." Kallista's voice cut across the other's words. "If you do not believe me, believe the spell." She pointed at the white opalescent mist overhead.

Chani snorted, refusing the possibility, but her eyes rolled to the mist, then to the corners of the courtyard, as if searching for signs of demons.

"Are you sure it has left her?" Kallista asked Fox.

"Search for yourself." His sightless eyes held her gaze. "You're better equipped for it than I am."

True. But without Stone's joyous magic . . . She fought back the agony of grief and called magic. It came willingly, but she had to fight it into the form she wanted and shove it hard to send it forth. The magic sauntered over to Merinda and hesitated, as if asking whether Kallista was sure this was what she wanted it to do. She gave it a hearty kick in its metaphysical backside, and the magic plunged into Merinda.

She shrieked, writhing in apparent pain in Keldrey's grip as the magic explored. She was changed, as Fox said. Twisted, stained, mad. No longer the woman who had married them six long years ago. But despite the lingering taint, the demon was gone. Kallista shared what she had learned. The mist glowed its beautiful white.

Chani snorted again, as if to say *Of course the demon is gone, since it was never there to begin with*, but she didn't speak aloud. Not about that. "So, is that all your trial?"

Kallista looked from one to the other of her iliasti. "You have all heard what happened. What Joh Suteny, Fox Varyl and Viyelle Torvyll witnessed. You have heard Merinda Kyndir's own words. What is your judgment?"

Keldrey cleared his throat and handed custody of Merinda off to Joh. "I have another question for the prisoner."

"Ask it." Kallista tipped her head in Merinda's direction.

Keldrey nodded and turned to face the half-naked servant. "When you were told your husband was coming to redeem you, why didn't you just tell the Habadra you wanted to stay? Why did you poison the wine?"

"Because I wanted him dead." Merinda's voice held vicious hate. "I want all of you dead."

"Even though murder is against the One's Law."

"I don't care. You should be *dead*."

Keldrey turned to face Kallista again and came to rigid attention. "Kallista Reinine, it is my judgment that the prisoner, Merinda Kyndir, committed these murders, and that she knew *exactly* what she was doing when she did them."

"Mine also." That was Aisse, cold and hard.

"And mine." Fox.

"I agree." The voices of her ilian murmured assent together.

"So. This is my judgment as well." Kallista took a deep breath and drew herself up to attention. She unclipped the Seal of Office from her belt. "Is there paper? Ink and quill?"

Habadra Chani stared, as if Kallista were more mad than poor Merinda, but she gave a hand signal. Someone at the back of the crowd trotted out of the courtyard. Moments later, the requested items were passed through the gathered champions into the hands of the Habadra, who handed them to Kallista.

In her turn, Kallista gave them to Joh—he had the best script of any of them—and Viyelle cleared a place on the nearby wine-stained table for him to write while Kallista dictated.

"As Reinine of all Adara, and in my role as Truthsayer and High Justice of Adara's Courts, I, Kallista Varyl, Godstruck of the One, find that Merinda Kyndir did murder Habadra Khori of Mestada in Daryath, and her own husband, Stone im-Varyl of Arikon in Adara and Tsekrish in Tibre. She did this in full knowledge of her actions, and without any influence other than her own will." Kallista paused to let Joh catch up.

"Therefore, it is my judgment that, as these crimes were committed in the city of Mestada, in Daryath, and in the House of Habadra Line against the Head of that Line, Merinda Kyndir shall be given into the hands of the Habadra Chani to carry out judgment according to the laws of Daryath."

Joh finished his writing. Kallista took a candle from the holder on the table and poured a fat puddle of wax at the bottom of the judgment.

Then, as it cooled, she pressed the seal with its symbol of the compass rose into the wax. She returned the seal to her belt, took the quill from Joh, signed the document and dated it: *Firstday, the thirty-fifth of Silba*—the last day of the first month of autumn. Joh blew on the wax to cool it, and handed the paper to Viyelle.

"For our records," Kallista said. "To make it official. Will you want a copy?"

"I have no need of such." Chani sneered, as if obeying law was beneath her.

"Now about the child." Kallista had promised. She could not leave Stone's son in this place.

"What child?" Chani looked blank.

"The son of my murdered Godmarked. The reason Stone was in this place." Kallista held onto her temper with torn and bloodied fingertips.

"The child stays. His father is dead. His mother will be before the day changes. He has no kin to redeem him."

"He has me." Fox stepped forward, his temper obviously more frayed than Kallista's. "I am his kin, his father's *brodir*."

"The boy is im-Varyl," Kallista said.

"The boy is in the Line of his mother. He is—what did you say? He is im-Kyndir. You have no standing."

"I have the standing of the Reinine of all Adara." Kallista couldn't stop herself, didn't want to stop. She grabbed the younger woman by the front of her dress and jerked her close.

The Habadra tried to knock Kallista's hand away, but she hadn't spent most of her life as a soldier. She couldn't break Kallista's grip. They scuffled, slipping on the paving. In Stone's blood.

The realization made Kallista let go, made her push Habadra Chani stumbling back a few paces. All around them weapons were raised, battle on the edge of breaking out. *Goddess,* what was she doing? And yet . . .

"I *will* have that child," Kallista snarled. "How much?"

"There is not money enough in all the world to purchase this child from me," Chani growled back.

"You would make an innocent child pay for the crimes of his mother?" Almost, Kallista leaped on Chani again. Only Obed's quick grip on her elbow kept her from it.

"He is mine," Chani said. "He will stay mine."

Then Obed stepped forward and slapped the Habadra Chani openhanded across her face hard enough to snap her head to the side. "I call upon the right of trial and the will of the One Who Rules Over Heaven, Earth And The Seven Hells to judge in the matter of the possession of the child Sky im-Kyndir."

At Obed's blow, the Habadra's champions seemed to relax, and his words backed them farther from the edge of violence where they'd been poised.

"Accepted." Habadra Chani lifted her chin belligerently. "The justiciars will call upon you within the week."

It was only Firstday. That gave a possible eight more days for the Habadra to do as she pleased with Sky before the justiciars got involved. If they would even care what happened to a servant child.

"I will have guarantees," Kallista said. "The child will not be harmed in any way. I will see him and speak with him daily to ensure this, beginning now."

"It is late. He will be asleep now. Morning is soon enough. And you will not enter this House again. Your people may see him, but none of these—" Chani sneered. "These Godmarked."

"If any harm comes to this boy," Kallista said, quiet and fervent, "I will destroy this House brick by brick. And his uncle will see him to be sure you do not try to palm some other child off on us."

"Once," Chani came back. "His uncle may see him once, then it must be another. One who has neither magic nor mark."

"They come together then, that once, so that the other knows the boy."

"Agreed." Chani gave her single, sharp nod. "Who? Choose now. Who will come with this uncle?"

"Keldrey." Kallista pointed.

He stepped forward and bowed. Keldrey wasn't marked, he had no magic, but he was ilias. Stone's son was Keldrey's as much as Fox's or any of theirs, though these Daryathi would not accept that argument.

"He is not marked? Is not nathain?"

"He's a bodyguard, one who protects the military naitani."

"Agreed. In the morning, no sooner than one bell after sunrise."

Kallista stepped close again to Chani who almost stepped back, then defiantly held her ground.

"I am not afraid of your threats." Chani's voice didn't sound as firm as it ought, if she truly did not fear.

"It is not a threat," Kallista said. "If that boy is harmed in any way, I *will* do what I have said. It is a promise."

Kallista turned away from the Habadra and saw some of her soldiers coming down the path through a gap in the clustered champions. They carried a stretcher, like those used to move the wounded—and the dead—from the battlefield. All of Kallista's feeble defenses, the things that had been distracting her, fell apart and grief crashed over her.

Stone was gone. He was not coming back, like Fox whom they'd thought lost to them twice over. Stone was gone and his son was lost and they had only—dear Goddess, how was she going to tell his daughter, Rozite?

Her knees almost buckled, but she didn't need Obed's supporting hand. She threw him off and went to take the stretcher from the soldiers. Fox and Joh took it from her.

They laid it on a clean spot on the paving, where the old Habadra had been. Keldrey and Leyja were already there, lifting Stone's body and head, placing them on the stretcher. They left the ornate robe in place over him as they moved the body, pulling it, once in place, gently over his head. Kallista watched, feeling helpless, useless. Lost.

Stone had been with them from the beginning. He'd hidden his grief over the brodir he'd thought dead in battle with teasing and laughter. Who would make them laugh now? Who would share his joy in living with the rest of them when they forgot, as they too often did, just how good life could be?

Fox and Joh, Keldrey and Leyja lifted the stretcher. Aisse and Viyelle gravitated together, hands finding each other to cling, following as the others bore their terrible burden down the path and out of the courtyard, leaving Kallista behind, bereft and alone.

"Kallista." Obed touched her hand, slid his into it.

She twisted free. He wasn't Stone. Stone was lost to them, his blood spilled across this foreign courtyard in a foreign land under a foreign sky. It was soaked into their clothes so that they wore their loss, a badge of grief and horror.

"Kallista, it's time to go." Torchay's familiar raspy tenor sounded in her ear. His hand in the small of her back gave a subtle but forceful push and she began to walk just to get away from him.

She didn't want comfort. She didn't want anything at all, except Stone. She would never, ever have him again.

And she had sent him to his death alone and comfortless.

Rumors flew all over Mestada. Of blood and death and armed foreign troops invading a House of one of the great Lines. Padrey heard them in the crumbling sector of the city where he lived, and he followed them, not sure why his heart pounded so.

He mingled with the crowd outside Habadra House, pushing his way forward to peer past the champions standing in the gateless gap into the outer courtyard, lit by dozens of flaring torches. He was so consumed by curiosity, by the *need* to know, that he only lifted one purse from a pocket as he passed. Once he reached his destination, the sight of so much blood slowly darkening to rusty brown on the white stone paving made him forget to merge back into the crowd. Padrey watched, and he worried.

He didn't want to worry. Who was the Reinine of Adara to him? What was the warrior woman Leyja but a source of income? He worried anyway. As if he had adopted these utter strangers as some sort of new family. He had to be losing his mind.

Padrey listened, but the crowd around him had no better idea of what had happened than he did, and the speculation grew wilder as they waited.

Only when the inner courtyard gate, which had been swinging idly on its well-oiled hinges, opened wide and soldiers in the brass-buttoned gray Adaran uniforms marched through did Padrey remember to fade away and pull up his hood. The soldiers gathered their horses, loose in the public courtyard, but only a few of them mounted. Those few rode at the gap in the outer wall, as if they meant to ride down the champions blocking it and anyone else who got in their way.

Their way cleared as if by magic, champions and populace melting away in the face of the soldiers' resolve. The rest of the Adaran troop formed ranks, leading their mounts, and followed behind those on horseback. Padrey had to stand on his toes and stretch to see those who came behind the soldiers.

Bareheaded, queues unbound so that their hair spilled over their shoulders and down their backs, the men and women Padrey had seen yesterday in their glittering finery trudged through the gate and into the public courtyard. They carried a burden that seemed to weigh more than they could bear. Padrey squeezed through to the front again. He had to know what they carried.

Four of them, one in plain unadorned clothing, bore a stretcher. The body on the stretcher was covered, face and all, with an ornate overrobe, jewels glinting in the torchlight. The black-clad bodyguard Leyja was one of the bearers, her face stark with her grief, so much that Padrey's own eyes filled with tears. Two women, walking with upright solemn dignity despite the way they clung to each other, followed the stretcher. Behind them walked the Reinine, with two more men at each of her shoulders. Everything and everyone was smeared, streaked and soaked with the dark coppery-smelling stain of blood.

Ilian, Padrey thought. All of them together were an ilian, like the five parents he could never speak of. And one of the Reinine's mates was dead.

Whispers buzzed through the crowd. Murder in Habadra House. No, it was a duel. No, the Adarans had attacked and lost one of their own men. No—

"People of Mestada!" A voice boomed from behind him, from the open courtyard.

Padrey was caught between the need to follow the Adarans and to stay and hear this news. He stayed, but on the edge of the crowd where he could see the slowly retreating backs of the Adarans in the ghostly light of the full moon.

"Murder was done this night in the House of Habadra Line." The Voice of Habadra had a fine carrying baritone. He stood next to a woman who was not the Habadra, but who looked very much like her, repeating the woman's words.

"The Habadra Khori and one of the Godmarked of Adara, a guest in this House, were murdered this night most cruelly. The murderer has confessed and has been tried by the laws of both Daryath and Adara. Witness now her execution."

A screaming servant woman was forced to her knees on the bloodstained paving. The woman who had given the Voice his words— the new Habadra?—raised a long, heavy, very broad scimitar.

Padrey turned his head. He didn't have to look, but he couldn't help hearing, and it sickened him.

He shoved his way through the crowd, trying to hurry after the Adaran Reinine, ignoring a purse that practically slapped him in the face. How could the Reinine have turned that woman over to such cruelty? What kind of people were these?

Padrey knew too well what the Daryathi were, but had clung to memories and to hope that the Adarans were different. Were they truly?

Chapter Eleven

Dawn slid stealthily into Mestada, bringing light where none had been. Keldrey stood in the draperies dividing courtyard from building, armed not quite to the teeth, but to both arms and legs and every other place he could easily carry a weapon. The doorways faced west, so the sun did not enter, but enough of its light did that Keldrey could see the sleepers inside.

They lay sprawled in every direction, some with their faces buried in pillows, others on their backs with arms and legs spread wide. One had even spun completely round in his sleep so that his head lay on his piled-up blanket and he'd pulled the bottom sheet loose to serve as cover. His children.

"I thought you would be here." Aisse slid her arm around Keldrey's waist, and he pulled her in close.

"And you were right." He bent to press a kiss to the top of her head. To hell with the servants. He didn't care who saw. "Lissta get you up?"

He marveled that one of this mob was actually his, that Aisse would have chosen to give him such a gift.

Aisse shook her head. "You did. I knew you'd be brooding."

"I don't brood."

Aisse merely looked at him.

"I don't." He couldn't stand up to that look. "I might worry a bit, but I don't brood."

Her snort was almost laughter. "Whatever you say. But you're 'worrying a bit' about the visit later this morning."

"A bit." Keldrey could admit that much.

He wasn't bad with this bunch, his own kids. He'd been around them since they were born, or not long after. They were used to him, to the way he looked and talked and did things. He tended to scare other children. He didn't mean to. He just did.

Problem was, he didn't know any other way to be, and he sure as hell couldn't do anything about his looks. He could only hope that Fox could pave the way for him with Stone's boy.

"I'm glad they were asleep last night when we got back." Aisse leaned into him.

"Don't make today any easier though." Keldrey deliberately used the crude grammar he'd grown up with, to tease Aisse. Adaran wasn't her native language, but she wanted to speak it perfectly, and she got annoyed when those around her didn't.

"No, it doesn't." She didn't rise to his teasing.

A faint cry rose from the next room, where the two youngest slept, announcing the waking of one. And where one was awake, the other would follow shortly. Keldrey followed Aisse, wishing the next few chimes were already behind them.

Telling their children about Stone's death went better than Keldrey had expected, and far, far worse. Because the children were so young, only the very oldest had any real understanding of what death was, and even then it was fuzzy. Rozite's twin Lorynda, and Niona, just a few months younger, gathered around Rozite, hugging her, patting her, holding her hand. Aisse and Joh's five-year-old son joined them for a moment, though he had less comprehension than his year-older sedili. All they knew was that Rozite's Papi was gone and wouldn't be coming back.

The older children cried because they understood their loss. The little ones cried because their big sedili were. The adults cried because they couldn't keep from it, even Keldrey who never cried. It hurt too much to see their children hurting. His own Lissta, just over a year old, stopped her crying for a moment as he held her, to stare in wonder at the tears on her Papi's face. She touched her little hand to his cheek and he had to choke back worse, which started her off again.

It was a good thing the new Habadra had said "Not *before* the first bell" for Fox and Keldrey to come. It took them nearly to the second bell to calm the children and eliminate the evidence of the morning's grief-festival.

The sun was already too hot on Keldrey's shaved head when he and Fox presented themselves at the barricaded gap in the Habadra House wall.

Fox announced their purpose and the cart was wheeled out of the way to admit them. They were left cooling their heels in the unrelieved heat of the outer courtyard. A bit of shade leaned over from the inner wall in the form of a young tree and Keldrey led the way to its shelter. The stones had been scrubbed clean, he saw. Fresh sand filled the gaps between them.

Keldrey deliberately turned his thoughts away from the sand and the reason for it. He'd seen death before, had lost his first ilian in battle against demons. Life still went on. Fox knew this as well, warrior that he was. They had a job to do, a task for their lost ilias. They had to pull away from the grief and concentrate on what had to be done. On almost anything but what had happened last night in this place.

They waited. Keldrey was used to waiting. He was a bodyguard. He'd spent much of his life doing little else. After a time, he rocked back on his heels. "Wouldn't a gate work better than a cart to block that gap?"

"Mmm," Fox agreed. "Probably why they had one yesterday. Fancy iron-barred thing."

"What happened to it?"

"Kallista."

"Ah." Keldrey nodded. "That would explain it."

Another space of time passed before he spoke again. "Blasted it off its hinges, did she?"

"Not at all." Fox shifted his weight to his other foot. Fidgety, he was. "She blew it to bits. Less than bits. Nothing left but dust. Habadra'll have to have a whole new gate made."

"Huh." Keldrey considered that a moment. "I take it our K'lista was a trifle upset."

Fox took his turn to consider. "You might say that, yes."

"So when she said she'd destroy the house brick by brick if Stone's boy is hurt, there's a good chance this Habadra woman'll take her serious-like."

"I think there's a very good chance, yes." Fox went alert, his whole body focused. "Someone's coming. I think it's them."

After six years, Keldrey was mostly used to Fox's ability to *know* without seeing. It had been a while since the talent had been put to more serious use than hide-and-seek with the kids.

"They're going to make us do this out here?" Keldrey didn't know enough about Daryathi customs to know if it was an insult.

"Apparently." Fox turned toward the inner gate. "I think Habadra Chani is afraid of our Kallista's magic."

"She should be. But Kallista's not here."

"I am. And I'm one of her Godmarked."

"Don't remind me."

Keldrey didn't actually know whether he was envious or not. Sometimes he felt left out, not being marked, especially during one of their whole-ilian-together times. When Kallista called the magic for pure pleasure. But they made extra efforts to make him feel included, which he appreciated *very* much.

The other times, when she used the magic for its more proper purposes, he didn't feel left out at all. He was rather grateful not to be included. What little he could perceive on those very rare occasions when he did sense something frankly scared the piss out of him. Magic was more than he wanted to deal with.

The inner gate rattled, and thumped. Seemed the Habadra had added extra security since last night. Keldrey hid his smile. Not that any added locks or bars would keep Kallista out if she wanted in. They hadn't kept her out last night. Nor had they kept death out. They'd harbored the murderer inside their locks.

Finally the gate opened and a very large champion came through, wearing a fancy painted kilt and leathers, bristling with as many weapons as Keldrey and Fox. He had his hand clamped on the shoulder of a very small boy in a white servant's kilt. The champion looked around the courtyard and the two Adarans stepped out from the minimal shade into the sun, making themselves visible. Black was entirely too hot for this climate, Keldrey thought, and he and Fox both wore bodyguard's uniform today.

The champion marched toward them with the boy till he was some ten paces away, then he stopped and shoved the boy onward with a hand between his shoulders. That was when Keldrey saw the leather collar around the child's neck and the chain leading from collar to the champion's meaty fist.

"Is this how the Habadra honors her word?" Keldrey said, fists working his anger.

"The boy is not harmed." The bass rumble of the champion's voice seemed to come from the vicinity of the paving stones. "He is a servant of the Habadra. You will not steal him."

"*Coward*. You and your Habadra."

"Merely prudent." The champion wouldn't be taunted into moving.

Fox touched Keldrey's arm. "Peace. You're scaring the boy."

Damnation. Keldrey managed to look past the collar and chain at the child himself. He was terrified, trembling. Keldrey dropped to one knee, to make himself smaller.

Was this Stone's son? He seemed frail, almost delicate, his ribs clearly visible through the golden-ivory of his skin. His hair was bleached almost white over a warm brown underlayer, and his eyes were blue. He was not Daryathi, that was certain. He stood balanced on his toes as if ready to run, poised halfway between the man who held his chain and the two who were waiting.

Bent over to put his face nearer the boy's, Fox eased a step toward him. The boy jumped, but held where he was.

"My name is Fox." Another careful step. "Fox im-Varyl. This is my friend, Keldrey im-Borr. We've come to visit you, but my eyes don't work. I have to use my hands to see. Will you let me touch you, so I can look at you with my hands?"

Hesitantly, still fearful, the boy nodded.

Keldrey cleared his throat and made him jump again. *Damn it.* "You have to say it out loud. Fox can't see you nod your head." Fox could *tell* it, but they weren't giving away secrets.

"May I?" Fox had eased several steps closer while the child's attention was focused on Keldrey.

"Yes." The boy cringed as Fox reached out, then relaxed gradually under the gentle touch on his face and shoulders.

"Will you come let my friend look at you? He's a healer. He can see how big and strong you are. He won't hurt you."

The boy looked skeptical, but he took Fox's hand and allowed him to lead him to Keldrey, the chain rattling along the pavement as the massive champion paid it out.

"What is your name?" Fox asked as Keldrey began his examination.

"Boy. Sometimes they call me Ti-Boy, or Useless Boy." The child scuffed a toe in the ground. "I'm not very big."

Keldrey had to clear his throat. "You're plenty big for five years old."

The boy's eyes went wide and he stared at Keldrey. "How do you know how old I am? Did Zyan-sa tell you?"

"We know how old you are," Fox said, "and we know that 'Boy' is not your name. Your name is Sky. You are Sky im-Kyndir and you are my *brodir's* son. Stone im-Varyl is your father."

Now Sky shifted his stare to Fox. "My father is dead. So is my mother. They told me. I didn't see her."

"No." Fox curved a hand over the child's head, his hair the same flyaway fluff as Stone's had been. "I didn't see her either. But I believe them."

Keldrey finished his examination, but pretended to continue so they could have more time. He tried to think of something to say. He wanted the boy to be used to him for the next meeting.

Sky's forehead wrinkled. "They said my mother was bad. She killed the Great Lady." His little pointed chin crumpled and tears welled from his eyes. "My mother said my father didn't want me. She said he did mean things. Bad things. That's why she was mad at me so much, because I'm bad like him."

Keldrey couldn't help himself. He wrapped the boy in his arms and hugged him. "That's not true. It's absolutely wrong."

"I knew your father all my life," Fox said. "He was a good man, and he *always* wanted you. He protected your mother from outlaws when they had to travel across Adara before you were born. He looked for you every day after your mother ran away from us. He was trying to take you home with him when he died."

Sky clung to Keldrey, sobbing into his shoulder. "They said my mother cut his head off and ran away with it."

Keldrey didn't swear, but it was an effort. Fox had to stand and walk away. Keldrey didn't believe in sugar-coating the truth, even for children, but there were still things they didn't need to know. Too late for that now. "She did," he said. "But we got it and put it back. Fox is your uncle. I'm your uncle too." Close enough for the child's understanding. "We're your family, always have been, always will be."

"Will you take me home with you?"

Fox was back. Keldrey turned Sky into the other man's arms to give Fox a turn to hold him. Fox wouldn't come again. The champion holding the chain was getting restless. They couldn't stretch this out much longer.

"We will," Fox said. "But not today. The new Habadra doesn't want to let you go. There's going to be a trial."

Sky went pale and clutched at Fox. "Will you die?"

"No. But I can't come back to see you tomorrow."

"I'll be back." The boy's sudden fear bothered Keldrey. What didn't they know about this trial business? "I'm going to come and see you every day until we can take you home with us."

Sky turned solemn blue eyes on Keldrey. "Promise?"

"I promise." Keldrey hooked his little fingers together for luck, then held one out to Sky who looked puzzled a moment before linking his tiny finger with Keldrey's. Then Keldrey showed him how to hook his own fingers together. "For luck."

"Remember your name." Fox linked his finger with Sky's and held it. "You are Sky Kyndir, or Sky Varyl, if you want to use your father's Line, no matter what they might call you here. Remember that. You're ours."

The champion rattled the chain, almost staggering the boy. "It is time."

"Right, then." Keldrey finger-combed Sky's cottony-soft hair into rough order. "What's your name?"

"Sky Varyl."

"Quite right. Don't you forget it." Keldrey turned him to face the Habadra champion and together the three of them walked back, Fox gathering up chain as they went.

He dropped it into the champion's hand, then put a finger to his lips as Sky gazed longingly up at him. "Remember," Fox said. "But don't tell."

"I'll see you tomorrow," Keldrey said. "Promise." He'd bring along a treat, too. Sky wasn't seriously underfed, but he could use some filling out. A meat roll to start, Keldrey thought. Until they could get him home and feed him up proper.

"Bye." Sky walked backward, waving shyly as his escort guided him back through the inner gate.

Keldrey and Fox lingered until the boy was lost to view, ignoring the restlessness of the waiting gatekeeper champions.

"He's definitely Stone's boy, then," Keldrey said when they'd passed far enough down the street for his comfort.

"Doesn't he look like Stone to you?"

"Yeah. Same hair. Same eyes. Different chin though."

"He's young yet." Fox raised a hand to rest on the hilt of his sword. "He *looks* like Stone to me too."

"So now all we have to do is get him out."

Viyelle rapped on the door to the private room Kallista shared with Obed. "My Reinine," she shouted through the door. "Kallista, you have decisions to make."

"Then make them." The voice was muffled, strained, oddly altered. But it was definitely Kallista's. The door stayed shut.

Viyelle picked up the nearest small object, an empty cup, and threw it across the room. It didn't shatter, since it was made of metal, but it did bend. Not as satisfying as shattering would have been. Not satisfying at all.

"Give her time to grieve." Obed folded his arms and leaned against the wall beside the door.

"Why should I?" Viyelle snapped. "Who's giving *me* time to grieve? Stone shared *my* bed, not hers."

She knew her words weren't fair when she said them, but she couldn't stop herself, as if hurting someone else might somehow ease her own hurt. She hugged her pain to her, wallowed in it. "You're just afraid to go back in there since she kicked you out. You're afraid she'll black your other eye."

Obed touched his swollen left eye. They'd all witnessed the shocking event, after the children had been herded out to play, away from the infectious grief of the adults. Obed had followed Kallista into their room and she'd turned on him, shouting at him to leave her alone, hitting him, throwing things. A cup like the one Viyelle had thrown had done the damage to his eye.

Joh hooked his arm around the back of Viyelle's neck and pulled her into an embrace. For a moment, she fought to break free before she realized it was the same behavior she condemned in Kallista. Viyelle sagged instead into Joh's embrace. At least *he* understood how much she suffered.

"Viyelle's right," Torchay said. "About the decisions needing to be made. Do we take Stone's body home for the funeral? Do we have the funeral here and just take his ashes home? Private funeral or public?"

"We can't leave till we have Sky out of that woman's hands," Keldrey said. He and Fox had missed Kallista's hysterics.

"So, funeral here." Viyelle turned in the circle of Joh's arms to keep their comfort around her as she faced the others.

"Private," Fox said. "Our grief has been displayed enough."

Viyelle made a face. "I agree, but I think there will have to be some sort of public . . . something. In Arikon when we get back home. A funeral service without the actual funeral?"

They argued over forms and functions, processions and intercessions and the impossibility of a temple service when the temple was closed to the public, until Viyelle wanted to have a set of hysterics of her own. She was entitled.

"This is useless." She threw the quill she'd been attempting to take notes with onto the table, spattering it with ink. "Kallista needs to come out of that room and make some decisions. We're not getting anywhere without her."

"You do it," Torchay said. "You heard her."

"Then stop arguing with me when I try. Damn it, Torchay—" Viyelle didn't get fully underway before he interrupted.

"I know you're hurting, love." Torchay reached across the table to clasp her hand. "We all are. But we weren't *bound* to Stone like she was.

She felt him die. That magic link she has to all of us—she felt it break. If she needs a wee bit more time and space to get over that, she should have it."

Viyelle swallowed her scream of pain and frustration. Maybe Kallista did feel him die, but she didn't love Stone like Viyelle did. He wasn't first in Kallista's heart.

"But she still has us." Aisse sounded confused and hurt. "We are not Stone, but we are us—ourselves. We are still here. I don't understand why—"

"She will remember us," Obed said. "Soon. But we have other matters to discuss."

"The trial," Keldrey said.

"Doesn't the embassy have lawyers?" Viyelle looked from Obed's grim face to Keldrey's. She was getting a bad feeling about this. "Truthsayers?"

Obed shook his head. "Warriors will be more use than lawyers. Justice in Daryath is decided by combat. Each side in a case brings a champion to the court. They fight, and the winner of the combat is the winner of the court case."

"B-but that's outrageous," Viyelle sputtered. "What about truth?"

"The One is the judge of the truth. The One ensures that the side of right is the winner."

"Let me guess—which usually turns out to be the side with the biggest purse to hire the best fighter." Keldrey's voice held all the cynicism Obed's only hinted at.

Their tattooed ilias smiled. "Or the side with enough sons to find those with the talent not only to become champions, but to become dedicat."

"What about the people too poor to hire a champion?" Viyelle's outrage grew with each further revelation. "Are they simply without luck?"

"Only those dedicat champions in their direct family line are sworn to fight for their Line. The others are sworn to justice. They fight for whoever has need. And the im-dedicats may do so as well, if they do not have other commitments."

"This was you?" Leyja's voice held the wonder Viyelle felt.

Obed inclined his head. "Yes. I did this."

"Kallista should be here," Torchay said. "She needs to hear this. Why have you no' told us before?"

"It is not a thing I am proud of. Murder done in the name of justice is still murder."

"Especially when it's done in the name of greed," Keldrey said.

Obed acknowledged that truth silently.

"Tell her," Torchay said. "You have to explain this to Kallista. We have to find another way to get Stone's boy back. She can't handle another death, not of one of us."

"None of us will die," Obed said.

"She won't let anyone else risk his life—"

"Trials are not always to the death," Obed interrupted. "It is a matter to be settled with the justiciars when they come."

"If it's not always to the death—" Viyelle spoke up, her horror mingling with awe that Obed had survived such a life. "Why is it *ever* to the death?"

His easy smile twisted. "Expense. The more serious cases—those involving serious crimes or large amounts of money—call for serious combat. It can be to death, or it can be multiple combat. A tournament, if it is not to the death. It costs more to hire more fighters, even if they know they will not die. Sometimes they still die. Many have killed without meaning to. And sometimes they die later."

"How serious is *our* case?" Leyja asked.

"I do not know." Obed looked worried as he shook his head. "It is over a small servant boy. He is not important. But the parties involved— the Reinine of Adara and the very powerful Habadra Line—they make it important."

"Why did you get us into this?" Viyelle demanded, horror rising to outweigh even grief.

"To get us out of Habadra's House without further bloodshed." Obed snapped his gaze to hers. "It would have come to this anyway. Neither Kallista nor this Chani would back down. It is the only way to get our son back without starting a war."

"Sounds damned close to war to me," Viyelle said.

"But it isn't." Torchay stood. "It's controlled, limited. It has rules. But no battles to the death. Agreed?"

Everyone nodded.

"Obed, you need to explain this to Kallista," Torchay said.

Obed sighed and stood. "I will try."

"If she starts to throw things again, duck this time." Fox attempted to tease, but his heart obviously wasn't in it.

"I would gladly accept another black eye," Obed said, "if only she would let us comfort her." He slipped through the door.

"We have to be careful," Joh said. "Sky is safe right this moment, but I've been talking to the embassy staff. They've told me about the Sameric sect of clerics, how they whip up mobs at the least hint of heresy. Habadra wouldn't protect him if the Samerics get hint of our ilian. And she could use it as an excuse for—well, who knows what she might do?"

Viyelle squeezed his hand. She wanted to sleep in a big pile with all of them together, as they sometimes did. It would be lonely with only Joh. Thank the One, she hadn't lost him too.

"*Kallista.*" The fear in Obed's voice carried through the open door. They all scrambled to join him. Chairs fell over, Fox nearly did. In moments, they were gathered around the chaise where Kallista sat staring into nothing at all.

"What's wrong?" Viyelle had to ask, her heart pounding.

"She won't answer me."

"Kallista." Torchay knelt beside her, waved his hand before her face. "Kallista, do you hear me?"

She blinked, turned her face in his direction but never quite made it before she subsided into her blank staring again. Torchay lifted her eyelids to peer into her eyes. He chafed her hands, pinched her wrists, and nothing happened.

Chapter Twelve

Cold rolled down Viyelle's back despite the heat building up in the room. She shivered, pulling Joh's arm around her.

He frowned, wrapping her close. "Cold?"

Viyelle nodded. "Scared. But cold too."

"So am I." Joh absently rubbed his hands up and down her bare arms. Viyelle recognized the subtle signs as Joh turned his analytical mind to matters she could only guess at.

"Viyelle is cold," he said after a moment. "So am I."

"Oh?" Leyja frowned and came to lay her hand on their foreheads. Having three bodyguard-trained iliasti gave them an embarrassment of riches in healing skills. Kallista had the magic and their bodyguards had the best non-magical medical training possible.

"Do any of the rest of you feel it?" Joh asked. "That chill?"

Aisse shivered. Obed rubbed his arms. "We feel it because you ask if we do," he said.

"No." Torchay shook his head. "It's not cold. It's the links. Kallista's cut us off."

"How do you know?" Obed's tone was scornful.

"Can she do that?" Keldrey asked.

"She can't do that," Aisse said at the same time. "She couldn't before."

"That was seven years ago," Torchay said. "And only three of you were godmarked. There's eight of us now and she's had time to learn."

"How do *you* know?" Obed repeated.

"Because I do. And if you'd get your head out of your arse and stuff that pride of yours where it belongs and pay attention to what the hell's going on inside you, you'd know it too." Torchay's face was in Obed's, both of them snarling and spitting.

Viyelle held her breath, hoping nothing more would happen, hoping that if something did, Keldrey and Leyja or Fox or someone could stop it. How could things be falling apart like this? So quickly?

"I *know,*" Torchay growled. "Before any of us were marked, even before she was struck with this magic, I could tell when she used magic. I still can. Compare how you feel now with how you felt this time yesterday. What's changed?"

"He's right," Joh said. "I can feel it. I think we all can. We just didn't realize what it was."

"I think she's been pulling back from us since yesterday," Torchay said. "A bit at a time, until now she's gone so far she can't come back."

"She has to," Keldrey said. "What about the demons?"

Fresh horror slid through Viyelle and she shuddered. She'd forgotten about the demons, about anything but her own pain. Could this mess have something to do with demons?

"What do we do?" Obed took Kallista's limp hand between both of his, quarrel forgotten. "How do we bring her back?"

They all looked at each other helplessly before Torchay finally said it. "I don't know."

"We keep trying," Joh said. "Whatever we can think of. We talk to her. We love her. We need her. We push that love and need down the links until we get through. All of us."

"Get rid of the Daryathi servants," Keldrey said. "We don't need 'em. We can take care of ourselves. All the locals in the whole embassy. Nobody comes inside who's not Adaran. That way, long as we're inside these walls, we don't have to worry about hiding the ilian in pairs."

"We can't send back that new champion of ours," Viyelle reminded them.

"He stays in the barracks."

"Maybe the funeral will help her," Aisse said.

"And maybe it won't." Leyja looked worried.

"It's got to be done though," Torchay said. "Soon."

"I'll take care of it." Viyelle didn't want to decide it all herself, but she would.

"I'll help," Joh said.

Viyelle nodded, smiled at him. "You always do."

"Since you're chief of staff, Vee, I think you'd better meet these justiciars with Obed." Torchay stood, hands on hips, staring down at Kallista.

Yet another task for her list. Viyelle needed paper to write them all down so she didn't forget one.

"Whoever isn't busy with something else, be in here," Torchay said. "Trying to get through to her." He sighed. "And I suppose I'll go let the ambassador know about the servants. She won't be happy."

"Too bad," Keldrey said. "What about the kids?"

"They might get through to her," Obed said.

"They might be frightened," Leyja fretted.

"Saints, what's got you so gloomy?" Keldrey grabbed her by the back of the neck and shook her gently. "Never mind. I know. You can't feel Kallista. Kids are smarter than you think. They'll know something's wrong, and if you don't tell 'em what it is, they'll be dreaming up something a thousand times worse than the truth. And they might help bring her back."

"We can work out a schedule," Torchay said, "so it's not a mob scene in here. Keldrey, you and Leyja can do that." He looked from one to the other. "All right then, let's get busy."

Endless days later, Obed strode through the embassy, his robes billowing behind him, scarcely pausing at the hurriedly constructed gate in the walls between the Reinine's residence and the embassy proper. He was in a hurry. Viyelle had to break into an occasional jog to keep up. Leyja merely stretched her long legs a bit.

The justiciars had finally come to discuss terms for the trial, and Obed begrudged every moment he had to spend with them. Kallista still had not returned from wherever she'd gone.

More than a week had passed since Stone's murder. It was Fifthday again. The justiciars had taken their time arranging this meeting. As usual.

The funeral had been last Fifthday, in the embassy's largest courtyard. They'd had to lead Kallista to her place at the head of the family. Torchay had placed the brand into her hand and held it there with his hand around hers when it was time to light the fire. Obed had had his own torch to deal with, but he still resented Torchay taking that place. He knew he had no right to resentment, tried to push it away, but it kept bubbling back up.

Kallista's body had attended Stone's funeral. Her spirit had been elsewhere. He wouldn't have thought she'd react like this, but— Obed only hoped she had not gone to be with Stone.

The embassy's truthsayer met them outside the council room doors. Obed didn't like this. At all. They needed Kallista and they needed all of her magic. But until they discovered a way to bring her back, they would have to get by as best they could.

He nodded to the truthsayer. Leyja opened the doors and Obed swept inside, playing the part of one-and-only-Reinas to the hilt.

The three justiciars sprang to their feet and bowed, looking from Obed to the obviously subordinate truthsayer, then to Viyelle and Leyja who were dressed in finery almost the equal of Obed's. Clearly, they did not know who ranked highest, whom to address. Obed gave an Adaran-style bow and let his robe slide a bit from his bare shoulders, exposing his body tattoos. He did not like to go about unclothed—he'd done far too much of it in his life—but sometimes the effect was worth it, as now. The justiciars could not seem to stop staring.

The head of the group, distinguished from her colleagues by the medallion of office that hung round her neck and the black trim on her white robes, introduced herself and her companions. Obviously, she hoped for a similar introduction so she would know whom to address. Obed was tempted to forego one—they knew perfectly well who he was. But good little courtier Viyelle stepped hard on his foot, so he did it.

"I was told the Reinine Kallista took a personal interest in this case." The head justiciar sat at Obed's invitation.

"My Reinine is indisposed." Obed flipped the tail of his robe out of the way as he took his place. "One of her Godmarked was murdered. But yes, she has a personal interest, which is why I am here, as well as her chief-of-staff."

"The matter is the redemption of a bondservant boy, child of a bondservant formerly named Merinda il-Kyndir?"

A battle with words, not swords. Obed took a moment to recite the dedicat's litany to clear his mind of all but his purpose here at this moment. No echoes from his childhood or the skola and arena. None of his desperate worry over Kallista. Just now. This.

He let Viyelle answer the question. He was here for the effect of his tattoos on the justiciars—these women had seen him in the arena-court many, many times—and to share his knowledge with the chief Adaran negotiator, Viyelle.

"*Tournament,*" she was saying, for the second time, louder. "Enough blood has been spilled already. My Reinine will not agree to more death."

"The Habadra has no dedicat champion in her Line to pit against yours. She hasn't the funds for a tournament. She has enough for one champion. It must be to the death."

"Absolutely not." Viyelle shook her head vehemently.

"Then you forfeit—"

"We will pay," Obed said. "We will provide prize money for four champions in addition to the one Habadra can provide."

"A case of this magnitude—" The head justiciar shook her head, not at all the apologetic she pretended to be. "Between two of the most powerful Lines in the world—if it is not a death trial, I do not see how it can be done with less than six combats. Eight would be better, to avoid unlucky seven."

"If Habadra Line is so powerful, they can pay for more than one champion. There are dedicats who will fight for nothing."

"Not for a rich and powerful Line like Habadra. But their riches are in land and crops, not in ready cash. Adara is the richest land in the world."

"But this case is not Adara's. It is a matter of the Varyl Line. Of family. We will pay for five champions for Habadra then, but we will not pay more than our share." Obed kept repeating his mind-clearing litany. This sort of battle did not allow him to leap across the table and choke the breath out of his opponent. Unfortunately. The twitching of Leyja's hands told him she felt the temptation as well.

The afternoon wore away and autumn's earlier evening set in as they hammered out agreement. The justiciars would go back to Habadra for her agreement and more hammering would doubtless be required. But the main terms were set. The trial would be a tournament of eight single combats, with a final mêlée battle the next day, the whole to be held three weeks after all the elements were agreed to and champions named.

Keldrey's continuing visits to Stone's son were added to the justiciars' trial order. Only the petty details were left, but in Obed's experience, the petty details often took longer to beat into submission than the larger elements of a thing.

At last, after interminable bowing and politeness, Obed was set free to return to Kallista's side. He flew through the embassy, whose corridors had never seemed so endlessly long. He found her sitting in the courtyard under the same tree where he'd left her, candles and torches providing gentle light.

The weather had changed in the past few days, a violent thunderstorm bringing cooler weather behind it. Pleasant weather, like summer in Arikon, rather than Daryath's oppressive heat. It made the courtyard an even more inviting retreat. Kallista sat passively, fallen flower petals decorating her hair, while their children played quiet games with chalk and buttons on the paving stones. Could nothing reach her?

"How is she?" Obed asked Keldrey who stood a casual watch on the scene from the doorway. "The same?"

"Yeah." Keldrey let a long breath sigh out through his nose. "Torchay tried calling her again. For a minute, I thought she might answer. But—" He shook his head.

Obed fought the wave of jealousy that swept over him, but it was relentless as the tide. He knew better, had conquered it in Adara, but the familiar sights and smells of his former home brought all his dreams and insecurities back again. Did she truly love him? Was he even worth loving? How could he know?

They all talked to her, called her, tried to bring her back from wherever she'd gone. Obed's voice had gone rough, his throat sore from all his calling and talking. But it was Torchay's voice she heard, *Torchay's* touch that roused her.

Obed knew he should be glad that someone could get through to her, but damn it, why couldn't *he* be the one?

"How did the meeting go?" Joh drifted over to join them.

Obed resisted the snappish response on the tip of his tongue. "After the children have gone to bed." He picked up Omri, who promptly laid his head on Obed's shoulder and popped his thumb in his mouth. Obed stroked a hand over his son's curls, breathed in his little-boy scent, taking what comfort he could.

"Yeah, it's time." Keldrey signaled to the hovering nursery servants who'd made the journey with them from Adara.

Obed carried his son to bed himself, needing to hold the child he and Kallista had made for just a little longer. They *would* bring her back to them.

Padrey sat on top of the courtyard wall in the shadow of a carefully watered winter oak, watching the royal Adaran ilian assemble below. It had been a job and a half getting here. The place was crawling with guards, alert and conscientious ones. But once he'd reached the tree, hidden himself in shadows made deeper by the torchlight below and stopped moving, he'd been able to watch and remain unnoticed.

Something was wrong with the Reinine. He couldn't see her well with that little tree shading the bench where she sat, but it wasn't natural, not moving like that. She wasn't a thief. Her life didn't depend on being able to stay still. Her ilian talked to her. The kids talked to her, wanted her to play. And nothing. She didn't answer them, didn't seem to see them.

Padrey had positioned himself close enough he could hear what they said, and the Reinine hadn't said anything since he'd found his hiding place while the servants cleared away dinner.

Now, with the children gone and the adults regrouping, Padrey went stiller than still and listened. The Daryathi in the ilian—unbelievable concept that it was—told the others about an upcoming trial while he, Leyja and another woman ate a late meal. They were trying to redeem a slave child from Habadra Line, the son of their murdered ilias. Padrey shivered as memories rose. No kin had come to redeem him.

"Can't we get him away from the Habadra any sooner than that?" Leyja asked. "Couldn't the justiciars take custody of him as the—the property in dispute?" Her disgust at the word "property" showed clearly. It made Padrey like her more.

"I worry what this Chani might do to him," she said. "Bad enough we had to leave Merinda to Habadra justice, but if they blame Sky for his mother's crimes . . ."

The existence of the boy-child changed all of Padrey's perceptions. The actions of the Reinine and her ilias had been taken to protect this boy, their son. They were emphatically not Daryathi. They were Adaran.

"The Habadra can't do anything to Sky with me coming to check on him every day," the man with the shaved head and bodyguard blacks was saying. "You came with me yourself yesterday. You saw him."

"Through a gap in the damned barricade." Leyja folded her arms and slumped sulkily against the fountain's rim.

"I don't understand why Habadra Chani is so set on keeping him." That was the brown-haired man with the waist-length queue. "According to embassy personnel, Chani was not close to her mother. Their quarrels tended to be public and of epic proportions. Why would she be so intent on revenge? And if that's not why she wants him, what *is* the reason?"

"Guilt?" One of the other women spoke, the one who'd eaten late with Leyja and their Daryathi, her brown hair pulled back in a short queue like the Reinine's. "Maybe she's glad her mother's gone and feels guilty for it, so she needs to prove that she's actually sad and upset by getting revenge?"

Didn't these people know anything? Padrey's fidgeting made the leaves of his tree rustle. Leyja and the redheaded man—also a bodyguard— looked sharply in his direction. Padrey froze, his mind a dust-devil of whirling thought. Even their Daryathi didn't seem to know the truth of what happened here.

If he told them, exposed his presence here, they could kill him. But he'd lived almost half his life running that risk. And they might *not* kill him. They might get him out of this place and back to Adara where he could truly be free.

He hadn't actually thought it all the way through before he moved, sliding onto a limb of the enormous tree stretching into the Reinine's courtyard, and dropping silently to the ground. Not silently enough.

The two red-haired bodyguards moved fast as thought toward him. Padrey spoke faster, hoping to keep from being run through. "I can tell you why Habadra wants the boy, and it isn't for revenge."

"Who are you and what are you doing here?" Leyja's knife quivered against his throat, close enough to shave those hairs he always missed on the occasions he bothered to shave.

Empty hands held carefully away from his body, Padrey answered, "You invited me."

"*You lie.*" The knife shaved a bit closer, taking a thin layer of skin.

Padrey needed to swallow, but didn't dare. He might cut his own throat if he did. "Truth. Do you deny offering to ransom a certain shiny red item?"

"A *thief.*" Leyja spat onto the paving. Her knife twitched again and Padrey could feel the warm trickle of blood down his neck. At least it was a trickle and not a gush.

"Leyja." The red-haired man took her wrist and eased the knife away. "Don't you think we should hear what he has to say before you kill him?"

"He's a thief. He stole Rozite's necklace."

"If he's clever enough to get himself all the way in here, don't you think he's clever enough not to bring the necklace with him? If you kill him, you won't get it back now, will you?" The man didn't take his eyes off Padrey, his sword never wavered, the one pointed just under Padrey's ribs where it could slide smooth as silk into his heart any moment it liked.

The bodyguard called over his shoulder. "Fox."

The tall blond man walked forward, eyes on Padrey, but eerily without seeing him. It made chills run shivering down Padrey's back.

"I'm not armed," he said. "Not even an eating knife."

"I don't see any sign of demons," the man called Fox said.

Demons. The young man without eyes, the one Padrey had guided back to the embassy, had spoken of demonshadow. Padrey had dismissed it as a naitan's poetic exaggeration. But now, here—more chills went shuddering through Padrey.

"Send for Gweric," the Daryathi ilias said. He was tattooed, like a champion. Like—*Goddess,* he had body tattoos, all three of them. He was a dedicat. Not just a dedicat, but one of the very, very best. He'd survived his oath.

Padrey was so shocked by the sight of all those tattoos in all those places, it took him a moment to realize he recognized the name. "I know Gweric," he said. "Or I met him. Last week. After the parade. Before—" He trailed off, not sure how to refer to the murders, or whether he should.

He cleared his throat. "I'm sorry for your loss."

"My loss?" The Daryathi's scowl on that tattooed face made Padrey more nervous than the sharp things so close to him.

"All of yours. Your ilias—" Padrey broke off, alarmed by the expressions on nine faces—eight. The Reinine didn't react.

Padrey was speaking fast again. "I'm Adaran. I had five parents myself. I don't talk about them here, but I *am* Adaran. I don't—I won't—"

"*Leyja.*" The shaved-headed bodyguard took Leyja's knife out of her hand before he picked her up and set her a few paces away. "If you can't control your temper any better than that, you got no business being so close to him."

He handed her back the blade. "Clean it off and put it up. You—" He grabbed Padrey by the back of the neck and marched him to the middle of the courtyard. "Don't give us no trouble and we might let you live. How did you meet Gweric?"

"I stumbled over him." Padrey went on to explain their chance encounter.

"Why did you spy on us?" the dedicat ilias asked.

"Because of her." Padrey tipped his head in Leyja's direction. He didn't dare move his hands to point. "She offered to trade for the necklace. I wanted to see what kind of person she was, if I thought she might trade for it fair or just toss me in a hole to rot. I was going to watch a while and come back tomorrow, if I decided it was safe."

"Why didn't you? Wait?" The red-haired guard hadn't put away his sword but he wasn't pointing it at Padrey any more. He had another one just like it on his back, the downward-facing hilt showing at his left hip.

"Because of the boy. The one Habadra has."

"Why?" This time the man Fox asked the question.

The Daryathi dedicat held up his hand to stop the answer as someone new entered the courtyard.

"You sent for me, Obed?" Gweric asked, moving unerringly through the courtyard despite his missing eyes.

"We need you to check for demons." The tattooed man was Obed, then. Padrey filed the name away.

Gweric shook his head. "None here. Kallista cleared everything out and warded it. You know that."

"But someone could bring it in with him, couldn't he?" Leyja said. "If it was riding him?"

Padrey shuddered. Demons *rode* people? *Goddess.*

Gweric nodded. "Yes, but there's no one here to— Is there?"

The young man's sightlessness suddenly showed itself as he turned his face in all directions, confused and clumsy.

A spurt of temper flared through Padrey, burning away his fear. "Here," he said. "I'm here, Gweric."

"Padrey?" The naitan smiled and extended his hand, evidently trusting Padrey to come and take it. "What are you doing here? I'm glad to see you again."

With a glance at the naked sword in the redhead's hand as he walked past it, Padrey clasped Gweric's hand. "At the moment, trying to keep myself from getting skewered, I sort of   came in over the wall."

"Why did you do that?" Gweric let Padrey lead him to one of the benches that curved around the fountain. "We'd have let you in at the door."

"He's a thief," Leyja said sourly.

Padrey sighed. "True, I'm afraid."

"I'm sure you have a good reason for it."

The red-haired man propped a foot on the bench beside Gweric. "So I take it you know this . . . Padrey, is it?"

In a few sentences, Gweric repeated Padrey's tale of their meeting.

"Why didn't you tell us?" Obed asked.

"Because I was afraid if I admitted to getting lost, I wouldn't get back out in the city to search. Not without a whole raft of soldiers and a local guide or two. And that wouldn't help. I have to keep looking. Especially now Kallista can't."

Padrey cleared his throat again. Gweric called Adara's Reinine by her given name? Heaven's saints help him, Padrey Emtal was in deep over his head.

"What—um—happened to the Reinine?" He asked it quietly, but he couldn't not ask.

"Stone was murdered." Gweric answered before anyone could stop him—Padrey thought some of them had meant to. The naitan looked around the courtyard as if he could actually see the others in it. Or *something*. He had said he could see magic. "The magic is still there, binding you. But it's dark. Dimmed. The light's gone out of it."

"Grief," the brown-haired man said.

"But it *is* still there." The redhead again. He set his hand on Gweric's shoulder as if he wanted to grip hard, but feared holding too tight. "You *can* see it. Right?"

Gweric nodded. "Yes, Torchay. I see it."

"And you *don't* see demons," the shaved-bald man said.

"No, Keldrey. There's not even a trace of demonstink clinging to him. Padrey's clean. I wouldn't have let him lead us anywhere otherwise."

"He might not be demon-ridden," Leyja growled. "But he's still a thief."

"Why?" Gweric turned his face to where Padrey stood. "Why are you a thief?"

"Because I'm a runaway slave. If I tried to get honest work, I would be caught and killed."

"There are no slaves in Daryath," Obed said.

Good thing they hadn't offered Padrey any drink, or he'd have snorted it up his nose laughing at that statement.

"There are bondservants, yes," the dedicat Obed was saying. "But they are freed in the year of the jubilee. Every nine years, they go free. Even if they were bound just a few months before the jubilee year, when that year comes, their debt is forgiven and the bondservants are set free. It is the Law."

"The law for Daryathi," Padrey said. "*Not* Adarans. There are Adaran slaves all over the city, and no Adaran is *ever* set free, jubilee year or no."

"That cannot be—"

The yellow-haired Fox cut off Obed's words. "Stop talking, Obed. *Listen*. Argue later."

Fox stared at Padrey, his gaze oddly blank. It disturbed Padrey, until he realized Fox was blind as Gweric, though he still had his eyes in his head. Then it disturbed Padrey more, wondering what this Fox could see.

"Why?" Fox said. "Why are the Adarans never set free?"

"Because of the magic," Padrey said. "Adarans have more magic, more naitani than anywhere else in the world. If the Daryathi have Adarans, then they have magic. Laws in Daryath apply only to the Daryathi."

"And the Daryathi with magic—" Torchay drew himself straight. "They're locked away in the temple, where their magic does no good to anyone but themselves."

"So—" the man with the long queue spoke. "So if the rest of the Daryathi want any magic to benefit themselves, they have to steal Adaran magic."

"How many Adaran slaves are there?" the dedicat Obed asked.

"I don't know. Hundreds. Maybe thousands." Padrey shrugged. "I haven't gone round to count."

"If so many Adarans are slaves," the bald Keldrey said, "why don't we know about it? If people are being taken, word would have been sent to Adara, to Arikon. We would have heard."

"How?" Long Queue spoke again. "Daryath is a long way from Adara. Traders are always being lost in storms or eaten by lions or wolves. Villagers go missing in the mountains. This is why our traders have been restricted to the coastal cities. What if those caravans or villagers weren't actually lost?"

He turned to Padrey. "How did you become a slave?"

Padrey took a deep breath, not noticing how his hands had clenched into fists until Leyja put her hand on the hilt of her sword, staring at his fists. He couldn't make them unwind, so he clamped them together behind his back.

"My parents were traders. They brought my sedil and me along on their last trip so we could start learning the business. They're dead now." He locked his fingers tight. "The three of them who came on the trading journey. They were accused of sacrilege, of adultery, and forced into the court-arena to defend themselves against trained champions."

"They had no champions to fight for them?" Obed sounded shocked. "There are dedicats who will—"

"They won't fight for blasphemers," Padrey interrupted. "No one would. My parents were slaughtered in seconds and Nanda and me were handed off to Penthili Line. Luckily, we were the only two of our sedili old enough to come on the trip. I was eleven. The Penthili was upset my second mother died. She had South magic, a fire-spark. They wanted more Adaran children from her."

"They're trying to *breed* naitani?" The small blond woman spoke for the first time, outrage bristling from her.

"Yes."

"Then—" Long Queue tapped a forefinger against his lips. "Why would they want to kill you? Wouldn't they want to keep you alive for—pardon, but for stud service?"

"I don't have any magic. When I was younger, they couldn't know whether I would or not, could they? But by the time—I think I was eighteen or nineteen. It was clear I wouldn't start magically setting fires or something. And I wasn't going to have any child of mine grow up like that. There was a girl . . ."

Padrey had to stop, take another deep breath, clear his throat. It had been a long time ago. Seven or eight years, if he counted right. But it still stung. "They *gave* her to me. She didn't understand why that bothered me. She was a baker, could put magic in the bread so it would keep longer—long as you liked. She'd grown up a slave, had already popped out a couple of kids who would grow up slaves. She wasn't any older than me.

"Her other kids had Daryathi for fathers. I guess they were hoping an Adaran, even one without magic, might have a better chance of breeding kids with magic. But I couldn't do it. So I ran off.

"And *that's* why they'll kill me. Because I ran off. I got away. I'm a bad example for the other slaves." He shrugged. "*And,* I'm a thief. Even your Leyja wants to kill me for that."

She scowled, but she no longer had a hand on her sword hilt.

"Why didn't you go back to Adara?" Obed asked. "It would have been a difficult journey, but—were you afraid to try?"

Padrey didn't bother to hide his scorn. "If I were afraid, I wouldn't have run away. I wouldn't have jumped out of your tree. Penthili Line still has my sedil. I won't leave her, and Nanda won't leave her kids, even if they were born of rape."

Everyone in the courtyard cursed when they heard that, some longer and more colorfully than others, but they all did it.

"She's the Reinine." Padrey tipped his head toward the motionless woman. "I saw her in the procession coming back from the Seat, and I saw her outside Habadra House that day, so I know. She's the Ruler of all Adara. She can get me and Nanda and her kids out of Daryath if she wants to."

The Reinine's mates were too busy exchanging worried looks with each other to meet Padrey's gaze for long, but they didn't avoid him.

"I'll help get your boy back from Habadra," Padrey said. "I'll bring back the necklace, no payment asked. Except—*please*—help me rescue my sedil."

"How could you help, thief?" Leyja demanded.

"Sneak in like I did here. Sneak the boy out the same way."

"He's too small to climb like you did," Keldrey said, "and too big for someone your size to carry so far."

"I may not be the biggest man around, but I'm stronger than I look." Padrey was generally grateful for his modest size—he was taller than all the women here except Leyja, even if he was shorter than all the men—but there were occasions it could rankle.

"You would make bargains with a thief?" Leyja swung a fist at Keldrey.

He slapped it away, voice quiet and full of power. "I'd bargain with demons if that's what it takes to get Sky out of those hands and into ours."

"Peace, Keldrey, Leyja," Fox said. "We all would. Quarreling among ourselves won't free him any sooner."

"Kallista would want to help him," the small blond woman said. "She would want to free all the Adaran slaves."

"You don't know that, Aisse," Obed said. "We can't make decisions on the basis of 'what Kallista would want' when she isn't here to tell us what that is."

"Isn't here?" Aisse pointed an accusing finger at the Reinine. "There she sits. Right there. She's with us. She could tell us what she wants. She just *won't*."

"It isn't that simple," Long Queue said.

"Shut up, Joh." Aisse rounded on the long-queued man now. "No one wants to listen to one of your lectures."

"Leave him alone." The brown-haired woman stepped between Aisse and Joh Long Queue.

Things were beginning to turn a touch chancy. Padrey thought he might need to nip back onto his wall out of the way.

"Bugger this." Torchay slid his sword into the double scabbard on his back, this hilt rising over his shoulder. He strode across the paving to Kallista Reinine, scooped her up in his arms and carried her toward one of the gauze-draped entries.

"What are you doing?" Obed hurried after him.

Torchay didn't lose a step. "We need Kallista. I'm going to bring her back."

Chapter Thirteen

"What makes you think you can?" Obed moved to block the path into the bedroom.

Torchay stepped around him. He would let nothing stop him. "She hears me sometimes, when I call. I'm going to *make* her listen."

"And you think that will—" Obed tried to block him again, but this time, Fox caught him, held him back.

"Let him try," Fox said. "What can it hurt?"

That was the thing that nagged at Torchay. Could it hurt? What if he drove her farther away? He didn't know, didn't know exactly how he was going to bring her back, or whether he could do such a thing. But he had to try. They needed her.

Her children needed her. The ilian needed her. Every Adaran in Mestada needed her, not to mention those back home in Adara. But mostly, *he* needed her.

He needed her to smile as she brushed the girls' hair at night. Needed her to laugh at Keldrey's pomposities and frown at her endless paperwork. He needed to feel her kisses on his mouth and her unseen touch on the magic that bound them all.

Torchay set Kallista on the wide soft bed she shared with Obed, where she'd shared their lovemaking with Torchay and Stone over a week past. She sat, her muscles working to hold her upright. That was a good thing, wasn't it? He wished he knew.

He eased onto the bed in front of her and brushed back the wisps of hair that had escaped from the simple queue he'd braided for her that morning. Where had she gone? *Could* he bring her back? He took her face between his two hands and tipped it up so she could see him if she would only *look*.

"Kallista," he murmured, but that would never do. He put more power in his voice, tried to send it down the link. Gweric said the links were still there, and she'd always said his magic held more power than the others. "*Kallista*. Kallista Reinine."

Being Reinine had never been one of her favorite jobs. Torchay changed tactics. "Major Varyl. Naitan. *Kallista*."

She blinked. Her eyes tried to focus and Torchay had to struggle to keep his hold gentle. Was it working?

"Come back to us, Kallista," he crooned. She seemed to drift away and he shifted his voice to whipcrack again. "*No*. Stay with me. Don't you leave us, Major."

She pushed feebly at his hands and he moved them to her shoulders. "Kallista, look at me."

He brushed his nose along hers, too close for her to look in his eyes, but touching her face felt right. He kissed her cheek, swept his lips along it till he found her ear. His voice quiet, he filled it with everything he felt for her. "*Kallista*."

"Tor—" She sounded slurred, couldn't find all his name, but she spoke. She hadn't spoken in more than a week.

Overjoyed, Torchay captured her lips in a kiss. It felt a bit like kissing a sound sleeper, or someone deeply unconscious from a blow. Her lips were warm, if utterly unresponsive. Unresponsive—until she twisted away from him, shoved at his chest with a fraction of her usual strength.

"No. Don't," she mumbled. Actual, understandable words.

He ripped his tunic off and attacked Kallista's. If kisses helped, perhaps more intimate touching would help more. Thank the One they'd dressed her in military issue rather than court dress or he'd be getting her out of it this time tomorrow.

"Stop it." She squirmed, her weakness worrying him. Had she harmed herself physically? Worry later. Bring her back first.

"*No*." Torchay upended her, hauling her trousers off over her feet. "If you want me to stop, you'll have to stop me. *Make* me stop."

He held her down easily with one hand while he kicked off his own trousers. Why hadn't any of them thought of bringing her back this way? The magic between them so often felt like sex, it should have occurred to one of the eight of them before now.

"Kallista." He lowered himself over her and groaned at the feel of her pressed naked along his equally naked self. It had been too damn long, magic sex or no.

"Leave me alone." Three words together.

"No." He pinned her hands over her head with one hand. Ordinarily it took him two hands and a lot of effort, if she wanted to play this game. With his other hand, Torchay stroked down her side once, twice, then came back to cup her breast. He nuzzled her ear, planted kisses across her face, found her mouth and demanded entry.

She turned her face away. He followed, abandoning her breast to capture her chin and hold her still for his kiss. His grip tightened on her jaw, forcing her mouth open and he plunged inside, begging with every sweep, every caress for her to kiss him back, to return from wherever she'd gone.

"*Kallista.*" He let go her hands—she'd stopped struggling to free them—and grasped her hips as he made a place for himself between her legs.

She planted a hand on his face and shoved, hard. He laughed, triumphant. *It was working.* "Go away," she cried.

He kissed her palm, then peeled her hand off his face. "*Make me.*"

Kallista bucked, fighting with her whole body to throw him off, and Torchay laughed again. He threw himself at her, magic and all, hoping something would get through. She hit him with her fist and praise be, it hurt. He captured that hand too and ducked his head to kiss her shoulder. She lifted her head and fastened her teeth on his ear. He ripped it free with a howl. *Damn,* she'd never played this rough.

He pinned her hands and body as best he could and lifted far enough to see her face. "Kallista? Are you with us?"

Her braid had come free so that her hair flew over and around her face as she fought like a wild thing, her mouth open to bite whatever she could reach. Her imprisoned hands reached for whatever she could claw, curled into weapons as if her clipped nails could rend and tear.

"Kallista." Torchay shook her.

She snarled at him. *Goddess, what was wrong now?*

He glanced over his shoulder at the others gathered in the doorway. Fox and Keldrey had a grip on Obed, as if they'd had to prevent his interference, but he stood quietly at the moment. Was Gweric still here? He wasn't ilias, but—it wasn't as if he could actually *see*, was it?

"Gweric, is this demons?" Torchay indicated Kallista's violent thrashing.

The others looked toward some invisible place behind them and after a moment, Gweric's voice drifted forward. "Of course not. She's Godstruck. But the magic's still dark."

"But it's working." Torchay had thought so. She was speaking, moving of her own will. Fighting him. "*Isn't it?*"

"But it's not finished."

Torchay looked back at his ilias beneath him, fighting so ferociously. This game was a bit of fun when they played it, but not so much now, when she fought him in earnest.

"Kallista!" He shouted now. "Kallista Naitan! Major Varyl, look at me! *See me*."

She paused for an instant, her gaze bright through her veil of dark hair. "Torchay?"

In that moment, he laced his fingers with hers and slid inside her on a cushion of liquid passion. "Kallista, *love*."

She screamed with mad rage.

She bucked, bouncing him up but not off. As they came down, he drove hard inside her, calling her name. She was wet, ready, so Torchay told himself she wanted this, wanted him. He nuzzled into her neck—it wasn't safe to kiss her—bringing as much of his weight down on her as he could to hold her still. Her struggles had him moving inside her more than any effort of his and it brought her name riding out of him on a groan.

"Kallista, please. Look at me." He groped for the magic, trying to recreate what he felt when she called it, used it. He felt like a blind, armless, legless cripple who wasn't quite totally deaf, hoping to find his way home by listening for the faint sound of mice digging in soft sand.

He kissed the place behind her ear that always made her quiver. He sucked her earlobe into his mouth and closed his teeth gently on it, and the tension in her body oozed slowly out of her. Torchay didn't bother pausing to check his progress. His magic still crawled around in the dark. She wasn't home.

He called her name over and over, between each kiss, with each thrust of his hips. She moaned and her body lurched, not to throw him off, but to welcome him in, to meet his motion. It was clumsy and uncertain, but it gave Torchay more hope. He dared let go of her hand and reach down to adjust her position, urge her to bring her leg up and wrap it around him.

"Look at me, Kallista," he whispered in her ear. "Where's your magic? I can't find you."

She whimpered, shaking her head as tears ran from her tight-squeezed eyes down her temples into her hair.

"I know it hurts, love, I know." Torchay kissed the tears away, his heart breaking with hers. "But you're stronger than this. We need you. And you need us. You *need* us, Kallista. We can make it better if we're together."

Kallista shook her head again, harder. Her liberated hand came up and tried to push him away. When he refused to go, she hit him with her fist, hard enough to snap his head around.

"Stop it!" He tucked his face back between her neck and shoulder, where it was a bit safer, and recaptured her hand. "Just stop all this nonsense right now. I love you too much to let you do this to yourself, but if you're determined to leave us, I'll be damned if I'm going to let you go alone."

Torchay had no clear plan, no true knowledge of what he was doing. He just did it. Somehow, he gathered up all of himself, that blind, legless, nearly deaf cripple, and threw himself out into that whispering darkness, shouting her name with something that wasn't his voice.

He fell, endlessly, into nothing. His cry became a wordless, voiceless scream as he plummeted. He reached out with his stunted, missing limbs, knowing that if he ever reached the bottom, reached the end of the nothing, he would have scattered all of himself across it until he was nothing too.

Terrified by the thought of that ending, Torchay flailed in the darkness, but he couldn't go back. He didn't know the way, didn't know where he was, didn't—couldn't—

Kallista caught him.

The magic snapped into place, as if she'd wrapped her hand around his forearm and enabled him to grab hold of her. He had arms again, and legs. He had eyes—it wasn't dark at all, but misty-gray, glowing with colors that weren't exactly colors.

None of that mattered. Kallista had caught him. She looked a bit thin, see-through almost, as if some of her had drained away. But she was *here*. Torchay used his hold on her to haul her into his arms and wrap her tight. "I won't let you leave me. I don't care where you go, you're no' going to leave me behind."

"Torchay—what are you doing here?" She caught his face between her hands and drew back so she could look at him.

"I haven't the vaguest notion." He looked around. "Where are we?"

"The dreamscape." Now Kallista took a look around. "Yes, the dreamscape. How did you get here? Why are you here?"

"I told you, I'm coming with you, wherever it is you're going. As for how I got here—I'm no' sure." He scratched his head, dislodging what little remained of his bedraggled queue. "I . . . jumped. Into nothing. And you caught me, and now I'm here, wandering round the dreamscape with you." He propped his hands on his hips and turned in a full circle as he stared. "Is this where you go then, when you do your true dreaming?"

Kallista shook back her hair, using the motion to try to shake a bit of order into her thoughts. She studied the dreamscape again. It was different somehow. Brighter. With more colors. "Sometimes," she said. "When I'm hunting demons."

But it wasn't the same. Where *was* she?

"Is that what you've been doing? Hunting demons?" Torchay reached for her hand, as if needing to be sure she was present. The touch felt warmer, better than it should. Or maybe that was simply the effect of the dreamscape—or wherever this was.

"No." She knew that much. But what had she been doing? She frowned, trying to remember. The instant she tried, *really* tried, it came to her. *Stone*.

The severed link ached. It was a burning, empty, bitter hole inside her that couldn't be filled, wouldn't be eased. She'd felt it even when she couldn't remember why.

"What were you hunting, love?" Torchay brushed a strand of hair back from her face, let his fingers trail down her cheek.

Kallista rubbed away the tears that followed his fingers. "Stone," she mumbled, embarrassed. "I was hunting Stone." She cleared her throat of its tightness, but it didn't help. "It hurts so much, Torchay. I can't make it stop hurting."

"All right, then." He laced his fingers with hers. "Let's go find him. Which way?" He looked around, seemed to pick a direction at random, and pointed. "That way? Or over there?" He pointed back over his shoulder.

"Torchay, you can't come with me. You're not a naitan."

"You're no' leaving me behind." He started to fold his arms and realized he held her hand. He folded one arm and held on as if he feared she'd leave him if he let go. He was right.

But what would happen to him if she left him here?

"Torchay, no. You have to go back."

He shook his head. Goddess, he could be so stubborn. "No' without you."

"You have no business going where I'm going. You couldn't get back."

"Can't get back now. I tried." He shrugged as if it didn't matter in the least. "I'm fairly certain it's impossible unless you take me. Doesn't matter. You're no' going anywhere without me. After sixteen years, I think you'd have learned that much. Besides, if I have no business going there, neither have you."

"But—" She turned away from him, needing to find what would fill that hollow burning.

"Stone's *gone*, Kallista. I know it hurts. I know losing the link to the lad must have been worse than anything I can imagine. But you can't fix it this way. You'll only bollix things up worse."

"You don't *understand*." Kallista tried to twist her hand free, but he held on tight, somehow stronger in this misty landscape than he'd ever been in the flesh.

Wasn't that wrong? She was the naitan. She should be the stronger, especially here.

"Maybe I don't," he admitted. "But I think there's a few things you're not understanding yourself. What about the promise you made Stone? To get his boy back *no matter what*? If you're wandering around here in the mists, who's going to do that?

"We've learned a few things as well, while you've been off wandering. Sky's not the only one. And they're not bondservants. They're slaves." His words fell like stones on her flesh.

"If you don't care about your promises, what about your ilian? What about your children? Do you want to leave Lorynda and Rozite without any blood parents at all? If you stay, I stay, remember? Are you really that selfish?"

His scorn ripped her open. *Goddess,* was that what she'd been? Selfish? So wrapped up in her own pain that she'd forgotten everything and everyone else?

Kallista looked down at her dreamself, at the gash above her heart pouring blood-red pain out to stain the mist. "I'm afraid," she sobbed. "It hurt so much to lose Stone, to feel that link snap. I couldn't bear to lose any of the rest of you."

"So you'll leave us behind to suffer instead?" His scorn didn't lessen. Couldn't he see her bleeding?

But when she looked at Torchay, she saw he was bleeding too. From two wounds, not just one, both of them heart-deep.

"Goddess, *no.*" She pressed her hands over his heart, carrying his along when he refused to let her go, trying to stop the bleeding. She didn't think he would actually bleed out here in the dreamscape. The blood wasn't real. It was a representation of their pain. But you never knew.

Events on the dreamplane sometimes had an effect in the physical world. You never knew which events, or what the effect would be.

"Why two?" Kallista had to know. "Why are you bleeding twice?"

"This one's Stone." Torchay touched her hand to it, his eyes locked on hers. "And this one's you."

"Oh, Goddess." Kallista moaned, sagging against him, still trying without success to stop the gushing flow. "I didn't know. I didn't think—"

"No, you didn't."

"I can't stop it. I can't heal it." Again and again she tried to call magic, to set it to mending what was broken. And every time, she failed.

"I don't think magic can heal this sort of pain." Torchay brought her in close against him, matching wound to wound, so that their pain flowed into each other. "At least, not that kind of magic. I think love's the only thing that can do it. Love's the most magical thing there is."

And as Torchay's pain, his love flowed into her through the awful gash in her dreamself, it began—just a bit—to fill up that burning emptiness inside her.

"I have been so stupid. Can you all forgive me?"

"Yes, you have been. But I should have expected it, you do stupidity so often and so well." He was grinning at her when she looked up at him. "As for forgiving, I suppose I have to, don't I? Since I'm in love with you and all. You'll have to go back and ask the others, though. Aisse is likely to smack you first, before she does, she's that mad at you."

Kallista pressed a hand over her own wound, and this time managed to seal it up, rather like pressing layers of soft clay together. It still oozed a bit, but it stayed shut. Torchay's injuries sealed up the same way, when he helped.

"Thank you for coming," she said.

He shrugged. "I couldn't let you go off alone, could I? I'm your bodyguard."

She tugged at a lock of his hair, laughing. "I think this could be considered beyond the call of duty."

Then she turned away to study the featureless dreamscape. Her smile faded. She didn't recognize anything. There was nothing for her *to* recognize.

"I don't know if I can find the way back," she said after several long moments of frantic searching.

"You'd better. I certainly can't. I don't know how I got here to start with."

"Weren't you dreaming?" Kallista started walking, sending up a quiet prayer for guidance.

"No. I was making love to you." Torchay held her hand as he stalked beside her, bristling with protectiveness even here.

"And you . . . jumped?" She cocked an eyebrow at him.

He shrugged, then stopped, pulling her around to face him. "You know the way back," he said. "Of course you know the way. Stone's gone, and I'm *here*, but you've got six other links. You've cut them off, but they're still there. All you have to do is grab hold, the way you caught me. They'll lead us home."

Goddess, how unbelievably stupid and selfish she'd been. The pain of her loss was no excuse. They'd all suffered the same loss. She'd been too wrapped up in her own misery to see it.

"Do you think the children will forgive me?" Kallista said in a small, contrite voice.

"Ah." Torchay looked worried as he shook his head. "That one's going to be tricky. You may have to work for it, before they decide to trust that you'll not abandon them again."

"But we have to get back first." She blew out a breath and held on tight to Torchay as she *reached* for her other links.

She'd squeezed them down so tight and so thin that she was almost afraid to touch them, for fear they'd tear and flutter away like spider webs on the breeze. She breathed on the links. They shuddered, but held, warming under her breath. Carefully, she opened the painful constriction and moaned as the cramped ache eased.

Half her pain had been self-inflicted, caused when she'd cut herself off from her iliasti. Yet more stupidity.

"Hold on." Kallista tightened her grip on Torchay's dream hand and grasped the links in her other as they plumped with magic, grew strong and resilient. Kallista pulled hard on them.

She didn't draw magic through them, but rather used them to guide her, Torchay flying behind her across the measureless distance of the dreamscape. Twice, she had to wrap magic around Torchay's self when he threatened to leave bits of it behind, but eventually, finally, she saw the opening in the dreamfog.

They were lying on their backs, she and Torchay, naked and helpless in the bed she shared with Obed. Their ilian had gathered as Leyja and Keldrey worked frantically over Torchay.

"What did you do?" Kallista glanced at him, alarmed.

"I told you. I have no idea. I just—came after you."

"Well, get back down there where you belong. Right now." She gave him a hard shove and followed him down to make sure.

He didn't seem to quite know how to put himself . . . back into himself.

"Like this." Kallista followed the umbilical that tied her to her body, flowing into it as if she'd never been away. She opened her eyes to see Keldrey's backside cantilevered over her as he breathed for Torchay.

What was wrong with him? She reached out to touch.

"Somebody stop her before she hurts him again," Keldrey growled, rising to give Leyja room to work.

Obed caught Kallista's hand and pulled her gently away.

"Wait." She struggled to sit up. "What's going on? What's wrong with Torchay?"

Everyone turned to stare at her, except Keldrey who bent to give Torchay another breath. Obed spun her in his arms and grabbed her face between his hands, searching her eyes as if scarcely able to believe what he saw. "Kallista?"

She smiled. "Yes, love, I'm back. I'm sorry I left you." But she didn't have time now to indulge in weepy reunions or extended hugs. She pulled herself out of Obed's embrace.

"What's wrong with Torchay?" Kallista crawled around Keldrey to Torchay's head and brushed his hair off his high forehead.

"You're the naitan, you tell us." Keldrey paused to give another breath. "We thought he was getting through to you. Then he collapsed."

Hadn't he got back into his body? Kallista didn't know, could see only reality. No, the dreamworld was reality too, just a different kind of reality. She couldn't see it now. But—she could see through Joh's eyes and her own at the same time. Why couldn't she see the physical and metaphysical the same way?

Kallista drew magic. She closed her eyes tight and opened them while leaving her eyelids closed. And there he was, hovering half an armslength above his body. "What are you doing?" she demanded.

"Floating?" Torchay rearranged himself to sit cross-legged in mid-air.

"I'm compressing his chest," Leyja said. "To keep his heart beating."

"Not you." Kallista waved a negating hand at Leyja. "Torchay."

"He's here?" Obed shivered as he looked around the room.

"Where?" Joh brightened, his looking eager and curious. He found every new thing fascinating.

"There." Kallista gestured toward her beloved's incorporeal self. "What—" She opened her eyes and peered with all her vision at him. "Did you cut yourself completely free of your body? Why in the world—"

"I told you, I wasn't letting you go anywhere without me." He shrugged, which made him bob up and down. "And I didn't know what in blazes I was doing."

"No, don't stop," Kallista said when it seemed Leyja would cease her laboring. "We have to keep him going till we can get him . . . reattached."

"We'll keep going till you say stop." Keldrey took over the chest compressions. "However long it takes."

"Next time," Kallista scolded Torchay, "don't take everything with you when you *jump*, or whatever it was you did. Leave something behind so you can find your way back."

"I had you to bring me back." Torchay arched an eyebrow at her. "Now, are you going to finish the job or no'?"

"Saints, you can't do anything for yourself, can you?" With a sigh and a weary, teasing shake of her head, Kallista called magic, reveling in the sensation as it flowed through the links to her. Without Stone, it was sluggish and resistant, like drawing mud from a well rather than water, but it came.

She reached *through* Torchay's body and out again to capture a foot-shaped bit and haul it into his well-loved, familiar body. It took a bit more magic to sweep all of him out of the dreamscape and back inside his physical self, but once there, he stuck nicely. Magic wasn't needed to keep him in place.

"Wait," she said. "Before you leave this place completely—*watch*. Learn." And she showed him how to make a safe shift into the dreamworld, so that he could find his way back to a body that only slept. "I hope you don't have to do it again, but if you do, I want you to know how. I want you safe. I love you."

"I love you." The words were spoken in his familiar raspy tenor as he opened his eyes to look at her.

Leyja and Keldrey scrambled out of the way before he raised onto an elbow and looked around at the rest of their iliasti. "Well. That was quite an adventure."

"What happened to you?" Joh asked.

Aisse climbed onto the bed to hug Kallista. Then she broke it off, clouted Kallista on the head, and hugged her again.

Kallista's vision, still as much in the dreamworld as in the physical, could see their weeping wounds bleeding into each other, beginning to fill up the empty space left when Stone was torn from them. She hugged Aisse tight, then reached for Fox, climbing over Torchay's legs to get to him.

Fox pressed his face against her. "Did you see Stone?"

"No." Kallista kissed his cheek, his eyes. "I think if we had, we couldn't have come back. He's gone too far for any of us to reach. But he's waiting for us, when our turns come—a long, *long* time from now."

Fox's laugh cracked, but it was a laugh. He pushed her toward Viyelle for more hugs, more kisses. Finally, she had hugged each one of her iliasti and was nestled again in Torchay's arms. Obed's dark eyes burned into her, with happiness and envy both. She could feel it hissing through the link, but she didn't know what to do about it. She was getting tired of the jealousy, so she ignored it.

Everyone crowded onto the bed while Torchay told the tale of his adventures. Then they had to explain to Kallista about the runaway-slave-turned-thief who had dropped into the family courtyard out of a tree and had now apparently vanished back up that tree into the darkness from which he'd come.

Leyja cursed and stomped around a bit when that was discovered, but finally admitted there was nothing to be done about it now, and if the thief returned, they'd know he was sincere in his offer. Maybe. Leyja seemed reluctant to trust anything having to do with this thief.

Then they told her what this Padrey had told them, about the slaves and the Daryathi breeding program. The news burned away the last of the dreamfog lingering in Kallista's brain.

Chapter Fourteen

"I told them you would want to rescue all the slaves," Aisse said.

"You were right." Kallista grabbed Obed's discarded robe and put it on as she got out of the bed to pace. She made a few circuits of the room before Keldrey stopped her and belted the robe around her.

"You're distracting the lads." He tipped his head at the others. "Makes it too hard for Fox and Joh to do their thinking."

"Right." They had to have their cleverest thinkers on the job. And Viyelle, with her creative, sometimes bizarre ideas that often actually worked. Kallista turned to face her ilian. "We have to get Sky out first, or we're too vulnerable to help anyone. But we're not leaving any Adaran enslaved."

"Are we taking the word of a confessed thief that this is happening?" Obed demanded.

"Do you have any real reason to believe it isn't?" Viyelle retorted. "Other than your experience of living here? Which you have yourself admitted was cut off from normal society."

"There is no proof either way." Joh stepped in to cut off the impending argument. "We need corroboration. Someone else to tell us whether it's true or not."

"That's easy enough," Kallista said.

"How? By sending the thief off to spy for us?" Leyja paced crosswise to Kallista's path. "Why would he tell us any truth but the one he wants us to believe?"

"Stubble it, Leyja." Keldrey pulled her back onto the bed, planting her there with a little shove. "You don't like him because he stole that necklace from you and got away. You're making it personal."

"All we have to do is ask Bekaara," Kallista said. "She's helped us already. She's an honorable person—everyone says so, and I have my truthsaying magic for just-in-case."

Obed leaned against the bed's headboard. "Yes. She will tell us truth, even if it is an uncomfortable one."

Kallista sighed, turning to look at her ilian all crowded together on the bed, looking back at her. "I'm beginning to think that everything in this place is uncomfortable."

"Oh, I don't know—" Torchay drawled, stretching out on the bed by shoving Joh aside. "Seems very comfortable right here."

"Speak for yourself." Joh shoved back, sending Fox nearly lurching off the other side.

"I am." This time Torchay's shove sent Joh stumbling halfway across the room to bump into Kallista.

Joh slung an arm around Kallista's shoulders. "Come along, love. There's obviously no room for us here. We'll find our own comfortable spot."

"Oh no, you don't." Torchay scrambled from the bed and joined them. "No' after I've gone to all the trouble of going after her and bringing her back."

"We're still in Daryath," Obed reminded them, arms folded in disapproval.

"No, we're not," Viyelle said. "We're in the Adaran embassy. On Adaran soil, as long as we're inside. We got rid of all the Daryathi servants. There's no one left to spy on us."

"You did?" A load of worry lifted from Kallista, then she frowned. "Won't that make them suspicious? And what about that boy? That gift?"

"Stone was murdered," Joh said. "By his 'wife,' true, but the locals still accept the need for heightened security, especially since you've been 'indisposed.'"

Kallista winced. "Has that caused any problems? Stone wasn't *my* husband."

"He's Varyl." Viyelle sat up cross-legged on the bed. "Im-Varyl, the way they've been reading it. In the direct line. And they don't quite know what 'godmarked' means, despite what you told the new Habadra—she's had her investiture ceremony, by the way—anyhow, they're apparently making allowances."

"And according to their laws," Fox said, "the 'gift', the man Habadra sent us, isn't Daryathi any more. He's Varyl-sa. Adopted into your Adaran Line. And in case you need to know, I got tired of calling him 'Hey You' during practice and named him. *Night,* because he's dark."

"River, Sky, Night—" Torchay listed the males their Tibran-born had named. "You keep going and no one will have names, just descriptions."

Fox threw a pillow at him, which was batted away. "I thought we were going to do sex. Or at least get to sleep all together for once. What happened to that?"

"I got shoved out into the cold," Joh said. "And captured the prize." His arm over Kallista's shoulders curled round her neck and he planted a smacking kiss on her cheek.

"Well, bring her back." Fox scooted aside to make room. "It'll be crowded, but we'll manage. We've managed with less."

"I don't think this is wise." Obed was squeezed up against the headboard as people shifted.

"Oh, Obed, don't be such a pooty-face." Viyelle grabbed his tunic and wrestled it off. She didn't have to wrestle hard.

"That's right." Aisse, already naked—Kallista didn't know how she'd done it so fast, but she always did—straddled Obed's lap. Aisse caught his face between her hands, her lips brushing his as she spoke. "Don't be such a pooty-face. Don't let Daryath rub all the Adaran off you."

She kissed him, mouth open, rubbing her full breasts against his naked chest, and after a moment, Obed kissed her back the same way, his hands settling on her hips. Kallista had to blink. He'd never gone so far with one of the other women in the ilian, not when she was naked.

"Hey." Viyelle jiggled Aisse's arm. "Share. Everybody kisses everybody tonight."

Aisse drew slowly back from Obed and looked at Viyelle from the corner of her eye. "Everybody?"

"Every single body." Viyelle punctuated her words with a decisive nod.

"All right then." Aisse patted Obed's cheek in a reluctant farewell, then turned and pounced on Viyelle, capturing her for an open-mouthed kiss. After a moment's startled laughter, Viyelle returned it.

"Well, that's not quite fair, is it?" Fox said, watching avidly. "I mean, we're already short of women to begin with."

"She did say 'everybody kisses everybody.'" Keldrey grabbed Fox for a loud, joking kiss.

When he let go, Fox took hold of his ears and brought him back. "*This* is how it's done."

"Looks like a good plan to me," Kallista finally managed to say. Viyelle was kissing Obed now, and Aisse and Leyja were trying to swap tongues.

Torchay and Joh exchanged a look, one of those very male ones Kallista didn't want to know the meaning of. Together they picked her up and tossed her onto the bed, into a bony tangle of knees and elbows, following close behind her. Then they kissed each other, leaving her to find her own partner. Keldrey just happened to be free again.

"Oh, Khralsh." Fox used the name of the warrior face of the One. "Aisse has gone broody again. She wants another baby. A black-haired one this time."

Kallista looked past Joh's shoulder to see Aisse with her hand halfway down the front of Obed's trousers and her tongue in his mouth. He had hold of her wrist, stopping her, but his resistance seemed to be softening.

"So?" Aisse abandoned her pursuit of Obed to roll over and sling an arm around Torchay's neck. "But if I can't have black, I'll settle for red."

"Will you, now?" Torchay slid his arms around her. "Will you settle for a kiss now and discussion later, after all this is done and we're back home in Arikon?"

Aisse stuck out her lower lip. "If you insist."

Torchay laughed and nipped her lip before granting the kiss he'd offered, and Kallista called magic.

It brought gasps from eight throats, including her own. She checked the contraceptive spells, making sure they were in place—they didn't need to be any more vulnerable while in Daryath than they already were—and she opened the web she had built over the years, binding each one to each of the others.

"Keldrey?" She still had presence of mind to ask. He wasn't part of the web.

"I've got him," Viyelle said.

Kallista opened her mouth to take in sleek, hot, solid strength. She wrapped the web of magic around her iliasti and swirled it round herself in a blanket of love, teetering on the edge. She checked again to make sure everyone was tucked in safe, then she let herself fall.

It wasn't a screaming, searing plummet into passion, not this time. The magic itself seemed to mourn, stuttering as it passed over the place where Stone should have been. They floated, drifting on a gentle river of comfort and rising desire. Stone was dead. But they, the ones who had loved him, were alive. Their love still lived, or it wouldn't hurt so much.

The magic swelled to its own crescendo. The stutter vanished, smoothing out. Not as if Stone had been erased, but as if he were still with them. It was, Kallista realized, the same thing she'd felt just before he died—Stone's love for them.

If not for you— the thought was Fox's, for the whole ilian—*he never would have known love, would never have understood what it was.*

Kallista bathed in the magic, wallowed, poured it over the others and scrubbed them with it. Stone was gone, but the love wasn't. Not while they still lived, still loved. As long as any of them was alive, any of their children, their children's children and beyond, the legacy of that love would continue.

On its own, the magic began almost to glow, stoking the fires of passion in slowly building waves. Kallista moaned, her hands sliding along sleek, warm flesh. She wasn't sure whose, but she knew it was one of the men. She'd never been so lost in the sensations before. She kissed, caressed, loved, riding with the magic in control as it carried them along, into the rapids to drop them screaming together over the cliffs.

Daylight was creeping through the gauzy draperies when Kallista floundered back to consciousness. All nine of them were crowded together onto a bed meant to hold no more than four. She struggled to breathe under the weight of five or six arms draped across her chest—no, that one was a leg. And the hair veiling her vision was not her own since it was a reddish gold rather than darkest brown. So the leg by her face didn't belong to Fox.

It slid up onto her neck—Obed's leg—and she shoved at it. "Get off. Get up. We need to go visit Bekaara today."

Torchay groaned. One of the arms across her middle was his, but Aisse was squashed between them. "How can you be so energetic? I'm flattened."

"Well, get your flat self up out of this bed and get yourself fed and dressed." Kallista squirmed through the tunnel of arms and legs—there were more across her lower body—to the foot of the bed and out onto the floor. Then she slapped the nearest backside to get Leyja moving. "Let's go, people. We have things to see. People to do."

"I thought we did them all last night," Fox mumbled, shoving his hair out of his face.

"Bloody hell." Keldrey sat up, his mouth working as if to rid itself of a bad taste. "I'd ask what I did last night, but I don't think I want to know."

"You were fabulous, lover," Joh teased, leaning in as if he meant to kiss Keldrey.

"Bugger off." Keldrey planted a hand in Joh's face and shoved him away. "I know I saw you with Vee."

Joh tugged his hair from beneath Leyja. "Part of the time, yes. The rest—is something of a blur."

"Stop talking." Kallista pulled on a toweling robe and clapped her hands in meager hope of actually getting them to do what she said. "Start moving. Go. Wash. Eat. Dress. *Now*."

She turned and walked out of the room. Maybe without her there, they would get moving. But even if they kept talking instead, she wouldn't be there to hear it.

"Hey." Torchay trotted barefoot down the corridor after her, a bit of cloth—a pillowcase?—clutched round his hips for modesty's sake. Though truth be told, he didn't have much of that virtue. "Are you all right?"

Kallista flashed him a smile. "Fine. Why wouldn't I be?"

"Let me think—Stone's dead. You spent most of last week wandering the dreamscape looking for him. You had to put me back together—*again*—before I died. This time I wasn't gutted, but I think it was a closer thing, wasn't it?" He raised an eyebrow at her, obviously waiting for an answer, so she nodded.

"If that's no' enough," he went on, "Stone's boy is still Habadra's slave. There are hundreds, maybe thousands of other Adaran slaves who need rescuing. And there's a trial-by-combat tournament coming up that we have to win if we're to winkle Sky out of that woman's hands."

"But I'm *fine*. Truly." Except for that weird feeling she had of something being . . . not right, that had started before Stone's death. Before they'd left Adara, perhaps. But she couldn't pinpoint what it was, and it always went away again. If the feeling got worse, she would deal with it then. She had enough to deal with just now.

She opened the bathing room door and went in, Torchay following her. "And if I'm not fine," she said, "you can sort me out when we figure out what it is."

"Right." He dropped his pillowcase, stepped into the pool and sank until the water closed over his head. When he came up again, he shook water from his face. "Come on then. Bathe. We've got things to see and people to do, I believe you said."

"Yes." Kallista stripped off the robe and laid it on the ledge before slipping into the hot water. Torchay tossed her a bar of soap.

The bathing room door opened and Fox put his head through. "Safe to come in?"

"Of course." Kallista tossed the soap in his direction. "Unless you're worried about drowning."

It only took two chimes of the clock to get everyone ready to pay their call on Bekaara. Besides getting eight of them dressed and ready and five queues properly braided—Aisse kept her hair short, Obed never wore one and Keldrey had no hair to braid—they had to send a messenger to ask whether it was convenient for a visit. It was.

Then Kallista had to change clothes when Omri greeted her with a big hug, and jam-coated hands and face. Finally, after Keldrey got back from his time with Sky, they left him with the children, and rode out to Shakiri House.

A young champion in Bekaara's service met them at the inner gate where their escort remained. He led them through the sprawling residence and up a flight of stairs to a suite of rooms tastefully if sparsely decorated. Kallista studied the wide expanse punctuated with low sofas and thick patterned rugs. She rather liked it. Liked it much better than the rabid ornamentation currently in vogue in Arikon. In the palace there, anything that held still long enough was in danger of being gilded. She had a few army-assigned bodyguards still washing gilt paint from their hair.

Bekaara came hurrying from one of the back rooms, drying her hands on a towel. Today she wore a simple pale blue dress ornamented only with embroidery at neck and hem.

"I hope we haven't disturbed you." Kallista bowed and took the hand Obed's cousin extended.

"No, no. I was writing letters, had to wash the ink off my hands." Bekaara squeezed Kallista's hand, patted it awkwardly. "I was absolutely sick to hear what happened to that nice young man. They said you knew the instant he— Well, if there's anything I can do—"

The open sympathy in Bekaara's face brought tears back to Kallista's eyes. She hated to cry, especially in public, but such a devastation as this . . . Kallista smiled—somewhat—nodded and squeezed back. "Thank you. I appreciate your offer."

Bekaara chuckled, gently. "That's why you're here, isn't it? Because there is something I can do for you. Come then. Sit, sit." She shooed them all to the sofas.

"May I offer you tea? Mother will be pleased to hear you've come. She may forgive me yet. The Reinine and all the Godmarked come to visit—well, except—" The expression of horror on Bekaara's face as she realized her misstep made Kallista smile.

"No need to walk on eggshells," Kallista said. "We miss Stone, very much, and we are more determined than ever to redeem his son, but we are not so sensitive as that."

Bekaara's champion brought in a tray with a steaming pot of Daryathi tea, prized all over the known world, and cups without handles.

Bekaara made a sweeping gesture. He bowed and went to do whatever she had bid while she poured tea and chatted about inconsequential things. When he returned to take up a post at the doorway, she set her cup down and folded her hands.

"Now." Bekaara smiled at Kallista, her eyes seeming to gain in sharp intelligence by the tick. "Danek has cleared away any listeners. What is it I may do for you?"

"I need information," Kallista said. "Confirmation. Obed has said that you will give me truth, even if it is an uncomfortable one."

Bekaara took a deep breath and let it out slowly. "Oh. Dear." She met Kallista's gaze. "Yes. I will give you truth."

Kallista leaned forward, intent. "I am told that in the jubilee year, when debts are forgiven and bondservants are set free, only the Daryathi gain their freedom. Is this true?"

Bekaara looked grim as she nodded. "Truth."

"I am told there are many Adaran slaves here in Mestada."

"Truth."

Piece by piece, Kallista went through the information her ilian had learned from the young thief and every word of it, Bekaara confirmed. The Daryathi bred their Adaran slaves in hopes of getting more naitani. Though only one in five women or one in ten men might be gifted with magic, those without magic were kept for the value of their labor and their children. This also meant that impoverished, indebted Daryathi had less opportunity for employment and more trouble paying off debt.

"Is this why Daryath wants a trade agreement?" Kallista paced the room, scarcely noticing how it agitated Danek, or that Fox had stationed himself beside the young champion. "So they can steal more of our people? Enslave us all?"

Bekaara sighed. "I think some of the Kameri truly wish to be able to *hire* Adaran nathains, but when others hold slaves . . ."

"Slaves are much cheaper than employees, aren't they?" Kallista didn't bother to keep the sharp edges from her voice. "Do *you* own any slaves?"

"I do not myself, no. But Shakiri Line—yes." Bekaara touched the fragile rim of one of the round teacups. "Sometimes I think this is why my mother is determined to live so long. Besides the fact that she hates to give up a single drop of power. She knows the first thing I will do as the Shakiri is to free all our slaves."

"Whereupon every other Line in Mestada will snap them up."

Bekaara's eyes held sadness when she looked at Kallista. "I would send them home, to you, on one of Obed's ships."

"I'm sorry. This just—" Kallista rubbed her aching eyes. She'd always had a temper, but lately it had gotten worse. And she wasn't the only one who'd noticed. Her iliasti complained about it. The worry was getting to her. "It makes me furious and you're handy. How did things get into such a mess?"

"When I was a girl," Bekaara said, "Adaran nathains were hired. But—they would leave for higher pay, or to go home. And they were always scarce, especially with all our Daryathi nathains going into the temple. So when magic was needed and no one would work for the pay offered, they began to be . . . taken."

Kallista bit down on her temper. "How long?"

"I wasn't of age when I first remember hearing of it, so—thirty-five years ago? Forty?" Bekaara scowled, letting go of the teacup she'd been toying with. "The first ones I heard of had been charged with blasphemy, adultery. They were tried in the arena-courts, but too many of them died. Most of the ones arrested after that were simply enslaved. Others, they didn't bother with arresting. Just took them."

"And you did nothing?" Kallista's temper got loose again before she could drag it back.

"What could I do? I was a child." Bekaara was on her feet now, but kept her distance, which kept Kallista's bodyguard iliasti seated. "What can I do now? I am the heir, not the Shakiri. The Shakiri can order my death and no one can stay her hand. By Law, I am required to kneel before her and bow my head for the blow."

"*Goddess.*" Kallista flung herself across the room, away from the temptation to attack, or break something. Fewer breakables at this end.

"When did all the Daryathi naitani begin to go into the temple?" Joh asked. "And why, if you want the magic badly enough to enslave Adarans for it?" Thank the One for cool heads and analytical minds.

"It began before I was born. Several generations back, I think." Bekaara returned to her sofa, picked up a teacup again. Perhaps handling the delicate porcelain helped her own temper. If she lost control, she would break the cup. "As for why . . ."

She sighed, brooded over her tea a moment. "Religion. The Sameric sect gained ascendancy some hundred years ago, teaching that the nathains, those gifted by the One with magic, were not just blessed, but holy. To be set aside and dedicated to the service of the One.

"Their sect believes that to be acceptable to God, a person must be separate from the daily evils of ordinary life. Only those with magic are blessed by the One. The rest of humanity can earn the remnants of the One's favor by setting themselves apart—joining the Samerics— or supporting those set apart. Gradually, Samerics took over all the temples in Daryath until now, few dare admit they don't follow Sameric beliefs." Her voice had gone sour.

"At first, the nathains lived together in special buildings, rather like a skola, coming out to do their work. But as the Samerics refined their teaching, that the nathains were too holy to even mingle with those denied by the One, they began moving into the temple here in Mestada, closing down all the other temples, and then they stopped coming out at all." She paused. "I am not Shathina's oldest daughter. Did you know?"

Obed shook his head for the rest of them. There was too much he did not know, and he hated the feeling.

"I had an older sister who was taken into the temple. As your sister would have been, Obed, had she not died of the fever. It struck about the time her magic appeared."

Kallista's lightning could not have stunned him more. "Sister?"

"Oh yes—" Bekaara looked stricken, as if she wished she'd said nothing. "How would you know about her? It happened after you entered the skola. Your mother was lonely with you gone and your father dead so long."

"He died when I was five," Obed said for those who didn't know. "I nearly died of the black-tongue fever as well." He barely remembered his father, only a deep voice and a sense of safety. The last time he'd felt safe until he found Kallista.

"That's right. So you were gone and Shaneen took a lover. One of the Shakiri-sa at the estate upriver where she lived. It wouldn't have been so bad, but there was a child, a girl. Mother was furious. She was pleased enough with the girl, but Shaneen had disgraced herself.

"She refused to break off with her lover as Mother ordered. Actually wanted to marry him—a Shakiri-*sa*. That had Mother absolutely frothing at the mouth. A *Sa* as her brother?" Bekaara stopped for a breath in the rapt silence.

Kallista returned to the sofas, took a seat beside Obed and put an arm around him. He scarcely noticed. How could he not have known this? What *else* had they not told him? He'd been devastated when he came for his visit to find his mother dead, but this—

"So," Bekaara went on. "The Shakiri ordered the Sa's death. When Shaneen found him, she came to Mestada for revenge, but Mother was surrounded by her pet champions. Shaneen's attack failed and she was injured. Mother planned to send her back to the estate, to forgive her, eventually, if she behaved herself. Of course, her baby would stay in Mestada with the Shakiri.

"Shaneen died before the week was out. She hadn't been injured so badly, but—" Bekaara sighed. "Without her lover or either of her children, I think she simply didn't want to live."

Obed dragged his hand down over his mouth, trying to wipe away all emotion. His voice shook when he spoke, giving away the earthquake inside. "I did not know."

He'd had a *sister*. And he had never known. Yet another thing Shathina had stolen from him as she had stolen everything else in his life. He was no more alone in the world than he had been. He still had his family, his son, Kallista. So why did he feel so much worse?

Chapter Fifteen

"Of course not." Bekaara poured more tea in Obed's cup, urged him to drink. "You were in—what? Your second—no, your third year at that skola. They wouldn't even let us tell you your mother had died. 'The students must focus solely on their learning.'" She mocked a pompous-sounding official. He heard echoes of the skola's grand master in her voice.

"By the time they let you out for your visit before you took your dedicat vows, your mother had been dead five years. What use would it have been to tell you all this then?"

"I might have met my sister." Obed ground the words through clenched teeth. He had never known, and the loss hurt the worse because of it.

"Shakiri Shathina forbade anyone telling you. You were qualified for dedicat, the first *im*-Shakiri dedicat in years. She wanted *nothing* to interfere with that. She wanted those dedicat skills sworn to fight in the courts for Shakiri."

"Why was I not told about my sister later?" Obed wanted to snatch up one of the teacups and smash it against the wall.

Bekaara wouldn't meet his eyes. "After she died? What purpose would it have served? I wish I had said nothing now—I forgot that you didn't know. It seemed mere cruelty, to tell you such a thing when you could do nothing about it."

The worse cruelty was not telling him from the start. He could have left the skola, given up his vows and become champion. Made a home for himself and his sister.

Dreamsmoke. Shathina would never have allowed it. Only the completion of his dozen years of vows and earning all nine tattoos had set him free of his aunt and her plotting. And allowed him to find his destiny. Kallista.

"Perhaps we should visit the temple." Kallista's voice brought Obed out of his thoughts.

"Only clerics and prelates go into the temple grounds," Bekaara reminded them.

Another reason for the Sameric clerics to preach against Kallista and Adarans, Obed supposed. Who knew what a free, uncloistered magic-user might do? Though none of the Daryathi seemed to know what "godmarked" truly meant.

"Do we have time for a visit now?" Fox asked quietly. "Before Stone's son is free?"

Kallista shook her head. "No. You're right. It would be a distraction. Later, if it's necessary, we can visit." She stood and pulled Obed to his feet. He still felt stunned.

"So," she said to Bekaara. "Can we do anything for you?"

"I am well enough." Bekaara bowed. "Thank you." She strolled with them back through the house, her young champion at her left shoulder just as Obed strode at Kallista's right. "My husband is away. He would love to meet you, I know."

"I thought—" Obed began before falling silent, wondering what else he hadn't been told.

"What?" Kallista walked sideways down the stairs to look back at him.

"I thought your husband died," Obed said. "After Thalassa was born. I never saw him after that, when you came to trials."

Bekaara's smile was thin. "The Shakiri ordered us divorced. We were too close. I spent too much time with him, too much thought on him. I loved him too much. But—" She shook her head.

"I have never abandoned my vows. He is still my husband, here." She touched her heart. "Shakiri Shathina could order us divorced. She can order my death, but she cannot make me marry against my will. I am already married. So."

"Saints." Obed added a few of Torchay's favorite oaths.

"Thiben, my husband, was married again by the Head of his Line. They live apart, he and his 'wife'—no children. He keeps his vows to me as well."

Kallista stopped to stare at Bekaara. "Is every life tragic in Daryath? Doesn't anyone have a happy story?"

Bekaara considered, standing there in the shadowed gallery beside an expansive courtyard. "I've never considered."

After a bit, she shook her head. "No, I don't believe so. Mother is happy on occasion, when she's moving the members of Shakiri House around like pieces on a queens-and-castles board, or when the en-Kameral does her bidding. But then Habadra or some other Line will do something, and she'll fly into a rage. Sometimes I think she's happiest only when she has something to be enraged about—but I am speaking out of turn."

Bekaara caught Kallista's arm, stopped her when she would have walked on. "What about you? Is yours a happy story?"

Obed held his breath, waiting, wondering what she would say. *Was* she happy?

"Yes," she said finally, tears overflowing once again.

"It's not happy right this moment," she said, "because we have lost our Stone. But we had him. We loved him seven years. We have his daughter. We *will* have his son. We were happy." She looked at those with her, at Obed, and smiled. "We will be happy again. Our hearts are broken, but they will one day heal."

"Then you have truly been blessed by the One." Bekaara's smile was wistful. Sad.

"The One's blessings be on you as well, Bekaara cousin." Kallista led the way outside to their escort.

Obed moved his horse forward as they rode through the outer gate, interposing himself between Kallista and the noisy crowds in the street. Torchay did the same on her other side.

Kallista frowned. "It bothers me, the naitani's seclusion. But I don't know why."

"I think I might," Joh said from behind them.

Kallista twisted in the saddle to see him.

He shook his head, gesturing at the increasingly rowdy crowds around them. "Wait till we get back to the embassy."

"At least we know now why the populace doesn't like us." Fox set his horse to dancing, forcing the people crowding too close to back away for fear of the flying hooves.

"It's not *our* fault *their* people have taken slaves," Aisse protested.

"But our people have the jobs they need," Fox said.

"We'll take care of it." Kallista's smile was grim with determination. "We'll give the locals all the jobs they want."

"Aye." Torchay said nothing more.

Kallista noticed the man loitering at the embassy gate with the hood of his overrobe pulled up against the sun, but she didn't pay him much attention. Ragged citizens roamed everywhere in Mestada and her escort guarded against trouble. Then he shoved back his hood to reveal gold-streaked hair no Daryathi ever claimed.

At the same time, Leyja snarled. "You."

"Me," he said. "I brought you something."

"What you stole." Leyja rode at him, as if intending to ride him down.

"Leyja!" Kallista had never seen the other woman so vindictive before.

"And more," the thief called, his gaze on Kallista. "News."

Leyja had stopped, but she wasn't backing up.

"Let him in," Kallista called to the guard captain. "I want to speak with him personally."

In the bustle of the outer courtyard, once again on foot, Kallista caught Leyja's queue and pulled her down so she could whisper in her ear. "Cool your temper, Sergeant, or I'll cool it for you. We need this man."

"He is a thief," Leyja growled.

"But not a liar. Let it go." Kallista pulled harder on the sandy red braid, bending the taller woman into an almost painful arc. "I mean it, Leyley." Now Kallista used the pet name Aisse had given Leyja, rather than her rank. "Leave him be. Let it go." Her lips brushed Leyja's ear as she spoke. When she finished, Kallista bit down hard on the earlobe.

Leyja shuddered. "Yes. All right."

Kallista released her. "All right, what?"

"My Reinine." Leyja bowed low.

"*What?*" Kallista raised an eyebrow and Leyja flushed, smiled shyly.

"Kallista," she said.

"Better have Aisse look at that." Kallista flicked a finger at Leyja's ear. "We'll be in the parlor with your thief. Don't be long."

As Leyja hurried off, Kallista sighed. It bothered her sometimes, the things Leyja liked, the things she responded to. But she was a good woman with a generous heart who wanted only to give. In some ways, she was too gentle to be a bodyguard, but in other ways—she would die before she would let any harm come to those she loved. Kallista couldn't help loving her back.

The guard captain held the thief by the entrance to the building. Not actually holding on, but with him, standing guard.

"Captain." Kallista acknowledged the woman's salute with one of her own. "Tell me your name." The captain had done excellent service both on the journey and here in Mestada. She deserved to be recognized for it.

"Ronda Kargyll, my Reinine." The captain swept into a low bow while keeping an eye on her charge.

"Viyelle, make a note. Make sure Captain Kargyll is on the promotions list."

"Of course, my Reinine." Viyelle inclined her head, smiling at the captain's second stammering bow of thanks.

"Pass the word, Captain," Kallista went on, her attention shifting to Leyja's thief. "This man is to be admitted to the embassy whenever he presents himself. At any hour. Send word to Torchay Reinas that he is here, understood?"

"Yes, my Reinine." The captain bowed once more and saluted.

"They tell me you are Padrey." Kallista studied him, trying to see past the scruffy surface to the man beneath.

He was Kallista's exact height, for she could look straight on into his eyes—grayed blue, like mist laid over the sky. He was thin, his straight blond-over-brown hair in need of cutting. His angular face was set in an expression mixed from equal parts defiance and reluctant hope.

"Padrey Emtal, my Reinine. This is an honor." He bowed, an unpracticed, awkward version of the captain's low bow. As he straightened, he pushed back his overrobe, reaching for something hidden beneath.

The point of Torchay's right-hand sword came to rest on his chest, stopping his action. Padrey went still, then spread his hands slowly away from his body.

"No harm meant," the young thief said. "Just fetching out the package. I'm not armed."

Torchay used his blade to move the overrobe aside. No weapons were visible. He patted pockets, and pulled out a rag-wrapped bundle which he handed to Kallista before finishing his check. "Truth." Torchay put away his sword. "He's no' armed."

"Shall we go in then, out of this punishing sun?" Kallista spread her arms, urged everyone through the doors.

"It's not as hot as it was," Padrey said, attempting casual conversation. "But the sun's still a bastard."

Kallista had to smile. He was a thief and a runaway slave, after all. Allowances could be made for rough edges. "So it is."

He cleared his throat. "I'm glad to see you're better than the last time we—*erm*—met . . ."

"Thank you." How could he amuse her so? "Though we didn't exactly *meet*, did we? I am glad to be better."

An embassy guard opened the door to the parlor and Kallista paused, looking for someone she could send on an errand. Finally she addressed the guard. "Go fetch Keldrey Reinas. And tell Sidris to go ahead and give the children their lunch. We won't have time for them until later. One of these will take your post till you return with the Reinas." She gestured at her duty bodyguards. Thankfully, Torchay would let her leave them at doors on occasion, rather than insisting they stay beside her. "And Gweric. We need Gweric Naitan, if he's in the embassy."

Inside the parlor, Kallista tossed the still-wrapped package to Leyja who was waiting there with Aisse. The thief was Adaran, but he lived in Mestada. He knew much they didn't, and Gweric vouched for him. She would let him stay for now.

She turned to Joh. "All right. We're at the embassy. What's so bad about the Daryathi shutting their naitani up in the temple? Other than their magic is useless there."

"Think about it," he said.

Leyja made a small sound when she pulled Rozite's necklace with its fat thumb-sized ruby from the bundle.

"See?" Padrey muttered. "Told you I'd bring it back."

Kallista silenced Leyja's attempted retort with a glare, then turned it on Padrey. "You are here on sufferance, because I hope you have something to contribute. If I am disappointed . . ."

Padrey cleared his throat and bowed, and Kallista turned back to Joh.

"What exactly am I supposed to be thinking about?"

"Magic," Joh said. "What *is* magic?" He walked around the sofa to the center of the room.

"A gift of the One." Kallista sat, stretched her arms along the back of the sofa, wondering where he was going with this.

"Exactly. Do you know of any naitani who have actually been possessed by demons?"

"Merinda," Obed said. "She refused the mark, but she was naitan and the demon took her."

"But it drove her mad." Kallista began to see Joh's direction.

"What about that wind naitan?" Viyelle said. "The Barb who flew that boat the day I was marked. Wasn't she a naitan?"

"Her gift was small," Joh said. "Barely registered, according to records. Perhaps that made it possible."

"We already know that demons and magic don't mix. Why else did the old Rulers eliminate all the naitani in Tibre?" Fox leaned on the back of the couch where Kallista sat. "Are you saying that demons have been locking up the naitani here, so they can have free rein in the rest of Daryath?"

"I don't know." Joh shook his head. "Gweric said the demons felt *old*. What if they escaped the final battle in the Empty Lands and ran *here* to hide? They'd have had thousands of years to work their subtle evil. Locking up their naitani has certainly caused evil to happen."

"Have you changed your mind?" Fox asked. "About visiting the temple?"

Kallista shook her head. "Not unless we have to. Perhaps the One will sort things out inside the temple for us. But my main worry is that we are only eight." She frowned.

"Without our ninth, I don't know that we'll have enough magic to deal with the kind of demons Gweric warned us about. I don't want to stumble over a demon somewhere we never expected it to be, but we might. We need time." She had to pause and clear her throat of sudden anguish. "We need our ninth godmarked."

Keldrey flushed under Kallista's pleading gaze. He was already their ninth ilias. All the iliasti who had married in unmarked were marked now—save for Merinda, and she'd refused. Surely the only reason Keldrey hadn't been marked before now was that they hadn't needed him. They had had their nine. And they hadn't been facing demons.

"I'm willing," Keldrey said. "I *am*. But—" He shrugged helplessly.

"I know." Kallista huffed a sigh. "The One moves as the One wills. And She doesn't tell us beforehand where She's going."

Kallista sat up straight and looked back at Padrey where he was standing behind her, hands locked behind his neck. "Come around here where I can see you and tell us your news."

Carefully, eyes rolling toward Torchay, Padrey lowered his hands and bowed. Then he moved to the center of the room.

"When I left here yesterday—" He blushed and cleared his throat. "It looked as if you lot were busy and I wasn't needed, so I thought I'd be off to collect the . . . package. On the way, there I was, passing Habadra House, and I thought I'd just nip round and take a peek at your boy, see he was sleeping okay."

"Was he?" Kallista had received full reports from Keldrey and Fox, but she craved every driblet of information she could get about Sky. She longed to hold him in her own arms.

"Dunno. Never found him. I heard voices and thought I'd see who." He paused, looking pleased with himself. "It was the new Habadra— ain't heard what her name is—and Shakiri Shathina."

Kallista wasn't shocked. She wasn't even very surprised. She'd have expected Shathina to be the "keep your friends close and your enemies closer" type. "And what was it Habadra Chani and Shakiri Shathina were discussing?"

"Your boy. The Shakiri wanted the Habadra to give him to you, to call off this tournament trial. Habadra wouldn't do it, not unless Shakiri replaced the boy with another slave. She—Habadra, that is—wants a proven magic user for the boy. Habadra says with his mother a healer and his father one of your Godmarked, the boy's sure to be a powerful naitan. Guaranteed.

"Shakiri says it's no guarantee. She offers another boy, pure Adaran, a year or two older. Habadra refuses. They snarl at each other a bit longer. Meeting ends."

Kallista threw herself to her feet, startling Padrey into stumbling back a few paces, bumping into Joh behind him. She couldn't hold still with all the emotions storming inside her. Had her expansive use of magic at Habadra House made Chani so determined to keep Sky? Had she caused this? Could she have done things any other way?

"It's done now," Torchay said. "You can only deal with *what is*, no' *what if*."

"Right." Kallista sighed. "*Right*. So, what's next?" She looked at her motley army of demon hunters. "I think we need to attack on both fronts—slaves and demons. Gweric and Padrey, you're our spies. Gweric, concentrate on the temple area for now, see what you can . . . see. We have to find those demons."

The Tibran naitan saluted, then shaded his empty eyes with his hand and pretended to look around.

"Padrey—" She turned to the young thief, who drew himself up to solemn attention. "I need to know where all the Adaran slaves are, and how many. If we're going to get them all out—and I won't leave a single one behind—I need a good count. That's your job. Find them for me, Padrey. Every last one."

She held his gaze a long moment, until his eyes began to shine and he almost seemed to transform into a different person than the grubby thief who'd been standing before them.

Padrey bowed, awkwardly. "As you will it, so shall I do." His voice quivered with the passion behind his words. Abruptly, he dropped to one knee. "I pledge to Adara and to you, my Reinine, in all the names of the One, to serve wherever I am needed, until breath leaves my body."

Kallista blinked, stunned. How did this young man, this lost son of Adara, come to know the ancient oath of the Tayo Dai? Once a company of the most loyal, the most talented in all Adara, the Tayo Dai had faded into the bodyguard corps. Still valuable, but nowhere near the level of devotion, commitment and skill of the legendary Tayo Dai. The stories were still told, the old oath a part of them. He'd obviously heard them.

Padrey remained kneeling, his gaze fastened on Kallista, filled with a hope and expectation that faded bit by bit every moment she stood there without responding. She couldn't take that hope away from him.

But she didn't remember how the rest of the ceremony was supposed to go. Improvising, she stepped forward and rested the palm of her hand on his upturned forehead. She called magic and wrestled it into a tiny blessing. "Adara thanks you for this generous gift of service, and gratefully accepts. The blessing of the One be on you." And she let it settle out over him.

A rustle of movement had her looking around to see everyone else in the room on their knees. Torchay led out, reciting the oath Padrey had just spoken. Tears choked off her voice, *dammit*. Of all the times to be unable to speak.

Kallista grabbed Joh, on one knee just behind her new Tayo Dai, and pulled him to his feet, into a hug. She had to hold him for a long moment before she could find her voice again. "You are my *ilian*. We have already sworn vows of devotion and service to each other. I do not need more."

She looked past Joh, past Fox, to Gweric. "*Your* vow, I will take." She strode to him, laid her hand and the blessing of the One over his eyes.

"And I'll take that of anyone else—who is not Reinas—who wants to give it. Later." Kallista motioned everyone to their feet. "Get up, get up. We have work to do. Padrey, Gweric, off you go. Stay out of trouble. You can't serve if you're locked up somewhere, or worse."

The two young men bowed and strode out together, obviously bursting to talk about what had just happened.

She blew out a breath. "Now. Torchay, somebody's going to have to be in charge of the new Tayo Dai. You just got the job. Find out what the insignia used to be—"

"A naked sword crossing a long-stemmed red rose," Torchay said. "I'll have badges made."

Kallista raised an eyebrow. "Seems I picked the right person for the job. Know all the old stories, do you?"

"Why do you think I became a bodyguard? I've been your Tayo Dai from the first."

"Why here?" Kallista didn't understand it. "Why now? It's been hundreds of years since—"

"Because now we have a Reinine worthy of the oath, and dangerous times that call for it." Torchay paused. "You can't take a Tayo Dai oath from just anyone, no matter what you said."

"It's your job to make sure they understand exactly what they're swearing, that it's not just the latest fashion. I can test them too, with truthsaying magic, for sincerity. But if they mean it, truly mean it, then yes, I'll take them." Kallista turned to Viyelle. "I assume the diplomatic staff have been busy with the trade agreement that brought us here."

"Yes," Viyelle acknowledged.

"That stops today." Kallista looked at the small, four-sided clock on the low table in the room's center. "They should still be at lunch. Send word, quickly. Our people do not go back into the meeting room. Recall them now. Until this situation—this 'trial'—is concluded, we do not negotiate."

"Isn't that putting personal matters ahead of the nation's?" Joh asked.

"No. Because Sky is only the first slave we will free. After the trial—*after,* because I won't risk his safety—we will demand the immediate release of all Adaran slaves."

"Oh saints," Keldrey muttered. "Did we bring enough troops to defend against the whole city? We *are* in the middle of *their* country, Kallista."

"We have a secret weapon, dearest Keldrey." She waggled her ungloved hands at him. "But, when the Daryathi ask why we have suspended the formal talks, tell them . . ." What truth would deflect greatest trouble?

She sighed. "It's a bit late to use Stone's death as an excuse, if the talks have continued afterward."

"We objected," Viyelle said. "But with you—*away*—"

"You didn't have the power to tell them no," Kallista finished. "So, our excuse: I am *outraged* by the lack of respect for my Godmarked's death. Negotiations will continue when I am no longer distracted by this trial. How does that sound?"

"Like you are weak, indecisive and easily distracted." Obed's voice was sour.

Kallista grinned at him. "Excellent. And when we prove them wrong, it will set them scrambling."

Obed shook his head, but he smiled. "Are we to the trial?"

She surveyed the others, but no one spoke. "We are."

Chapter Sixteen

Quickly, Obed told Kallista what the others already knew. "Now we have to select those who will serve as our champions."

"I fight," Leyja said.

"No." Kallista shook her head hard enough to send her queue flying.

"You can't hold back your best fighters out of fear we'll be hurt," Torchay said.

"*Are* we her best fighters?" Keldrey asked. "We were losing steps six years ago, Leyja. And it's been six years. We're all older than we were."

"I'm younger than you are." Leyja seemed on the edge of striking out until Aisse touched her arm, quieting her.

"We need eight champions," Obed said. "We are eight, but not all of us can fight on the level needed for this trial."

"And what level is that?" Torchay sauntered toward Obed, a smile on his face and challenge in every line of his body. They'd been trying to best each other since they'd met, and neither had managed it yet.

"High." Obed's smile answered the challenge with its own. "Very, very high."

"No fighting in the house," Aisse scolded. "How do you expect your children to follow the rules if you don't?"

They glanced at her and the challenge dissolved in laughter. "But it is a good idea," Obed said. "Test our people against each other. Only the best to fight in the trial."

"Can we be sure our best will be good enough to win?" Fox said. "We *have to win* this trial."

"I have contacts in my old skola. I can arrange for a test against their best." Obed ran his fingers idly along the hilt of his sword. Kallista was sure he didn't realize it. "We do not have to be showy," he said. "We only have to win."

"Without killing," Kallista said. "And no one gets hurt in these tests of yours. Not a scratch."

"Bruises aren't scratches." Fox shrugged away Kallista's worry.

"You can't fight your best if you're banged up." She grabbed Fox by the base of his queue and shook his head gently. "Use that sense Stone was always going on about."

"The testing will be good training," Torchay said. "Get us ready for trial."

"Do we have a date yet?" Kallista squeezed under Fox's arm and he obligingly draped it around her.

"Three weeks after we both name our champions," Obed said, scowling. At Fox? Why? Goddess, please, not more jealousy.

Kallista scowled back. "Can Habadra delay this indefinitely by not naming champions?"

Obed shook his head. "A trial can be delayed only if both parties fail to name champions. Once one side lists names, the other has a full week, less the three virtues, to file their list with the justiciars, and the trial is scheduled."

"We'll start testing in the morning," Torchay said.

"What's wrong with this afternoon?" Kallista wanted Sky home as soon as possible, but she didn't want anyone hurt.

"Tomorrow's soon enough." Torchay planted a kiss on her forehead where she stood with Fox's arm around her. "Today, we'll be passing the word, explaining what it's about and asking for volunteers."

Kallista took a deep breath and hugged them both. "Yes, you're right. Tomorrow's fine. I just—"

"Shall we begin?" Obed's voice boomed across the room, interrupting them. His jealousy was getting worse, but how bad would it get? Enough to disrupt the magic? They couldn't afford to let that happen, but Kallista didn't know what else to do to make it stop.

The weekend was relatively peaceful, spent playing with the children and taking oaths from a double-score of new Tayo Dai—all the bodyguard corps and Captain Kargyll. In the middle of the night, as Peaceday slid quietly into Firstday, a rumbling crash in the near distance brought the entire embassy awake. Anyone who had lived through the gunpowder explosions of the invasion and the Barinirab rebellion knew that sound.

With everyone on alert and the Reinine tucked away with her family behind layers of guards, Padrey checked in with the Tayo, Torchay Reinas, to see if he had any orders. The Reinine sent Padrey to see what was happening. He'd have been gone already—he hated not knowing things—but he was Tayo Dai now. Better to go with orders.

The whole of Mestada's center was filled with people running all directions in the dark, all of them shouting impossible, contradictory things. It wasn't until Padrey reached the temple square that he saw what had actually happened.

Both walls around the temple lay crumbled to the ground in two neat rows, opening the temple grounds and the temple itself to the public. Crowds gathered despite the hour to gawk, a few of them pocketing bits of rubble as souvenirs.

"What happened?" Padrey pulled his hood forward as he caught the arm of a ragged beggar, one of those who lived near the temple where the begging was good.

"The walls fell straight down. They just fell." The man looked Padrey in the eye and straightened his gnarled fingers. "Nathains came out of the temple. Six of them, or seven. One of them healed me. *Look.*" He stretched his arms wide and twisted from side to side, his back straight. Padrey remembered him now. This man had been hunched over, curled into a ball by the disease that had twisted his back and crippled his fingers.

"She healed me," he said. "And the walls fell down and the nathains ran away."

The beggar hunched his shoulders, ducked his head. Padrey looked back, around the edge of his hood, and saw the shaved heads and white robes of Sameric clerics as they scrambled over the fallen rubble. Some stayed to guard the walls. Most fanned out into the crowd, obviously hunting the runaway magic-users.

Padrey beckoned the man closer. "Do you know where the nathains were going?" he asked, just loud enough to be heard.

The ex-cripple tightened his lips, refusing to speak.

"You know me." Padrey slid his hood back for the beggar to see his face. "You know I wouldn't betray anyone to *them*."

The man looked over his shoulder—a motion he couldn't have made before—and leaned even closer to Padrey. "They went to your people." He nodded knowingly. "I heard them say something about the free nathains."

"Right. Thanks." Padrey didn't know if this was good news or bad, but it was news his Reinine needed. Before the runaway naitani reached the embassy. Fortunately, he knew shortcuts.

"They wore robes like the clerics," the beggar said before Padrey took more than a step. "But in colors. Like the compass."

"Right." Padrey gathered all the coin he carried for bribes, and dumped it into the man's hands. He needed to be lighter for this run, anyway.

Along the tops of narrow walls and across roofs and balconies, dropping to the crowded streets only when absolutely necessary, Padrey flew back to the embassy. The guard on the alley door knew to let him in quickly and quietly, and moments later, Padrey was gasping out his report to the Reinine.

She frowned as she paced. "This is good, that their naitani are breaking out of the temple. It's nothing *we* did. But if they come here, it will cause trouble. Everyone would *think* we did it, knocking down the walls and such."

The Reinine stopped and swung on Padrey, her lightning blue gaze locking onto him. He couldn't help his flinch.

"Can you find them a place somewhere else?" she asked. "Somewhere the clerics can't take them back easily?"

Padrey started to deny the possibility, until he remembered the beggar's behavior, his willingness to hide the naitani from the clerics. "I might know a place."

"Good. Then go. Stop them before they get here."

He nodded, took a deep drink of the water someone had given him, and slipped back out the door. Where did one go to find runaway naitani? People who had no idea how the world worked? Gweric fell into step next to him.

"What are you doing here?" Padrey glowered over his shoulder at Gweric's oversized bodyguard shadow. "Anyone sees you two, they'll know Adarans helped the naitani get away."

"We have robes." Gweric shrugged into his, pulled the hood up over his bright gold hair. A moment later, Kerry did the same. Though his hair was brown, his military queue and bodyguard uniform marked him as Adaran.

"We won't approach. Once I help you find them, we'll leave you to it." Gweric waited for Padrey to open the alley door.

The plan made sense. Gweric would easily see the naitani magic in a city with all the other magic-users locked away for the night. Padrey plunged into the alley's darkness, the other two on his heels.

They wandered a while before Gweric led them down Kameral Street toward Cotton Road. Where they crossed, the broad paving of Rose Square was inlaid with a stylized compass, a rose-fountain rising at its center. "There." Gweric pointed.

Dawn's faint glow gave color to the robes of the young people clustered nervously by the fountain—blue, yellow, green and unrelieved black. Padrey nodded to Gweric and Kerry as they faded away, and he approached the nathains.

He dipped his head for a drink, rinsed his hands in the waterflow, and spoke without looking at his targets. "Greetings from Adara's Reinine to the free nathains of Daryath."

Those nearest him startled when he addressed them as nathains and the men scrambled to push the women behind them—three men, four women. "*You're* the Reinine?" one of the women asked, disbelievingly.

"Course not. She sent me to find you." He tipped his head as if for another drink and drew his hood back enough to show his sun-bleached hair just as the man in black spoke.

"Truth," he said.

Truthsayer, then. That made things easier.

"What does she want?" the woman in green, who'd spoken before, asked. "Why did she send you?"

"To tell you not to come to the embassy." Padrey put up a hand against the aura of despair even he could sense coming off them at his words. "It's the first place the clerics would look, and already they're preaching against us. Against Adarans. But I know where you can go. It won't be too comfortable but it's big enough to hold you all, and if you help the folk there like you helped that beggar outside the temple, they'll protect you."

"Where is it you're taking us?" the truthsayer asked as they started off.

"My old place. Down by the river docks and the main canal. It's an attic—be getting colder now, so you'd best be getting blankets and such to keep warm, because it's drafty. I still have my stuff there, so no one new'll have taken it up yet. And if they have, they'll vacate for nathains."

"Isn't it dangerous by the docks?" The South nathain woman almost quivered with nerves.

"That's why they need your help." Padrey shrugged. "Most of the people aren't bad. They're just poor and desperate, and they can't protect themselves against the folk who *are* bad. If you help them, they'll protect you with their lives."

"Sounds perfect," the truthsayer said.

Kallista spent the rest of the week stopping fights in the city. She sent out misty veils of good sense and calm again and again whenever tempers seemed to flare too close to the embassy. It amused her to imagine how frustrated the Sameric clerics must be when their attempts to stir up riots kept deflating. And with every veil of magic she sent out, Kallista felt herself growing stronger along with the magic.

The magic came in huge, billowing waves, more than she had ever obtained in a single call. So much, it was almost unwieldy. Would she need so much to handle these demons? Did it mean she could do it without a ninth? Without adding Keldrey to the mix?

She also stopped fights inside the embassy on occasion, when she wandered into the courtyard that had been filled with trucked-in sand and roofed over with tight sail-canvas against the autumn's increasingly frequent rains. If she stayed behind the half-wall barricade to watch, her bodyguards would allow the competition to continue until the battle spun too close. Then they would call break.

The whole of the bodyguard corps—the new Tayo Dai—with the new man, Night, had volunteered for the trial. Only Keldrey had not, saying he was needed with the children they already had, and he was too old besides. By Fifthday, the number had been pared to twelve, with Torchay, Obed, Fox and Leyja at the head. Obed and Torchay were almost even, Fox and Leyja not far behind. Fox's loss of vision kept him from anticipating an opponent's moves and Leyja's age put her a step slower.

The other eight possibilities were a notch or two below the four godmarked, each with his or her own strengths and weaknesses. So on Sixthday, an enormous caravan assembled early in the morning to ride the thirty or so leagues out of Mestada into the desert to visit Obed's old skola.

Just before the trip, Leyja informed Kallista that she had decided not to participate in the trial. She claimed she was needed more at Kallista's side as bodyguard. Kallista suspected that Torchay and Keldrey had ambushed her after one of the practices and "convinced" her of it, but she had to admit she was more comfortable with one of her iliasti bodyguards nearby.

With so many of her bodyguards making the trip, Kallista's entire ilian rose up and refused to let her stay in the embassy without them. They also decided it would be good to bring the children along and let them loose outside the confines of the embassy buildings. Which meant the hordes of nursery servants had to come too, as well as the massive troop escort. Only Keldrey stayed behind—yet again—to keep his daily appointment with Stone's Sky.

He was also appointed to receive the odd-sized scraps of paper with their laboriously written-out names and numbers that arrived regularly from their spy. Padrey didn't spend much time in the embassy, coming in just long enough to leave his reports. As long as he did that, Kallista allowed him to work his way. The numbers in his reports were climbing high enough to chill.

Kallista also got verbal reports, relayed usually from Padrey through Gweric—they seemed to meet regularly in the city—about the welfare of the runaway naitani. They had taken to dockside life as if born to it, clinging to their attic even when offered better quarters elsewhere. They did accept the food and clothing, blankets and threadbare rugs offered in payment for the sharing of their magic. Clerics had come to the docks at least twice, hunting their missing nathains, but the denizens of the area had spirited their own magic-users away to safety.

One report mentioned that the local crime lord had tried to appropriate the nathains' magic for himself. He'd been thwarted by the East nathain's gift. She could heal or harm with her magic, and she had the Daryathi ruthlessness when attacked. After that, a number of four-marked champions had attached themselves to the group to act as bodyguards.

Everything else progressed as it should, allowing Kallista to make this trip to the country.

The Edabi Skola had been founded almost three centuries before, during the Troubles, the times of chaos between the fall of the last Tyrant and the establishing of the en-Kameral. Line had fought Line for preeminence and advantage, street duels and assassinations the preferred tools. Not totally unlike today, Obed said with a smile as he told his tale. But during the Troubles, the fighting often spilled over onto the innocent, and assassinations were messy public acts that killed as many bystanders as targets.

Under the Tyrants, the Edabi—which meant "the faithful"— had been an elite, highly trained group of warriors dedicated to the principles of the One. During the Troubles, they had banded together to patrol the streets and protect the innocent. The Edabi established their skola outside the city as a safe haven for themselves, and a place to train their replacements. Gradually, the Lines learned to deal with each other in more peaceful ways. The system of justice by combat was set by custom because, too often during the Troubles, the only justice anyone received came at the edge of an Edabi blade.

Over the years, more skolas were established, but this was still the oldest and the best. The Edabi Skola produced more dedicat champions than any other, because that was their intent—to produce dedicats, not merely champions. Its graduates were as known for their devotion to the One as their skill at arms.

A village had grown up around the skola, sharing the water of the spring that ran even in the driest months of the year. The village provided the things the skola needed, including large guest houses and inns. Representatives from the Lines came to hire champions and dedicats for trials. Sometimes parties of the young and frivolous would ride out to watch the champions and dedicats in training.

Shakiri Line had its own residence in Edabi village. Shathina had offered it for their use the instant she heard of the trip, but Kallista turned the offer down. Best not be too beholden to any Daryathi. They hired out an entire inn instead.

It didn't seem too politic to dismiss the staff of the inn, including the owners, so Kallista and her ilian were back in their pairs again. They would only be in Edabi for the three days of the week's end. They could endure that long.

Chapter Seventeen

On Graceday morning, the entire village stopped to watch the parade of champions in red Daryathi-style kilts as they walked together from the inn to the skola. The tattoos on the bodyguard's arms—tattoos of rank with a crowned rose added to indicate their position in the Reinine's household—especially on the women, created a great deal of whispering as they passed. Children ran on the grassy common. Most of them belonged to the ilian, though a few locals had joined them. A few of the children stopped playing to wave as they passed.

The white-plastered mud brick homes dwindled away and they walked down the road under tall trees with leaves that whispered, though many already lay in golden drifts underfoot. A stream murmured alongside the road, watering the trees as it ran from the spring inside the skola's walls to the village and on to the Iyler before it reached the city. It was a pleasant walk, one Obed had not often made on foot.

The dun-colored walls of the skola seemed to grow higher as they approached. The walls sprawled in all directions, turning at odd angles, built to enclose buildings at random. But this occasion was different from all the other times Obed had approached this place. He was returning more wildly successful than he—or anyone else—had ever dreamed possible.

"I have arranged," Obed said, "as a favor to me, a tour of the entire skola. Normally, outsiders would not be allowed within the cloister walls, but as you are the Godstruck, and not related to any of the young scholar-champions, and because you are my wife, allowances have been made."

"For all of us?" Kallista peered at him, as if trying to see inside his head.

Obed had felt the dedicat's mask harden over his face as they neared the heavy wooden gate in the dust-colored wall. He tried to crack it, to let his heart show, but the instinct was too strong. The mask meant safety. "Yes. All of the godmarked, all of our champion-candidates."

"Just how much clout do you have in this place?"

He pulled the rope that fed through a square opening in the gate and the familiar muffled clang sounded.

"Much," he said. "I have all nine marks of the dedicat vows fulfilled. I left the skola with all I had been gifted, a wealthy man. And I have married well." Satisfaction flooded through him. He'd married for love, his own choice, not that of his Line's Head. "This is my triumphal return. I survived. I *thrived*. And those who said I would fail are proved wrong."

The gate swung slowly open to show a stocky, white-kilted champion with tattooed hands and face who stood blocking the gap. His eyes widened when he saw Obed's body tattoos, warmed when he looked up at his face.

Obed bowed, Adaran style. He no longer belonged here, but to Kallista's Line, Kallista's land. "The Reinine and Godstruck of Adara, with her mate, with all of her Godmarked and her champions, to see the grand master."

Old Jaget bowed respectfully and opened the gate wider, backing with it. Obed tucked Kallista's hand into his arm so that they entered the outer, defensive courtyard together. A boy of perhaps fourteen with a thick scruff of short black hair waited to escort them through the inner gate and beyond.

"When you said you survived, just now," Kallista spoke for Obed's hearing only. "You meant that literally, didn't you?"

"Yes." Hadn't he explained that to her? Hadn't she understood?

"How many usually survive these dedicat vows?"

"Very few."

"Numbers, Obed. Specifics." Kallista held his arm a fraction tighter. "How many made dedicat vows when you did?"

"Nine. Five here at Ebadi. Four from other skolas."

"How many are still alive?"

"One."

A shiver raced through her and she tucked him even closer. "How many survived from the year before you?"

Obed let out a quiet breath, finally realizing how little she had understood about everything. "None."

"And the year before that?"

"None."

"So, say, in the five years before you finished your vows, how many others completed them?"

He shoved his loose hair back with a hand and met Kallista's eyes. "One."

"One other than you?"

"Yes."

"And where is he now?"

"Here. Teaching."

"He didn't leave the skola?" That seemed to surprise her.

"He had nowhere else to go." Obed's smile reached only his eyes where the mask let it out. He might have been like Carrek, but for— "I did. I was coming to you."

"Do most dedicats who complete their vows stay on?"

"Most, yes. Or they return after a short time. The world outside can be a strange and frightening place." He gave her a sideways glance. "I know you recall how I struggled to adapt. How I still struggle."

"I imagine you had more to adapt to than most." Kallista squeezed his arm. "I'm glad you came to find us."

"As am I." His smile, a true one, flickered as he bowed her through a door into the main arena. He ruled the mask.

Floored with deep sand, it was lit by clerestory windows high above. Polished wood columns divided the central arena from the wings off to either side, and a wide, smooth plank walkway encircled it two steps above the thick sand footing. The scent of wood polish, sweat and dust swept him back. Obed loved this place, and he hated it. The boy led them along the decking to a room tucked behind the columns on the left, separated from the arena by a protective screen of fine metal.

Inside, a man waited, small, wiry, with an open robe exposing a full set of body tattoos. What hair he had left was snow white and his face held lines laid down by his living. A scar bisected his right eye, the pupil white with scarring. The left eye glittered with sharp intelligence. *Murat*.

Obed hid his hatred in reflex, but his hand tightened over Kallista's, bringing her closer as they entered the room. Obed started to bow, but Kallista's pinch stopped him before he did more than incline his head. He'd almost forgotten. His vows were to Kallista now. The old man inclined his head in return.

Obed waited until everyone had crowded into the room behind them and turned to Kallista. "My Reinine, this is Murat, the Grand Master of Edabi Skola." He paused and the old man bowed deeply, but without respect, to Kallista.

Scowling, Obed spoke again. "Grand Master Murat, this is Kallista Reinine, Ruler of all Adara, Godstruck by the very hand of the One. My beloved, my mate, the mother of my son."

Murat's face showed no outward emotion, but Obed knew it roiled underneath. The old man was not happy to see her, and he was still less happy to know she had given Obed a child. Murat hated anyone who had claim to those he thought his own, as Obed had once been. Kallista held his gaze as she bowed, not so deeply, throwing back her own unspoken challenge. Obed clung to the warmth her attitude gave him. She claimed him as hers.

"Allow me to introduce you to the rest of Adara's Godmarked," Obed said. "Those of us who did not need to be marked by men because we have been marked by the One's own hand."

The grand master's disapproval grew, though it didn't show in his expression. It seemed he did not trust the One to do Her own Choosing. Obed knew from experience that Murat did not trust any but himself. After Obed presented their godmarked iliasti, he presented the eight champion-candidates.

"You cannot be serious," Murat said when Obed finished. "Put women in the arena?" The grand master shook his head. "No, women cannot fight."

"I'll take you on, old man," Leyja snarled.

"I am sorry." The old man bowed. "I did not mean that you are not capable of fighting. I have heard of Adara's woman fighters. But a woman's blood is too precious to waste in the arena. A man—" He flicked his fingers dismissively. "A man's death is a small thing. Men are born to die in the service of the Line that has given them birth. But—"

"*No* death is a small thing," Kallista interrupted. "No life is less valuable than any other. But are we not all born to die? Does any of us escape death? So if these have the talent and the will to enter the arena, if that is their calling, who are we to deny them?"

Murat's expressionless mask cracked with displeasure. He must be very angry indeed, Obed thought, to show this much. "On your head be it," the old man said, almost evenly. "Their death is on your hands."

Kallista's eyebrows flew up with her alarm. "Death? No one dies today, Grand Master. That was the agreement for this contest. First blood only, no serious injury."

Murat shrugged, a sly, secret satisfaction rolling off him in waves so thick Obed almost choked on them. Goddess, he hated this man.

"It is the arena," Murat said. "One cannot always control what happens."

"Yes," Obed spoke up. "One can. A true champion is in control of his blade and his actions at all times. Did you not teach me this yourself?"

"True, true." Murat seemed even more satisfied. He had to be looking forward to deaths this afternoon. He would not get them. "But I have not had the training of your champions."

"I have." Obed's scowl didn't change as he felt the pleasure of Kallista drawing magic.

"No one dies today," Kallista said it again.

"I share your hope." Grand Master Murat bowed politely and Kallista jumped, as if the magic she drew had kicked her. It must have told her Murat lied. Obed did not need magic to know. Murat always hoped for death.

"Thank you," Obed said. "May the One grant that it be so."

"Please," Murat gestured toward a door in the far wall. "Show your brothers and sisters our skola. Let your—your wife see where you lived so many years." He seemed to have trouble saying the word 'wife.'

Obed reveled in the old man's struggle. *You have no more hold on me, old man.*

When they had all filed out of the screened-in viewing room, their boy-guide brought them to a man with tattooed face, hands and one foot, also unfamiliar to Obed, who held a fat ring jangling with keys. He unlocked a door at the end of the corridor and folded it back, revealing a shallow chamber lined with racks of pole weapons—quarterstaffs, pikes, bills, halberds and such. Obed was a swordsman. He didn't know all these.

After viewing a fraction of the armory, which extended down both sides of the very long corridor, Obed took them to see the practice arenas. Row after row after row of enclosures, both indoors and out, held champions-in-training, beginning with awkward, clumsy twelve-year-olds whacking at each other with sticks up to the slashing grace of those on the verge of leaving their teen years.

"When they come here, the boys' heads are shaved and they receive their first tattoos." Obed indicated the marks on his face. "Their heads remain shaved until they exchange the wooden weapons for metal and win their first contest with a true weapon. Then, they may begin to let their hair grow."

He brought them to the last arena. The young men here wore their hair braided close to their heads, the braid doubled back on itself into a thick difficult-to-grasp club. Sweat sheened on their bodies as they practiced their combat with bright, sharp steel.

"These will face examination soon," Obed said, "to see whether they will go on to make dedicat's vows, or qualify for further training, or go out as champions to keep the peace."

"Why do they seem so . . . ?" Kallista frowned.

Obed flicked a surprised glance her way. Could she sense their desperation? "Some of them will not survive the examination."

"Some?" Viyelle crowded close, her gaze on the fighters. She had Kallista's appreciation for the masculine form.

"Many," Obed amended. "Many of them will not survive."

"Goddess," Viyelle murmured. "What a waste."

Obed felt the tug of magic again as Kallista called it, the ready rush of power through his body. She seemed to struggle with it, gasping for breath.

"Are you all right?" Worried, Obed sent a glance Torchay's way and instantly her red ilias was there, peering into her eyes, counting her pulse.

"Water here, for the Reinine!" Torchay called out. Five people—their young guide, three Adarans and one of the Daryathi champions-in-training—leaped to serve.

"What is it?" Torchay plucked aside a strand of hair that had stuck in the sweat on Kallista's face.

"Sending out magic. Demon-hunter. Cleaning out demonshadow." She fought to control her breathing, without much success. "You know how much of an effort it is without Stone." Her voice cracked on grief, but she refused to give in to it. Obed didn't dare offer comfort. She wouldn't welcome it here.

The Daryathi dedicat-candidate brought her water in a wooden cup. Kallista smiled as she accepted it from his hands, and a ruddy blush rose on his dark skin. Another conquest for Adara's Reinine. Obed crushed the upwelling of fresh jealousy. He didn't need to be manufacturing new rivals.

"What is your name, champion?" she asked.

The young man blushed again, bowing low. "This one is called Ruel Dobruk-sa, my Reinine." Ruel fidgeted, looking back over his shoulder at his comrades who had clumped together, making faces at him.

Kallista drank again. "Can I do something for you, Ruel?"

"I—that is—" He stammered another moment, then bowed again. "My Reinine—"

Did he understand what that meant—adding the "my" to "Reinine"? That he offered her his allegiance? Obed thought perhaps he did. He didn't blame the boy.

"May I ask a question?" he finally managed to say.

"Of course." She nodded, smiling a little.

"Is it true that this—that the nine-marked is your mate? That he left the skola after his vows were complete, and found you and you married him?"

Kallista looked at Obed and her smile grew, warming his heart. She did love him. She'd said so a hundred times. Why did he ever doubt?

"Yes," she said. "It wasn't quite so simple as that, but yes. He is my mate and the father of my son."

"When I was finally free of my vows, I left the skola," Obed said, driven to tell them his tale. "I journeyed for a year, seeking the call of the One. Finally, I was led into the Mother Range where the One marked me with His own hand." This time he turned, bowed his neck and moved his loose hair aside to show his mark. All the dedicat candidates crowded round to see.

"The One led me across the mountains, across valleys and rivers until I reached the fabled white city of Arikon. And there, I found my fate. My Kallista."

"I wasn't Reinine then," Kallista said. "Just a captain in Adara's army." No one paid attention to her. They were lost in the truth of Obed's tale.

"So *live*." Obed gripped Ruel's shoulder. "All of you *live* so you can receive the treasures the One has waiting for you." He hoped they would take his advice.

With another smile, Kallista handed the cup back to young Ruel, and Obed led her beyond the wall to the residences. He tried to see them as a stranger would. As she would.

The cluster of oddly shaped buildings contained an internal maze of tiny cell-like rooms. No two rooms opened onto the same corridor without a turning between. Each doorless room was just enough larger than the narrow cot it held to have space to walk around it. A small chest was tucked beneath the cot and a rack for weapons hung on the wall of each identical room. Only in the type of weapons on each rack did the rooms differ.

"Students are to focus on their studies," Obed said as he led them unerringly through the narrow, twisting hallways. "They are allowed no distractions. Rooms are given at random, first-years scattered among their elders in the places that have become vacant." Deliberately, to make it difficult for friendships to form. But he had survived anyway.

He stopped outside a cell no different from any of the others, save for a single, scarlet silken cord that stretched across the doorway. "This was mine."

For twenty years, he had lived in this place. Alone. With nothing but the possibility of death—his own or another's—waiting every time he ventured forth. No wonder he had turned to the comfort and the promises of the One. But even now, even when he had received more than he ever dreamed, he had trouble believing it could last. Because it never had before. Goddess, he had been so very alone.

His cell did have one or two differences from the others. The long curved saber over the bed bore a knotted cluster of multi-colored tassels dangling from its hilt. Around the rack on the white plastered wall someone had painted the same nine symbols Obed wore on his body, and a bright blue blanket covered the cot, rather than a gray one.

"Achievement has its rewards." Obed's smile took on a wry twist. "The tassels were won in various tournaments. The blanket, a gift from a grateful client."

"*This* was all the reward you received? A bit of color, a dash of decoration for your room?" Kallista sounded horrified. "How long were you here?"

"Twenty years." Obed stared into the doorless room, his mind lost in memory. "The eight years of my training, and the twelve years of my vow."

"Is this the door they gave you?" Torchay flicked the cord stretched over the opening with a finger and set it to swinging.

Obed gave a soundless laugh. "Hardly. The only privacy here is in the turn of the corridor. The cord was set in place when I left, walked out naked leaving this place behind. I fulfilled my vows. *I won.* Only the rooms of the nine-marked, those of us who finish our vows, are set aside this way."

"I don't understand." Joh was frowning. "Where did all your wealth come from? If you lived like this, why is it so expensive to arrange a trial?"

"Ah." Obed smiled as he moved down the hall to allow the rest of the crowd to see into his old room. "The gifts—it's not actually called 'payment', though it is. Champions who are not cloistered like the dedicats keep their pay, of course. Many of them live well—very well— because they do not know how long they will live.

"A champion may remain at the skola, earn the hand and foot tattoos, but may leave at any time. Only the dedicats may earn the body tattoos. Only the dedicats stay in the skola for the full twelve years of their vows, leaving only for trials.

"Dedicats do fight for those who cannot pay. There is a rotation to determine who fights next. But when there are gifts—some of it goes to the skola. Most of the rest goes to the winning champion. A dedicat's gift is held until his vows are complete. If the losing champion has been hired for pay, they get a percentage, if they survive the combat."

"And you won," Joh said. "Frequently."

"Yes." Obed nodded. "I won. Bekaara invested my winnings. As I drew near the end of my vows and could have a monthly visitor, she began to teach me how to run the business she created for me. By the time the visits became weekly, in my last year, I was making many of the decisions. What to buy, where to sell."

"And we are all most grateful to Bekaara for her teaching." Torchay touched the hilt of his Heldring short sword.

Obed had bought nine Heldring blades as gifts before he ever met Kallista—ten, if one counted each of Torchay's pair. The weapons were rare and astoundingly expensive because of the magic hammered into each blade. A Heldring sword bonded with its owner. It never broke, never rusted, never went dull, never failed its owner. Obed's enormous wealth had provided that much, and more, he hoped. Perhaps using it for his new family would help erase the taint of the way his wealth had come to him, through the deaths of so many he had faced in combat.

"What if you hadn't survived?" Kallista asked. "If you died before completing your vows? Where would your wealth have gone?"

"A generous portion would have come to the skola. The rest would have gone to my family, to Shakiri—they gave most of it, since I fought for them most often." Obed glanced at Kallista and lost himself in her gaze.

"No wonder Shathina let Bekaara invest it," Joh said. "I don't imagine she was best pleased when you finished your vows."

Obed's smile flickered to life, his eyes never leaving Kallista's. "Especially since I did not return to Mestada to allow her to arrange my marriage. Fulfilling my vows set me free of Shakiri and the skola. I would not bind myself to anyone or anything again unless it was of my own choosing." Surely Kallista understood this much.

"But what does the skola do with the gifts it receives?" Viyelle asked as they began moving slowly along the corridor again. "If everyone lives like this. *Does* everyone live this way? Even the masters? What do they spend the money on?"

"I have been in the masters' rooms. They are much the same as their students'." Obed walked backward a few paces to watch them before coming to another turn. "There are many mouths to feed, and they feed them well. A man cannot fight if he is hungry. A boy must grow as well as fight. Weapons break and must be re-forged or replaced. More money buys better weapons."

"Heldring?" Torchay asked.

"No. I had heard of the legendary blades made in the Heldring, but I never saw one until I purchased these." Obed touched his own hilt, gestured toward Torchay's double scabbard.

"The metalsmith naitani seldom sell outside Adara," Kallista said.

Obed led the way out of the maze of chambers, through another gate into a vast vegetable garden. A scattering of boys worked picking produce, hoeing or pulling up spent plants.

"Discipline." Obed smiled as he tipped his head toward the nearest boys. "I spent many bells in the garden over the years. And I hated every one of them."

Kallista laced her fingers through Obed's, as if offering comfort to the boy he had been. But he needed more for her to love the man he had become. He had to trust that she did. It was time to return to the arena.

Chapter Eighteen

Fox *looked* around the arena when they entered, familiarizing himself with the space. Backless benches had been set up on all sides of the arena and strangers stood on one side, chatting idly, pretending not to notice as the Adarans entered. He couldn't afford any distraction. Obed had warned them that this competition could be more difficult than the trial itself.

They had debated long and hard whether Fox should participate in this contest, whether keeping his skill a surprise or letting the knowledge out to intimidate would be more effective. The decision had finally been left up to Fox, and if the choice was between doing or watching, his choice would always be to do.

He removed his belt and scabbard. Champions would enter the arena clad only in kilt, and shoes if they wished. Fox wore the light lace-on shoes. Most of the others did not, but he had grown up in Tibre's colder climate. He wasn't used to fighting—or doing much outside the bed and bathing rooms—without shoes.

The Heldring blades were fortunately not an issue. A champion always fought with his own weapon. Fox's sword was long and straight, sharp on both sides, what Adarans called a mountain sword. He used a dagger in his left hand. Obed fought with a long, curved, single-edged saber, using it with both hands, and Torchay had his short swords.

The other eight Adaran champion-candidates fought with an assortment of weapons, primarily mountain swords like Fox's, though two used paired short swords and one of the women had a halberd rising over her head and banging against her legs where she carried the pole weapon on her back. The long wicked ax with its razor-sharp spear points behind and above was a weapon Fox had no desire to face, even if he was a head taller than Genista. The shaft's length made up for the difference in reach.

"These will meet in the arena for combat to first blood," Grand Master Murat said in his strong, old man's voice, "in the order that your name is called."

"Genista Fynli." Obed named the halberd-wielding bodyguard.

"Ruel Dobruk-sa." Murat called the name of the young dedicat-candidate they'd met as Genista's opponent, and they each took a step down onto the level just above the sand.

The matching-up went on, moving as planned up the skill level, though in fact the differences between fighters were small. Fox noted his designated opponent, but could tell nothing about him.

Then Obed called out the last name. "Torchay Omvir."

The echoing chamber already buzzed, but now the babble grew louder. Torchay and Obed had pitted their skills against each other almost since their first meeting, and neither had yet been able to win over the other. Obed had explained that the vanity of the skola's masters would have them believing no Adaran could hold his own against a Daryathi dedicat, much less best him. Naming Torchay last, after Obed, could do any number of things, from instilling false confidence that Obed's skills had fallen so far that a foreigner could beat him, to wondering whether the Adarans were actually that much better.

The combatants moved back up onto the decking, save for Genista and young Ruel. They stepped down into the sand of the arena. Fox reviewed the procedure Obed had drummed into them as he *watched* Genista and Ruel perform it. Three strides across the sand. Stop. Bow and bring weapons slowly up to ready.

The lower end of Genista's halberd was weighted to counterbalance the ax head, creating a club very nearly as deadly as the sharp pointy end. Sometimes Fox wondered how she could wield the thing, but she managed, to devastating effect.

The old man gave the signal and the combatants began a slow, circling advance. *You don't have to be flashy*, Obed had said. *You only have to be good*. Was Genista good enough?

Ruel used a pole weapon too, Fox noted. The young Daryathi seemed reluctant to close, as if fearful he might injure the woman opposing him. He'd have to get over that right quick or—yes, there she went, spinning past him, smacking him on the backside with the flat of the ax hard enough to stagger him.

"Come on, boy, *fight*." Genista's voice was a purr, not a taunt. "It's only to first blood. A little blood won't hurt either of us. I've been hurt worse. Shall I show you my scars?"

She made as if to raise the hem of her kilt and Ruel did something—shook his head, perhaps. At this distance, Fox's *knowing* sense wasn't good with the finer motions, especially when they weren't aimed at him. The young candidate swung his weapon at her, a half-hearted threat, and Genista laughed, swaying out of the way without bothering to move her feet.

"I know you can do better than that, sweet Ruel." She circled him, forcing him to turn with her. "I know what you really want, darling Ruel, but you have to prove you deserve it. If you beat me, I'll give it to you freely, no holding back. But first, you have to win."

If that didn't inspire the lad to fight, nothing would. His questions on the practice field had betrayed a wide romantic streak. Even Fox could tell Ruel wanted to fall in love.

Finally, the young man attacked in earnest. Genista parried just in time. The weapons flew, spinning in attack and defense, clashing, ringing, scraping along each other in odd squeals of sound. The fighters whirled apart, breathing hard. Ruel gave her only a moment before he charged, spear point out. Genista ducked, swept his feet out from under him, but when she sprang up and spun to end it, he was already standing again.

They exchanged another flurry of blows. Ruel was younger, stronger, larger. Genista was faster, more expert, had more stamina. The young man already panted, began to falter. And she had him.

Both of them went utterly still in the arena, the endpoint of Genista's halberd touching the skin of Ruel's neck. Fox held his breath, concentrating hard to *see* whether this match would end as Obed had said it should. Ruel let go his weapon. Very carefully, he leaned into the point of Genista's halberd until the steel pierced his skin. Fox couldn't *sense* whether blood flowed down the young man's neck, but he could smell it.

In the silence, the strangled sound Genista made echoed across the arena. She walked hand over hand up her halberd until she reached her opponent. She let her own weapon fall to the sand as she thrust her fingers into the waist of Ruel's kilt and hauled him hard against her. Stretching onto her toes, she caught the club of hair at the back of his head and pulled him into a kiss so searing, Fox could feel the heat where he stood.

The grand master shouted, but everyone else stared as Genista ran her tongue up Ruel's neck—licking away the blood, Fox thought, given the way she lingered. Old man Murat was stamping his feet, making the decking boom, and shouting like a maniac. Fox thought he might jump into the arena—strictly forbidden for any but the combatants and the medics standing by on either side in their robes.

The Adaran competitors began cheering and hooting at Genista's behavior. As Ruel's companions broke out of their shock to harass their comrade, Genista took a step back. Her hand lingered on her defeated opponent's face a moment longer before she bent, picked up her weapon and walked away, hips swaying in that way of women who know they have achieved exactly what they intended.

"I thought you said I had to beat you to get what I wanted," Ruel called after her.

Genista looked back over her shoulder. "I did say it."

Ruel picked up his weapon. "Then what was that?"

She paused, one foot on the bottom step, and turned to look at him. "What *I* wanted, sweet Ruel." She blew him a kiss and sauntered off to stand beside the non-combatants.

"Just so you know," the next Adaran competitor, Sandrey, called out before stepping onto the sand. "I'm not kissing you, no matter who wins."

The entire arena burst into laughter—save for Grand Master Murat. Fox kept his face turned toward the arena, but focused his attention on Murat. There was something wrong with him, but was it demons? Or was it Murat's own twisted soul Fox *saw*?

Fox eased back from the arena's edge. There were six more bouts before his turn. He could wander where he liked within the building. He came to kneel beside Kallista.

"I do not like this Murat," he said softer than the clang of metal on metal.

"Didn't you say you saw no demons?" Kallista never looked away from the arena.

"I never see demons," Fox said. "Gweric does that. I see—I *know* things. It's how I tell one person from another. I can't see what they look like, but I can know . . . who they are. What kind of person they are. A demon twists people when it rides them. I usually can't *see* much twisting until after it leaves them. But some people are just twisted, just wrong. It doesn't take a demon to do it, they get that way on their own."

Obed and Torchay had drawn close for this whispered conference, joining the rest of the godmarked already listening.

"Is that what you see in Murat?" Obed asked. "His own evil?"

"I don't know." Fox shook his head. "My knowing isn't that delicate. I can tell *what*—that he's wrong—but I can't tell why."

A shout went up from the Daryathi champions and Fox turned with everyone else toward the arena, though he didn't need to. Sandrey was looking down at his arm.

"What is it?" Fox asked.

"The other got through Sandrey's guard," Leyja said. "Long scratch up his forearm. He fought well. An instant of bad luck."

Sandrey lowered his sword and bowed. His opponent dropped his sword and began to stride forward with intent. Sandrey sent his sword spinning into the sand near the Adaran side and yelled as he turned to run. To the accompaniment of much shouting and laughter, the Daryathi champion chased the Adaran bodyguard until he cornered him behind the colonnade and planted a teasing kiss on his mouth. Fox was not the only one convulsed with laughter when Sandrey emerged, swiping his forearm across his mouth and spitting into the sand as he retrieved his sword.

"*Enough*," Grand Master Murat bellowed as the Daryathi champion collected his weapon on his way to rejoin his companions. "Will you desecrate the holy purposes of the One with your jokes? This is *combat*, not play!"

"Did the One not create laughter?" Kallista stood as she spoke. "And play? The combat was finished. There is no harm."

Even Fox could sense the white-hot anger boiling off the man. Murat's fists opened and closed as if he wanted to do Kallista injury.

"Let us continue." Kallista gestured for the next in line, one of the short-sword men, to step into the arena and begin the next match. But the moment had ended, all sense of play fled.

The matches continued. Some of them whirled from one side of the arena to the other, both combatants exhausted and slippery with sweat before the finish. Some ended in mere moments. The Adarans lost almost as many as they won, but Fox wasn't worried. Obed had told them it would be thus, and the three iliasti had not yet entered the arena.

Finally it was Fox's turn. He drew his long sword from its scabbard, found his left-hand dagger, and stepped down onto the sand where his opponent waited. *Three steps into the arena. Bow. Raise your weapon slowly to ready.* Fox concentrated on his opponent, his eyes focused who-knew-where. It didn't matter since they couldn't see, had nothing to do with his *knowing*.

"Athen." Fox spoke the other man's name, using it to focus.

"Fox." The other man lowered his saber. He took a step toward Fox who circled the top of his sword in case this seeming halt to the action was a ruse.

"This man is blind!" Athen accused. "Aren't you." It wasn't a question.

"What does that have to do with anything?" Fox slid to the side, daring the dedicat to test him.

"I can't fight a blind man. Where is the honor in that?"

"Are you afraid?" Fox taunted. "Your Ruel wasn't afraid to fight our Genista. He learned she knows how to fight. So do I."

"Knowing how doesn't matter if you can't see where your opponent is or what he is doing." Athen threw down his saber in disgust and started off the arena floor.

"Pick it up."

Athen stopped, turned to stare over his shoulder.

"I said, pick it up, Athen, unless you are afraid." Fox showed his teeth in a mockery of a smile. Stone had always claimed it a frightening sight. "I do not need to see. I *know*. I am godmarked, Athen. My lack of faith cost me my sight when I was marked." Kallista denied it, but Fox believed it was so.

"My naitan gave me something else with her magic. I did not see you drop your sword, but I know you did."

Fox advanced, dug his sword into the sand beneath Athen's gently curved weapon and flipped it toward the dedicat. "Pick it up. Try me. Discover what I *know*. I dare you."

"You heard it fall," Athen said, uncertain.

"Perhaps." Fox shrugged. "It is magic. I don't know how it works." He dropped into his ready position again, knees bent, sword and dagger pointing at Athen. *"Begin."*

Wary, eyes on Fox as he bent, Athen picked up his sword, wrapped both hands around the hilt and adjusted his stance. Fox didn't wait longer to launch his attack.

Athen was good, as Obed had said. More than once, Fox got his dagger up to parry just in time. The saber tactics would have given him trouble, save for all the practice against Obed who used the same sword, same skills. The mountain sword gave Fox a thrusting attack as well as fore- and backhand slashing, but Athen had practiced against his weapon as well. This would be one of the long bouts.

Athen attacked, driving Fox across the arena under relentless blows. Fox allowed Athen to think he was winning, and watched for weakness, for some fault that would give Fox the edge he needed to win. And there it was, the key.

Thus far in the fight, Fox had used his left-hand dagger strictly for defense, so much that Athen seemed to have forgotten it was a weapon as deadly as the sword in the right hand. Fox stopped retreating, closed, and had to whirl away again to avoid a slash at his torso. A few more attack-parry-advance-retreat exchanges, and the opportunity opened again. Fox engaged the saber with his sword, closed and pricked Athen's sweat-glistened chest with the dagger, just over his heart.

Both men froze, breath hot in each other's faces, taking the moment to recognize the end of the fight, the winner, the loser.

"Your magic is strong," Athen whispered. "I am honored to have known a man so touched by the One." And he dropped his full weight on the dagger Fox held, burying it deep in his heart.

Fox jerked his hand off the dagger, shouting in horror as he caught Athen, lowered him to the sand. "Kallista! Kallista, come quick—see what he's done. Save him!"

She flew across the sand, Leyja at her heels, the other medics running from the Daryathi side. But when the others saw the dagger's hilt protruding from Athen's chest, they slowed, stopped. Kallista kept coming, dropping to her knees.

"Look what he's done—" Fox's throat ached, so tight he could scarcely force words through. "Do something."

"There's nothing to be done." The satisfaction in the old man's voice sickened Fox. "He honored the One. He is gone."

"Not yet, he's not." Kallista laid her hands over Athen's awful wound, surrounding the blade that pierced him. "There's life in him yet."

"It flows out onto the sands with his blood." Murat walked along the decking, around to the side to be closer to the scene on the bloody sand.

"No." Kallista drew magic, packing it around the mortal wound to stop the blood flow. She had only a few ticks of the clock to save him, to repair his heart and get it beating again, according to the naitani who had trained her in this use of her magic. Otherwise, Athen as he was would be lost to them. "His blood is not flowing. He is not dying. I told you, old man, *no one dies today.*"

She hoped. She had never yet healed anyone so grievously wounded who was not ilias. The blood loss was halted but his heart was not beating, could not beat as long as cold steel speared it.

"Fox." She could feel his horror through the link. It would be good for him to help. "I need you to pull the dagger out, on my signal."

"Aye." He grasped the hilt and waited.

Kallista squeezed the magic closer round the blade so it would slide into the wound as the blade slid out and keep Athen from losing any more blood. "Now."

Fox drew the dagger out exactly along the path it had gone in, not opening the wound any further. As the magic flowed into Athen, Kallista went with it. It was hard work to match up the cut edges precisely and urge them to heal at a speed far greater than natural. She had only moments before Athen-who-was would begin to lose bits of himself. But perhaps the magic would heal that too, if need be.

The tear in his heart was sealed if not fully whole when Kallista sensed Athen somehow . . . coming loose. She kicked his heart into beating again with a tiny shock of her lightning—she'd learned that trick back in Academy, that lightning could start hearts to beating as well as stop them—and grabbed for him the same way she'd grabbed Torchay during his dreamscape adventure. "You stay here," she ordered, pinning him back into his body.

"How can I? I have failed," Athen's spirit said. "I have disappointed my grand master and the One above all."

"You lose a single fight and you're ready to quit?" Kallista took a moment to start the rest of Athen's injury healing along the dagger's path to his now-healing heart, and to send a surge of reassurance to her iliasti before stepping with Athen into the dreamscape.

"Is there anyone who has never failed?" she demanded. "Is not the One a God of second chances? And third chances, and twenty-seventh? There is forgiveness and beginning again, even for failure much greater than yours. Do you truly believe that you have accomplished all the One has for you to do?" Kallista touched his cheek, let her hand rest on his shoulder. "Perhaps that's why I am here today. So that you can have the chance to live long enough to fulfill your purpose."

"But—I failed. Didn't I?" Athen sounded more bewildered now than despairing.

"Did you? Fox Reinas has been touched by the One. He uses magic instead of sight. How is a loss to him worse than any other loss? Is it not *less* that losing to another? And if he can be used by the One, blind as he is, do you not think the One has a use for you?"

"I—" Athen blinked at her. "Suppose . . ."

"Smart boy." Kallista eased him back down into his body, checked that the healing had settled in nicely and stepped back into her own.

"Welcome back," Torchay murmured at her shoulder, wearing a hastily donned medic's robe.

Kallista tossed him a quick smile and lifted her hands from Athen's bloodied chest. He wasn't completely healed, wouldn't be for a good while yet, but it was well under way. He would not die, not today. Not for many years to come, she hoped.

Athen opened his eyes and smiled at her. Kallista smiled back, then stopped him as he struggled to rise. "Leyja, clean him up," she said. "Bandage his wound. You need rest, Athen. In bed, for several more days before you begin much walking. The dagger pierced your heart. It will take time to recover."

"Thank you." Athen captured her hand and brought it to his mouth for a kiss, his soulful gaze holding hers. "I will not forget anything you have said to me."

Leyja fastened his bandage down with a bit of the naitan-made stickum she carried, and the Daryathi-side medics helped Athen to his feet and off the arena sands.

"What have you done?" the grand master snarled at Kallista as Athen was helped off. "You have gone against the will of the One."

"If it were the One's will that Athen die, I could not have healed him. I have gone against *your* will, Murat. Do not confuse the two. It could be dangerous." Kallista took Leyja's hand to rise to her feet.

"Death is part of the arena." Murat reached for Athen as he neared the steps and the dedicat flinched aside, almost falling.

Kallista tried to send him strength, but without touching him, without Stone's joyous magic to help, she could not. "Death is part of life. This arena is . . . something apart. And no one dies today, out of his time. Without necessity. No one dies in this arena today. I told you this, and I have been given the magic to make sure it is so."

She held Murat's gaze a moment longer until, with a grimace, the old man whirled and marched back to his place at the head of the arena. Kallista trudged back across the sands with the rest of the healers.

Obed met them at the steps to offer his hand. Kallista didn't need it. She hadn't gone feeble yet. She was only forty, for the One's sake—forty-one. But she took it anyway. Obed seemed to need her to. "What did you say to the dedicat?"

Kallista gave her dark ilias a sharp look. But at least he was asking, rather than hiding his fears behind an emotionless mask. "I didn't propose, or declare undying love or anything, if that's what you're asking. I just told him he wasn't dying today. The One isn't through with him."

"He's in love with you." Obed led her to the bench.

"They all are," Torchay said with a crooked grin. "Those that aren't in love with Genista."

"Well, I'm not in love with them." Kallista scowled at both her men. "Don't you have a contest to fight?"

In the end, the day's score tipped in the Adarans' favor, six bouts to five, when Torchay and Obed both won their duels. The grand master snarled and snapped, trying to keep his dedicats and candidates from the traditional farewell in the arena's center, but to no avail. Everyone, including the watchers on both sides, met in the middle to congratulate the winners, hash over tactics and, in the case of at least a few, to flirt.

Ruel Dobruk-sa was not one of them. Though he cast a lingering sidelong glance at Genista, who seemed to be watching for him, he made his way through the crowd to bow to Torchay.

"Master, this one has achieved the rank of champion. This one would dedicate himself to your skola, to learn further." Ruel bowed again.

Kallista heard him, for she'd been listening to Leyja and Torchay explain to the local medics how they combined healing with fighting. Was this a common request? Kallista grabbed Obed where he stood talking nearby, and hauled him closer.

"Say that again," she ordered.

Flushing a dull crimson, Ruel glanced at Torchay and at Obed for confirmation of the order.

"She's the Reinine," Torchay said, tipping his head at her. "She's the one in charge. My rank is sergeant, no' Master." He turned to Obed, not waiting for the young champion to repeat himself. "Seems the lad wants to leave this skola and join ours. Even though we don't have one."

"Is this allowed?" Kallista asked.

"It does not happen often," Obed said. "But it is permissible. You are champion, correct?"

Ruel blushed and bowed agreement.

"So?" Kallista looked from Obed to Torchay and back again. "We *can* take him with us, apparently. *Should* we?"

Those nearest the small conference at the edge of the arena had stopped to listen, and more turned their attention every moment. It worried Kallista a bit, how others might react.

"Why not?" Torchay shrugged. "He's a good man with a weapon. If he's willing to swear to you—Tayo Dai never limited itself to Adarans. Penrith Ko was an Islander. Hoban Felessan came out of the far north beyond Tibre." Torchay named two of the heroes from the old tales. "Why not a tattooed Daryathi?"

"Obed?" Kallista needed his counsel in this. He was the one who understood the skola, these people. And she didn't like the feeling she was getting. She couldn't pinpoint its source, or exactly what it was, but it was ugly and it frightened her.

His eyes on Grand Master Murat, Obed hesitated a long moment. "Yes," he said finally. "I see no reason not to accept Ruel. But he should wait until morning to join us. The grand master is in a chancy mood. Best not to make it worse, if you intend to wait until later for your search."

She'd already searched the skola, but not inside people. They tended to notice. Obed was right. If she didn't want to search Murat now, it would be better not to upset him any more than he already obviously was.

Kallista nodded. "Ruel Dobruk-sa, I accept you into my service. Report to Sergeant Omvir at dawn."

Ruel bowed, backed away With a spring in his step, he finally approached Genista, who met him with a smile.

"What do you call it," Torchay mused, watching them, "when it's faster than a whirlwind romance?"

"Thunderbolt," Obed said. "What happened to me when I met Kallista."

"Oh? Well, finally something we have in common then." Torchay winked at Kallista and sauntered away to begin gathering up the bodyguards for departure.

As the gates opened and the Adarans left the skola, Kallista called magic and sealed the walls. It worried her, especially since she might be sealing the demon inside with all those boys. But if a demon was in the skola already, hiding inside one of these men as it had hidden inside the last Reinine's high steward, she didn't want it getting out.

And if it wasn't there, she certainly didn't want one getting in, now she'd cleaned everything up.

As an afterthought, she added a warning bell, a bit of magic that would alert her if things started going badly wrong. Not just demons, but anything. She did *not* like that Murat.

Their children had spent a wonderful, exhausting day running and playing like a pack of little wild things, and either fell asleep early, or were cranky and demanding because they should have done. Kallista dispensed hugs and kisses to the few who stayed awake past the adults' dinner and sent them off for the servants to deal with. There were times she truly appreciated being Reinine. And didn't that make her feel guilty.

It was late, the crescent moon riding high in the sky, when Kallista retreated to the room she shared with an already sleeping Obed, and called magic. Time to scour a few souls while hunting for demons.

She took a moment to scrub away the demon stains from the village, fewer here than in the skola. Then she sent her magic arrowing for that walled community. She had always been able to send her hunter magic ranging a long way even without the dreaming. Kallista hoped she might be able to grapple with any demon hiding in the skola, even from her comfortable spot seated cross-legged in the bed at the inn.

The magic slipped through the warding around the skola, like recognizing like, and went sniffling through the maze of residence buildings, hunting for the *wrongness* she and Fox had *seen*. Was it demons? She intended to find out.

The warping lay scattered at random throughout the living quarters, with the occasional cluster. More of it than she had hoped, or wanted to count just now. It didn't matter how many there were. She would search them all. Whatever was required, however long it took, she would find the demons.

Kallista gathered her magic and sent it plunging into the nearest twistedness. No demon. Just a deep torrent of often-indulged rage. The next held a love of inflicting pain. One at a time she searched out all the different twists, offering healing to those who wanted it. Few did. They hugged their perversity close, cherished it, indulged it, told themselves it was normal, ordinary. Virtue, rather than vice.

Murat was one of these. She found the mark of demons on him, imbedded so deep it had become a part of him, woven into his very nature. But Fox had guessed right. Murat bore no demon now. Years ago, a demon had ridden him, had taken a flaw in his nature—one he might have struggled with, but perhaps could have managed if he tried—and had strengthened it. Brought the fault forward until it overpowered whatever else Murat might have been. And when he had come to love his flaw, the demon left him.

It left him to do its work, to gather others with their own flaws, teaching them to indulge, giving them opportunity to develop their twisted tastes. The demon might have begun this work, but Murat's own will and that of those he gathered had continued it. They had made this place into what it had become.

Kallista sat slumped in bed, drained dry and sick to her heart at what she had found. She felt grubby. Nasty, as if the awful things her magic touched had leaked through to her. She ached all over, in places she couldn't name, the parts of her that lifted, pushed, carried this magic. Searching so many had exhausted her, but she was too tired, too soul-weary to sleep.

"K'lista?" Obed's arm fumbled its way round her waist where she sat tucked against his sleeping form. "What're you doing?"

"Nothing. Magic. It's all right. I'm done."

"Then come to sleep." He tried to pull her down beside him, but asleep as he was, couldn't find the right leverage. "You need rest."

"All right, don't fuss." She slid down into the bed beside him, snuggling her back into his front.

"Fuss if I want to," he mumbled, nuzzling through her hair until his lips touched her neck. "Love you, K'lista."

"Love you, too, Obed. Go back to sleep."

"Will if you will."

She smiled as a soft snore told her he hadn't waited. Kallista tucked his arm more securely around her middle and wished for someone to put her arms around. Any of them would be nice. Just as sleep stole up on bare feet to claim her, she realized that Obed had chased away the nasty, grubby feeling.

Night had grown even darker when Kallista jolted straight up into darkness, every nerve jangling.

"What?" Obed was on his feet, sword in hand. "What is it?"

She scrambled out of bed, hunting her clothes. "The skola. Something's gone bad wrong at the skola. Wake up the others. Everyone—except the children. Don't wake the children, but everyone else. *Everyone.*"

Torchay burst in, wearing his smallclothes and his sword sheath, both blades in his hands. "What's wrong?"

Obed went to the door, relaying orders to the bodyguard just outside it.

"We have to get to the skola." Kallista tried to pull her tunic on and pull magic at the same time.

With an exasperated huff, Obed tossed his saber aside and came to put Kallista in her clothes. "Do we have time to dress?"

"If we hurry. Get Leyja. She's in charge of protecting the children. I don't know if what's wrong at the skola will come here—there's no demons. We don't have to worry about demons. I looked. But there's trouble. I want our babies safe."

Torchay nodded. "I'll get my trousers after I tell her."

"Tell the others. Half the troop stays here, half with us to stop the trouble there." Kallista threw Obed's trousers at him, dressed now, and tied her hair back without bothering to braid it. "I want all the guards who went to the skola to go with us. Be ready. I won't wait. They'll just have to catch up."

"Bloody hells, Kallista, you can't—"

"I'm not waiting, so you'd better move right sharpish, love." She buckled on her sword as Torchay dashed back out into the inn bellowing orders.

When Kallista trotted up the road to the skola, Torchay was shirtless, still fastening up his trousers, but at her side. Obed stalked at her other shoulder. Fox led the way, scouting ahead with his peculiar senses while Joh followed at the head of the Tayo Dai and the dozen or so soldiers who'd been ready to march. Aisse and Viyelle had decided to lend their swords to Leyja, defending the children, and Captain Kargyll was chivvying the rest of the troop into order.

The moon still rode high in the sky but now on its downward slide, a crescent sliver of light that didn't penetrate the shadows beneath the cottonwood trees lining the road and the stream beside it.

"How do you know?" Torchay winced, his stride skipping as he stepped on something sharp with his bare feet. "That there's trouble in the skola?"

"I set an alarm. Magic." Kallista dropped her pace a bit so she could walk and speak at the same time. "After I cleaned out the demon stain, when we left, I sealed the skola off. No demons in, none out. And I set an alarm, in case there was a demon hiding. Or in case that chancy mood of Murat's went bad. There's no demon. I looked before I slept. But there's a lot of bad. I just—I don't know what might have set off the alarm—"

"Someone's coming," Fox called back to them. "A party from the skola—" He paused. "They're boys. Young ones."

Kallista hurried to reach Fox. Ten or twelve terrified boys with shiny shaved heads cowered naked in the road. Some of them shared blankets. Some fought tears. They were in the care of two older boys of sixteen or so with hair down around their ears and weapons in hand to shield the youngsters. One of the older ones had managed to grab a kilt before they ran. He stepped up, frightened but defiant in his determination to protect.

"Are you the Reinine?" His voice cracked.

"I am. What's happened?"

"I—Yanith said to bring the skints to you. You'd keep 'em safe. The grand master's gone mad. He's— The medics—there's—" He choked on the tears he refused to release.

"Go." Kallista pointed down the road toward the village. "Take the young ones to the Red Toad. Help guard the children. And tell my captain to *hurry*." She motioned her people on.

"Where are you going?" The boy sounded surprised.

"To help your Yanith. Now you go. You're in charge of the skints. See them safe."

"Wait." Genista stopped the boy. "Have you news of Ruel?"

His chin crumpled before he stiffened it. "Dead. Grand Master Murat killed him. Killed them all."

Chapter Nineteen

"No." Genista whispered the word, her face white.

"I'm sorry." The boy repeated it several more times as he followed the stream of younger boys toward the village.

"Steady, Corporal." Torchay gripped Genista's shoulder. "The Tayo Dai hold. We serve. And nothing's certain till we see him cold. Not with our Reinine. This Reinine."

Kallista broke into a run, motioning the younger, more fit guards ahead. They needed to get there fast, not at her forty-year-old naitan's speed. Forty-one. "Stop the fighting," she ordered. "We'll sort it out when that's done."

Genista put on a burst of speed, unlimbering her halberd as she ran. Kallista called magic. It made her stumble, but if she could keep any alive—she shoved the magic out, shaped only to stop bleeding, and felt it take hold, some of it. Most of it. Pray the One it would help.

She *reached* for the warding magic and stumbled again. Torchay and Obed took hold of her arms and carried her between them, allowing her to shatter the protection on the walls and shift it to protect boys and those who fought to protect them.

Fox's shout told her those who'd run ahead were inside.

"Let me go." Kallista got her feet working properly again. "I'm through with magic till we reach the injured. That's where I'm needed. Obed, you find Murat. I leave him to you."

"Isn't there magic you can use to stop this?" Torchay led the way through the first gate, then the second.

Kallista took a moment to check the gatekeeper, but he was already gone. "Without demons involved, the veils are unpredictable. How do I shape it? What if I put the wrong ones to sleep?"

"Put everyone down. We can sort it later."

That made sense. She should have realized it herself. "I need to be in the middle, so it doesn't miss anyone."

"I go to find Murat." Obed saluted Torchay. Not Kallista. He turned her over to Torchay like some courier's packet, but for Kallista, he had no salute, no kiss, not even a mumbled "Ta." And she had bigger things to fret over.

Joh stayed with them, guarding her other side. He had to fend off a crazed dedicat who charged screaming, kilt and sword dripping with gore, before leaving to find easier prey.

Kallista ran to the sand pit behind the big arena. There, hopefully in the center of the skola grounds, she planted her feet, caught a shoulder on either side for balance and closed her eyes to call the magic. Torchay's strength, Joh's understanding surged forward, under her hands. Kallista reached a bit farther for Fox's order, Obed's truth, and farther still for Aisse's loyalty, Viyelle's creativity, Leyja's love. Together with the will her own magic provided, it needed only Stone's joyful eagerness to be whole. But surely for this, it would be enough.

She shaped the magic for sleep, excluding all her own people. With a prayer that it would work, she threw her hands wide. Then she gave the magic a hard shove. And a kick. She threw a noncorporeal shoulder into it and heaved. It wobbled a bit and rocked back into its rut.

"Damn it, *move!*" she bellowed, and blasted it out of dead center with a burst of sudden power.

The shouts and screams cut off almost instantly. Kallista scrabbled for more magic to send out a quick reassurance to her people that this was what was supposed to happen.

"Now." She looped her arms through Torchay's and Joh's, hoping they wouldn't notice her trembling. Surely she had strength enough left to heal those who needed her particular ministrations. "To the sorting out."

Captain Kargyll organized the work parties. The injured were brought to the infirmary where the bodyguard-medics worked over them. Too many of the injured—and the dead, who were laid out in the sandpit—

were the skola's medics. The youngest boys still in the skola, those with the barest fuzz of hair, were brought to the dining hall. Everyone else went to the arena.

Kallista was in the infirmary, located beside the arena, working on a young dedicat with four just-severed fingers. Kallista's mother had pioneered the reattachment of such losses some years ago, and since the bodyguard-healers seemed to be handling the other injuries perfectly well, Kallista had decided to see whether she could help this young man. It was delicate, painstaking work, but she had got three of the fingers back on with the blood flowing nicely through and bones beginning to knit when she heard a keening cry from outside.

It rose and fell and rose again, laden with howling grief. It tugged at Kallista, almost a physical grabbing hold. She looked at the tattooed hand she worked over. One finger left, the smallest.

The wailing cry pulled at Kallista again. The dedicat would be fine with three fingers. She could not ignore that cry.

A pair of young soldiers stood awkwardly to one side while a woman in white-trimmed blacks knelt on the ground, weeping over the body in her arms, Genista mourning for her Ruel.

Kallista sent the soldiers back to their duty with a gesture. Her own eyes near blind with tears at this vision of her own loss, Kallista wanted to turn away, to run and hide and mourn her Stone. But she couldn't. She literally could not walk away, could not even turn into Torchay's comforting arms where he stood at her back. *Why?*

"Give him to me." Kallista walked forward, toward the grieving woman, not understanding the impulse that drove her.

Genista clutched Ruel tighter. "Will you deny me the chance to say goodbye? We never got more than hello."

"*Give him to me,* Bodyguard." Kallista knelt beside Genista, touched the young champion's body, and she finally knew what drew her. "He's not gone. He still lives. He doesn't want to leave you. But you must let me have him."

If Kallista could keep another from facing the pain of such a loss, she would do everything in her power to make it happen. Wild hope rose in the young woman's face as she tumbled Ruel's body into Kallista's arms.

His wound was obvious, a deep slash that laid his thigh open and severed the artery to set his blood spilling life out onto the earth. Kallista's stop-gap magical patching that she'd sent during the dash from the village had saved his life. It hadn't stopped all the blood loss, poorly targeted and slow-moving as it had been, but it had thinned the gush to a seep.

"Help me." Kallista laid Ruel's head gently on the ground. "Help me pull the edges together."

"But the dirt—" Genista protested.

"The magic can clean it out. The wound is spread too wide. I need you to pull it together so I can heal it properly."

"Yes, my Reinine." With both hands, Genista pressed the gaping wound closed, kneeling beside Ruel in the dusty path.

Kallista used her newly practiced skill at matching blood vessels together, and tendons and muscle. She got the artery sealed tight, and worked her way to the surface, flicking away everything that didn't belong, until she closed the skin over the top. When she was done, she sensed more than saw Ruel settle happily into his body, and tears blinded her again. Stone would have done the same had it been only the poison killing him.

She fought back the tightness in her throat until she could speak. "Cherish him well," she told Genista. "He lives because he would not leave you. If he had died before we found him—"

"He lives because of your magic." Genista lifted Ruel's head back into her lap. "We have seen how slowly the wounds bleed. You have given him back to me."

"His own determination kept him alive long enough for my magic to do some good." Kallista saw Joh approach from the arena. She beckoned a pair of soldiers over, sent them for a stretcher to move Ruel inside, and stood to see what Joh wanted.

"Obed thinks we've found them all," he reported. "Kargyll's troops are conducting a room-by-room search, but we think they're all accounted for."

"How many dead? Too many, I know, but how many is that?" She took Joh's hand as they walked to the arena, needing the touch and knowing Torchay wanted both his hands free.

"I don't have the final count, but last I heard, it was well over thirty."

Kallista shuddered, outraged by the carnage, the waste of so many lives, and for what? An old man's madness? "How many were boys? Children?"

Joh shook his head. "I don't want to know. I might kill someone—the wrong one, or the right one at the wrong time."

"Aye." Torchay breathed the word, his voice rougher than usual.

The sleepers were laid out in rows along the arena floor. Murat and several of the bloodiest lay in a bunch at the far end of the arena. Another small group lay nearby. The rest of them, some forty or fifty dedicats and champions, lay between.

"These are the ones we found defending the skints and fuzzheads." Obed used the skola's slang for the youngest students, gesturing to the nearest group. He flicked a finger at Murat's bunch. "Those are the ones doing the slaughtering. The ones we are sure about. The rest—"

He indicated the big bunch in the middle. "We don't know which side they were on, or if they took any side at all."

"Let's find out." Kallista considered her options. She was tempted to wake the defenders first, leave the rest of them asleep, but it would better to have witnesses to the tale. And an idea presented itself to her.

"Are there any villagers here?" Kallista strode to a bench still placed along the side decking of the arena.

"I think so." Obed looked confused.

"At the gates," Fox said. "They haven't come inside."

"All right. This is what we're going to do."

Dawn was breaking by the time everything was ready. The villagers filed in through the gates, escorted by fuzz-headed boys, first to the sandpit where the dead lay in their rows, then to the infirmary where the wounded moaned in pain, and finally to the arena. The youngest boys came with them, leaving only children and their caretakers in Edabi village.

The headwomen of the village took the bench set up for them at the end of the arena farthest from the main doors, the honored place.

The rest of the villagers lined the arena decks on either side, crowding in with the younger students. The dedicats and champions still lay sleeping on the arena floor, though they had been rearranged to face the elders' bench.

Kallista sat near the elders, off to one side, about to drop with weariness. Once, this would not have tired her. Age had its price—she was fairly sure it was age. She leaned against Fox standing behind her, her eyes closed for the few moments of rest she could get while waiting for everything to be ready. Her godmarked were with her, around her. The rest of her people either tended the wounded or protected the children. She wanted this to be a Daryathi event, not one imposed by Adarans. Mostly.

The buzz of conversation grew until Obed bent and spoke into her ear. They were ready. Kallista opened her eyes with a sigh, and took a deep breath. Time to begin.

Obed pounded a staff he'd appropriated from somewhere on the raised wooden floor. The echoing boom was muffled by all the people standing on it, but it made enough noise to stop the talking, turn everyone's eyes his way.

"I am Obed im-Shakiri a-Varyl, once dedicat of this skola, a nine-marked who fulfilled his dedicat vows and lived to depart into the world." He pulled his overrobe back to make sure everyone saw all nine of his tattoos. While he went on to give his credentials as someone with the right to be involved in skola matters, Kallista began to bring the sleepers awake.

She wrestled with the magic, shaping it carefully to keep the captives from speaking out of turn, from attacking anyone. As long as their intentions were peaceful, they could move, but they could not hurt anyone. In afterthought, Kallista barred them from leaving the arena floor.

Sweating with the effort, trying hard not to pant, she gulped the water Leyja handed her and tried to find where Obed was in his speech. He'd reached the part about the godmarks already. Kallista took another sip of water and let Torchay and Joh help her to her feet. She gathered magic and held it in her "hands," waiting for Obed to pass her the staff.

It took effort to keep from leaning on it when he did, she was so tired. She released the magic, sent it to finish waking the sleepers. "These masters, dedicats and champions are only sleeping," she said. "The magic bestowed on us by the One, as Obed Reinas explained, allowed me to stop the . . . disturbance here in the skola so that together we can discover the truth of what happened and so that you can decide what to do about it."

A murmur rolled around the edges of the arena.

"I know this is not in your usual practice of justice, but is it not possible that the One has a better way than death? Would it not be better to determine the truth of a matter and together use your own judgment to decide matters? Why else would the One have given us truthsaying magic?"

Kallista had to pause for a louder sweep of shocked conversation. Most of the sleepers were awake, and those who weren't were almost so. She drew more magic, slowly, to keep from straining herself worse. "Yes, there is even now one of your own truthsaying naitani at work in the city of Mestada, not cloistered away in the temple. Will you listen to what these men have to say? Will you judge for yourselves what happened here and how this kind of justice can work?"

"How will we know they speak truth," one of the elders asked, "if this nathain is in Mestada?"

"I will act as truthsayer." Kallista shaped her magic into the truth mist she'd used at Habadra House and sent it to hover above the arena. "The mist will show you if someone speaks truth. Do not expect other truthsayers to create this mist. I know of none who can. I believe it was given to me so that you can see the truth and believe it, even though I am Adaran."

"How does it work?" one of the fuzzheads piped up in a high, clear voice. "The mist?"

Those around him tried to hush him up, but Kallista smiled at the boy's youthful bravado. "Try it. Tell us a lie."

"I love beetroot." He grinned, then laughed out loud as the mist went instantly black, his laughter echoed by others.

"Now, a truth." Kallista caught herself leaning on the staff and straightened.

"Kassid Penthili-tha is my best friend."

The mist turned white again, and a babble of talk broke out across the chamber. Kallista remembered to hand the staff back to Obed. Her part was done, except for managing the magic.

"With your agreement—" Obed bowed to the elders on their bench. "The nathain Kallista will act as truthsayer. I, as nine-marked dedicat of this skola, will conduct the investigation into the truth. And you—" He swept his arm around the arena, taking in all of the observers. "You will sit in judgment."

"Do you bring—" The elder who spoke, the oldest of the three women, with scant wisps of white hair above bright black eyes set in a crinkled face, was interrupted by a commotion at the far end of the arena.

The doors had opened and a contingent of injured champions hobbled in, led by Athen im-Noredi and Ruel Dobruk-sa who was supported by Genista Fynli. Hands reached out, boys ran to support them, to lead them to the steps and help them sit.

Ruel remained standing. "We have the right to be here," he said, his voice shaky. "To tell what we know."

"You do," Obed said. "Welcome. Please sit."

Kallista reached for the staff, but Obed apparently knew what she wanted to say, for he said it. "Do not speak unless you have been called upon. Don't interrupt anyone while they are speaking, even if you believe they speak lies. The mist will show us what is truth."

The oldest of the elders stood. "Do you bring your weak foreign ways to impose on our Daryathi strength? Our way is—"

"Is it strength—" Ruel clutched at Genista's shoulder, trying to rise from his half-way down position. "Permission to respond, Lord Dedicat," he said belatedly.

Obed nodded, holding the staff at an angle, pointed toward the injured man.

"Did you see the dead?" Ruel asked. "Did you walk by that place and see? All those boys, those strong men? How can it be strength to kill so many of our best? All respect to you, Elder Sothi, but that is weakness, not strength. Strength is in *life*, not death. It is in truth. Hear the truth, and then decide."

"I will not—" Old Sothi was interrupted again by the boom of Obed's staff. Reluctantly, pouting, she asked permission to speak and was granted it.

"I will not take part in this travesty. You violate Daryathi tradition as it has come to us through the years. I demand that you end this now, Cori, Lutha. This is wrong."

The middle elder, the apparent leader, signaled Obed with an upraised finger, got his nod and a shift of the staff toward her. She stood. "I agree with Ruel. Death is not strength. I see no foreigners here, save for the nathain and her people offering her magic, and the medics aiding our injured champions. Before the Troubles, our ways were different, and that was not so very many years ago. I say we find the truth and decide. Sothi says no. What do you say, Lutha?"

The third woman, the youngest but still older than Kallista, stood. "I say aye. We listen. We decide."

"I will not abide this!" The old woman shook her fist at the other two and stamped her feet.

"*Then leave.*" Elder Cori's voice boomed over the arena.

Old Sothi shot her a poisonous glare and stomped away, out the side door near that end.

Obed handed Elder Cori the staff and she raised her voice. "We will not decide today who will take Sothi's place as elder, merely who will sit with us for this deciding. Do I have names?"

In a quick, rough-and-tumble session, someone was selected to share the bench with the two town elders, a male metalsmith from the village. Finally, Obed received the staff back and the investigation into the slaughter at the skola began. Ruel and the injured with him spoke first.

They had been awakened in the night by the grand master screaming with rage, demanding everyone get up and assemble with weapons, as they were. Those who took time to dress became the particular focus of his anger. He ordered them to pair off, begin fighting in the flickering torchlight at the practice arena, spurring them on despite the danger.

The other masters began to join in, and some of the dedicats and champions, shouting at the younglings, beating them with the flats of their swords if they did not show sufficient enthusiasm for the combat.

Anyone who protested was immediately set upon by those encouraging the mêlée.

Then Grand Master Murat came upon Ruel. Until this point, no one had been seriously injured. A few scratches, some sprains, bruises and such from stumbling in the dark, but no real injuries. But when Murat saw Ruel, it was as if a spark caught in gunpowder.

Murat attacked, screaming that Ruel should have died, that he had disgraced himself losing to a woman, allowing himself to be mauled in public—on and on. Ruel fought hard, but Murat's frenzy seemed to give him strength. Ruel fell, mortally wounded.

His blood spilling black in the torchlight seemed to set loose the bloodlust, according to others who took up the tale. Murat ran for the infirmary, screaming Athen's name, while those who had joined his madness began to lay about them with sharp edges, rather than the flats of their swords.

Yanith, the dedicat who had lost in the arena to Torchay in the last combat yesterday, best against best, managed to send the brand new skints out of the skola. With some of the others, he had organized a group to defend the fuzzheads at the dining hall, though it was too late for many of the boys.

As the wounded champions spoke, they pointed out those they had seen among the men gathered on the arena floor, the ones who had participated in the slaughter and those who had fought to stop it. The mist stayed white.

After a time, Elder Cori raised a hand, asking a turn to speak. "May we not speak judgment for some of these now?"

Obed glanced at Kallista, who shrugged. This was no Adaran trial. The three justiciars were in charge. "That is your choice," he said. "I act only as investigator. Kallista Naitan—Nathain Kallista is only truthsayer." He handed over the staff.

Cori conferred with the other two for a moment before speaking again. "Dedicat Yanith, did you defend those who could not defend themselves, sending the younglings to safety?"

Yanith stepped forward a few paces from the group on his side of the arena. The dedicats and champions in the arena had sorted themselves, some joining Yanith, some Murat, a few others loitering in the center. "Yes, Elder Cori, I did."

"Did you kill or injure anyone who was not attacking you or those you defended?"

"No, I did not." The mist remained the same pearly white.

"What say you?" Cori addressed the crowd. "Shall we bring him out among us?"

"Aye," thundered back from half a thousand throats.

Kallista freed Yanith from the magic that bound him, save that which prevented attack. She wasn't sure of his actions toward Murat and his cronies.

As Yanith trudged across the arena to join Ruel and the other champions at the back of the chamber, Elder Cori asked the same questions of the others who had been named as defenders, and one by one they were released from the arena.

Cori handed the staff to Obed and seated herself again. "Proceed."

Obed seated the heel of the staff on the deck, braced it against his foot and looked out over the arena. Heartsick and weary, he considered the next step in the hearing of the night's events. Best to leave Murat and his associates to the end.

"You." Obed spun the staff and pointed it at one of the lingerers in the middle, a man whose name he could not remember, if he had ever known it. "Tell us your name and your tale."

"My name is Farrin Chosida-sa, and I have no tale." But he did. Farrin told of how he had run away, had pretended to be on first this side and then that, protecting only himself.

Obed concentrated on maintaining his dedicat's mask. He was out of practice, his discipline weak, and he liked it that way. Obed had never wanted to be a man who could look at death and feel nothing. The killing had always felt like a stain on his soul. Obed had perfected his self-discipline in the years he had spent here under the old man's authority. Murat had always somehow sensed the disgust Obed had for him and his teaching, but once Obed had learned not to show it openly, Murat could do nothing. The punishment had stopped. Obed's only true defiance had been his success. And his continuing life.

Kallista had taught Obed to feel again, and he never wanted to go back to what he had once been. The memories existed, but they could no longer hurt him. Still, playing the role of investigator as he did, he had to hide his reactions. He remembered Farrin now and the others with him. They should never have been sent to the skola, were unsuited to a champion's life. But they had survived. Perhaps they did know something of value. Or perhaps not. It was not his place to judge.

When all those with Farrin had spoken, Elder Cori asked that they be held in the arena, apart from those still remaining. She reserved the village's judgment on them.

Now, at last, it was time for those accused of the killing.

The sun was rising high, and Elder Cori called a break for refreshments. Villagers worked with the skola's servants—the few left alive—and the skints and fuzzheads to brew cha, bring out cakes and biscuits, and water for the injured. They refused to return to the infirmary, so pallets were brought and places made for them to lie down. Water was left on the arena sands for those held there. After half a chime or so, when most of the people had returned to their places, the elders signaled Obed and he pounded his staff on the deck to call everyone to order.

Obed twirled the staff as he considered whom to question next, scarcely aware of the hum it made as it spun faster and faster. Better to start with the leader, he decided, but how? He had clashed with Murat a thousand times, almost from the moment he had walked through those gates, a scared and scrawny twelve-year-old. Perhaps it would be better for someone else to question him. But no one else had the nine marks, and certainly no one had his ten.

The staff slapped against his hand as Obed caught it, pointed it at the old man. Spattered and streaked with blood, Murat stood defiantly at the forefront of the men now in the center of the arena. "Grand Master Murat," Obed said. "I call you to answer for your crimes."

Chapter Twenty

The old man spat in the sand. "They were not crimes. They were justice. I righted a wrong."

The mist, which had stayed white since the fuzzheads' testing, churned as it turned a dark red-brown. Everyone in the arena gasped and stepped back from the sand at the sight.

"*Lies,*" Kallista called out, acting as official truthsayer, though everyone could see.

"Murat." Obed gripped the staff tightly, pinning it between arm and body in an attempt to hold back his anger. "Did you attack the champion Ruel Dobruk-sa and give him mortal injury?"

"He is here, is he not? How could it have been a mortal wound?"

"Evasion," Kallista said, though anyone could know that.

"Did you cut open the leg of Ruel Dobruk-sa and sever his artery?" Obed gave the staff a slow twirl as he dropped the end onto the decking. He wanted to crack Murat's head open with it.

"Yes." Finally, with Murat's answer, the mist cleared back to white. Kallista pronounced it truth.

"Did you intend his death?"

"Yes."

Obed wanted to ask why, but it wasn't important now. "Did you then proceed to the infirmary with the intent of killing Athen im-Nuredi, and did you kill the medics who tried to stop you?" Obed read their names from the list he had been given.

"Athen still lives," Murat said.

"I did not ask whether you killed Athen. I asked whether you killed these others." Obed took pride in the level tone of his voice. He did not even clench his teeth—while he spoke. He ground away layers when Murat answered.

The old man shrugged, unconcerned. "I may have. If they got in my way. I do not know these names."

"They were medics. Healers in the service of your skola, and you do not know their names?" The metalsmith spoke without asking permission.

Obed turned the staff quickly his way, giving leave. Then he spun it back for the answer.

Murat shrugged again. "There are many in service to the skola. I can't be expected to know all their names. Medics should not be needed in a skola. You live." He made a chopping motion with his hand. "Or you die. There is no in between."

A horrified buzz went around the arena as the mist whirled ominously and darkened to a purple-brown-maroon color.

Murat shook his fist at the mist. "It is truth!"

"Murat believes it to be truth," Kallista said. "But the One declares it a lie."

"May I speak, Nine-marked?" Yanith walked carefully along the step around the arena, balancing between the crowd above on the deck and the sand below. "May I ask my questions?"

Obed sent the staff spinning across the arena to the six marked dedicat who snatched it out of the air and twirled it to point at Murat.

"You have said you intended Ruel's death," Yanith said. "Did you also intend the death of Athen im-Nuredi?"

"You know I did," Murat snarled. The mist faded to white.

"*Why?*"

"Because their failure demands death."

Back to maroon again. Kallista pronounced the lie.

"If their failure demands death . . ." Yanith looked around, as if puzzled. "Why are they not dead? Why has the One declared this a lie?"

Murat growled but did not speak, for Yanith had spun the staff away. Kallista must have tied her silencing magic to the staff. Obed took the chance, now the arena's attention was on Yanith, to move next to

Kallista, lay his hand on her shoulder, draw comfort from her, offer her his strength.

The staff halted, pointing at Athen with his bandaged torso and head. "Athen," Yanith called. "Why are you not dead? You were stabbed through the heart, were you not?"

Athen stood to answer, a bandage round his head as well as his torso. He'd fought in the night's mêlée despite his injury. "I was. The Chosen One, the Godstruck healed me."

"How did you come to be so injured?" Yanith asked.

"I lost my match, against a blind man. Instead of conceding defeat by piercing my skin, I conceded by piercing my heart. I thought I deserved death. That is what we have been taught. Great failure requires great payment."

Athen struggled to stand straighter. "But I no longer believe this. The One provided healing so I could live. Life is demanded of us, and service, not death. I will leave my life in the hands of the One and not snatch it into my own."

"And you—" Yanith aimed the staff at Ruel. "How did you live?"

"The Chosen One, Nathain Kallista healed me." Ruel's voice rang out, but quickly lost its strength. "The Nine-marked Obed told me to live. I—" He glanced at Genista. "I had just found love. How could I leave her?" The mist continued to glow its perfect white.

"So." Yanith twirled the staff slowly, pacing in the small space that had opened up around him. "The One does not seem to demand death for their failure. Why then, Murat, do you?"

The staff slapped into Yanith's palm, pointing at the grand master. Murat remained stubbornly silent.

"*Answer me!*" Yanith shouted.

Murat flinched but pressed his lips tighter together. Yanith started to step into the arena sands, but stumbled over something that was not there, and fell. Murat charged, and tangled in the same invisible something that tumbled him head over toes and left him lying with his face buried in the sand.

"You cannot attack each other." Kallista stood and beckoned for the staff. A dozen hands took it gently from Yanith as they helped him up and passed it hand over hand to her. Obed could see how she struggled not to lean on it, but before he could offer his support, Torchay was there. Again.

"The magic will not allow it," she said when the staff reached her. "This is a public hearing so that we can all hear the truth, not a combat trial to see who is stronger or more skilled." She paused, pointed the staff at the men on the arena floor. "One of you, help Murat before he smothers in the sand."

Reluctantly, a few of the bloodiest began to move, eyeing each other as if willing someone else to take action so they wouldn't have to. Then they jumped, as if Kallista had goosed them with the magic, and hurried to flip the old man over, clear his mouth of sand.

"Where was I?" Kallista muttered.

Obed gave her a worried glance. Was she too tired for this? She had been hauling magic around for hours. Magic she claimed was more difficult to use without Stone's contribution.

"Oh yes." Kallista lifted her head and spoke to the assembly. "I will not use magic to force Murat to speak. If anyone does speak, their words will submit to truth testing. But they may remain silent if that is their wish. We do not need him to speak. These others have spoken truth. We know what he did. We do not have to know why."

"But I want him to say it!" Yanith howled out his anger and grief as he fell to his knees on the decking. "I want to hear him admit what he is."

Murat snarled, his mouth working as if he attempted speech. Obed took the staff from Kallista and pointed it at the terrible old man. He wanted to hear Murat say it too.

"I am a dealer in death," Murat shouted. "Is that what you want me to say? Then I say it. I deal out death. I teach death. How to kill. How to die. It is the way of the champion, of the dedicat. To *win*. To kill and watch death flow out into the arena sands, watch it creep up into the eyes and steal away their brightness, and to glory in the beauty of that death. Yes, I take pleasure in watching death. It is our way!"

"It is not my way, old man." Yanith removed his kilt and cast it aside, standing naked in the arena. "Never mine again."

"Nor mine." Athen cast off his clothing.

Moments later, the arena was filled with more than a hundred naked men and boys.

It took considerable effort for Obed to hide his laughter at Kallista's wide-eyed stare. He had to clear his throat several times before he could speak without laughing. "Gather them up to burn," he said, stripping off his overrobe and offering it to the nearest naked boy.

The villagers followed his example and soon everyone was more-or-less clothed again, though some wore only blankets shared out from the injured.

Elder Cori gestured for the staff and Obed handed it over. One by one, she questioned the men standing with Murat, getting confirmation that they had participated in the slaughter. One by one, the assembly pronounced them guilty of the crimes.

When it was done, the three justiciars put their heads together, discussing their judgment. Finally, the metalsmith accepted the staff from Cori, as all three of them stood.

"Farrin Chosidi-sa." The smith went on to name all those who had avoided the carnage. "It is the judgment of this court—"

Obed smiled. They had named themselves a court. The change had already begun, away from justice by combat back to the old ways. Back to the ways of Daryath before the Troubles, before the Tyrant. Back to the ways the dedicats and champions had longed for and discussed in the rare moments of leisure they had together. This was a court where truth determined justice rather than strength. Pray the One the change would spread from here.

"—That while you did not kill anyone yourselves here last night, neither did you try to stop the killing or help protect those who needed your protection. You do not deserve the name of champion. Your marks will be barred and your names stricken from the list." The smith exchanged a look with the other justiciars. "You're all welcome to stay in Edabi village while you figure out just what it is you are suited to do."

That was unexpected. Most who had the crisscrossing bars tattooed over their champion's skola marks were shunned, cast from their Lines and forced into whoring or crime for lack of any other work. The elders showed unexpected mercy.

"Nathain Kallista." The smith bowed to Kallista, clearing his throat nervously. "Your mate has said that your magic comes from all points of the One's compass."

"Yes, this is true." Kallista struggled to her feet again, assisted by Fox and Torchay.

"Tales say that in the Before, West magic could sentence criminals to suffer the crimes they committed. Can you do this?"

Obed watched Kallista's eyes grow distant as she searched her magic.

"I have never done such a thing," she said after a moment. "But I think that I can." She gave a crooked smile. "I have recently done many things I never tried before."

In a corner of the arena, Obed noticed a small section of the mist turning a muddy purplish-gray and called Kallista's attention to it. Immediately, she dissolved the mist.

"My truthsaying is for serious matters," she called out. "Not for questioning your wife as to whether she truly met with grain sellers last night." Kallista paused. "She did not, as the mist verified. But she did not meet with a lover. She visited your son. You should mend that quarrel."

The crowd's laughter faded quickly as Kallista turned back to the justiciars with an apology.

"Then that is our sentence." The metalsmith-justiciar pounded the staff three times on the deck. "The crimes you have done will be turned back on you, Grand Master Murat Konethi-ti, Master Koben . . . "

Obed listened with less than half an ear as the twenty-seven names were called out. All of the remaining students, the champions and dedicats had cast off their belonging to this place, but was it right that the skola be completely abandoned? It had existed for more than two hundreds of years, teaching honor and discipline. Only under the rule of Murat had the teaching become so twisted.

". . . sentence to be carried out at the soonest possible time," the smith finished.

"Here," Kallista said. "After the arena is cleared."

"There should be witnesses," Elder Cori said. "To see it done properly."

"Choose your witnesses, then."

"Myself and Sadim." Cori indicated the smith. "Lutha? No? Then Dedicat Yanith. Three should be enough."

The crowd began filing slowly out of the arena. Uninjured dedicats collected those to be barred to escort them to the tattooist. Yanith made his way against the flow to join those at the head of the arena.

"A word, if you will." Obed gathered those remaining. "Daryath still needs champions. Not for trial, though I think it will take years for enough truthsayers to be found for proper trials. But champions are needed to keep order, protect the weak, deal with outlaws and bandits. To teach your children honor and discipline and duty. The things this skola once stood for. It should not die here."

"What are you saying?" Yanith frowned.

"That this skola could be what it should have been from the first. The evil has been cleansed from it. Not just Murat's evil, but the stink of demons that overlies all of Daryath. Kallista Naitan has laid protection around this place. Bring in your boys—and girls too, if they want to learn these things, or make another skola for the girls. Teach them. Not how to kill or how to die, but how to live and serve."

Obed thumped his shoulder tattoos. "Let me be the last dedicat. Be champions instead. Allow *yourselves* to live."

Yanith remained motionless a long moment, then he bowed. "Are you naming me grand master of this skola, Nine-marked?"

Was he? But who else had the right? "Yes, Yanith, I am. Make it what it should be."

The arena was almost empty, a last few stragglers nearing the wide doors at the far end. Obed was ready for all this to be over. He was weary to his soul. Kallista had to be even more so.

"Let's finish this." She echoed Obed's thoughts, and pushed at his shoulder. "Go on. This won't take long."

"Kallista, no." Obed protested. She could barely stand.

"I'm no' leaving you." Torchay squared off against her, making Obed feel weak and inadequate yet again.

"I want you to go. You shouldn't have to see this." Kallista pushed at Torchay, who stood like he'd been rooted.

"Nor should you, but you are. I'm no' leaving you alone, no' in here with that lot. No' in the state you're in." Torchay crossed his arms, glaring at her.

Obed wished he dared stand up to her that way. Instead, he resorted to his usual persuasion. "You're already so exhausted you can't stand without leaning on something. With us farther away, you know it will be harder to call the magic. We'd have to come back and carry you out again. And if the magic slipped—"

"I just—I don't—" She broke off, fighting for composure.

Goddess, she was that tired, that close to giving in to tears. Obed swept her into his arms. "You can't even stand."

"Can't you work the magic from that door?" Aisse waved at the door where the Tayo Dai waited. "We could be just outside. *I* do not want to be witness if I don't have to. And you could be just inside. With Torchay and Obed and whoever else insists."

"I," Leyja said. "I insist."

"All right, yes. I'll do it Aisse's way." Kallista's agreement was reluctant. "Obed, put me down."

"No." He strode along the decking, trying to maintain the control he'd once been celebrated for, while emotions clamored inside him. But he was not the same man he had been the last time he'd been in this place. Then, he stood alone against a grand master who had prophesied failure, who had mocked his remorse for the deaths he had caused.

Now, Obed was alone no more. He had found what he'd never had. A home where his love was welcomed and returned. Which was why he was so terrified of losing it. Kallista was all he had.

"Obed, put me down," she said again. "I thought I could count on you at least to do what I asked without arguing."

And see what his little rebellion, his tiny defiance had got him?

Sick to the heart, he set her on her feet. "If that is what you want, that is what I shall be. I am yours, Chosen." He moved away, ready to catch her if her strength wasn't sufficient.

"Nathain, are you ready?" Elder Cori approached, her manner as brisk as her stride.

"Yes, of course." Kallista swayed as she turned to face the other woman.

Obed reached out, but Torchay was there before him. He braced Kallista until she could stand alone, then took his place behind her. Obed folded his arms to wait. Leyja took up a similar stance beside him as the other four filed through the door with the Tayo Dai.

He felt Kallista's touch deep inside as she drew magic once more, felt the surge of energy it left behind. It always felt good when she called their magic, but it didn't always feel the same. It depended on her purpose when she called it, like the difference between touching someone to caress and touching him to add strength to a task. This was work.

The magic seemed to move slowly, though Obed didn't know what made it feel that way. He willed it to speed up, to cooperate, but didn't know what effect his meager will might have. Then the screams began.

Kallista shuddered. Obed moved to hold her, but Torchay was already there, gathering her in, as always. He held her, murmured in her ear, then turned her into Obed's arms. Would she ever be there if Torchay did not hand her along? Only Torchay had been able to bring her back from the spirit world after Stone's death. How could Obed compete with that? Could he survive on the driblets that trickled down to him?

"Let's go," Torchay said. "If they're not dead already, they will be soon. It's only getting worse."

Kallista huddled against Obed, almost as if she wanted to crawl inside him and hide. He wrapped her in his arms, against his bare chest and held her tight. "It is only what they have done to others," he murmured as he eased her out the door. "Nothing of your doing."

She shuddered. "That's what Torchay said. But—"

Of course Torchay had said it first. Torchay did everything first and left nothing for the rest of them. Obed tried to throw off his bitterness. None of the others believed Kallista could love only one of them, but he'd grown up with the idea of One True Love and he kept sliding back to that idea. She was in his arms, but only because Torchay had put her there. She *had* come willingly, though. She clung to him, welcomed the comfort he offered. He had to focus on that, on what he had rather than what he didn't. What else could he do?

———

They took an extra day in Edabi to rest so that Kallista wouldn't fall off her horse riding back to Mestada, but by the end of Firstday, they were back in the embassy. Kallista had sent a message by way of Taylin Farspeaker with a list of the trial champions to be presented to the justiciars. Torchay, Obed and Fox would be joined by five of the new Tayo Dai, including Genista, Night and Gweric's bodyguard Kerry.

Keldrey met the family with back-slapping hugs and enthusiastic kisses, especially for the little ones who had missed their Papi Kel. He inspected the newest Tayo Dai, for Genista's Ruel had already taken the oath. Keldrey reported that Sky continued well, growing stronger with the extra food brought him. The count of slaves in Mestada had reached over five hundred, and Padrey had word of a few score in the countryside.

Clerics had turned up that very morning, demanding to search the embassy for their missing naitani. With the place virtually empty, Keldrey had let them search as they pleased, insisting only that each cleric be accompanied by an Adaran escort. Nothing had been found, of course. The naitani were happily practicing their magic by the canal docks, under the protection of their champions, their magic and all those who benefited from that magic.

The city's residents seemed not quite to know what to think of the collapsed temple walls. The clerics tried to rebuild them, but the stones would not stay one atop the other, the work of one day undone before the next day's work could begin. Arguments flared as to whether it was the Hand of the One preventing the rebuilding, or ordinary vandals knocking things over every night. The clerics even set guards, but after the guards kept falling asleep and the stones sliding back to the ground while they slept, the "Hand of the One" side of the argument seemed to be winning. The rebuilding was abandoned.

On Hopeday, some of the more daring among the populace— perhaps encouraged by the dockside naitani, for the brave were mostly among the poor—ventured across the rubble onto the temple grounds to participate in the day's worship. They didn't quite dare enter the temple itself—it might not have held them all had they tried—but they were in the gardens. Keldrey hadn't heard whether any of the still-cloistered naitani had made an appearance, but there was no retaliation against those who dared "sully" temple soil with their unsanctified presence. So perhaps things were beginning to turn back to the way they had been before the demons' interference.

·Life fell into a routine. Or as much of a routine as was possible while in a foreign country with a child missing and a trial by combat hanging over their heads. And that was without mentioning the rumbling turmoil in the city. Habadra Chani took a few extra days to name her trial champions. She was reported to be extremely unhappy to learn that Edabi dedicats refused all requests to participate in any trial, including hers. But at last the trial date was set.

It would begin with the individual contests on Firstday, the eighteenth of Forende, as fall began to shift into winter, the mêlée battle to follow the next day.

While the Adaran champions practiced, honing their skills on each other and anyone willing to step into the courtyard with them, Kallista played Reinine. It was a role she played, a job she did. Inside the fancy clothes, she was still Kallista Varyl, soldier. And a soldier always did her duty.

So she met with all the Kameri who begged audience, bringing them into the embassy proper for luncheons and afternoon teas, and attending as few outside events as Viyelle and Namida Ambassador thought prudent. Each of the Heads Kallista talked with had their own interests and concerns, but after the first five or six, she began to see a pattern. They wanted magic, but they wanted it without having to change their comfortable, profitable way of life—that comforted and profited so very few. The changes that followed Kallista like a flock of ducklings disturbed, upset or outraged them, depending on just how resistant to change that particular Head of Line might be.

Obliquely—and sometimes directly—they accused her of wanting to destroy their entire society. And, so far as their society was influenced and guided by demons, that was true.

Kallista did find it interesting that when she mentioned the possibility of having their own Daryathi naitani—nathains—working in society, outside the temples, most of the Kameri stopped sputtering. They listened intently to her reports of the young nathains living near the docks, building a new temple there, gaining support from the populace who protected them from those who disapproved. The potential for change kept Kallista talking long after her voice became a frog's croak, kept her meeting with one Head of Line after another. If they could break apart the things created here by demons, perhaps it would drive the demons out of hiding to defend their work.

Gweric attended all her luncheons and teas, despite the snubs and cruelty dealt out when the Daryathi caught sight of his scars. He sniffed for demon presence so Kallista could send her magic into those he marked. She didn't want to search everyone she encountered. For one thing, people noticed when they had magic rummaging around in themselves, and they usually did not react well even if they were not demon-possessed.

Grand Master Murat might have gone on his rampage even if he had not been magic-searched, but Kallista had to accept the possibility that her search might have set him off. It wouldn't keep her from searching those Gweric indicated, but she didn't dare go round shoving magic willy-nilly into just anyone. Not yet. Not until necessary.

Besides it was exhausting. Even when they'd had their ninth, using the magic required effort. Without Stone, it took immense amounts of strength to move the magic, especially as powerful as it had somehow grown. It was disrespectful to think this way, she knew, but Kallista wished the One would hurry up and mark Keldrey already. It was time and beyond.

Chapter Twenty-One

As the first week of waiting for the trial passed and the second began to wear away without Gweric finding a single new person for her to search, Kallista found herself wanting to scream with frustration. Nothing moved. Time itself seemed suspended. The demons refused to be found, though their stink was everywhere. They even hid from her dreams.

She stalked the dreamscape, rapier in her hands, demon-hound at her heels. *"Where are you?"* Her cry set the mists to quivering with its fury.

You think we are so stupid as to tell you? The whisper came from all directions and none, slithering out of the grayness.

You think you are so powerful, that you can defeat us, but you can't. You are flesh and blood, born to die. One mortal being who can do nothing without those who cluster round you like fat gathering on a scummy pond. Already we have weakened you, taken part of your strength.

Suddenly Stone lay in front of her bleeding onto the paving stones, his head rolled a little distance from his body. Kallista cried out, turned away, but the sight moved, staying before her eyes. *It wasn't real.*

It had been real, yes, but it was past, his body burned, the ashes waiting for the journey home. She had coped, accepted the death—not well and not completely—she still cried at night when Obed was asleep and couldn't hear. But she didn't have time for more grief. Not now. She was needed.

"I've weakened you as well," she retorted, more bravado than anything. "I took away your skola, and the temple walls are down. Nathains are in the city, doing their work among the people. You are losing power."

You've done nothing. You cannot harm us. We have taken this one, and we will take the rest, the insidious whisper came back.

A vision of Torchay flashed into view beside Stone. He was spilled open on the sands, split from neck to nethers.

All of your strength.

Obed lay beside him, in pieces. Aisse joined them, and Fox and Joh and Viyelle and Leyja, until all of them lay dead and bleeding across the dreamscape.

Kallista refused to scream. *It's not real. None of it.*

She lashed out with her magic and the vision burst, exploding into a few ragged shreds of mist.

We will take everything from you. The whisper returned. *Even those little pustules of humanity you call children. We will strip it all away until you are exposed, naked, vulnerable, powerless. And then we will destroy you too.*

"No!" Kallista cried. "You won't. You can't. *I won't let you!*"

But the voice was gone, leaving behind no hint as to where it had come from and no way to track where it had gone. She screamed her fury into the dreamscape and woke to find herself whimpering, held tight in Obed's arms.

Torchay stroked a hand down her shoulder. "It's been a while since one of us woke screaming from a dream. Did you find the demons then?"

"No, curse it." She laid her cheek on Obed's shoulder, needing to feel it attached to the rest of his body. "But they talked to me." She tugged Torchay round to where she could see him. "You *are* all in one piece, right? No gaping holes? No internal organs trying to escape?"

"Perfectly grand." He spread his arms, displaying his torso, whole and healthy. "And I've no plans to be gutted again, thank you. Three times is quite enough for one lifetime, even if I did survive them all." He paused. "Is that what you dreamed?"

Kallista nodded, tightening her arms around Obed. "You were all dead. Obed was in pieces. You were gutted. Aisse was—"

"No need for details. Once had to be bad enough."

"It was." She checked that Obed's legs were still attached. Yes, he was holding her, breathing warm into her ear. Yes, she knew the dream wasn't real. But she had to check.

"Why?" Obed seemed reluctant to speak. "Why did you dream this? Why did the demons not simply continue to hide?"

"Good question." One she hadn't considered. Kallista sat back and subjected Obed to a more complete inspection, touching as well as looking. Every well-loved part of him was present, including the ear she'd seen sail through the fog and land at her feet. She turned and sat with her back against him, pulling his arms into place around her again. "Maybe because our tactics are working. Maybe the demons have figured out that we're not going to just go away. So they're resorting to threats."

A rap sounded at the door and Joh looked in, his waist-length hair spilling through after. "Everything all right?"

"Fine," Kallista began.

Torchay walked his words over hers. "She's dreaming demons."

"I'll get the others." Joh left before she could stop him.

Viyelle arrived first, her eyes red and swollen. Kallista held her arms out and the younger woman fell into them with a sob. Torchay folded her into the middle of an ilian embrace.

"I miss him so much," Viyelle said, her choked tears bringing on Kallista's. "It's worse at night, with just Joh and me and no one on my other side."

"Oh, love." Kallista wept with her, all of them rocking together. "My poor darling."

As the others arrived, they joined the embrace until it was a tangle of arms, legs and tears, with Viyelle in the middle. When the storm finally ended, Kallista wiped away Viyelle's tears, then her own, with a corner of the bed cover.

"Come to us," Kallista said. "You and Joh, or ask one of the others to join you, if you think this bed too small for five."

"I'll come," Keldrey said. "The beds here are too small for four, much less five."

"Joh said you dreamed demons." Aisse leaned back into Keldrey's solid form.

"I didn't see them, but I heard them." Quickly, Kallista shared what she had dreamed. "I think it means they're still trying to scare us into going away and leaving them alone. But they won't succeed."

"They succeeded in killing Stone," Viyelle said in a small voice.

"And because of that, we're warned. We take extra care. We can't tuck tail and run. If the demons aren't destroyed, they won't stop trying to destroy us." Kallista stretched her arms as far as she could, trying to touch each one of her iliasti. "They will go after us one at a time, because together we are more than we are separately. We cannot let anything drive us apart, and we cannot turn back."

"No one goes anywhere alone," Torchay said. "Even inside the embassy."

A yawn caught Kallista suddenly. "Why are we talking business in the tiny chimes of the night?"

"Because that's when the demons come." Torchay gave Aisse an affectionate squeeze, then handed her off to Fox. "Now go back to your own beds and let me sleep. Morning comes early."

Two days later, on his visit to check on Sky's welfare, Keldrey found himself escorted into Habadra House, to the courtyard where Stone had died. Habadra Chani waited there with a Tibran pistol which she proceeded to use in a demonstration of her power. One after the other, she executed an adult son of her Line and Sky's burly champion-escort for failing to fulfill her expectations. She ended with a threat to execute Stone's son in the same way if the court case was not dropped.

Keldrey told Kallista of Habadra's threats as soon as he returned, but when they complained to the justiciars, Chani denied it all. The only living witnesses were a small boy, a bondservant and Habadra's two pet champions. However, the justiciars agreed to take the disputed property into custody until after the trial in one more week—nine long days.

Justiciar's custody was scarcely better than Habadra's, especially for a five-year-old boy. The only place they had to keep him was the jail where they held those accused of crimes and bound over for trial. They did give him a cell to himself in the better part of the jail, where there was light and Kallista could pay for extra comforts, like a blanket and better food. But it was still a solitary, barred cell for a very small boy.

The best thing about the move was that now, only Kallista was forbidden to visit to the boy—Kallista Varyl and Habadra Chani, the parties to the lawsuit. Despite Chani's protests, everyone else was allowed, including the godmarked.

Kallista sent Joh to visit nearly every day, at a different time from Keldrey, so Sky would spend less time alone. She could ride Joh's vision, see Stone's son for herself, but it was almost worse this way. She could see, but not touch. Most of the others went along at one time or another.

Riots broke out in that last week of waiting, confined mostly to the areas near the trade canals, and where the hovels of the poor bumped up against the better-off parts of town. They kept raging, and they spread.

Rumor said the rioting began at a small trial in the east canal district. A dockworker claimed he'd been cheated of wages by a barge captain. Unable to find a champion willing to fight for the pittance he could pay, the screwsman—a specialist in "screwing" cotton into holds—would have been forced to fight his own trial against the barger's champion. The truthsayer nathain had appeared at the trial's opening when the parties made their claims. He'd declared the barger's claim a blatant, bald-faced lie, and produced others she'd cheated—not just dockworkers but merchants and craftsmen as well. The barger's champion had struck down the screwsman anyway, declaring a victory, and the whole district exploded.

The people rioted against the injustice, against a system where all the magic, the wealth and the power was concentrated in the hands of a few, the Heads of the Hundred Lines. They rioted to spur on the changes that now seemed possible. Or they rioted to stop them, because the changes were against the teachings of the Sameric sect. But everyone seemed to believe that whatever was wrong could be blamed on the Adarans.

One bunch seemed to hold Adarans at fault for allowing the Lines to enslave them and monopolize all the employment. Others hated Adarans on principle, for their perversions and blasphemy and letting their magic-users run around loose. Whatever the cause, few in the city were friendly.

And so the day arrived for the trial between Kallista Varyl and Habadra Chani.

Champions lined the streets shoulder to shoulder guarding the route between embassy and arena from any disturbance. Kallista rode behind the escort troop, ahead of the trial champions, with Torchay and Obed at either shoulder as always.

Over their kilts, the Adaran champions wore scarlet overrobes trimmed in the colors of the compass rose—blue for the lightning arm of the North, green for the East twining vine, yellow for the flame pointing South, and black for the thorny briar of the West. The robes kept them warm against the drizzling rain that had the horses slipping on the slick paving. Kallista wished she had a robe of her own to go with her broad-brimmed hat. The rain was cold on her neck. But she refused to have servants carry a canopy over her. She wouldn't melt from a little damp.

The trial arena was new, built outside the city's governmental center across the Bafret Canal in the main commercial area. Merchants had donated land and funds for its building, according to Namida Ambassador. The trials brought people into the sector and the excitement encouraged them to spend freely. As they rode across the arched bridge over the canal, Kallista saw the massive building rising ahead.

Drum-shaped, its granite construction gray and gloomy in the rain, it seemed to promise blood, death and pain. How many had died just bringing the granite from the mountains for its construction? And now folk flooded through its gates for the entertainment of watching more men fight and possibly die. And now folk flooded through its gates to watch men fight for their entertainment.

Oh, they claimed it was justice, a way for the One to determine which side was in the right. But justice had nothing to do with this spectacle.

Immediately around the arena court, wide plazas opened up. A distance away, Kallista saw Chani with her purple-clad champions riding in their own procession to the arena. All across the plazas, traders hawked their wares from awning-protected carts or sodden blankets spread on the ground or from the depths of their overrobes. Champions made paths through the chaos and others were scattered through the plazas to keep order, but for once, few paid the Adarans any attention. They were intent on business, or on getting into the arena before they got any wetter.

Finally, Kallista's party rode through the plaintiff's gate out of the rain and dismounted. The horses were taken away and justiciar's apprentices waited to escort Kallista and the other non-combatants to their seats. She couldn't make herself leave, not quite yet.

"Finish it quick," Obed was saying to the red-robed others. "If you can. The crowd won't like it, but you're not here to entertain them, no matter what they think. This is a trial. You *win* and end it."

Kallista couldn't say "stay safe." They were going into an arena to fight. "Take care. Nobody dies today."

"What if they want us to die?" Night asked.

"You'll just have to make sure you win, then, won't you?" Torchay winked. "Yeah, we've all heard Habadra retained a bunch of the most brutal fighters in Mestada. We're better than they are. We don't have to kill them to beat them." He looked up at Kallista. "But stay close, Naitan, just in case."

"I have my healer's robe." She showed the garment that would allow her access to the arena to heal any of the injured. The justiciars had found it an odd request, for a party in a case to be allowed to participate as healer, but as long as she agreed to heal the wounded on both sides, they would allow it.

One of the waiting apprentices pointedly cleared her throat. Those not fighting needed to go to their places, but Kallista couldn't make herself leave, couldn't tear her gaze from her iliasti. Black-haired, red, gold—she'd dreamed of them before they'd become hers, fought against loving them, and now she couldn't imagine life without them. And she had to send them into a fight without her beside them. She didn't like it, it wasn't right, and she couldn't do a thing to change it. Yet.

The others—Aisse, Viyelle, Joh, Leyja—had all wished them luck. Only Kallista delayed. She reached up to brush her fingers across Fox's sightless eyes, wishing she dared kiss him, and spoke a single word. *"Win."*

She tucked a coil of scarlet hair that had come loose from the clubbed queue behind Torchay's ear and whispered the same word. Then she curled her hand into a fist and touched Obed's shoulder tattoos. She opened her hand and pressed it over the tattoo around his navel, the tattoo that proclaimed "Victory comes from the One."

"Win," she whispered, and stepped back.

She turned to the rest of her champions then, moving from one to the next, holding each gaze. "Live," she told them. "*Win*. Bring Stone's Sky home."

She could delay no longer. Kallista turned to follow the justiciars through a maze of narrow corridors until they emerged into a huge chamber shaped like a flat-bottomed, steep-sided bowl. The sides rose in tiers that provided seating for several thousand spectators; the floor was filled with sand to provide footing for the combatants as well as to absorb blood. The open roof was covered over with an enormous tight-laced canvas to keep the rain off and the cold out.

It succeeded, for the most part. The dim light filtering through the rain clouds and canvas was supplemented by strategically placed torches and a gigantic lighting fixture that hung from the thick beam crossing the open space overhead. Its many branches held more than a hundred candles, all blazing away.

The justice-apprentices led Kallista to a box on one side of an area raised above the lower levels of the seating. Habadra Chani and her party already occupied the box on the far side. A fanfare sounded from a brass horn, its mellow tones filling the arena, and everyone rose to their feet. Obed had told them what would happen, but still the ceremony, the ritual of the thing, caught Kallista off guard.

Below them, literally under their feet, doors opened in the arena wall. Kallista could barely see the door below Habadra's box and the one below her not at all. The champions walked out, eight from each door, clad in kilts of their sponsor's colors. When they reached the center of the arena, each group pretending the other didn't exist, they turned and faced the boxes.

The horn sounded again. Kallista turned to see a trio of white-clad justiciars, one of them with hair almost as white as her robe, walk onto the central platform from the gilt archway behind it. They took the three benches at the front of the platform. Behind them, dressed in his slave's kilt, came Sky, escorted by a pair of younger justiciars. They'd had clothing made for the boy for this event—a plain tunic and trousers—but the justiciars had apparently banned it.

"Easy, love." Joh gripped Kallista's shoulder, quelling her impulse to leap onto the platform and snatch their son away now. Or at least smother him with hugs and kisses.

She'd ridden Joh's vision a dozen times on visits and she was tired of it. She wanted her own time with him, not to borrow someone else's. She'd probably terrify the boy, blubbering all over him. She couldn't stop the tears now, finally seeing him with her own two eyes rather than Joh's. Stone's boy. The last little bit of their lost love they could hold on to.

A gong sounded, one of Mestada's great bells, vibrating the bones in her body. When it faded away so she could hear again, the youngest of the justiciars in white was reading the official petition. Kallista tried to listen, but her mind kept drifting. To Sky. To Stone. To her men standing on the arena sands.

But the petition was short and before she expected it, the champions trudged back across the sand to their respective doors and the spectators rustled back to their seats. The escort justiciars indicated that Kallista and the godmarked should take the chairs set up across the front of their box.

"Is every trial held in this place?" Kallista asked the apprentice who seated herself just behind her.

"No, Your Majesty. Many are, of course—all the trials for serious crimes, and civil cases between the Hundred Lines. But there are smaller courts across the city and in the districts outside Mestada."

Kallista unfolded her healer's robe and put it on, awkward while sitting, then tried to smooth out the wrinkles. "If I'm needed, how do I get down to the arena?"

"Er—well . . ." The justiciar had apparently never been asked that question before.

"Never mind." Kallista shook her head. "If it's bad enough I'm needed, I can jump."

"Over the wall?"

Kallista ignored the young woman's shocked exclamation, for the doors had opened again to admit the first two champions in single combat. The justiciars had called for a "dedicat bout" to begin, apparently to get the crowd enthused. Kallista didn't approve, but though she was Reinine, this wasn't Adara and she wasn't a justiciar.

Chapter Twenty-Two

Fox was the first. The spectators murmured over his tattoo-less state and his golden hair and skin. The murmurs grew to a loud buzz when they realized he was blind. All across the arena, bets were laid. Fox's opponent had his height, but easily twice his weight. He held his hand-and-a-half sword, a third longer than Fox's mountain blade, in tattooed hands.

"Fox's people don't do tattoos," Kallista murmured to the justiciar. "He's Tibran-born, from their Warrior Caste."

"Ah." The justiciar nodded as if she knew exactly what Kallista meant.

It took some time for Fox to wear his opponent down, amazing the audience with his nimble escapes, his flashing parries and ripostes. Finally, the courtside judge called halt just before the dedicat ran himself onto Fox's blade. A flag was hung from one of the eight posts below the front of Kallista's box. This was how they determined matters of law? The Reinine did *not* approve.

The next two contests went quickly, a win for Habadra and a win for Kallista. Then the crowd went wild when Genista marched out onto the sand, halberd over her shoulder. They'd seen her parade with the champions at the beginning, of course, but this was absolute confirmation that she would actually fight.

Ruel hadn't come. He'd stayed at the embassy with Keldrey, taking Genista's place guarding the children. He'd said that while he fully expected her to win, he couldn't watch her in the arena with another man.

The other man was a massive brute. His only tattoos were on his face, but his body was crisscrossed with marks—scars from previous combats.

"Kerik hasn't lost a match against any champion not dedicat," the justiciar murmured.

"Must have fought a great number of dedicats to get scarred up like that," Kallista muttered back.

The scarred champion roared, showing his missing teeth, and swung his pole weapon in a circle over his head. While he was swinging and roaring, Genista darted in and poked the upper point of her halberd under his chin. Three flags to one. Kallista tried not-so-hard to keep the smirk off her face.

The combats wore on. More flags went up in front of Kallista's box. The audience thinned out. Apparently they found the quick victories boring. Two more Habadra champions won their matches—one through sheer mismatch, the other when his Tayo Dai opponent allowed himself to be distracted. Torchay and Obed won the final two flags.

Kallista was ready to go meet her champions and congratulate them on their victories, have lunch. But there was yet more ceremony to endure. The three white-clad justiciars had their heads together, discussing something. Finally, their spokeswoman stepped to the front of the platform.

"Varyl is the winner of the day's trial, five to three. Tomorrow, at first bell, the mêlée combat will begin. Varyl is handicapped by five. The three dedicat-level champions will face Habadra's eight."

"What?" Kallista jumped to her feet, knocking over her chair, shouting at the justiciars on their platform. "What do you mean, *handicap?* Three against eight? What's fair about that? What kind of people are you?"

The justiciars ignored her, retreating through their archway to wherever justiciars went. The apprentice in the box caught Kallista's arm, tried to restrain her, and found herself facing bodyguard's steel in at least three hands.

Kallista threw her off. "I want to talk to the justiciars."

"It's not allow—"

"To all the seven bloody hells with what's allowed." Kallista shoved the young woman toward the exit of the box. "Take me to them. *Now.*"

Scowling with disapproval at every step, the apprentice did as Kallista demanded, taking her to a room one level up in the bowels of the arena. The door opened onto a large chamber filled with every luxury Daryath's wealth could provide. The justiciar's speaker looked up. "What is the meaning of this?"

"Exactly what I would like to know." Kallista pushed past her guide into the room. "What in all the names of the One is this handicap?"

"How dare you disturb the workings of the court? I'm calling out the guard." The speaker yanked on a bell rope.

"This looks more like lunch than court, and while I know you'd rather watch others spill their blood than do any honest—"

"*Kallista.*" Viyelle's fingers dug hard into Kallista's arm, and she realized Vee had been squeezing for a while.

Kallista also realized Viyelle was thinking more clearly than she. They did not need to antagonize the very people who could determine the outcome of this trial. She took a deep breath, reaching for control. A trickle of magic seeped through the links without her calling it, tasting of Viyelle's worry and Joh's cold anger. That helped more.

"I beg forgiveness for this disturbance." Kallista bowed low, Adaran-style. "But I know nothing of this *handicap* business. You claim justice in Daryath is fair, but three men fighting against eight? How is that fair?"

"Ignorance of the law is no excuse for—"

The white-haired justiciar cut off their speaker. "She is from another land that does not know our laws and she is ruler there, where she can demand and receive what she demands."

That was far from how it worked, but Kallista didn't owe them any explanations. They owed her.

"It does no harm to answer her questions." The old woman looked then at Kallista. "Is it fair to force those who have faced each other once already and *lost* to fight again with nothing altered? Circumstances must change to even the odds."

"Why? Why must circumstances change? How does 'evening the odds' benefit anyone but the betting shops? How does it show 'the will of the One'?"

"By removing the influence of money. One side may have been able to buy better champions. This eliminates that advantage, so that the One's will may more clearly be seen."

"*My* champions do not fight for money." Kallista let Joh grab her hand, used his grip to keep her seething rage under control. From the corner of her eye, she could see Aisse holding onto Leyja the same way.

The old one's response was a shrug. Nothing more.

"Why bother to win in the individual combats then?" Kallista demanded. "Why should anyone win if they're going to be penalized for it?"

"Today's wins are still credited to your case." The old woman sipped at her cha, her quavering hand taking its own time about it. "Tomorrow's results will be weighed against today's victories. If your dedicats are as skilled as today's matches showed, they should have no trouble against these opponents."

"But—" Kallista cut off the temptation to shout that they were all mates and she loved them. The justiciars would likely just shrug again and go back to their meal. If they didn't call out the mob, or have them all tossed into the jail with Sky.

"You have had your questions answered. We are done." The white-haired justiciar waved a hand, dismissing them rudely.

But then it had been rude for Kallista to barge in on them, and it had done no good whatsoever. Might even have done them harm. Nothing had changed. Torchay, Obed and Fox would stand alone in the arena tomorrow against all eight of Habadra's ruthless champions.

Kallista bowed in grudging apology and allowed Joh and Viyelle to escort her out of the room. Aisse had to almost drag Leyja out. The little justiciar-apprentice led them back through the warren of corridors to the space inside the plaintiff's gate where the champions waited with the horses.

"Where were you?" Torchay demanded when Kallista finally let go of him. "We've been waiting an age."

She grabbed Obed by the shoulder of his robe and shook him. "Why didn't you tell me about the handicap?"

"Handi—?" His eyes narrowed. "*What* handicap?"

"It seems that since you won today's matches so easily, tomorrow, the three of you will face all eight Habadra champions by yourselves."

"*What?*" Shock and outrage came from a hand of throats at once, Obed's foremost among them.

Kallista could sense his surprise through the link, now Leyja had calmed a bit. "You didn't know, did you?"

"No, of course not. What—How—?" Obed's mouth opened and closed another time or two without finding the words he wanted.

"Let's go. Back to the embassy. We can talk about it there." Kallista swung onto her horse. "They must have changed the rule since you left Daryath."

"Yes, but *why?*"

"No reason that makes sense to me, but I'll tell you what they told me when we're out of all this." Kallista clucked to her horse, heading for the gate, forcing Obed and a few of the others to scramble to keep up.

That night, during all the explaining and all the complaining, Obed let everyone know exactly how senseless and unfair he thought the rule change was. His opinion: they'd changed it to increase the likelihood of someone actually dying in a tournament, for the thrill of the crowds. Kallista thought it likely inspired by the demons still hiding from them. Demons fed on death, destruction and misery. The three remaining fighters held strategy sessions late into the night to develop three-man tactics rather than eight.

The next morning, they retraced their path through Mestada's center, over the Bafret Canal, through the busy market squares to the court arena. All those who had made the trip on Firstday were back again. The champions not in the arena today wore their red robes over their Adaran uniforms. Kallista suspected they might be wearing those robes the rest of their lives as a boast that once they'd had the honor of fighting for their Reinine in a foreign arena.

Their young escorts were back, eyeing the black-clad, red-robed Tayo Dai with suspicion. "Why are they here?" one of the justice-apprentices dared ask. "They do not fight today."

"They are bodyguards," Kallista said. "Adaran soldiers. Not free-lance champions. They are part of my household."

The young woman didn't seem to know whether to be impressed or disdainful. Kallista turned to embrace her kilted iliasti.

"Stay safe." She couldn't get her arms around all three of them at once, so hugged them one at a time. "We can find another way to get Sky away from that woman."

"Are you saying you don't think we can win?" Horror and hurt shuddered in Fox's voice.

"No, of *course* not." Kallista rushed to reassure him before she saw the tiny quiver at the corner of his mouth, and clouted the back of his head for teasing her so. "Mean, cruel man."

"Me? You're the one that's hitting." Fox rubbed the back of his head piteously.

"We will win," Obed said. "We are that much better. Habadra's champions are stupid, clumsy and slow."

"They're also brutal and ruthless," Kallista added.

"And we're not?" Torchay lifted an eyebrow at her and she had to admit his truth.

"We're soldiers," Fox said. "Not champions."

"Which means?" Kallista looked from one to the other for an answer.

"We know how to fight together, as a team," Torchay said. "Even Obed, who *was* champion and dedicat and spent his life fighting alone. He's learned soldiering these past seven years. He's one of us. Part of us, like we're part of him. It's no' eight against three today. It's three against one and one and one, to the end of them. Those other lads, Habadra's champions—they're each one of 'em standing alone. They're no' soldiers. They're no'—" He broke off, but she still heard the word he wouldn't say. *Ilian.* The others weren't ilian.

Silence ruled in the plaintiff's yard a long moment, seeming the more profound because of the hum of voices coming through from the public areas.

"Right." Fox broke it. "Exactly. What he said."

"It is time," the escort called from her place.

"Yes. So—" Kallista took a moment to hug them all again.

"Be especially careful," she whispered to Fox. "I can't lose any more of my Tibrans." She brushed her fingers over his eyes. "I wish I could help you somehow."

He smiled, captured her hand and pressed a kiss to her palm. "And I wish I could see you. Any of you. All of you. But we don't get everything we want, do we?"

"We get what we need." Kallista called magic. She shaped it for vision, quickness, cleverness, wisdom, and she let it go. She didn't direct it. Any who had need of those things was welcome to them, even if they were Habadra's champions.

The world seemed to pause while the magic settled out over it. Then Kallista made herself walk away to go watch her beloved defend themselves against more than twice their number.

The opening ceremony was much the same today as yesterday, save only three in red kilts stood on the arena's sands. Habadra's box seemed more crowded today than yesterday, and it heightened Kallista's sense that something was not right.

She beckoned her duty-guard over. "Samri, does Habadra's box look different to you today?"

"There are twelve more people, my Reinine."

"Ah. Would you have Night take a look to see if he knows who they are, and why Chani might have brought them with her? Have him report to me, yes?"

The young guard bowed and stepped back a pace, beckoning the red-robed ex-Habadra over so Samri wouldn't have to leave his post guarding his Reinine.

The petition had been read. The spectators were rustling back into their seats. The champions stepped out to return to their respective arming chambers and retrieve their weapons when the justiciar speaker held up her hand. *"Hold."*

The champions stopped. A buzz rippled through the arena. What was this? More rule-changing? Kallista held her temper. Time enough to let it go when she knew what was happening.

"It has come to our attention that one party in this trial is a nathain of very powerful magic," the speaker stated. "One who could easily interfere with the working of this court."

The crowd's hum grew louder as a young man in black robes over black Daryathi shirt and trousers strode onto the justiciar's platform, a staff in his hand. "This man is Nur im-Nathain," the speaker said. "One of our own, a truthsayer. He will determine whether unauthorized magic is being used."

He had to be one of the naitani who had fled the temple. Automatically, Kallista looked around for the shaved heads and voluminous white robes of the Samerics. One or two. No more. They seemed cowed by the justiciars' peace-keeping champions scattered thickly through the crowds. The clerics had no legal power, only persuasion, and it looked as if the justiciars had no intention of allowing them to use it today.

Nur strode to the front of the platform, right up to the wrought-iron railing at the edge, to look out over the champions on the sands below. After a long moment, he looked back at the justiciars. "Magic has been worked this morning—"

"Forfeit!" Chani jumped to her feet. "I claim forfeit. Varyl has broken the rules and lost—" The rest of her rant was smothered by the noise of the crowd.

Nur Truthsayer slashed his staff through the air and the sound subsided abruptly. "The magic clings to more than the Varyl champions. Three of Habadra's have been touched by *the same magic*," he added before Chani could cry foul again.

He turned his back on Chani, pointing his staff at Kallista. "Varyl Kallista, did you work this magic?"

Kallista stood and bowed deepest respect to the young truthsayer. "Nur im-Nathain, I did."

"*Truth.*" He was good, powerful, to be able to read truth at this distance. "What sort of magic did you work?"

How to describe it? She didn't quite know. "It is—I—"

"You see?" Chani shouted. "She seeks to lie already."

"*Silence.*" Nur slashed his staff at Chani and she fell back a step from the sheer force of his will. He thumped the heel of his staff on the floor beneath him. "You will not speak without permission of this court. You will not disrupt this proceeding. Another word from you when the staff is not yours and I will have Varyl Nathain weave it shut. Do you understand me?"

Kallista could not see the Habadra's expression clearly across the space between them, but she saw Chani bow. Then the Head of Habadra raised her hand asking permission.

"The Varyl does not seek to lie," the truthsayer said.

Chani raised her hand higher and with a sigh, Nur pointed the staff at her.

"How do we know *you* tell the truth?" Chani's voice carried across the arena. "How do we know you are actually nathain?"

Nur's smile was crooked as he looked out at the spectators. "Ask them." He waved his hand at the audience. "I have worked among them four weeks now. Am I nathain?"

The crowd burse into a roar of approval, of "Nathain! Nathain! Nathain!"

He had to wave his staff several times to stop the noise. "I am truthsayer. I cannot speak anything but truth." His crooked smile returned. "And damned inconvenient it can be."

"Then tell me this truth," Chani said. "Which side do you favor in this trial?"

"The child's," Nur said without hesitation. "And there is no doubt that Sky im-Varyl—"

"Habadra-ti!" Chani howled, then shut up as Nur jerked the staff to point skyward.

"—Sky *im-Varyl* will have a better life as a son in the household of the Varyl Reinine, *but*—" He gestured with his staff, cutting Chani off before she got started. "*But*, I am *truthsayer*. I am nathain. I will speak the truth without bias or favor to anyone, whether the Head of the richest line in Daryath, the Ruler of half this continent, or a beggar on the street. *I am nathain*"

"Enough." The speaker for the justiciars cut off any more argument. "We brought in this truthsayer at your request, Habadra. Let us get on with it."

Nur took a deep breath and turned to point his staff at Kallista. "Nathain, what was the magic you worked?"

"Perhaps the best description of it is a blessing." She'd taken the time spent in argument to work out her answer. "Good will. Benefit bestowed on—wherever it falls. Which is likely why it clings to some of the Habadra champions."

"Truth." Nur frowned. "Why not to all of them?"

"Blessings can be ignored. Rejected." Kallista paused. "I can do it again, if you like. For everyone. You can watch me."

"I want none of her poison," Chani burst out, ignoring the scowl sent her way by the justiciars.

"It is *blessing*. For good sense and wisdom and vision to see true. Magic, straight from the hand of the One."

"Truth." Nur's voice held more than a touch of wonder. He turned to look a question at the three presiding justiciars.

"I'll take it!" One of the purple-kilted champions stepped forward. "I felt it last time—like the best wine ever made, without the morning after. An angel's kiss. I'll take more."

The white-haired justiciar looked up at Nur and nodded. He looked at Kallista, anticipation in his eyes.

She bowed to him, bowed to the justiciars, and turned to bow to the crowd. Then she called magic, called the great billowing waves of it pouring from her seven godmarked. Torchay's head fell back where he stood on the arena sands, his expression almost rapturous as she called. She struggled to shape it, hauling against the massive weight to shape what she wanted. Good sense, wisdom, true sight.

"I see it." Nur's whisper barely reached her. "I see her calling the magic. It's beautiful."

Finally, Kallista had it balanced, perfectly formed for the purpose she intended. She bent her knees slightly, the physical action echoing the greater unseen action as she centered herself beneath the mass of magic, and thrust up hard, sending it up and out, moving majestically in all directions at once.

A thousand throats gasped, a thousand bodies stood as the pearlescent mist burst over the arena. A few screamed, but most lifted their faces to watch as it wafted outward, then drifted down over them. Even the champions, those who had rejected it before, turned their faces up to receive this Godstruck magic.

Profound silence fell, punctuated by the occasional soft rustle as someone's knees gave way and they plopped onto their seat. A quiet sigh echoed across the stadium.

Finally, Nur cleared his throat. He pointed his staff at the Habadra champion who'd spoken before. "Was that the same magic you experienced before?"

"More." His voice scraped over gravel. "Better."

"Look at Chani," Night whispered from where he stood just behind Kallista. "Does she look well to you?"

She didn't. The Habadra had gone pale, seemed struggling to breathe. Kallista frowned. "Gweric—"

But he hadn't come, had picked up a bad cough from somewhere. Fox was in the arena, and if she spun out any magic to look herself, Nur would see it and wonder what she was doing. Kallista could not look inside the Habadra for demons now.

"If we are satisfied?" At the justiciars' nod, Nur Truthsayer retreated to the back of the platform where he took a seat on the bench beside Sky.

The justiciar's speaker stood. "Retrieve your weapons, champions. The trial begins."

Kallista stood to peer over the stone parapet of her box at the doors set in the wall below. Obed was already armed and out, the other two on his heels. They trotted together out to center arena, their hair spilling black, red and gold over their shoulders from their unbraided queues, a taunt to their opponents. They could tie their hair back loosely rather than binding it into the champion's difficult-to-grasp clubbed queue because their opponents wouldn't get close enough to grab it.

Obed had never thought to find himself here again, standing on arena sand, waiting for the justiciar's signal to begin. He had been very good at it, but he had regretted the killing. He did not think he would regret it today, if they forced him into it. And today, for the first time in his life, he did not stand here alone.

Justiciar Maathin—he remembered her well, despite the pure white her hair had gone—waved her hand. The lion flag on its pole came sliding down and Obed turned with his iliasti to face their opponents. The purple-clad were charging, obviously intending to overwhelm them with mass and numbers.

Obed stepped aside, away from Torchay, to let the big one rumble between them. Torchay slashed as the man passed while he parried another attack with his left-hand sword. Obed fought off his own opponents, folding back against his iliasti until they stood shoulder to shoulder, back to back to back.

"Status?" Torchay rasped.

"I'm bleeding," Fox said. "A scratch. Nothing."

"Hm. So am I." Obed discovered the graze along his upper arm, scarcely deep enough to bleed. "You?"

Seven of the Habadras attacked again. Torchay had caught the big runner across the back of his leg deep enough to take him out of the match. All seven attacking together got in each other's way. One of them tripped, fell but scrambled back quickly enough to escape injury. Obed saw him past the flashing steel he parried, the man's long halberd waiting to dart in from a distance and—Obed caught it on his blade, shunted it aside as Torchay dealt with the attack coming in under the halberd at Obed's stomach. Fox stopped an attack on Torchay, and Obed had to leap to knock aside a sword sliding toward Fox's side.

Finally, the Habadras fell back, bleeding from as many places as the three godmarked. But there were seven Habadra champions to spread the cuts across. The lion flag went up as arena judges consulted.

"Status?" Torchay leaned back and they all took a moment to relax, leaning into each other for support.

"Fine. What's *yours?*" Obed demanded.

"Bleeding, like the rest of us. *Fine.*"

Obed didn't like the snap in the man's voice, but forgot it when Fox shook his head as if dazed. "Fox, trouble?"

"I don't—" Fox rubbed his eyes, leaving streaks of blood across them like a mask. "There's—shapes. I—"

"They're taking another off," Torchay said. "Six to go."

"Only two to one now." Obed glanced up at the box where Kallista sat, saw her rise and wrap her green healer's robe around her as she hurried away, her bodyguards behind her. The injured man must be hurt worse than he'd thought.

"Flag's gone down," he said. "They're coming."

"I can see that," Torchay growled. "I'm not blind."

"I am," Fox said. "And . . . *I* can see it."

"What?" But Obed had no time for questions. The purples were on them.

He'd fought against Habadra champions too many times to count— their families quarreled often—but he didn't know these. They fought without honor, using every low tactic they knew. Obed fought back the same way. Honor didn't matter today. Winning did.

He saved Torchay's life a dozen times, Fox's almost as many, and they saved his life twice that. Sweat rolled into a hundred cuts, making his skin sting all over. *Damned purples.* Why wouldn't they just *die?*

Fox shouted and he stumbled, falling awkwardly onto his backside and dropping his sword. Obed and Torchay held the purples off, taking on more of the shallow cuts while Fox groped for his blade like—like a blind man.

"*Here.*" Torchay got his foot under the blade, shoving Obed aside, and flipped the long sword to Fox who caught it as if nothing was wrong.

Fox stood with all his usual fluid grace, fighting as if he'd never stumbled. One of the Habadras staggered back, blood welling through the fingers he clutched over his belly and Obed laughed aloud. Another down.

As he watched from the corner of his eye for the flag to go up, Obed felt Fox lurch into his shoulder, almost as if he'd flinched. But Fox never flinched. Obed spun and slashed across the chest of the man pulling his sword out of Fox.

"Oh saints and bloody murder," Torchay rasped, "it's Fox they've gutted."

Chapter Twenty-Three

Torchay attacked, holding off the four remaining Habadras on his own as Obed lowered Fox carefully to the sand.

Obed looked toward the flagpole. Why didn't they raise the damned flag? Couldn't they see the three men bleeding into the sand? This wasn't a death match, for the One's sake. *There*. Finally. It was up.

The Habadras pulled back from their half-hearted attack—they'd likely been waiting for the flag too. Medics ran out into the arena to collect the injured.

Fox grimaced as they lifted him, set him on a stretcher, then he smiled. "Kallista's already working. I can feel it."

Good. Obed swiped his forearm across his face, wiping on more than he wiped off. It burned, stinging his eyes and lips. Blood didn't burn like that, did it?

Obed grabbed a cloth from one of the medics and wiped his face, then tossed it to Torchay who ignored it. Rude bastard.

"Nice of them to give us these rest breaks." Torchay brushed at the sand caught in the hair on his barrel chest.

"It's not a death match." Obed struggled to even his breathing. "They have to at least pretend to keep us alive."

"Kallista'll make sure. And keep your great oversized feet out of my way. You nearly tripped me." He wasn't joking.

"Wish I had," Obed muttered, quiet enough Torchay would have to listen close to hear him.

"Is that what you want? Because I'll give it to you—soon as we finish these bastards off, I'll take you on. I'll be glad to finish you too."

"Keep dreaming. You couldn't finish me if you had four swords to fight with and a week to do it. You'd be flat on your back, crying like a baby, begging mercy."

"I don't need four swords. One is plenty—" Torchay broke off. "Flag's gone down."

Obed turned, laid his back against the other man's and waited for the purples' attack.

In the infirmary, just behind a barred gate opening on the arena, Kallista met Fox as he was carried in, leaving the others to the medics. Fox was hurt the worst and he was hers.

"What happened?" She laid her hand over his wound, walking blindly beside his stretcher as the bearers carried him to one of the tables, using her magic to see what was torn. "Never mind. Don't tell me yet. Not till I'm done."

He smiled his crooked, foxy smile and closed his eyes, alarming her for an instant. But she felt the beat of his heart in her magic, the whisper of his breath under her skin. He was healing. The magic was healing him.

When veins and organs were knit together again and Fox's skin sealed over it in a pretty pink new scar too much like those Torchay bore, Kallista glanced at the other injured to see whether she was needed. An East magic healer "escaped" from the temple and the medics seemed to have things well under control, the life threatening injuries healed to the point where non-magical care would cure. Kallista squeezed water from the cloth in the basin beside her and began to wash the blood from the scores of shallow cuts adorning the front of Fox's body.

"It's as if they thought enough of these little cuts would bleed you dry." She ran a finger along one of the deeper ones, healing it shut.

"The others—Torchay and Obed look worse than this." Fox opened his eyes and looked at her.

Kallista smiled. "By now they do, I'm sure. Is that why you let yourself get skewered? To keep yourself pretty for us?"

He stared, his eyes seeming to actually be focused on her face. "You're smiling," he said finally. "I can see your smile."

Her heart squeezed, and she turned to rinse the cloth in the basin, still smiling. "I didn't know your knowing sense could recognize smiles."

"It can't." Fox touched her chin, turned her face toward him with a gentle finger. "I can hear smiles, when you talk. But—I *see* you, Kallista."

He stroked his finger along her cheek. "You look just like you did in my dream, that time we dreamed each other, when I was prisoner of the rebels. Are we dreaming now?"

Too choked with sudden emotion to speak, Kallista shook her head. What was happening here?

"Don't cry." He wiped away an escaping tear with his thumb. "You hate to cry. Do you think this will go away? I have a lot of things I want to see before it does."

"Did regaining your sight cause this?" she managed to ask, touching the just-healed wound in the center of his body. "Did you see in the arena? Did it confuse you? Blind you?"

"I was blind before," he reminded her with a smile, still watching his hand explore her face. "It surprised me. I forgot to pay attention and the sword slipped by my guard."

"I'm sorry. My fault. I should have—"

Fox's fingers pressed against her lips, stopping her speech. "Done exactly as you did. Do you think I wouldn't trade a few moments of pain for this? To see you? To have the possibility of seeing the faces of my iliasti, my children? The wound is gone. You healed it. And I can still see you. For however long it lasts, I'm glad it happened."

"But—" She tried to protest around his fingers when the roar of the crowd outside drowned all ability to hear.

Fox sat up, looking with Kallista through the open grille of the gate to the arena beyond. She could see only a fallen champion struggling to crawl away from those still fighting. The little healer ran to peer through the grate. She turned to shout something, but the crowd's noise drowned her out. The alarm in her face had Kallista running to join her, Fox at her heels.

The roar of sound was fading but the healer didn't try to speak again. She pointed.

All the purple-clad champions were down, two of the four ominously still. Kallista spun off magic to stop their bleeding. Torchay and Obed alone still stood, so covered in blood, they had the same color skin—scarlet. But they didn't stand wearily, accepting the accolades of victory. They fought each other, swords flying as if this time, this combat would be to death.

"The lion flag is up!" a medic shouted in Kallista's ear, pointing at the fluttering bit of irrelevant cloth. Flag or no, they shouldn't be fighting each other. Something was wrong.

"Fox, can you still sense the demon-touched?" Kallista unfurled her magic and sent it flying out into the arena. "Why isn't anyone stopping them?"

"They are dedicats, God-touched," the healer said. "No one dares go near them."

"I dare." Kallista started out the gate.

Fox caught her, pulled her back hard against his chest. "Why bother? They want to kill each other, let them. They've been wanting it since the beginning. Why stop them?"

Shock held Kallista speechless as she looked over her shoulder at Fox. That wasn't Fox speaking. She yanked her magic from its sniffing round the arena and sent it whipping through the infirmary. No hint of demonstink, nothing new since she'd cleared it earlier. Fox was only Fox but . . . something was wrong.

She poured magic down her link to him, searching him roughly enough to make him shudder and swear. And there it was, seeping subtly through his veins. Not demons—demons couldn't touch the godmarked—but drugs.

More than one drug, she thought, acting together to produce an unnatural madness, so close to a body's natural function as to be almost undetectable. But how had it reached him?

Kallista shaped the magic to sweep the stuff from his blood but too much of it slipped between the bristles of her broom, refusing to leave him. She refined the magic, chasing the elusive drugs through Fox till she found where it was concentrated strongest. Nearest his myriad wounds.

"Their weapons—" She caught the healer-naitan's sleeve. "The Habadras' weapons are drugged. They drugged my champions with every cut."

"I'll collect them," the young woman offered. "So you have proof."

"Have your bodyguard do it. I need you to rid my Fox of the drugs. *Look*." Kallista grabbed hold of the woman's healing magic and swept it through Fox's contaminated blood alongside her own, showing her how to filter out the drugs. "Do you understand?"

"Y-yes." She nodded, gripping Fox's blood-streaked arm tightly as she led him back into the infirmary. He already began to come back to himself.

Kallista turned to hurry out onto the arena floor. Torchay and Obed circled each other, death in their eyes, riding the edges of their swords.

She got only a few steps onto the sand when strong hands caught hold of her again—this time, her bodyguards. "Let me go! I have to stop this." Kallista clawed at their hands.

"They are drugged. They could kill you. We cannot allow that, my Reinine." Samri's voice was quiet, matter-of-fact, calm in contrast to the fury with which she fought him.

"They are mine," she wailed. "They could die."

"You are the Godstruck," Night said. "They are godmarked like the Fox you healed. Can you not heal them from here?"

Could she? Kallista gathered magic from her undrugged four and sent it flying down the links to Torchay and Obed. The drugs were so subtle, so very like the body's own processes. It would take time to clear them away, time she was not sure she had.

Torchay stepped carefully over the sand, over the legs of the fallen, his eyes never leaving his opponent's. "You will die," he said casually, hiding the harshness of his breathing. He should not be so winded, or so angry. His mind should be clear for fighting, shouldn't it?

"Perhaps. Or perhaps it is you who will die." Obed sounded just as calm. He had to be hiding the same rage, the same weariness. They had walked onto the sand at the same moment.

On the same side. Hadn't they? Torchay shook his head and his hair came loose, whipping round his face. He snarled, the small annoyance feeding the hot blaze of anger filling up his skin. He launched himself at that sneering expression but Obed knocked the twin swords aside, his saber flashing faster than any single sword had a right to.

Obed broke off, spun away. Torchay let him go, his heart trying to pound its way out of his chest. "I should have killed you years ago." He gasped the words out, unable to hide his panting any longer. "You brought her nothing but pain with your Southron ways and your jealousy."

Obed glared past the sweaty strands of black hair spilling across his face. "You want to kill me?"

He threw his sword away, sent it spinning end over end across the arena, torchlight flashing along its polished steel length until it thudded onto the sand with a soft shush of sound. Torchay dragged his eyes back to Obed to see him standing with arms spread wide, offering himself up. "You want to kill me? Then kill me.

"*Do it,*" Obed said. "You are the one who always knows what she needs. You are the one who can bring her back from the land of the dead. You are the one she loves. So do it. Kill me. But first admit that I am not the only jealous man in this ilian. You know I could not hurt her if she did not care for me a little, and *that* is why you want to kill me."

Someone was shouting, screaming his name, and it joined the buzz in Torchay's head, the roar of anger consuming him, confusing him. "She loves you, not me. I'm the one got banned from her bed."

"You're back in it now, aren't you?" Obed sneered. "She loves you. Perfect Reinas, always there, always right." He slapped his chest with both hands. "Come on. Kill me. Get me out of your perfect way."

"I have to be perfect just to hold my own against her fascination with Obed im-Mysterious," Torchay snarled. "With your black eyes and your damned tattoos. It took nine years for her to notice me, but you—you stroll in the door and she's falling over herself. *Yes.*" Finally, he admitted it. "Yes, damn it, I'm jealous. I am *exactly* like you."

He took a step, and looked at the swords in his hands. He'd almost forgotten he still held them. He opened his hands, let them fall to the sand and launched himself at Obed. Killing him with a blade was too impersonal. Bare hands were needed.

Torchay tackled him to the ground. Obed offered no resistance, toppling like a fallen soldier. Torchay straddled him, fist raised to strike. Obed lay gazing calmly up at him.

"Why aren't you fighting me?" Confusion held back Torchay's blow. Something was wrong here. He couldn't think.

"She loves you," Obed said. "She needs you. I don't matter."

That wasn't right. Torchay slumped to one side, sitting in the sand. "She loves *you*." He frowned. "And I—I want to pound you into the dirt."

"Then do it."

Torchay looked at Obed lying sprawled on his back, bleeding from a double score of cuts. "I think I just did."

"Why won't you kill me? I want you to."

"Perhaps that's why. To thwart you." Torchay shook his head, carefully. It didn't feel quite proper, as if it were full of things it shouldn't be. Thinking was too hard. "Because as angry as you make me, jealous as you make me—and I admit it, you do. But you're my ilias. You are—"

He looked at Obed, understanding squeezing through the confusion. "You are my closest friend. More than that. My brodir. I can pound you into the dirt, but I can't kill you."

Others were in the arena now, kicking the weapons out of their reach, carting away the wounded. Obed paid them no attention as he groaned his way up to sit beside Torchay.

"Next time," Obed said, "I will pound *you*." He hesitated before speaking again. "She loves me?"

Torchay smacked him on the back of his head. "Yes, you idiot. You'd know that if you'd pay attention to your link. And you couldn't pound me if I had both arms tied behind my back." He paused, then amended. "One arm. I'd need at least one."

Kallista appeared in a flutter of green robes. She dropped to one knee between them and peeled back Torchay's eyelids, peering into his eyes.

"How do you feel?" she asked as she subjected Obed to the same treatment, ignoring the myriad cuts blooming with blood.

"Like a roast pig carved up for dinner." Torchay cocked his head as he studied her, groping inside himself for the magic link between them to double-check what he saw on her face. "You're not angry we tried to kill each other?"

She gestured for the medics to help them to stand. "You didn't succeed." She flashed a brief smile at him, before sobering. "You were drugged. Something subtle on the Habadra weapons so no one noticed until you attacked each other."

Torchay reached over his shoulder for his sword and found nothing. Oh, right. He'd thrown them down. Nor had he worn the sheath into the arena. "Where's my blade? I need to kill a Habadra."

"You need to go home and get rid of the rest of those drugs." Inside the infirmary, Kallista beckoned to the little healer and handed Torchay the cup she brought, filled to the brim with water. "Drink. I don't like the way your heart is pounding. Or yours." She gave Obed a cup as well. "The drugs affected your body as much as your mind. Where's Fox?"

"He went to collect the boy," Samri said. "And the rest of the godmarked."

"Good. We need to get back to the embassy as fast as possible."

This time, Torchay managed to gain his feet on his own strength when Kallista moved away. *Drugged.* He'd think about it later, when his head was clear and he could control the anger he felt boiling up again. At least they'd won Stone's boy free. He would think about that instead.

Fox strode through the back ways of the arena, enjoying the way folk backed away from him. It could be Night who parted the crowds—the former Habadra led the way to the viewing box—but it wasn't until they saw Fox with his blood-streaked skin that their eyes widened and they cowered away. Of course, it could be the naked sword in his hand that sent them scurrying.

He *saw* them scurry and cringe and stare. He couldn't see them clear until they came close, not like his sharp-eyed vision of before, but he could see. The One be praised, *he could see.*

As they left the crowds behind and entered the official sector of the arena, Fox closed his eyes, wondering whether he still possessed his odd magical *knowing* sense, or if it had left him when his vision returned. He experienced a moment's disorientation, as if he'd been concentrating too hard on seeing, before he could take in what was there—walls to either side, Night pulling ahead of him. Fox sensed a confused flurry of action beyond the point where he could see clearly.

He hurried to catch up with Night. "Have you a scarf, or a handkerchief? Any strip of cloth?" Fox opened his eyes to see the younger man shake his head.

"Help me." Fox tore at one of the useless bandages round his forearm. Trouble lay ahead and he didn't need any distraction in a fight. In moments, they had the bandage off his arm and a single layer tied over his eyes to help him keep them shut. It muffled the *knowing* a bit, but not enough to matter.

"Now, *hurry.*" Fox turned Night and propelled him forward, toward the uproar in the boxes ahead. "Be ready for anything."

"Yes, Godmarked."

The champion kept pace with Fox's rush, a saber appearing in his hand.

The three official court boxes were in chaos. The justiciars cowered against the front rail of their platform, away from the conflict that filled the rest of it. Habadra champions fought Adaran bodyguards, both sides trying to reach the little boy cowering against the Daryathi truthsayer.

The nathain kept trying to lead Sky to safety, but the Habadra had him cut off and blocked every gap the Adarans made. Fox's heart stopped when he *saw* Aisse swarm over the barrier into the box to lunge her rapier into a purple-kilted thigh.

Her attack left the Adaran box empty. Habadra's wasn't, until the last person in it jumped the barrier. Too late, Fox shouted his warning. Nur Naitan had moved too close to the Habadra side. The woman slashed, knocked him out of the way and snatched up Stone's son, holding her dagger to his throat.

"Hold!" she shouted. "Or I kill him."

Fox knew that voice. The Habadra, Chani. She *would* kill the boy, right here in the court if she decided to. He groped for a solution as the Adarans obeyed Leyja's nod and disengaged.

Chani handed Sky to her nearest lackey who held his sword to the boy's throat. "I will leave now with my property—"

"He's not yours," Leyja snarled. "We won the trial. Your justiciars said it."

"The trial is flawed. Your own champions fought each other."

"*After* they won. After—"

Fox sensed men moving through the corridors behind them. "Who?" he asked Night. "Who's passing?"

"Justiciar's champions," Night murmured. "To keep order in the arena."

Fox frowned, sniffed as they came nearer. "I smell gun oil. Muskets?" The Tibran army had conquered the whole northern continent with their muskets, Fox one of them. He knew muskets.

"They use muskets in instances such as this. They are not very good with them."

"I am." Fox sheathed his sword. He stepped into the corridor and appropriated the musket from the champion hurrying behind the others by bashing him in the face and taking it.

"Night." Fox checked the weapon, made sure it was loaded properly. "Get over there. Warn them to be ready. When the man falls, we snatch the boy and run."

Night moved. Fox slid into place just past the entrance to the box, close enough that the notoriously inaccurate musket fire ought to strike his target. With luck and the blessing of the One. He felt the stir of magic and sensed the change in Joh that meant Kallista was looking through his eyes. She knew what was happening. They'd have to intercept her on the way up here.

Fox blocked out the crowd noise, which was growing again as people noticed the battle and flowed back into the stands to watch. He tipped his head, aiming all his senses down the barrel of the musket. He could not afford to miss.

Sky was tucked beneath the champion's arm. Leyja stood close, her face in Chani's as she argued. Fox brought the firing hammer back to full cock and slid his finger through the trigger guard. His focus narrowed. He let his breath out slowly and in the quiet before he took it again, he squeezed the trigger.

The explosion roared in his ear, recoil bucking the musket hard against his shoulder. The champion dropped, the back of his head blowing outward. Joh caught Sky before the boy's feet touched ground and tossed him to Night. Night passed him to Fox who had pitched the empty musket back into the corridor where its owner still sprawled. The bodyguards threw all the godmarked over the barrier and followed, just as Habadra Chani screamed and drew a pair of pistols from beneath her robe.

Fox handed Sky back to Joh and appropriated another musket from the justiciar's champion who had come back to find his comrade. Fox spun back into the box and brought the muzzle down as Chani fired her first pistol.

One of the bodyguards yelped and crumpled sideways a moment before the man next to her got his shoulder under her arm and half-carried her out of the box. No time for careful aim. Fox fired an instant before Chani took her second shot. He missed, the musket ball ripping a hole in her sleeve. But so did she.

Fox let the last bodyguard shove him back into the corridor where he paused to hand the musket back to the bewildered champion. "Tell your captain to secure and protect the justiciars. *Now,* before Habadra takes her madness further."

He pelted after the others, bodyguard at his heels. Kallista was waiting with the horses, Obed and Torchay looking a bit befuddled, but no longer attacking anyone. Fox didn't want to think about his own moments of madness. The return of his vision had lessened the effects of the drug, he thought, and the sword through his belly had bled off much of it.

Fox threw himself onto his horse and dragged the bandage off his eyes, tucking it under his sword belt in case he needed it again. Then he held a hand out to Joh. "Give him to me," Fox said, drinking in the sight of the boy in Joh's arms. "Will you ride with me, Sky? We're taking you home."

Sky gave him a wary look. "You were fighting."

"Yes. So we could take you home. Because you're our *son*." Fox turned his hand palm up to the boy. "Will you ride with me?"

"We need to go." Kallista's voice held barely suppressed impatience.

Abruptly, Sky held both arms out to Fox who swung him onto the saddle in front of him. Joh mounted and they rode out of the arena at a fast clip. Fox wrapped one arm around Sky's middle, though such a close hold wasn't truly necessary. He could scarcely believe the boy was theirs. Fox's new vision wasn't good enough to have clearly seen Sky's features while Joh held him, and now, Fox could see only a head full of gold-over-brown curls. But soon, when they were safe behind embassy walls, he could look his fill, find Stone's features in this child. Stone's son, finally home.

Padrey was in the embassy, on his way to deliver another report to Keldrey Reinas, when the whole place burst into uproar. People ran in all directions, some of them heading first one way, then stopping short to turn and run in one completely different. A guard in white-trimmed black ran smack into him, nearly knocking them both down.

"What is it?" Padrey steadied himself and her with a grip on her arms. "What's happening?"

"We've won the trial." The guard grabbed Padrey's arm in return and dragged him along with her. "But Habadra cheated. Her champions' weapons were drugged. Then she tried to take the child, even though we won— Eight against three and we *won*."

"And?" That wasn't all the story, Padrey knew. Couldn't be.

"The Reinasti took the boy back. Now they're on their way here and everyone's called out in case there's trouble. *Everyone*." She shook his arm a bit, giving him a look full of some kind of meaning. "Especially the Tayo Dai."

"Right. O' course." Padrey nodded like he knew what she meant. "What can I do? I'm a spy. A thief."

"You take this." She handed him a wicked dagger from her own belt. "You *have* been going to the training, haven't you?"

"Aye. Yes." When he could, when he wasn't busy counting slaves. Padrey nodded.

"Then you go out there—" She pushed him toward the courtyard outside the family's quarters. "And you make sure no thieves sneak in to steal any more of our treasure."

"Set a thief to catch a thief?" He repeated the old proverb.

"Exactly. Now go." She opened the wide, multipaned window-door and shoved him through it.

Chapter Twenty-Four

Padrey looked round at the bodyguards and soldiers swarming the courtyard and felt more than superfluous. He felt useless. Still, none of those others knew how thieves thought. Padrey slid through the daylight shadows to the tree where he'd first entered the embassy. He leaped, caught hold of a low-hanging branch and swung himself up. This was a thief's only way in. He'd tried for days to find another.

He found himself a perch, dark and shadowy even in the brightening autumn daylight, and took a moment to wonder what sort of treasure he was guarding. More jewels like the one he'd stolen? Gold? Pearls? Or all of it? Wouldn't it be grand to see such a treasure? He didn't want to steal it, nothing like that. He just wanted, rather badly, to *see* it.

Padrey wasn't in his tree long enough to stiffen up when the window-doors were opened and left open after the Reinine came through. She was holding the hand of a small boy dressed in a rust-stained kilt. Most of her ilian followed, save for the three who had fought in the arena today. Padrey assumed they were off cleaning up, changing clothes. He eased farther out on the broad branch where he hid to hear them better.

"I got my kilt dirty." The child's voice was almost too quiet to hear.

"Doesn't matter." The Reinine crouched beside him, making herself small enough to look the boy straight in the eye. "We're going to throw this kilt away. You're our son. Sky Varyl. You'll wear a son's clothes. Adaran clothes."

The boy peeled out of his kilt right there in the courtyard. "My clothes from the jail?"

The Reinine's chuckle sounded a bit choked as she shook her head. "New clothes. Made just for you."

She looked toward the nursery at the same time the banging caught Padrey's attention and he looked too. A chubby brown-haired toddler, the next-to-littlest girl, had apparently spotted her parents through the glass in the window-doors and was not happy about the barrier. She beat on the panes with both open hands, shouting "Mami," at the top of her lungs.

The Reinine laughed. "Do you want to meet your sedili, Sky? Your sister? I don't think we can hold them back much longer."

Her prediction proved correct when one of the bigger boys opened the door and children poured into the courtyard, swarming the adults, staring shyly at the new boy in their midst. After the others had been outside for several ticks, two more children appeared, the two eldest, the Reinine's twins. They ran to their mother where she knelt beside Sky and stopped short, suddenly bashful. Padrey listened hard to hear over the general babble.

The red-haired girl elbowed her fair-haired twin, making faces and pointing at the boy. The blonde poked her sister back, then thrust a bundle at Sky. "We brought your new clothes, so you could put them on right away, Lorynda and me. That's Lorynda. She's my twin."

The girl took back the garment Sky held and gave him another. "Smalls first, silly. Trousers are too scratchy, else. I'm Rozite. I'm your sister, not just your sedil, 'cause my father is your father too."

Sky took the trousers from her and pulled them on over the smallclothes he'd just put on. "Papi Joh taught me to tie," he said. "My father is dead."

"I know." Rozite nodded, her face solemn. "I cry sometimes, 'cause I miss him a lot. You can cry with me if you want."

"Don't cry." Red-haired Lorynda put her arm around her sister. "It makes me sad when you cry, 'cause I miss Papi Stone too. You can have my Papi for your first father. He doesn't have any little boys and no girls besides me. And he already loves you bunches. He said so."

Motion diverted Padrey's attention to the Reinine; she was wiping away tears. Most of the adults were, though Aisse Reinas didn't seem to be bothering. She just let them flow.

Sky poked his head through the neck of his tunic and fought his arms through the sleeves. "My mother is dead too."

"You can have our Mami," Rozite said quickly, as if to keep up with her sister's generosity. "The people wouldn't let her come see you in the jail and it made her mad." She giggled. "Mami said bad words. And she threw a cup so hard she bent it."

The children's laughter at the Reinine's misdeeds was interrupted by the entrance of the morning's champions, transformed into shrieks as most of the children rushed them. Padrey had seen the Reinine's ilian with the children before, enough he could tell them apart and match them with birth parents, but briefly and never in unguarded moments like this. He felt as if he should turn away, grant them what little privacy they could have, but he couldn't. He had to watch.

Torchay Reinas strode to the Reinine, a twin in each arm. Fox Reinas carried his smallest son under his arm while his daughter Niona clung to his back like a monkey. His other son rode his leg until Obed Reinas peeled him loose and tucked him under his free arm, the other already filled with squirming black-haired little boy.

"So." Torchay Reinas set the girls down near the just-dressed boy. "You're giving me away, are you? To this fine lad?"

He bowed with full Adaran court flourish. "I'd be proud to stand as father to you, Sky, and I'm pleased to be finally making your acquaintance." He knelt between the twins and offered his hand. "I'd have come before, but I'm head of the Reinine's bodyguard and I could no' leave my duty for so long."

When Sky gave his hand, the red-haired Reinas used it to draw him in for a careful embrace. "Besides," the bodyguard said with a wink, "it didn't seem quite fair that your Mami Kallista be the *only* one not to meet you. So I waited with her."

"Torchay—" The Reinine touched his shoulder. "Let Fox see."

What was this? Padrey switched his focus to Fox Reinas, only now noticing the way the man stared at his trio of offspring. Fox cupped his daughter's cheek as he gazed another minute, then dropped a kiss on her forehead and turned to their new-found child. *He could see?* What had happened?

"You said you can't see." Sky's voice wasn't suspicious, exactly.

"Today I can. Kallista worked magic and I can see. Not very well, though. You have to be close." Fox Reinas beckoned and slowly Sky stepped nearer, until the Tibran could brush the tousled hair out of the boy's face.

"You look grand in your new clothes," Fox Reinas said. "Like the Reinelle you are. You have your father's eyes . . . and your mother's smile."

"My mother was bad," Sky said. "She killed my father."

"She did a bad thing. She listened to bad people and after a while, she believed what they told her. But when she made you, she wasn't bad. None of those bad things got into you, only the good parts of your mother. She was good when we knew her." He smiled. "And you got the very best parts of your father, who was one of the very best men I've known. And I knew him since we were the same age you are now, so I know. I know you, Sky Varyl, and I am very proud to have you for my son."

"Don't you have boys?"

"I have two, and a girl, and all the rest of this mob." Fox cocked his head, looking at the child. "You don't have to pick. Not today, or ever, if you don't want to. You have five fathers. And four mothers. You are our son. You belong to all of us."

As little Sky hugged the golden-haired Reinas, Padrey had to grab hold of a tree branch to keep himself from falling when understanding smashed into him like one of the Reinine's lightning bolts.

Leaves that would stay green all winter rustled with the violence of his reaction, but fortunately, no one below noticed. Padrey had to crawl back to the main trunk and huddle in the fork of two great branches, it hit him so hard. The treasure he helped to guard was not gold or jewels. It was the children.

Power and wealth meant nothing to these people, except as it could be used to protect the defenseless, to help those who needed it. He had sworn oath to the Reinine because she'd promised to free his family, and he'd meant it.

But still, he'd held a bit of himself back, waiting to see whether she would keep her promise, or forget it when it became inconvenient or unprofitable. He hadn't understood. Not who he had made his oath to, or who she truly served. Now he did, and it made him feel all peculiar inside. It made him want to be part of it, whatever the cost. He wanted what they had.

Kallista watched the nursery servants herd the children away after the chaos some called luncheon. Sky seemed to be fitting in nicely. Meeting Joh and Aisse's son Tigre, just his age, had helped.

She shook her head and turned it to business. "Two things. Send somebody for the embassy's lawyer. We're complaining to the justiciars about those drugged blades. We did get them back home with us, didn't we?"

"The East healer took them," Obed said. "To give to their truthsayer. She thought it would be better for a neutral party to hold them. I believe she obtained five of the weapons."

"Good thinking. We'll ask Nur Naitan to send one to the justiciars but hold back the rest. Second thing." Kallista pushed back from the table to pace. "We have Sky back safe with us. I think it's time we presented the en-Kameral with our demand to free the rest of the slaves."

She thought out loud as she paced. "Viyelle, you and—Obed? Or Joh—or hell, both of them—get with Namida Ambassador and come up with a demand to be presented to the en-Kameral. I'd like it done today to present tomorrow. And Vee—" Kallista caught the prinsipella's gaze. "Don't let Namida soften it. It's a *demand*. If they don't release the slaves, we will take them."

"Both of you, then," Viyelle addressed Obed and Joh. "*Help*." She made a joke of her plea, and chuckling, the men rose from the table to join her.

"My Reinine."

The unexpected voice of a bodyguard just behind her made Kallista jump. She raised an eyebrow in question.

"My Reinine, the embassy guard sends word that justiciars are at the gate with demands."

Her eyebrows went higher and she cocked her head. "What demands, Bodyguard?"

"I do not know, my Reinine. I was not told."

"Well, go back and ask." Kallista's first inclination was to slam the gate on any hint of Daryathi "justice." She might do it yet, but with everything else going on, she would at least find out what they wanted first. *Then* she could slam the gate in their faces. "And tell that lawyer to hurry."

The lawyer arrived before the answer did, a tall, lean gray-haired woman in scholarly white. Kallista was in the midst of explaining what she wanted when Jondi Bodyguard returned.

"The justiciars will address their claims only to 'one Varyl Kallista,' my Reinine." The barest bit of sour mimicry crept into Jondi's voice as he repeated the words.

Kallista sighed. "I'm busy. Let them wait. In the street, preferably. I don't want them on embassy soil."

"*Yes,* my Reinine." Jondi couldn't quite suppress his grin as he went to relay the message.

It took some time before the lawyer had all her questions answered, so that she understood everything. Allanda Vartain was ilias to Namida Ambassador and had studied Daryathi law all the years Namida had been appointed here. Once satisfied, she went with Kallista to the gate. Most of the godmarked trailed along to see what might happen.

Kallista strode up to the iron scrollwork gate that separated the embassy's outer courtyard from the street and stopped, glaring through it at the justiciars on the other side. They looked weary and out of patience. They should be glad the rain had stopped and the air had warmed. Kallista had a none-too-large supply of patience left herself.

"I am Kallista Reinine." She planted her fists on her hips. "My family name is Varyl. What do you want?"

"You have unauthorized possession of the property in question in Case Varyl Kallista against Habadra Chani, one boy Habadra-ti, also known as Sky im-Varyl." They pushed a sheaf of papers through to Kallista who handed them to Allanda.

"The presiding justiciars declared Varyl victorious," Allanda said. "And gave possession of the child Sky to Varyl."

"There has been an appeal. The law states—"

"I don't care what your law states," Kallista interrupted, so angry she was certain steam rose off her skin. "Sky is *ours* and we will not give him up. Your law—"

"Has no jurisdiction within the Adaran embassy." Allanda dared to interrupt Kallista. Probably a good thing.

"This is Adaran soil. He is under Adaran law." She waved the papers. "This appeal claims the trial was invalid because the victors began fighting each other. That does not negate their victory."

"That is a decision for the head court to make. And until that hearing, the property must—"

"The *child*. The son of one of our Adaran Godmarked who was murdered in your city will remain on Adaran soil," Allanda declared. "We will present our answer in due time, along with proof of a crime committed by Habadra that caused the situation at the end of the trial. The Habadra perverted the course of justice in this matter, and she *is* under Daryathi law."

With a whirl of white robes, Allanda spun and walked away, leaving Kallista to stare after her. She followed, quick as she could gather herself, not wanting to weaken the impression left by the lawyer.

Kallista beckoned to the embassy captain when she reached the inner gate. "I know your forces are stretched thin, but tighten security as much as you can. No one but our people in or out. Don't let any Daryathi through these gates for any reason whatsoever. Get with Captain Kargyll and see what you can do."

"Yes, my Reinine."

When Kallista neared the family quarters, she could hear Namida Ambassador "discussing" with Viyelle and Obed the document to be presented to the en-Kameral. The whole district could likely hear them. So of course, Kallista had to open the door and see what the trouble was. Allanda rolled her eyes and went off to compose her own documents. Fox, Leyja and Aisse had business of their own, but Torchay stayed to join the fun.

Kallista rather liked the stark, two-sentence demand Viyelle came up with. "Release all of the Adaran slaves and the offspring of any Adaran slaves to the Reinine of all Adara. If you do not release them of your own accord with one week of this reading, Adara will take them from you."

Namida, being the diplomat she was, did not approve. She wanted flowery words and euphemisms like "bond servant," skirting around the target before finally taking aim. Only because Obed agreed that an oblique approach might possibly be more effective did Kallista relent.

It took the rest of the afternoon to hammer out something satisfactory to all. The statement took an unconscionably long time getting there, but it made the same point as Viyelle's original version. Namida took Joh's clean copy off to be copied again for the Reinine's seal. It would be handed over to the en-Kameral after Namida's reading. They had perhaps half a chime left to spend with the children before dinner.

Obed stood behind their new son, stopping the ball when it got past him, which was most every time Omri threw it. Even sitting in Kallista's lap, with her help in the throwing, Omri sent it flying in bizarre directions. Not that it mattered. Sky wasn't any better at the catching, even when the ball came toward him. The boys didn't care. They laughed like lunatics whatever happened. It made Obed laugh too.

The whole family was gathered to play. Torchay had the trio of oldest girls all crowded onto his lap while he read to them. Keldrey made faces at their littlest in Aisse's arms, playing peekaboo. The rest of the family growled and wrestled and chased each other. Playing bears, Obed thought. Joh made a fine bear.

These were the moments he lived for, what he had endured all those years in the skola to have. Aisse watched him over her daughter's head, a familiar look in her eye. She wanted another child. His, or Torchay's. She'd admitted it, made no apology for it. And as Obed put out a foot to stop the ball yet again, he realized that he wanted to give Aisse what she wanted. Because he loved her.

Not the same way he loved Kallista, but the way he loved Aisse. Which was different from the way he loved Viyelle, and the way he loved Leyja, and all the rest of them.

How could he think Kallista was all he had when he was at this moment looking at all his riches? And how could he expect to be the only one she loved when she was not his only love?

But Obed could tell Kallista still worried about what had happened during the trial, when he and Torchay had turned on each other. She wanted to talk, but they didn't have a chance until late, after they had retreated to their sleeping room for the night.

"What happened?" Kallista pulled off her soft-topped boots and tossed them toward the wardrobe. "In the arena. What—"

"The Habadras' blades were drugged." Torchay paused, his tunic trapping his arms, only half off. "Weren't they?"

"Yes, but they were drugs, not magic." Kallista frowned, reasoning her way through what she had seen. "It's possible they were meant to drive you to fight each other, but I don't know how Chani could have predicted that. The drugs mimicked natural bodily functions too well. They interfered with your reasoning power, your control over your emotions. They also caused your heart to race wildly. I think, if you had not stopped when you did, your hearts might have burst from the strain."

"But we did stop." Obed kissed her forehead. "Our hearts did not burst. You cleaned the drugs from us. We're fine."

"Except for being marked up a bit." Torchay winked at her.

Kallista didn't wink back, though she knew he wanted it. Their fight worried her too much. "But why did you *start*? Do you really hate each other so much? If the drugs ate away your self-control, then—" She bit her lip, fighting tears. "I can't force you to be together like this if that's how you truly feel."

"*No.*" Obed's cry came a breath ahead of Torchay's denial. Obed took her in his arms, then opened them to allow Torchay in, to envelop her between them.

"Yes, there is a rivalry between us," Torchay admitted. "We can't either of us let the other get half a step ahead. In anything. And jealousy—Goddess, I was so sick with it when he had your bed and I didn't. Even after, even now, it makes me sick to think of it. But I couldn't admit it, even to myself, until Obed bashed me over the head with it. I had to be the perfect bodyguard, the perfect ilias."

Obed brushed back Kallista's hair, kissed each of her eyelids. "I was raised to believe that it is possible to love only one other, and that all else is sham. I learned better in Adara, but coming back here . . . I forgot what I had learned. And Torchay was so perfect it drove me to madness. What need could you have of me when he can even follow you into the spirit world and bring you back?"

Kallista swallowed down the tears choking her throat. "So I was right. You do hate each other."

"*No.*" Both of them spoke at once.

"When you took away the drugs," Obed said, "I threw away my sword. I would not fight. How can I be jealous when I myself love you *and* Aisse and Viyelle and Leyja? How can I say you should not love Torchay?"

"It was the drugs, Kallista." Torchay turned her to face him. "Just the drugs. When they were gone, I couldn't kill him. Beat that pretty face bloody, perhaps, but no' kill him."

"Wait. You mean while you were still in the arena?" Kallista twisted so she could see both of them at once. "But the drugs *weren't* gone then. I could barely touch them, much less sweep them away, until you started drinking the water. The water allowed me to start ridding you of them. The healer-naitan discovered it while she took care of Fox."

Torchay lifted an eyebrow as he looked at Obed. "We were still drugged."

"So truly, in your heart of hearts, you do *not* want to kill me," Obed said thoughtfully.

Torchay's eyes narrowed. "But you want me to."

"I *dare* you to." Obed's teeth flashed in a wicked smile. "It is not at all the same thing."

Kallista made a disgusted noise. "You sound like my brother-sedili."

"But we're no'." Torchay nuzzled the sensitive spot under her ear. "We're your iliasti." He kissed her cheek and stepped out of the three sided embrace. "And now, I'll go see whether Aisse and Leyja have room for a fourth. You two haven't made love alone together since we've been here. I think it's time—"

"No." Obed grabbed Torchay's wrist. "You are not playing Perfect Reinas again. You haven't been alone with her either."

"Excuse me." Kallista put her hand up. "When did I become invisible?"

"Never." Obed leaned forward to kiss her. "You are with us even when you are not."

Kallista felt a shiver of magic along his link as his lips touched hers, made softer, warmer by the scritch of his day's beard surrounding them. She opened to him, deepened the kiss, abandoned herself to the wonder of holding him, kissing him, when she thought she might have lost him forever.

Obed pulled away, left her reaching for him until he turned her round, urged her into Torchay's arms. She didn't need urging. Kallista wrapped her arms around her other ilias, tangled her hands in his tumble of red curls and demanded a matching response to her needy kiss.

"Don't leave me," she murmured into his mouth. "Don't you ever leave me."

She stretched an arm behind her and caught a handful of Obed's loose black waves to pull him in. "Either one of you. Don't ever scare me like this again."

She leaned back and twisted to kiss Obed as Torchay kissed his way down to her breasts. Somehow, by means of all-too-mortal magic, they were in the bed together, naked, while true magic whispered through their links.

"Love me." Kallista hooked a leg over Torchay's hip, opening herself to him.

"Always. Forever." He surged inside her with a quiet groan.

Against her back, Obed shifted as if to move away. Kallista clutched at his rough-haired leg. "No. You love me too."

"You know I do," he breathed into her ear. "Always. Forever."

"Then love me now." She needed him here with her, a part of her as Torchay was.

"There's no room."

"Then make room." She said it without quite knowing what she meant by it, knowing only that she needed them both, now.

She sensed the two men exchanging a look past her, then Obed was pushing his way inside her too, stretching her wide, making room for himself as she'd bid him. Magic surged through the link from Torchay, leaving her slick with arousal.

"How do you do that?" Kallista gasped as Torchay pulled her leg higher over his hip, opening her wider. "How do you send me magic when I don't call it?"

"Don't know exactly. It works?"

The men began to thrust in unison, leaving Kallista unable to reply. She grasped the magic she'd been given and sent it rippling between them.

It was awkward, almost uncomfortable to have both of them shoving inside her at once, and it was so erotic it made her tremble. She let the magic go, unable to hold it, much less control it. The sensations bleeding through the link were not the magic. She could feel what they felt, sense how every slide of flesh against flesh against flesh aroused each of them. Intense. Outrageous. Uncontrollable.

She grabbed for the magic in a too-late bid to hold out longer, and kicked them all into cascading, screaming climax.

Eons passed before she could move again, or perhaps just a moment. Kallista rolled to her back and hooked an arm around each man's neck, drawing them in until their faces touched hers.

"I love you." She kissed Torchay. "And I love you." She kissed Obed. "Please don't force me to choose. I can't. I couldn't bear to lose either one of you, and I know our other iliasti feel the same."

"We couldn't bear to lose you either." Torchay kissed her cheek. "And I've been thinking."

Kallista gave him a wary look. "That sounds ominous."

"It's not. At least I don't think so." He sat up and folded his legs. "I want you to teach Obed how to go to the dreamscape and back. If something happens and you get trapped there again, I don't like being the only one who can follow. It would be better if you could teach all of us to do it."

"Now?" She could feel weariness eating away her strength.

"Obed now, yes, I—I'm afraid to wait. Now we've got Sky back and the drugged swords failed to take any more godmarked from you, the demons could be desperate enough to attack directly. I don't want you dreaming without at least two of us able to come after you."

He was right. And two of them could help each other if need be. "Go fetch Jondi," she said. "Or whoever's on duty. Tell him what we're doing, to watch without interfering unless the sun rises and we still haven't woken. Then he's to fetch the godmarked and Gweric. When you've done that, come back and lie down." Kallista patted the empty pillow beside her.

Torchay eyed her with suspicion. "I can watch."

"You're coming with us. You need the practice." Kallista looked at Obed as Torchay padded naked to the door. "We didn't ask whether you wanted to learn this, did we?"

"Whatever you ask, you know I will do it, if I can." He smiled as he brought her hand up to kiss her fingers. "And I agree. I should know how to do this. I want to know." A shadow crossed his face. "But I fear I will not be able to learn."

"You will. It doesn't require magic, and our link will make it easier."

Leaving the night guard just inside the door, Torchay returned and stretched out next to Kallista, drawing the bedcover to his neck. She found his hand beneath it and twined her fingers with his, her other hand still clasped in Obed's.

"Listen to your heartbeat." She closed her eyes. "Feel your breath whisper in and out of your chest, your blood pulse through each part of your body. Sense each part of your physical self. Know it. Accept it. Love it."

Kallista sank deeper into her own body, sensing her men settle solid into theirs. "This is home," she said. "Where you belong. It will be here waiting for you when you return. Now that you have anchored yourself, you can let go. Body and spirit are one whole, but spirit can leave for a short time without harm. Listen to my heartbeat now, and step out."

She wanted to help them, to take that step with them, for them, but they had to be able to do it on their own. So she sat in the dreamscape, watching anxiously.

After a moment, Torchay exhaled and bobbed up into the dreamfog beside her, a cork rising to the surface. "That was easier than last time." He looked around curiously. "Is it always like this?"

"When you've got yourself properly anchored, yes." Kallista watched Obed struggle. "Don't wander off."

Torchay gave her a sour look. "What sort of bodyguard do you think I am?"

Kallista ignored him, satisfied he would stay close, and focused her attention on Obed. "Relax," she whispered. "Let go. Gain control by giving it up."

He tensed, then his lips moved as if he repeated some meditation. His body visibly relaxed. Kallista felt a tug on his link, and Obed slipped out of his body and into the dreamscape.

"See?" Kallista hugged him tight. "Not so hard after all. Now, to get yourself back."

"But I just got here." Obed turned in a circle, staring at the multi-colored glows flaring within the gray mist.

"Practice first. Explore later. Back you go." She swatted Torchay's backside and with a wink, he dove back into his body.

Obed stepped down with more dignity, settling in without trouble. Kallista had them do it twice more, up and back, before she declared them proficient.

"What are the colors?" Obed reached for an azure bubble floating by. It dodged his touch, bobbing higher out of reach.

"I don't know. Other people's dreams?" Kallista shrugged. "My own dreaming is enough to deal with."

"Are we dreaming now?" Torchay had clothed and armed his dreamself, apparently deciding that if he played the part of bodyguard, he ought to look like one.

"Not exactly. When we dream, a smaller part of ourselves comes here." Kallista surveyed the dreamscape, itching to search it for demons. But she would not drag her magicless iliasti after her. Not in this place.

"What is that?" Obed pointed.

Not far from where they stood, a golden glow speared through the mist, growing in brightness until they had to hide their eyes from its brilliance. When it faded enough to see, the light had become a glowing tendril, groping blindly in the dreamscape as if looking for an anchor. It called to Kallista, and she eased closer. She reached for it, but her hand closed on nothing. The slender thread seemed to dissolve.

"What is it?" Torchay asked this time, staring in wonder.

Kallista started to shake her head, then stopped as the possible answer hit her. *"Hurry!"*

She didn't wait for them, flying back to her body. The men scrambled after, stumbling as they followed her out of the bed.

"Wait!" Torchay cried. *"Stop."*

She couldn't. Without pausing to grab her houserobe, or anything else, Kallista ran naked through the embassy, her nightguards trotting impassively after her. Her iliasti staggered behind, holding each other up as if they hadn't quite got themselves shoved all the way back down to their feet.

"Damn it, Kallista," Torchay shouted. "What's going on?"

Elation bubbled through her and she spun in a celebratory circle, allowing the men to catch up. "I know what we saw. Keldrey's been marked!"

Chapter Twenty-Five

Kallista threw her arms around Torchay and Obed and even the startled bodyguards, hugging them each in turn, before darting away again. She threw open the door to the room where Viyelle slept with Joh and now Keldrey too, snoring in his place nearest the wall. It brought Kallista up short a moment. Wouldn't he have been awake for his marking?

She crawled onto the bed and up his blanket-covered form, not bothering to keep from waking the other two sleepers. "Keldrey," she crooned. "Darling Kel, kiss me."

"Mmm." He obeyed before he came fully awake, pursing his lips, bringing up his hand to the back of her head to hold her as he deepened the kiss. The kiss that was just a kiss.

On the verge of tears, her elation crumbled into despair, Kallista struggled to free herself. Jerking out of Keldrey's hold, she swiped her hand across her mouth as she sank back onto her heels. *It couldn't be.*

"Hey," Keldrey protested. "That's not right. To come in here while I'm sleeping all peaceful-like and kiss me and get me all hot and stand-up, and then push me away like that." He reached for Kallista and she batted his hand away.

Then she reached for it. Maybe she hadn't done it right. "You have to be marked," she muttered, clasping his hand between both of hers. *"I need you to be marked."*

Her agitation growing, she grabbed Keldrey's head and pulled him forward, down, till he almost lay in her lap, searching for the rose-shaped mark on the back of his neck, the one that had to be there. And wasn't.

"Why aren't you marked?" She flew at him in a rage.

Shock held Torchay motionless for too long while Kallista rained openhanded blows down on Keldrey, following as he tried to retreat. This wasn't like her. Surely even delayed grief couldn't have sent her this far out of control.

She screamed incoherently in her attack. Keldrey shouted at her, telling her to stop. Joh swept Viyelle out of harm's way. Obed caught Kallista's flailing arms and pinned them to her body, but couldn't stop her kicking at Keldrey as he lifted her off the bed. Too late, Torchay came to help, imprisoning her in the houserobe he'd thought to bring, taking her from Obed.

"What in all the seven bloody hells is going on?" Keldrey touched his split lip and frowned at the blood he found.

"*Kallista.*" Torchay shook her gently. She'd stopped screaming finally, but the weeping didn't reassure him.

"She thought you'd been marked," Obed said.

"I gathered that." Keldrey looked at the others in the room. "You okay, Vee?" He crawled from the bed and went to use his bodyguard's healer training to check on her.

"Fine. Never better." Viyelle turned Keldrey's face to the lamp Joh had lit. "Is your lip the worst of it?"

"You don't understand," Obed said. "We saw it. The marking. Or we saw something." He explained what they had been doing and what they had seen while Torchay tried to get Kallista to talk to him, to do anything other than weep. What was wrong with her?

"If it wasn't me being marked, which obviously it wasn't 'cause I ain't marked, am I? Then what was it?"

"I don't know." Obed shook his head.

"Kallista? Look at me, love." Torchay tipped her face up, lifted her eyelids. "Help us out here. What did we see?"

She shook her head, tears still flowing, silently, uncontrollably. "I need him to be marked, Torchay."

"I know." He tucked her head against his shoulder, holding her close, and gave Keldrey a helpless look. Torchay didn't know what to do for her. Maybe the other man did.

"What if . . ." Joh began and all eyes turned his way. He didn't finish. He was watching Kallista. "I have a thought," he said. "But I don't think our ilias will like it."

Kallista pushed out of Torchay's embrace and turned on Joh, eyes blazing. "What?" she demanded, shoving her arms into the sleeves of her robe. "What is your thought? What won't I like?"

"Kallista—" Torchay caught her arm and she threw him off. This wasn't what he'd had in mind when he asked for a response. Her whiplash moods worried him.

"*Kallista.*" Keldrey stepped between her and Joh.

"Oh for—" She rolled her eyes. "I'm not going to hurt him."

"You'll excuse us if we don't exactly trust your word right now." Keldrey pushed his swollen lip out farther.

"Fine." She backed up, then her eyes filled with sudden tears that spilled over as she looked at their oldest ilias. "I'm sorry," she whispered. "I'm so sorry, Kel."

"I've had worse. Doubtless will again." Keldrey pulled her into a forgiving hug, then kept his arms around her as he nodded to Joh. "Tell us."

Joh cleared his throat. "What if it *was* a godmarking you saw? What if someone other than Keldrey was marked?"

"What? No!" Kallista began to struggle in Keldrey's grip. "*No.* Keldrey's ilias. He's one of us. I won't have a stranger in Stone's place!"

Oh Goddess, not this. Torchay's heart broke for her, for all of them. Hadn't they endured enough pain?

Kallista fought so hard, Torchay feared she would hurt herself, but Keldrey's hold never slipped. It never would.

"Take her back to our room," Torchay felt thick-headed. His worry for Kallista made it impossible to think, not good for a bodyguard. "I'll get the poppy syrup. Perhaps if she sleeps—"

"Perhaps we should search," Fox said. "In case Joh's thought is correct. Or in case it is not. You saw *something* in the dream world. Perhaps we should try to find it."

"Search the embassy," Obed said. "What we saw was close."

"I'll get it started." Fox tied a scarf over his eyes. He had kept the delicate strip of red silk with him since the arena, tied round his upper arm when it wasn't over his new-seeing eyes. He claimed it helped him focus his *knowing*.

The three in the doorway backed up to let Keldrey through with his struggling burden. Torchay ran to collect the medicine from his room, then caught up with Kallista as Kel crashed over onto the mattress with her. Obed had to pry open her mouth while Keldrey pinned her down and Torchay poured the syrup down her throat. Keldrey held on until the drug did its work and soothed her into sodden sleep.

Most of the tension leaked out of Torchay when Kallista finally stilled. The problem remained to be dealt with later, but for now, she could rest. Perhaps the sleep would help her accept the situation, whatever it might be.

"*Goddess*," Obed groaned.

That brought Torchay's head up to meet his ilias's gaze across the bed. Torchay nodded. Thank the One Kallista had taught them both dreamwalking in time.

With a sigh, Torchay turned to Keldrey who was sitting on the bed next to Kallista, brushing back her hair with his fingertips. "Good," Torchay said. "I don't think we should leave her alone. She always does better with someone beside her, touching her."

"You want *me* to stay?" Keldrey sounded surprised.

Torchay considered, his shoulders shifting in discomfort. "Aye, I do. You need to be here when she wakes. She needs to handle it, you not being marked."

Kel had as much medical training as he did. Torchay didn't have to stay. She didn't need both of them. He stretched his shoulders again. "I can't settle. I can't—I need to move. *Do* something. Find out what happened." He looked at Keldrey, his burly arm draped across Kallista's waist. "Obed, are you staying?"

"Do you truly think it was a marking we saw? That it is someone else?" Obed held Torchay's gaze, as if asking him to deny it.

He couldn't. Torchay shook his head. "I don't know. I don't even know what to hope for. We need our ninth. Kallista's right about that. She canno' face these demons without all nine. But if it's no' Keldrey—" Torchay met Obed's bleak expression, knowing his own face looked much the same.

Obed beat him out the door. Torchay turned the other way. He loped down the corridor, heading generally for Viyelle's room, though he didn't truly expect to find anyone there. Both Vee and Joh would be out searching. Torchay hadn't gone far when he saw one of the oathsworn, a Tayo Dai wandering as if lost.

"Padrey," Torchay called as soon as he recognized him.

The young thief didn't answer. Didn't seem to hear.

"*Padrey.*" Torchay caught his shoulder, turned him round.

Awareness rose slowly in Padrey's gray-blue eyes, and he blinked. "Reinas."

Dread crawled under Torchay's skin. "What are you doing here?"

"Oh." Padrey blinked again. He looked around as if surprised to find himself where he stood. "Erm— Right. Sorry. I should go."

"Oathsworn, do you know why you came here? Do you remember?"

"I—" The young man's forehead creased. "No, Reinas."

Torchay let go a heavy sigh. He had been afraid of this, had been waiting for it since Joh put forth his theory. Not Padrey, necessarily, but someone. "Come here, lad. Tip your head. Let me see your neck."

"My—?" Padrey frowned, suspicion in every line of his body. "Why?"

"Just do it. You are Tayo Dai, are you not?"

"Yes, Reinas." Padrey bowed his head.

Torchay brushed aside the gold brown hair straggling over Padrey's neck and sighed again. The mark was there, identical to the one on the other seven of Kallista's godmarked. Kallista would not be pleased. Nor would Leyja, who had barely moved from outright loathing of the man to grudging tolerance.

"Welcome to the family, lad." Torchay clapped him on the back and propelled him forward. "I hope you don't regret it."

"Wait. What are you talking about?" Padrey dragged his feet, trying to slow down.

Torchay kept him moving. "You're not Tayo Dai any more."

"You're kicking me out? Why? I didn't do anything?"

"Ah, but you did. And you haven't been kicked out." Torchay's smile felt grim. "You've been promoted."

"To what?" Padrey didn't look as if he wanted any promotion. Too bad.

"To Godmarked."

"I— What?" Padrey broke free to stare at Torchay in shock. "You're mad."

"Afraid not." Torchay caught the young man's arm and bore him along again. He glimpsed a flutter of red in the corridor beyond and called out. *"Aisse."*

She popped back around the column where she'd vanished, face wrapped in question.

"I've found what we're looking for. Tell the others. Gather in Kallista's room."

Aisse grimaced. "Oh dear. Leyja won't be happy."

"Hope for the best. I'll see you there."

"Wait, *wait* a minute." Padrey struggled against Torchay's grip. "I don't understand. What were you looking for?"

"You, apparently." Torchay felt weary to his bones and beyond. "I'll explain once we're all together."

"In the Reinine's— *Now?*" Padrey fought to a standstill.

"Aye." Torchay let go. He was tired of dragging the man. He was just flat tired. "It's been a long day for all of us. Will you just come? Without balking, without arguing? We can explain what's happened, what needs to happen next, and then we can all get some rest. All right? Will you do that much?"

"Yeah, all right. I can do that." Padrey trailed at Torchay's elbow as he started off again. Padrey didn't argue, but he wasn't silent. He spoke, barely loud enough to be heard. "The Reinine's own room? *Me?*"

Padrey tried to hang back when they reached their destination, quailing at the thought of entering the Reinine's private chamber, but Torchay Reinas, the Tayo, pushed him through the door. The Reinine herself was there, in the bed *asleep,* with Keldrey Reinas stretched out beside her, playing with her hair. It made Padrey even more uncomfortable. He did *not* belong here. But he didn't think the Tayo would let him leave. He sidled into a corner, hoping to escape notice.

It didn't work. All the other Reinasti stared openly at him as they entered the room. Padrey folded his arms, hunched his shoulders, trying to make himself invisible—or at least smaller. It didn't help that he couldn't stop watching the Reinine. She drew him, moth to flame, and he had no doubt he would be crisped black if he came close enough to touch. He had to fist his hands against the urge to cross the room.

Leyja Reinas was the last to arrive, stalking through the door, shoving it shut so hard that Fox Reinas got his fingers slammed when he caught it to keep it from banging.

"What?" She glared around the room at her mates. Then she spotted Padrey fidgeting in his corner. "What is *he* doing here?"

She went pale so suddenly, both Fox and Torchay Reinas jumped to steady her. "No," she whispered, staring at Padrey with horror. "*No.*"

Padrey edged toward the door. "Why don't—I'll just go."

"*Stay,*" the Tayo ordered.

Padrey stayed, but he didn't like it. Well, he did. It felt right being near the Reinine like this, but he didn't belong here. He was her spy, nothing more. He was a reformed—mostly—thief, an ex-slave. A grubby trader's boy.

"Show them your neck." Torchay Reinas touched Padrey's shoulder with surprising gentleness, urging him to turn, lower his head.

They all came to look, the ones not sleeping. Even Keldrey Reinas got off the bed and looked. Some of them touched, making Padrey shudder. When they'd finished, Torchay Reinas rested his hand on Padrey's shoulder. Padrey glanced up at him, but the scarlet-haired Reinas watched his mates. "You all saw it."

They all nodded, their expressions grim or resigned or—did Aisse Reinas look relieved?

"But—" Padrey whispered to the man beside him. "What is it? What did you see? What does it mean?"

Torchay Reinas turned his attention to Padrey who had to stiffen his spine not to shrink at that regard. "Sorry, lad. I know this must be confusing to you."

He gestured Padrey into a chair. Thank the One Padrey had on the new clothes they'd given him or he'd fear getting the delicate upholstery dirty. He perched on the edge, crossing his arms in a self-protective gesture. It wasn't good for a thief, or a spy, to be the center of attention.

The others—the *Reinasti of Adara* for the One's sake—disposed themselves around the room, in chairs or the fat round cushioned footstool or on the bed with the Reinine. Torchay Reinas pulled a chair close to Padrey's, but rather than sit in it, he went down to one knee. Padrey would have popped to his feet in protest, save for the Reinas's hand holding him down.

"Don't argue. Look." The Tayo bowed his neck and pulled his loose, shoulder-length hair aside to reveal a raised, red birthmark on the back of his neck. A mark that resembled the stylized rose in the center of the One's compass rose symbol.

"That is the godmark." Torchay Reinas slid into his chair and shook back his hair, "Kallista's is different, but all of us—" He indicated his fellow Reinasti. "All of us have a mark just like it." He touched the back of his neck, then touched Padrey in the same place. "And now, you do too."

Padrey began to shake, crossing his arms tighter to keep it from showing. "Wh-what does it mean?"

"You're one of us now." Aisse Reinas smiled at him. At *him*. She rose from Fox Reinas's lap and came to take Padrey's face between her hands. She kissed him. Right on the mouth.

Too stunned to react, Padrey could only stare and blink as she released him and sat back on her heels.

"Go easy, Aisse." Torchay Reinas smiled at her. "I think it's going to take him a while to grab hold of all this."

"What it means," Obed Reinas said, "is that the One has marked you, set you apart and poured into you *magic* for the Godstruck—Kallista—to call and use in the service of the One. We have come to Daryath to destroy demons. And now you have become an essential part of that task."

"I—" Padrey blinked again as inside him, something seemed to resonate to the dedicat-Reinas's words, deeper and stronger than the thing he had felt when he first saw the Reinine. Something that said this was right. This was his new purpose. "Good." He nodded his head once, accepting the role. *"Good."*

"He's a *thief*," Leyja Reinas burst out.

"And I'm a murderer," Joh Reinas retorted, surprising Padrey. Shocking him. The tall quiet man, a murderer? "Or I would have been, if not for Kallista's magic."

"You didn't intend murder—" Leyja Reinas began.

"I'm just saying," Joh interrupted her. "He's no worse—"

"*Enough.*" Obed Reinas cut across the threatened argument.

"It's done." Aisse Reinas rose gracefully to her feet. "The One has accepted what he offered and now it is for us to accept this gift. Padrey has the magic Kallista needs. You've seen her struggle. You know how it tires her."

"We don't need to fight you too, Leyley." Torchay Reinas sounded as if the weight of the world rested on his shoulders.

Leyley? Padrey eyed the warrior woman, but she didn't react to the silly name. Then he paused. Had the Tayo said—

"Torchay Reinas." Padrey ducked his head when the man swung toward him, but kept talking. "Did you say—*too?* What—?"

The Tayo sighed. He'd been sighing a lot. "The Reinine—"

"She still grieves," Obed Reinas said. "We had our nine, the number needed to complete her magic, to make it whole so she could face these demons. When Stone was murdered—" He seemed to lose his train of thought, gazing down at the Reinine, stroking his fingers along her face.

"When Stone died, it shattered the magic," Fox Reinas said. "And it broke her heart."

"Broke all our hearts." Tears streamed down Viyelle Reinas's face. The others went to her, put their arms around her, wiped away the tears.

"She's no' healed." With a last touch of Viyelle's cheek, Torchay Reinas walked to the bed to gaze down at the Reinine. "And I hate to say it, lad, but she's no' likely to welcome you. I don't know what she'll do when she sees your mark." He lifted his head, turned his bleak gaze on Padrey, who shivered.

"Couldn't we just—" Aisse gestured between the ex-thief and the Reinine. "Take care of it now? While she's sleeping? Let him touch her and bind the magic?"

"And that wouldn't fire her temper, would it? Not at all." Keldrey Reinas's sarcasm came through clear even to Padrey.

"Besides," Joh Reinas spoke up. "Who's to say it would work? Could be she has to be conscious for the binding to work."

"Binding?" Padrey hoped someone might hear him and explain.

"She has to touch you," Aisse Reinas said. "Skin to skin, so the magic can join, so her magic can call yours. Once she touches you, you won't be able to move more than ten paces from her for a few weeks. Until the link matures and she can call your magic without touching you."

"What happens if I get too far away?" This was beginning to sound too complicated for Padrey.

"You collapse." The Tayo clapped Padrey on the shoulder. "But not to worry. We've gone through this eight times already, and until the magic touches—yours to hers—you don't have to worry about any collapsing."

"Just going mad." Joh Reinas spoke so softly, Padrey almost didn't hear. "The magic pulls at you, pulling you to her."

"Mad?" Padrey twisted round to look at him. He didn't like the sound of that either, not at all.

Torchay Reinas glared at his ilias, speaking through clenched teeth. "Only if the binding is delayed too long."

"*Mad,*" Padrey repeated. "How long is too long?"

Fox Reinas laughed as he strolled over to clap Padrey on the shoulder. Padrey's shoulders stung from all the clapping. "Relax, ilias," Fox said. "You've got at least a week, and I doubt the demons will give us that long. Once it's done, we get to fight demons, and likely the rest of Daryath too."

Padrey struggled to sort through all the impossibilities he'd just been told. "Wait—*ilias?*"

"It's late." The Tayo held up both hands, forestalling any more revelations. "Some of us have spent the past two days in the arena. We can't do anything else until Kallista's awake. I suggest we all try to get some sleep and finish this in the morning. Aisse, do you know where we can get a cot for Padrey?"

"Why don't I just go back to my room?" Padrey pointed toward the door and the room beyond it he shared with Gweric.

"You're godmarked. We can't afford to lose you now you're finally here," the Tayo said. "I want you well guarded. You'll be bound soon enough and you'll have to stay close. May as well begin tonight."

Surely they didn't mean for him to—but apparently they did. Servants brought in a narrow cot like the one in the quarters Padrey shared with Gweric. Much nicer than the pallet in his old attic. They set it up there, right in the Reinine's room, and made it up with piles of pillows and soft blankets. He shouldn't be in here. But when he tried to walk away, to step outside the door and leave, he couldn't make himself do it.

Or the magic wouldn't let him. Joh had said the magic pulled him to her. Padrey's muscles locked up, shaking violently. His stomach churned, so raw he feared emptying it all over the Tayo's bare narrow feet.

"Don't fight it, lad." Torchay Reinas led him to the cot and pushed him down. "And don't let this Reinine business get your hair on too tight. She's no' been Reinine but a few years now. She's been an army naitan most of her life. We're none of us so very grand. Except maybe Keldrey and Leyja, who were bodyguards and Reinasti to the Reinine that was before."

"Leyja Reinas hates me." *Goddess,* could he sound more pathetic? The Tayo had hold of Padrey's feet, pulling off his boots. "Stop." Padrey struggled, but didn't have the strength to break free. "That's not right. You shouldn't—"

"*You* shouldn't." Torchay Reinas pushed Padrey back down with one hand. "We're all godmarked here, but you're the new one. And *I'm* the Tayo. So do what I tell you. Lay yourself down, get some sleep and we'll finish this in the morning."

It was obviously no use trying to talk sense to anyone tonight. And Padrey's head did hurt. Stomach too, though it felt better now he was still. "All right, fine." He turned on his side and punched a pillow into submission.

"Keldrey, Obed, do you need me here?" The Tayo stood.

The tattooed Reinas shook his head. "Our new godmarked will not give us any trouble."

"Right then. I'm off." Torchay Reinas gathered up a small kit. "Kel can't sleep anywhere without taking up all the room. I'll be with Vee and Joh—she needs someone on her other side."

Padrey closed his eyes, determined not to see or hear anything that was none of his business. Yes, he had watched from the tree, but that was in the embassy courtyard, where anyone passing could see. This was *private*. He knew the difference. Sleep caught him before he knew anything more.

Kallista opened her eyes to see Keldrey's solemn gaze staring back at her.

"How you feeling?" He brushed back her hair with his long fingers, incongruous given his otherwise stocky build.

Daylight filtered through the sheer curtains over the doors to the courtyard. Bright, sunshiny daylight, not pinkish-gray early dawnlight. Kallista shoved Keldrey's arm up toward the pillows so she could lay her head on it. When she was snuggled in, comfortable and safe, she took inventory. How *did* she feel?

Groggy, not quite ready to wake up, for one thing. She yawned and pulled his other arm around her. Physically, she was tired and hungry. She'd heaved a great pile of magic around yesterday and it took a toll on her physical reserves. Her metaphysical muscles were tired as well, but not aching, as they would have been not so long ago. She was getting stronger. A few of her twinges made her smile and wriggle a bit closer to Keldrey.

"K'lista?" Keldrey kissed her forehead. "Are you awake?"

She hummed a little in her throat and let her hand slide down his naked chest to curl around another naked part of him. "Do I have to be?"

She could feel his smile against her face as he removed her hand. He pinned it against the pillows when he rolled above her.

"No." The smile sounded in his voice. "Not just yet. Not if you don't want to be."

She made a place for him. "I don't. Love me, Kel."

"Is that what you really want?"

"Yes." Kallista hooked a heel around one of his heavy thighs, curling her hips in an attempt to bring him inside.

"Even if I'm not marked? Even if I'm *never* marked?"

Her eyes flew open and she stared into his amber-flecked eyes, his expression serious, almost grim. She wanted to touch him but he'd trapped both her hands under his. She strained to lift her head and he brought himself down, let her give him the kiss she wanted. "Don't think like that," she said. "It will happen. Give it time."

"What if it don't?"

Tears gathered and she fought to keep them from escaping. "It *will*, Keldrey. I know it will."

He looked away, his mouth tightening, expression going hard. *"But what if it don't?"* He turned back, flaying her with his gaze. "Am I out? Done up? Finished? Cast off?"

"Oh Goddess, this is about last night, isn't it?" Kallista struggled to free her hands, and after a moment, Keldrey let go.

He shifted as if to move off her and she tightened her legs around him, threw her arms around his neck and held on. The stupid tears got away from her, but Keldrey didn't.

"I'm sorry. I'm *so* sorry." She repeated it again and again until some of the tension left him. Not all of it, but some. Enough that she thought he'd decided to stay.

"I shouldn't have done that. I never meant to hurt you." Kallista dared loosen her hold on his neck enough to pull back and look him in the eye.

"No, you shouldn't have," Keldrey agreed. "But you did. An' I'm not talkin' about my lip."

Goddess, he was going to make her talk about it. He was worse than Torchay about "clearing the air." Keldrey never let her get away with anything either.

"I been part o' this ilian for more than six years now, and I never minded bein' the only one not marked. It's come in handy now an' again, especially here. I told you I'm willing to take the mark. I offered. A hundred times, I've offered. A thousand. Kallista, I will do *anything,* I will give *everything I have* to protect this family. Up to and including my life.

"But, after so long with nothing happening, I got to accept the fact that my future prob'ly won't include a mark. I need to know if you can accept that too." He paused, gazing into her eyes a long moment before looking away to clear his throat.

He swallowed down some emotion, his throat bobbing with the effort it took, before he looked back at her, determination in every line of his face. "I gotta know, Kallista. Do you love me enough that it don't matter?"

Chapter Twenty-Six

She nearly choked on the tears fighting to get free, unable to force words past them. She laid her hand along his cheek and he leaned into it.

"I know you don't love me as much as you do Torchay or Obed," he said, his voice not quite a whisper. "Maybe not even as much as Joh or Fox or the women. But—"

"Shh." Kallista stroked her thumb across his cheek to press it against his lips, hating that he might have worried for one instant that his place in the ilian, in her life wasn't secure. "It doesn't matter. *It doesn't*. I do love you, Keldrey. You've made your own place in my heart and I need you to fill it. Mark or no mark."

He pulled back, searching her face. "You mean that?"

Words weren't enough. Kallista reached between them, guided him into her body. He groaned as he pushed deep inside. "I love you, Keldrey Borr," she whispered into his ear. "Love me."

"You know I do." He withdrew and surged slowly, powerfully back into her.

Kallista moaned. He had no magic for her to grab hold of, nothing to help her hold back or hurry ahead. She was helpless under his sensual assault, wholly in the physical, the possibility of more lost to her, forgotten. Keldrey played her body like a master, coaxing sounds from her she never knew she could make with familiar sensations that felt somehow completely new. And he did it again, and again, and again.

Finally, they collapsed, limp and satiated. They couldn't have lain there more than half an eon, when Keldrey sat up. He gave her a sharp slap on her hip and bounded out of bed.

"*Now* you have to be awake." He opened the wardrobe and rummaged through it. He looked at her over his shoulder. "What're we doin' today? What do you wear for chasin' demons?"

Kallista levered herself to a sitting position. How did he do that, jump up with all that energy after they'd just—

Torchay came into the room. Had he been listening, waiting for them to finish? Had she screamed? She couldn't remember.

"This will do for now." Torchay tossed her a houserobe, handed a bundle to Keldrey. "Things have been happening while you slept."

Kallista frowned and pulled on the robe. Keldrey dressed in trousers and tunic, plain bodyguard's blacks. Why did he get clothes? What was he going to be doing that required them? Or she, that didn't?

"What things?" she wanted to know.

"Us putting you to sleep for one." Keldrey didn't look up from tying his laces. "You were a bit hysterical, if you'll recall."

She nodded, hating the blush. She'd rather not recall, truth be told.

"I stayed with you," Keldrey continued. He frowned at her. "Wouldn't have hurt if you'd slept till afternoon. Don't she look like she needs more rest to you, Torchay?"

"Aye, but we can't wait longer." Torchay took over the tying of her robe. She had far too many ends to her belt and not enough fingers—or perhaps the other way round.

"Wait longer for what?" She asked the question idly, wondering whether breakfast would have those flaky, honey-layered pastry things. Until something about the looks her two bodyguard-iliasti exchanged got past her hunger.

"Breakfast's waiting." Torchay took her elbow and marched her through the door.

"For *what?*" Kallista twisted in his grip, trying to catch Keldrey's eye. "What has happened?"

Keldrey didn't meet her gaze. Neither did Torchay.

Kallista pinched Torchay's side, hard. *"What has happened?"*

"Breakfast first," he said grimly. "Stop fretting." He ushered her into the dining room where Keldrey went to the sideboard to fill plates for both of them. "It's nothing bad, and you'll know soon enough."

"That does not relieve my mind." Kallista glowered at him, then included Keldrey in her glower when he joined them.

He pushed her plate closer. "Eat."

"Torchay, what—"

Her red-haired ilias picked up a raisin bun and shoved it in her mouth. "Viyelle says the en-Kameral will 'hear our petition' at the first bell after noon."

"The whole group?" She talked around the food till she got it swallowed. Saints, she felt hollow with hunger. "Not just the governing council, correct? The whole en-Kameral will be there?"

"That's what I was told."

"Good. I don't want the council to be able to pretend we never said anything." Kallista knew Torchay was distracting her from whatever they didn't want to tell her about yet, but she would allow it. For now. She needed to know these other things. "What about the complaint to the justiciars?"

"That went out already this morning, since the messenger had to go to the docks to collect Nur Truthsayer first."

Kallista paused half a moment in her eating. "Nur? Why?"

"Because he can deliver the altered blade without it passing through Adaran hands. And because he's a truthsayer."

"Kallista, slow down." Keldrey caught her hand, the one with the fork. "The food isn't going anywhere. Neither is whatever's happened. I don't want to send for that healer-naitan because you ate too fast and choked."

She glared at him. But he was right, which was mostly why she glared. She set her fork down, picked up her cup of tea and sipped. "Can we use this complaint to get Habadra's slaves away from her? Since she's the one most likely to kill them rather than let them go, according to our spy."

"Don't ask me." Keldrey got up to fetch more sausage. He gave one to Kallista, since hers had all somehow disappeared. "I'm no expert on law, Daryathi or Adaran. But I do know that Habadra woman wouldn't think twice about slaughtering 'em all."

Kallista looked up to get Torchay's opinion. He met her gaze briefly, preferring the view in his teacup. "I know less about the law *or* the Habadra than Kel does."

What did happen last night? She ate the sausage Keldrey had brought her and the last half of her last raisin bun, and drank off her tea—except the bit with the leaves. "All right. Breakfast is over. No more stalling."

Torchay looked her in the eyes, medically intent. After a long, searching look, he nodded once as he stood. "It's time."

Keldrey took a last sip of his tea as he followed them to his feet, leaving the cup with a little clatter.

Curiosity and dread mixed in equal parts as Kallista strode down the corridor in Torchay's wake. What could possibly have him acting this way? She tugged her houserobe closer, trying to decide whether she wanted to turn back and put on clothes. She would feel less vulnerable, but it would take time.

Torchay nodded to a brace of bodyguards outside the family gathering room and they opened the doors. The rest of their ilian waited inside, but none of the children. So it wasn't something the children had done. Kallista looked around the room, confused. What in the wide world was going on?

And she saw him. Standing in the corner, in the shadows, his arms wrapped round himself, one who didn't belong. His eyes met hers for an instant and flinched away.

A sick feeling grew in the pit of her stomach and she reached for support. Hands caught hers and she threw them off, taking hold of good, solid, honest wood, the back of a chair.

"What we saw in the dreamscape last night—" Obed approached, but she wouldn't let him touch her.

"It was a marking," Torchay said, his voice gentler than she'd ever heard it. "But it wasn't Keldrey being marked."

Kallista jerked round to look at Keldrey, saw the bleak expression on his face, and felt herself shatter inside. Only her skin kept the bits of herself from scattering to the winds.

"You *knew*." She let out all of her anger and none of her pain. "And you said *nothing*. That's what this morning was about. Manipulating me—"

"No manipulation," Keldrey growled. "You needed to—"

She turned her back on him. She didn't want his excuses, his lies. They had all lied to her. Every one of them.

Torchay reached for her. "Kallista—"

"Don't." She slapped his hands away. "Don't you touch me. Don't any of you dare." She took a step away from them, but all the broken pieces of herself grated against each other, threatening to burst through her skin in a screaming gout of pain, so she stopped.

She looked at him again, the interloper. His jaw twisted to the side when he frowned, the way he did now.

Her loss crashed over her again. He wasn't Stone. She remembered how Stone's link had stretched so impossibly thin before it snapped, slicing her to bits as it rebounded through her, leaving her empty. She staggered, grabbing for the chair, knocking away all the lying hands that reached to help her. They didn't care. How could they care and betray her like this?

But it was the One God's betrayal that bit deepest.

How could She send Kallista *this* as a replacement for Stone? How could the One force another stranger on her when Keldrey was already part of them? Hadn't she endured enough?

"No." She shook her head, holding her skin tight together over her shattered self. "I won't have it. I won't have him."

"He has the mark, Kallista," Torchay said. "We've seen it. We all miss Stone, but you can't—"

"I *can*." A tiny piece of her vicious agony snarled out of her mouth, before she got the rest pushed back. "I can do anything I want. I am Reinine of all Adara. *No one rules me.*"

She couldn't stay here any longer, couldn't keep holding her skin closed like this. Kallista spun and walked out of the room, ignoring the pain that raked through her at every step. It would be worse if she let it out. Her whole being was nothing but pain, and if she let it escape, the only thing left to her would be an empty, flapping skin.

"*Kallista.*" Viyelle followed her. "Please. This won't help. You're not the only one who misses Stone. He shared my bed more nights than he did yours, but the—"

"He shared my *soul*." Kallista whirled on the younger woman. Sparks hissed at her fingertips, called by the depth of her anger and pain. She shook them away and pressed her hands against the place in the pit of her stomach where she felt the links the strongest, trying to push away her anguish. "He was here, inside me. A part of me. I will not replace that with some—some grubby thief."

In her peripheral vision, she could see the thief in question, in the crowd that had spilled into the corridor, saw him wince at her description. She didn't care. He didn't matter. She walked away from the traitors.

"The demons—" Obed followed. They all followed, curse them.

"Put these on." Keldrey thrust her gloves at her. He must have pulled them from Torchay's belt.

Kallista ignored him, hissed at him when he grabbed her hand and slapped a glove across her palm.

"Put them on *now*," he ordered. "If you're so far out of control you're throwin' sparks, I'm not havin' you without gloves even were you the One Herself. Put 'em on."

Snarling at him, Kallista pulled her gloves on with swift, sharp jerks, still walking. She hated him. Hated all of them. She would hate them forever.

At least—she wanted to. And she would. If she didn't love them so much. That's what made it hurt like this.

"Kallista, *think*." That was Joh. Mighty fond of thinking, he was. "You have to look at this sensibly. If—"

"No." She shook her head so violently, she lost her balance for a moment. "I don't *have* to do anything I don't want to do. I'm the Reinine. The Godstruck. Sense and logic and reason have nothing to do with this. It's *magic*." Hurt and anger overcoming her, she spun and shoved Joh away, hard enough to send him stumbling back. He'd have fallen if Fox hadn't caught him.

"Go. Away," she said, very calmly and coldly. "I do not want to hear anything you have to say. Any of you. I don't want to look at you. If I could pull these links out by their roots, I would do it." She stopped the quiver in her voice before she got any more shrill, before more than the one sob could escape.

"You don't mean that." The anguish on Obed's face reflected the broken pieces inside her and Kallista shuddered.

"No." She shivered again, but warded off Torchay when he would have come to her. "I don't know. Maybe. Maybe I do mean it. I just—"

She shook her head, deliberately refusing to look at the stranger in their midst. "I can't do this now. I can't—I just—I need to be alone."

She held up her hand again, forestalling protests. "I know. I'm the Reinine, I have to have bodyguards. But Samri and Bay—whoever's on duty. I need to be alone, without any of you."

"Kallista—"

She saw the plea in Torchay's face, felt their concern and worry through the links. Somehow, it made everything worse. *"Please."* She backed down the hall. "Give me this. I won't—but if I do, you know how to follow. Please, just leave me alone."

This time, when she fled, they let her go. She could feel them, standing bunched together there in the corridor, feel them getting further away. She bathed and dressed, trying to keep her mind busy with Reinine's matters, but it kept circling back to Godstruck things. *Why* had the One done this to her?

Kallista kept moving, and gradually the sharp edges of this betrayal wore away enough that she could think. She'd been doing just fine with the magic she had. Granted, she hadn't actually faced any of the demons yet, however many there were. But her magic had grown stronger. She had more power now than she did when they'd faced the seven demons of the Barinirab rebellion.

"Namida Ambassador hasn't left yet to present our demand to the en-Kameral, has she?" Kallista addressed her bodyguard. The noon bell hadn't rung yet. "Send word that I'll be going with her. And Gweric. I want Gweric with me."

"Yes, my Reinine."

The attendant flurry of action to her order told her everything would be ready. Kallista contemplated ordering her iliasti to stay behind, but decided they could suit themselves. She didn't have to talk to them to draw their magic against demons. Leyja peeked in while Kallista ate lunch on a tray in her room, but she just went quietly away again.

All the godmarked were waiting in the courtyard, already mounted, when Kallista appeared for the ride to the Seat of Government. Including the man they were trying to foist on her.

"He stays." Kallista tugged her gloves tighter.

"Who?" Torchay tried to pretend ignorance.

Kallista just looked at him.

"He's *marked*, Kallista. If you'd just look—"

She cut Torchay off with a gesture as she mounted. "He stays here. He is not one of us."

"He should be." Torchay's mutter was just loud enough for her to hear it.

"No. He should *not*."

"What if the demons are there?" Obed edged his horse closer as Kallista signaled the captain. "Won't you need all your magic? You needed all nine to deal with Khoriseth before."

"Who says that Khoriseth is here? I have enough magic. I can do this." She rode ahead, trying—and failing—to leave them behind. Except for *him*. He stayed in the embassy as ordered.

This time, the en-Kameral was inside when Kallista and her party arrived. Namida Ambassador scurried up the stairs beside Kallista, whispering instructions the whole way. "The escort must remain outside—but close, in case they mislike what we have to say—and I do not expect smiles and cheers."

Namida almost wrung her hands in her agitation. "The bodyguards can accompany you, thank the One. After all, the Kameri have their champions. And be silent. Please. Let me read the document. You merely add the weight of your presence. We go in. I read the message. I hand the paper to the page. We go out. Short and simple. Agreed?"

"Agreed." Kallista found a grim smile for the ambassador and gestured her to lead the way.

Namida stepped up to the podium facing the executive council's dais. Kallista seated herself in the throne-like chair behind the podium, Obed at her side. He was still officially her Reinas in this place. This time, the Godmarked did not sit, but ranged themselves with the bodyguards around their Reinine.

The paper did not take long to read. Though couched in diplomatic language, it clearly stated the Adaran demand. Halfway through it, Gweric came to crouch beside Kallista's chair. "I see demon's workings."

Kallista sat up straight. She should have expected it, but she hadn't, not truly. She had done all those things at the skola and the trial arena, and nothing happened. Why now?

She opened her eyes to the dreamplane and saw the dark glow of fresh demonstain. It was working to influence the minds of the Kameri, harden their hearts. But where was the demon?

Kallista called magic, hauling it out of her godmarked fast enough to make them gasp. She was stronger, her magic-using muscles more fit. She could do this with the magic she had. She didn't need anyone else. Anyone new.

She shaped her demon-hunter, added on the destroyer magic so that what it found, it would destroy and what it destroyed, it would track to the source and leave nothing behind. She centered herself under it, like a laborer preparing to lift a heavy load, and shoved with everything she had.

The magic crept out. It didn't slide back, kept moving outward, but it was in no hurry. It had power, understanding, truth, will—everything it needed but eagerness. Joy.

How could that thief replace Stone's bright joy in the magic? He couldn't. Impossible.

Kallista rolled onto her metaphysical back and kicked at the magic with both metaphysical feet, moving it along a bit faster. It began to pick up speed, humming with purpose. Just as it passed the outermost person in her circle of godmarked—Viyelle—it burst against an impenetrable wall, flaring so bright, Kallista had to look away.

Gweric and Joh hid their eyes from the flash, and Torchay, and some of the Daryathi in the chamber. But most paid no attention to the magic's death.

"*No.*" Kallista squeezed the cry between her teeth. Only those nearest her noticed. She called magic again, more of it.

"Time to go." Torchay signaled her duty guard who lifted her from her seat. "The paper's been presented," he said. "They have their copy."

"Wait. I—" She sent this magic out, willing it to break through the barrier. Instead, the magic was broken upon it. Again.

Her second duty guard took Kallista's other arm and together they half-carried her from the chamber. Not so fast they appeared to be fleeing, but fast enough.

"There were demons," she protested. "Gweric saw them. I have to—"

"Get to safety before the demon can stir them to attack. Or attack us itself." Torchay directed the retreat with a lift of an eyebrow, a tilt of his head.

"It hasn't, not the whole time we've been here." She let him push her out the doors to the building.

"Goddess, Kallista, don't—" Torchay's voice held strain.

"Taunt it? Why not? It's *afraid*." She twisted in his grip. "Come out, Khoriseth! I dare you. Zughralithiss, come fight me!" She'd been given only two names from the same unknowable source where the names had come before. That should mean there were only two demons.

The air outside the Seat of Government seemed to pause, hovering motionless as if time itself waited to see what happened. The moment stretched. Kallista gathered magic into her hands, just in case.

Torchay hustled her down the steps, the others close behind, weapons in their hands. When they reached the bottom, Kallista laughed. She let the magic go. "You see? *Cowards*."

It hit her. Slammed her flat inside her magical shields.

Kallista screamed, drawing magic fast and hard, wrapping it around her godmarked, around all her people. The pull of magic on the heels of the attack staggered Torchay and she broke away from him to run back up the stairs. She needed to get inside, close enough to see the demon, to crush it.

She shaped her magic and shoved it out, unable to send it flying. The tendrils of demon stuff coiling out from the building snapped at her magic, quenching some of its power, but couldn't keep her from cutting off great chunks of its dark essence, shredding them into nothingness.

Fox caught her, kept her from dashing into the building as more of the demon came boiling out after them. She grappled for magic, struggled to shape all that came pouring into her. The demon's inky darkness built higher, blacker. Gweric cried out, voicing the dread she felt, but she couldn't give in to it. She had to direct the magic, form it into a weapon that would rid the world of this foulness.

The demon shrieked, shattering her concentration. She lost her hold on the magic, and the demon fell on them, on all eight of them at once.

Kallista felt their pain as she felt her own, magnified through their links. She fought to keep from feeding it back to them again, the way she shared out the pleasure. She fought to take hold of the magic, to use it, to—she couldn't think, could only send a wild, wordless, desperate prayer to the One for help before she lost all consciousness.

Thank heaven. She was down. Torchay took Kallista's limp body from Fox, passed her to Obed who passed her to Joh already mounted. They had to get out of here before anything worse happened, before the demon could organize a physical attack. So far, Kallista's protective veil held against the demon, but Torchay didn't want to trust it too long. Nor did he think it would hold up against musket balls or crossbow bolts.

As Torchay swung onto his horse, he noted with approval that all the troopers had their weapons loaded and held at the ready, pointing down past their stirrups at the street. Joh had had the foresight to insist their escort receive the first of the new cavalry carbine pistols. They only carried a single shot, but their greater range ought to keep the mob at bay a little longer. The escort hadn't carried them until recently, when the riots had spread.

Gweric looked with his missing eyes back at the Seat.

Torchay didn't like that look, not at all. "Let's ride," he shouted. "Before it decides to take another slap at us."

"Why isn't it?" Fox pushed his horse into a non-existent gap beside Torchay. "Kallista's out. She can't help us. Why not finish us off?"

"She hurt it." Gweric held on with both hands as they hurried through the cobbled streets as fast as the horses could manage. "I saw that. When she went down, the magic flared."

"Destroyed?" Obed asked hopefully.

Gweric shook his head.

"Does the demon have to be close to attack directly?" Torchay asked. "The way Kallista does? She can't hurt it if she's too far away. Is the demon the same?"

It was half a block before Gweric answered. "I don't know."

"What *do* you know?" Obed snapped.

"Very little."

Chapter Twenty-Seven

When they reached the embassy and dismounted, Gweric spoke again. "This is what I *know*," he said. "The demon that attacked us is very old and very powerful. Stronger than any I have seen before, including, I think, Khoriseth. I never actually saw Khoriseth in Arikon, but I saw what it left behind. This demon makes Khoriseth look like a mewling kitten. I also know that Kallista hurt it. She didn't destroy it, but it is damaged."

He kept talking as they moved into the building. "This is what I *believe*, but do not know for certain. I believe Torchay Reinas is right, that the demon must be close—I do not know how close—to attack directly. Which likely explains why it has not attacked before now. Whatever the reason, I believe the damage Kallista dealt it gives us some time. How much time, I can't say." He paused, suddenly looking his very young age. "I would plan for less and hope for more."

"Thank you, Gweric Naitan." Torchay bowed to him, grateful for every bit of help and information they could get. "Could you perhaps stand watch? Warn us if the demon comes this way?"

The young naitan gave a brusque nod. "I will, Tayo."

Torchay blew out a gusting sigh, striding after Joh as he carried Kallista deeper into the embassy. Leyja trotted at his side, trying to check their Reinine's condition. *Now what?*

"Goddess, what a mess." Obed voiced Torchay's own thoughts, scowling at the floor as he stalked along beside him.

"Truth." Torchay heaved some of the burden onto his ilias. "What should we do? What *can* we do?"

"The embassy is as secure as arms, men and warding magic can make it. What's left is—" Obed hesitated.

Torchay waited for him to admit the truth to himself.

"It's Kallista," the dark man finally said. "She is our weak point. Her stubbornness . . ."

"Could get us all killed." Torchay followed Obed into the room they both shared now with Kallista, where the ilian had gathered. All the players were present, though Kallista was still unconscious. This behavior wasn't like her. He did not understand it. Nor did he know what to do about it.

Joh laid her carefully on the bed. Torchay looked round. "Where's Padrey?"

"Next room," Keldrey said. "He kept tryin' to follow. Actin' wild. I finally had to lock him up."

Torchay glanced at Joh, then to Fox. Their long-queued ilias had been in prison when he'd been marked, had tried to claw his way through the walls to reach Kallista. Fox had walked hundreds of leagues, most of them in a daze of compulsion to find the Godstruck. "Did it hit you so quick?" Torchay asked.

Joh frowned. "It's hard to remember that time, but no—I don't think so."

"Fox?" Torchay asked for confirmation.

"I couldn't tell you. I was injured, healing. It was weeks before I could move at all. Who knows what was injury and what was the mark? But the need to find her seemed to build slowly."

"If the madness *has* hit him sooner than expected," Aisse said, "what does it mean?"

Torchay didn't know, didn't want to say what he suspected.

"It means we are out of time," Obed said. "I think that if we had the luxury of time, Kallista would eventually accept what has happened. She knows that this is the One's choice, the One's gift. Her heart is sore, but it is soft. And she is wise. Her resistance would wear away in a few days' time."

"But we don't have a few days," Joh said. "Do we?"

Torchay sighed. He didn't want to do this. Only the One knew whether Kallista would ever forgive him. "We may not have even a full chime of the clock. We also have no choice."

"No choice about what?" Leyja's eyes narrowed in suspicion.

"We have to force it. We have to make sure she . . . links with Padrey." Torchay felt sick at the thought, as if he would disgrace himself on the nearest boots.

"We should at least give her the choice first," Viyelle protested. "Wake her up, explain. Then, if she still doesn't . . ."

"Should we wake her?" Obed brushed his fingertips across her forehead. "*Can* we?"

"I agree with Viyelle," Keldrey said. "Give her one more chance."

"Yes." Aisse climbed onto the bed, patted the unconscious woman's cheek. "Wake up. Kallista, wake up."

Consensus apparently reached, for no one tried to stop Aisse, Torchay leaned against the wall, arms folded, trying to control the sick feeling in the pit of his stomach. Over the years he'd done thousands of things "for her own good"—forced food down her, slipped sedatives into her wine so she would sleep, carried her to safety over her furious protests. He had been her bodyguard for almost a decade before he became ilias. But he'd never gone this far.

Because it had never mattered so much. And she had never been so stupidly stubborn.

They wouldn't be doing this if she hadn't forced them to it. Ironic it was, given that Torchay had usually been the stubborn one before. He pushed himself off the wall.

"*Kallista.*" He used his sergeant's voice, loud without shouting. "It's time to wake. Duty calls."

He didn't know whether it was his old call from their army days or Aisse's cold, wet cloth on Kallista's forehead and neck, but their Godstruck ilias struggled to consciousness.

"Stop." Kallista pushed Aisse away. "Why are you getting me all wet? Stop it."

Torchay glanced round at the others, but he couldn't lay this task on them. He'd been with her longest, he knew her best. The whole palace, including their ilian, acknowledged him as her second, no matter what Viyelle's official title might be or who bore the name of steward. He had to do this.

"Kallista." He sat next to her on the bed, took both her hands in his. "You're out of time. I wish we had more to give you, but we don't. You *must* link with Padrey."

"Must?" She set her jaw and glared at him. "There is no *must* to it. I don't need him."

"Yes, you do. The demon's no' destroyed, and it knocked you flat. Knocked you out. We could have done nothing to stop it, if it decided to—to do anything at all. You need Padrey. You need what his magic will give you."

"Why *him?*" She jerked her hands out of Torchay's and flung herself off the bed to pace. "Why him and not Keldrey? Kel's already one of us. Why couldn't he have been marked?"

"I don't know, Kallista." Torchay's patience felt more like weariness. He was simply too tired to fight any longer.

"I've had a thought about that," Joh said, and all eyes turned his way. "Perhaps there's a quality in the person that has to mesh with the magic they carry. You say Fox's magic carries order—and our Fox has a very strong sense of what's proper. Perhaps Padrey fits better with the sort of magic you need him to carry. Perhaps Keldrey is—well—"

"Goddess knows, I'm nothin' like Stone," Keldrey said.

"If anything, you're too much like Kallista," Leyja said. "Both of you stubborn and hot-headed."

Kallista came close to them in her pacing, her eyes snapping sparks. "That—that *thief* is nothing like Stone. *Nothing.*" She spun away again. "No. No. We don't need him. I can do this with what we have."

Torchay took a deep breath. He'd reached the end of his patience. "I'm no' going to argue any more."

"Good. Now what we need to do—" Kallista swept past him and he snagged her wrist, pulling her in.

The contact with Padrey had to be skin to skin. Harder for her to avoid it if all she wore was skin. Torchay slid his hands under her tunic to peel it off her.

"What—what are you doing?" Kallista struggled to free herself and Obed came to help undress her. "We don't have time for this." She tried to pull her tunic back down, her trousers up. "Sex is a very bad idea right now. Demons, remember?"

Aisse was at her feet, hauling off her boots. Fox picked her up to make things easier, and in seconds, Kallista hadn't a thread of clothing left her.

"I remember." Torchay hoisted her, rump up, over his shoulder. "That's why." He headed for the door and Kallista understood what he meant to do.

"No!" she screamed, kicking out, twisting her body to throw herself free. She wasn't a small woman, almost as tall as the men in the ilian, and strong. Torchay lost his hold. Obed caught her. They carried her between them out of the bedroom and a short distance down the corridor.

Kallista fought them viciously. Fox, then Joh and Keldrey had to help, keep her from breaking free, from hurting anyone. Viyelle ran ahead and unlocked the door. It took all the women to open it against the weight of the man slumped against it.

At the sight of him, Kallista fought harder, desperate to stop this. She couldn't do it, wouldn't touch him, refused to know him. *He wasn't Stone.*

"No-oooo!" Her scream became a wail as they carried her to the bed, tossed her down, holding her there. "Please don't do this to me. *Please*. Torchay, please."

He lifted his head without loosening his grip a fraction and looked her, his eyes soft with pity, his face hard with determination. "Will you do it yourself then?"

"*I can't*." She wept, ignoring the tears. "Don't, please don't make me."

"Goddess, Kallista." He looked away, across the room. His throat moved as he swallowed something down. When he looked back, she could see no softness at all, only grim determination. "I have to."

"*We* have to." Obed's voice called Kallista's attention past Torchay to his dark, sorrowful face. "*You* have to. There is no other choice."

"We always have choices."

"And you made yours seven years ago, on that broken wall in Ukiny," Torchay said.

"*I can't*." She knew she was whining, but she couldn't help it. It hurt too much.

"*Stop this.*" Keldrey crawled up her body, grabbed her shoulders and shook her. "You're the Reinine, for the One's sake! Before that you were the Godstruck, and before that a soldier, a naitan in Adara's army. You're the only one who can destroy this demon. The. Only. One." He punctuated each word with a little shake. "Without you, we all die. *All* our kids will be slaves, just like Sky. Is that what you want?"

"No!" How dare he suggest that she did?

"Unless you have all your magic, that's what's going to happen. So just stop this stupid messin' about and do it." Keldrey flung her down and rolled off the bed.

In the gap between Torchay and Obed, Kallista could see Padrey. The women had stripped him down, with Joh's help for the heavy lifting. Now, Joh held Padrey up at the edge of the bed, the dazed look in the young man's eyes fading as he focused on her. He was lean, but not as thin as she'd thought, his shoulders broad, arms and chest well muscled. Her magic stirred, scenting him on the air. It liked the way he looked. No, *she* liked the way he looked, especially as the flush of arousal crept over him.

She turned her head, hating herself for betraying Stone this way. "I can't," she whispered.

"It's not betrayal." Viyelle knelt at the side of the bed, murmuring in Kallista's ear. Had she read her mind? "Do you truly think Stone would begrudge you any pleasure? Would he want to see you like this, or would he be teasing you out of it?"

"Stone was a Warrior," Fox said. "He knew that when one warrior falls, another must take his place."

Kallista squeezed her eyes shut. They were confusing her. The magic churned, making her dizzy, even lying down. The emotions seeping through the links confused things more, filled with worry and determination and—and love. So much love.

She felt for the empty place, the stump where Stone's link was severed and found more love. Faint and sweet, with a hint of distant laughter and a taste of "what are you waiting for?"

Your approval, she thought.

Silly woman. You know I always approve of sex. Even if I don't get to play.

Her choked laugh ended in a sob as she felt that last, faint touch of *Stone* leave her. She couldn't go back, couldn't have things like they were. Not ever again. Moving on wasn't a betrayal of what had been. No one could ever take Stone's place, but—the One had marked this new man. The One's judgment had never failed yet. Perhaps they could make a new place for him.

Kallista sighed and opened her eyes. "Touching his hand would have worked just fine. Don't you think all this is a bit overkill?" She gestured at her own nudity and Padrey's.

"I figured the more skin exposed, the more likely it would actually happen." Torchay searched her face. "You'll do it?"

"Padrey." Kallista tried to sit up, and warily, they let her. She reached out to the naked ex-thief. "Padrey, come here."

He blinked, shook his head. Not in a "no", but to clear it. "My Reinine?" His eyes went wide as he seemed suddenly to realize his state of undress and hers. "*Oh shite*. Saints and all the holy sinners, I—"

With a laugh, Joh caught him round the middle and tossed him onto the bed as Obed scrambled out of the way. Padrey bounced, giving Obed time to prevent his attempted escape.

"I shouldn't be here. I shouldn't—I can't—Oh Goddess. Oh Ulili and Khralsh and—" Padrey babbled, calling on all the names of the One as he tried to scoot away.

"Shh," Kallista eased down into the bed again.

"We should leave," Leyja said. "Shouldn't we?"

Aisse shrugged. "We will be part of it, I think, whether here or elsewhere."

"I'll just go. I should go. Really." Padrey crawled toward the foot of the bed. Fox blocked that escape.

"Padrey Emtal." Kallista used her Reinine's voice, which was nothing more than her major's voice, six years older.

He went still, peeked at her over his shoulder. "My Reinine?"

"Did you, or did you not pledge yourself to my service?"

He swallowed hard. "I did. My Reinine."

She offered him a smile, fleeting because she feared he would try escaping again if she softened too much. "And did you offer yourself to the One, for whatever use you might be?"

"Not in those exact words. It was more like—"

"*Did you?*" she interrupted, insistent.

"Well . . . yeah. I guess I did. More or less."

"And the One accepted the offer and marked you, correct?"

He shrugged, looking around at the other godmarked. "That's what *they* said. But I don't—"

Kallista held up a silencing finger. "Who is the Reinine here?"

Padrey subsided, flushing red. "You are."

She had to use his awe of her position while she could. If he had anything at all in common with Stone, it wouldn't last long. "Then come here."

"Where?" He gave her a wary look. Nope, not long at all.

"Here." She patted the space beside her. "*Now*, Padrey."

Eying the men and women ranged around the room, Padrey scooted slowly up the bed until he occupied the farthest bit of the place she had patted, his legs drawn up to hide the fact that he was still aroused.

"Should we leave?" Torchay murmured from his place at her back.

Kallista shrugged. "Suit yourselves."

This moment had been different with each of her previous eight marked mates. Some of them had been bound in almost seamlessly, at the moment of their marking. For others of them, the binding had been a bit more . . . spectacular. The greater the length of time between the marking and the binding, the more spectacular the binding seemed to be. Padrey had only been marked yesterday. Surely the magic wouldn't go so terribly wild. Still, better not to take chances.

"Whether you stay or go," she said. "It might be a good idea to sit down. We haven't done this in a while."

"Done what?" Padrey seemed caught between worry and suspicion.

"This."

Kallista planted her hand in the middle of Padrey's chest. She had time to push him flat on his back and slide over him, breasts to chest, before the magic woke. It lifted its shaggy great head and shook it, shuddering Kallista. Then it seemed to realize more magic lay just beyond her skin, and roared with delight as it burst from her to snatch up Padrey's magic.

There was a moment's pause, a wrenching pain that had both Kallista and Padrey crying out, clawing at the bedcover as the magic he carried was twisted to fit with the rest. Then the magic leaped up in a whirling, *joyous* dance, thrumming through Kallista and Padrey in perfect step.

The magic loved the full-body touch between them, spinning back and forth, sensitizing their skin to the faintest whisper of pleasure and then screaming along it. Kallista moaned, Padrey shouted, grinding himself into her.

"Take him," Obed said. "Take him inside you."

"If you want." Torchay touched her at the same time Obed did, at the instant the magic reached for them.

It tumbled them both into the pleasure and joy, their intent lost. Kallista caught them, bound them into their places in the web of magic with the efficiency of years of practice. Padrey pushed up against her again and she shifted, sliding forward, up and then down, sheathing him inside her.

Her eyes rolled back in her head at the feel of him filling her, as if he poured magic directly into her with this more intimate touch. She tucked him close, both physically and magically, next to her heart, so she wouldn't lose him as the magic reached out again. It spilled in rapid order into Fox, Aisse, Joh, Vlyelle and Leyja, and as it brought them into the dance, Kallista bound them swiftly into place, letting the magic send its joy between, around, through them.

The magic had a different flavor. This was a quieter joy, one that sprang from a darker place and flowed all the brighter because of it. Stone's joy was a fountain, spraying high into the air, splashing everyone who came near. This bubbled up like a mountain spring, forcing its way free of all the weight that tried to hold it prisoner. Kallista reached out, her godmarked reaching with her in a faint echo of hands, and pulled away the heaviest stones so that the spring could run free, clear, cold.

Padrey gasped. Kallista laughed and gave the magic a nudge to spin it faster as she began to ride him. All the strength developed by moving the magic without a ninth almost sent it out of her control now their new ninth was bound in, but she didn't try to slow it. She grabbed hold and rode the magic as she did Padrey, making sure everyone was tucked in safe before she lost herself to the sensations sweeping through in wild waves.

Rough, helpless noises came from Padrey's throat, echoing those in Kallista's mind, in her own throat. He bucked beneath her, beginning to lose the rhythm. Aisse cried out, or maybe it was Viyelle, but Kallista wasn't ready to let go. She wanted to push it farther, see how far, how high she could take this.

With a violent lunge of his body, Padrey rolled, somehow staying inside her as he took her with him, until he rose above her onto his knees. He lifted her hips, her legs over his arms as he used them to haul her closer, higher. Bracing one hand on the bed for leverage, he adjusted his position and thrust. The new angle touched that perfect place deep within.

Kallista screamed as the wave of magic crashed over her. Padrey managed another thrust before his climax brought her again. One after another, the others cried out, as if the magic wanted to give each of them his or her own distinct, separate climax, with all of them sharing in each moment.

If there were only nine moments. Kallista didn't count. There might have been more. Afterward, she only knew they had seemed to go on forever.

She stroked her hand over Padrey's fine, silky hair, and heard Torchay huff a breath of laughter through his nose.

"Aye then, it's right and done." Torchay touched Kallista's cheek with a long forefinger. "You're petting him, like you always do the new ones."

"Do I?" Kallista felt limp and achy but . . . right. Whole.

She smiled, content under Padrey's comforting weight. Her eyes drifted shut and she peeked inside herself at the echo of the web she'd built. She built it new each time she called the whole magic, but each of them always fit into the same place. When she'd woven this one, it had not seemed the same framework she'd used before. She wanted to look at it again, to be sure.

Padrey hadn't been simply plugged into Stone's old spot. He wouldn't have fit. Not because he was larger or smaller. He simply wasn't Stone.

He wasn't the same . . . shape. She'd made a new place for him, tucked between Torchay and Viyelle, next to herself. Stone had always fit in next to Fox, somewhat above Obed. His place was still there, beginning to smooth over with new threads of magic and of love. Stone would always have a place, even if his magic could no longer fill it.

The bed jostled and Kallista realized the rest of the ilian had decided to join the four of them already on it. She opened one eye. "Is this the smartest thing for us to do?"

"Why wouldn't it be?" Aisse asked from her comfortable-looking spot cradled against Keldrey.

Kallista stroked her hand across Padrey's broad shoulder. He was the leanest of their men, but she thought it was his natural build rather than any lack of food. He hadn't put on any weight since living in the embassy. "For one thing, we don't want to terrify Padrey."

"Too late." He tucked his face deeper into the hollow of her neck, as if hoping that since he couldn't see anyone, no one could see him.

Kallista chuckled. "It's all right, Padrey. No need for terror."

All right? *No need?* Padrey squeezed his eyes tighter shut. Maybe he could put off the moment of reckoning. *Goddess,* how had he come to be here? *Here,* in the Reinine's bed, in her *body?*

He remembered—oh, he remembered being inside her with her dark-haired, warrior queen beauty rising above him, driving down onto him, and him caught in the grip of the wildest, fiercest pleasure he'd ever known. And that had been only the beginning. He didn't have words for the rest of it.

A hand, rough-textured and slender, settled on his back and he startled, relaxing as it stroked down his spine. *Wait.* The Reinine's hands—one was in his hair and the other on his shoulder. That was an extra hand. Someone else's hand. Whose? He wanted to know, and he didn't.

A masculine chuckle made Padrey flinch. "You canno' hide forever, lad." And that raspy tenor voice belonged to the Tayo, Torchay Reinas.

Padrey groaned. *The Tayo* was here? So why was Padrey still lying naked on top of the Reinine, slipping slowly out of her? Why wasn't he skewered through and hung out on the banner pole?

Another hand, a larger one, popped him on his bare backside. "Time for lazing's past. Up with you now."

Saints and all the holy sinners, was the Reinine's whole ilian in here with them? Padrey slitted open one eye, saw a strand of dark hair curling beneath the Reinine's ear.

"It's all right." The Reinine touched her lips to his ear, making her murmur a sort of kiss. She shouldn't—but he loved it. "You don't have to move yet, if you're not ready," she said.

"What's going to happen when I do?" He couldn't help asking, but quietly, so only she would hear.

"Tonight?" She paused, then took a deep breath, lifting him a little with it. "A wedding, I should think."

"A—*what?*" Shock had Padrey jerking back to stare at her.

"A wedding?" The Reinine bit her lip, suddenly looking uncertain, vulnerable. Like a woman rather than a ruler. It made Padrey want to cuddle her, tell her everything would be fine, even though he didn't know any such thing and had no business telling her anything, much less cuddling.

She squirmed from beneath him, coming up onto her knees. The sway of her breasts distracted him. Someone brought a houserobe, helped her into it, and Padrey could hear again, could think. Someone—*Goddess, Viyelle Reinas*—put his arms into the sleeves of a red silk houserobe and tied it around him. He'd never felt anything so fine against his skin. Well, except for the skin of the Reinine.

Padrey dared to glance at her. She gazed back at him as if waiting for something. Perhaps for his look, for she took both his hands in hers.

"Padrey Emtal." The Reinine looked deep into his eyes, her expression formal. "Will you marry us?"

He swallowed, hard. Was this a joke? He looked from the Reinine to the Reinasti positioned around the room. Some of them smiled. Keldrey Reinas—he *winked*. Leyja Reinas wasn't one of the smilers but she held his eye a moment, then nodded. She *meant* it? Obed Reinas nodded. So did the Tayo.

The Reinine seemed to take his confusion for reluctance, for she gripped his hands tighter, drew them closer. "We need you, Padrey. *I* need you. Desperately. What happened just now was the magic of your mark binding with the rest of us. You are our ninth, completing the magic."

Padrey nodded. "Yeah, they told me that. You need my mark to fight demons. Whatever you need, my Reinine, it's yours."

"Good. And it's Kallista, not 'my Reinine.'" She leaned forward and kissed him on the mouth, too quick. "Vee, can you get everything organized? We have Gweric for the ceremony, I think he'd like that." She looked at Padrey as she slid from the bed. "You and Gweric are friends, aren't you? Is there someone you would like to invite?"

She made a face. "I don't think we can wait till we get your sister-sedil free. We need to do this now, tonight. But I'm sure we'll have to have another ceremony once we get home. Your sedil can come to that."

The Reinine's flow of speech slowed, halted as she looked at him. Then she smiled hesitantly and held her hand out to him, palm up. "You did say yes, didn't you? You will marry us? Some of our others— Stone first, and then Joh—didn't have a choice. They were married *di pentivas*, by order of Serysta Reinine."

Padrey didn't know what she meant at first, until he remembered the stories his sister-sedili had liked to read, about war prizes, men married without choice. Joh Reinas was *di pentivas*?

"But I'm Reinine now, and I—" She cleared her throat. "I won't force you. I only ask. Will you?"

Chapter Twenty-Eight

Padrey stared at her, at that plea on her beautiful face, her hand stretched toward him. His heart thundered in his ears, making everything even harder to comprehend. "Why?"

She didn't pretend to misunderstand. "We are already bound by the marks, you and I, all of us. What we just did, *that* made us an ilian, together. In a sense, you already are ilias. But I think the ceremony somehow . . . *seals* the binding, perhaps by making the commitment we've already made a public one. I'm not exactly sure what it does, to be honest. But it does *something*."

"So, it's important?" Padrey still didn't completely understand, but he trusted the Reinine and she did.

"Yes, Padrey, it's important."

He flicked his eyes to the others in the room before returning them to the Reinine. "And everybody's okay with it? With marrying me?"

The Reinine didn't take her eyes off him. Leyja Reinas stepped forward on her own. Padrey goggled as she bowed to him.

"Padrey Emtal, I would be pleased to have you marry us," she said. "You were a child, trapped in a terrible place, and despite all, you have become a good and honorable man."

"For a thief." He added the words he knew she was thinking.

"For *anyone*." Leyja's fierce retort startled him. "I didn't understand how it was. Now, Kallista's magic has shown me. Shown us all. I *know*." She took a step closer, slid her hand under the Reinine's, supporting her appeal. "Will you say yes?"

The others moved, joining her, adding their hands so that they all reached out with the Reinine's hand.

Overwhelmed, Padrey couldn't speak, could scarcely meet their eyes. But his muscles worked, some of them. He nodded. He took the hand offered and in the next instant, he was lifted off the bed and tossed into the middle of a ten-way embrace.

Everyone hugged him. The women all kissed him, and some of the men. Padrey didn't know how he felt about that. The women kissed him again, even Leyja Reinas, then the Reinine wrapped her arms round his waist and waved the others off.

"Go on. Get busy." She laughed as she clung to him. "I want the ceremony at the nineteenth chime, so the children can attend without being too cranky. Aisse, can you find something suitable for our Padrey to wear? Joh, the location is up to you. Find something—"

"Suitable, yes." He tipped his head in acknowledgment, his long queue sliding forward, a smile in his eyes if nowhere else.

That first day, Padrey made the mistake of straying too far from the Reinine once and collapsed into the fit they'd warned him about— fortunately just *after* he'd got out of the bathing pool, so he wasn't in danger of drowning. It hurt though. A lot. Bad enough he made sure not to do it again.

The Reinine—*Kallista*—she corrected him every time he called her "my Reinine," but it was deathly hard to remember. Kallista kept touching him, and when she did, he forgot everything including his own name. She would sling an arm over his shoulders, or pat his hand, or stroke a finger around his ear, and every time, something inside him sizzled, or sparked, or glittered, or came awake. Though the waking wasn't entirely inside him.

Torchay Reinas—just Torchay, the Tayo insisted—kept teasing her for petting him. She'd tease back, saying she had to get acquainted with his magic. That's what the glittery sparks were. His magic. Joh Reinas said it would stop reacting like that eventually, would only rise and sparkle when she called it. Padrey didn't know whether or not he hoped that was true.

Aisse Reinas started calling him Padrey Reinas every time he forgot to leave off the title. It sounded strange—but good. Who would have thought? *Him*, one of the Reinasti.

The others touched him too, patting his back or squeezing his shoulder mostly. Fox Reinas kept scruffing up Padrey's hair, and Viyelle would smooth it down again for him. Aisse leaned. She would lean past him for something, or into him, or over him. She kissed too. His cheek or the top of his head, usually, but sometimes his mouth, always too quick for him to kiss back.

Aisse was exactly his age, or around there. She nor Fox knew exactly how old they were, but Fox thought he was a couple of years older. Aisse was glad to have another "youngest."

They found him a red tunic done all over with gold braid and real jewels, so fancy it made his guts quake at the thought of getting something on it. The servants were setting the last stitches in the hems of his trousers while he wore them, as the nineteenth chime sounded. Everything was ready, or would be by the time everyone was assembled and the servants and troopers pressed into service stilled their scurrying.

Padrey waited with the men of the ilian in a small antechamber off the embassy's ballroom. The night was too chill to have the ceremony in a courtyard as Viyelle had suggested. The head of the bodyguard corps put his head in the door. "It's time."

With Jondi in the lead, they strode into the ballroom in the order they had joined the ilian. Torchay came first, as one of the original four creating the ilian, then Obed, followed by Fox. They had joined in that first year. Joh came next—he'd been marked and married the next year—with Keldrey behind, married in after the last Reinine died and before Kallista was selected Reinine. Padrey trailed them all, feeling incredibly young, terribly ignorant and unfathomably grateful.

The ballroom blazed with hundreds of candles, glittering in the mirrored walls. The candelabra were draped in gauzy red, the Reinine's color, and a floor cloth painted with the design of the compass rose had been rolled out onto the hardwood floor. In a masterpiece of timing, Kallista was moving to her place on the north arm of the compass, just far enough ahead of Padrey to keep him from collapse. Padrey followed her around the arc to his place, nearest her on the east. Each of the other women stood on one of the compass points—Aisse to the east, Leyja, west and Viyelle, south. The men spaced themselves out between.

Gweric stood in the middle, in his black prelate's robe, looking nervous. He kept clearing his throat. The three oldest girls stood a pace behind Kallista, trying to keep the bands they held from chiming together too much. Sky and Tigre stood behind Torchay, who was closest to Kallista on the West. Beyond them, around the large chamber, the Tayo Dai, the embassy staff, servants and escort troops ringed them with solemn faces. On the front row, the rest of the ilian's ten children were gathered.

"This is my first wedding." Gweric's voice cracked and everyone chuckled.

It was Padrey's first wedding too. The first time to see one—a proper one—and his first time to marry.

"I suppose that's obvious to everyone," Gweric went on, "but I am overjoyed to have this opportunity. I have known this family since Captain Naitan Kallista Varyl refused to leave me, a crippled Witch Hound, in the Ruler's palace in Tibre, and Fox, Warrior vo'Tsekrish carried me out because I could not walk."

Padrey listened, fascinated. Gweric had told him some of this the few times they were in their shared room at the same time, but not all.

"I am sure all of you know, as I do, how fortunate Adara is in her choice of Reinine. We mourned with them when this ilian lost one of their own, and now we rejoice with them because the One has brought them someone new to love." Gweric paused to clear his throat. "We have a new Godmarked."

A spontaneous cheer broke out among the crowd of witnesses, and faded quickly under Gweric's glare. "Once, when I was young and foolish, or younger and more foolish than I am now—" He got a chuckle. "I was jealous of the magic binding the Godstruck with her marked ones. You all know, I think, that magic is all I can see, and the magic that flows between the godmarked—"

He paused to turn his scarred face upward, an expression of joyous awe spreading across it. "This magic is the most beautiful I have ever seen. And I wanted badly to be part of it. But over the years, I have come to accept that the One knows what She is doing, knows much better than we do.

"Those brought to this ilian are exactly the persons who need to be here. The magic that binds them together is based on love, and it binds all of them, marked or not." Gweric smiled. "Yes, Keldrey Reinas, I can see you also, though perhaps not as clearly as the others. The magic is still there. The love is there. And that being said . . ."

He moved into the vows portion of the ceremony. The women went first, beginning with Kallista. Aisse came next, because though she was the youngest, she was one of the ilian's original four, then Viyelle and Leyja. One at a time, they went to one knee before him, placed a band on his right ankle, recited the vow, kissed him and returned to their places. When the women were done, the men came, placing their bands on Padrey's left ankle, until he wore nine anklets, five left and four right.

Then it was Padrey's turn. Gweric had agreed to act as attendant as well as prelate, so he moved outside the circle behind Padrey and handed him the first bracelet.

Obed had offered to provide the ilian bands, but Padrey refused. He had the money he'd been saving first to buy his way free, then to buy his sister and her babies. Maybe some of the money—most of it—was made by thieving, and maybe the bands he'd bought weren't as fancy as the ones they'd given him—though the one from Torchay was plain chased silver like what he'd bought—but it was his money that he'd more or less earned. The bands he gave were from his own efforts, his own heart.

Padrey crossed the few paces to Kallista and went to one knee, slipping the slender silver band onto her left wrist with the six already there. "I come pledging myself to you," he said. "Heart to heart, my body for yours in whatever comes our way. We, above all others, joined as one before the One who holds all that is, was and will be. So I swear with everything that I am."

He stood and with trembling hands touched her face as he leaned in for the kiss. *This was real.*

He was actually, seriously, truly marrying into the royal ilian of Adara. *Him.* Padrey Emtal, trader's boy, slave, thief, spy—now godmarked Reinas of Adara. It still felt more like dream than reality. He touched his lips to Kallista's and drew back, searching her face.

"Yes." She smiled. "This is me, and that's you." She laid her hand over his heart. "But remember—" She laid her other hand over her own heart. "*Here,* I am only Kallista Varyl. A soldier naitan. Don't let all this blind you with its glitter. Please."

Padrey blinked. That sounded like an actual plea. Did it matter so much to her? The thought that it might made him smile. She smiled back and he couldn't help but burst out grinning.

"Kallista." He said her name. It seemed important to her. He bowed, and yeah, maybe it was just a bit cocky, a bit of a tease. It made her laugh, and when he walked back to get the next bracelet from Gweric, he walked with a touch of swagger.

Padrey made his vows to the rest of the ilian, twice nine trips in all across the compass rose. Kallista had to take a few steps into the center when he crossed to Viyelle on the southern-most point to keep him from collapse. They'd made the compass rose symbol as small as possible, but with ten of them to space around it, it couldn't be too small. Finally, he worked the last anklet over Keldrey's foot, made his last vow, gave his last kiss, and it was done. Nine vows taken, nine given. No wonder the ceremony seemed endless. It was.

Gweric stepped forward, not into the center of the circle, but into the space between Kallista and Padrey. He took their hands and nodded for the rest of them to hold hands as well. When they were joined in a circle, Gweric spoke the final words.

"As you have each vowed today, giving and receiving these bands in pledge and in symbol of the vows you have made, as a prelate of Arikon in Adara, I recognize this ilian."

He smiled, looking at each of them. "May the One bless you with love, with loyalty, with grace, hope and peace."

"May it be so." Everyone in the ballroom spoke in response.

And now it was really done. He was married. To *these.*

Gweric stepped back outside the circle and placed Padrey's hand in Kallista's. The instant the circle closed, something slammed into Padrey, a crashing boulder of pure pleasure. His body went tight and hot, and he cried out.

Welcome, Godmarked, our Padrey.

It was Kallista who said it, he knew that, but not with her voice and he didn't hear it with his ears. Nor did he know how he knew it was Kallista, except that it simply *was*. She was inside him somehow. Or he was inside her. Or—

Kallista chuckled. *It's the magic, sweet Padrey. We are together inside the magic.*

Somehow she wrapped herself completely around him as the magic stretched, rushing on. Torchay was there, and Obed and Fox, tangled up inside Kallista and the magic. Aisse and Viyelle and Joh and Keldrey and Leyja, all of them together with the strange delight that was the magic. Padrey couldn't see them or hear or even touch them, but they were there. Part of him somehow. His. Like he was theirs. Part of them.

The magic drew them tighter, bound them closer, until Padrey couldn't tell where he ended and they began. He was still himself, and they were each definitely their own selves, but the edges between were hard to find. Not that he tried very hard. The magic felt so good. A bit like yesterday, with Kallista.

Padrey's thoughts dissolved. He felt stretched out, his body pulled up onto tiptoe, arms stretched wide, hands holding tight. The magic burst, showering their conjoined selves with cascading pleasure. He heard his shout echoed by other voices. Kallista let them slip away from her as the magic faded until last, she poured Padrey back into his body. He shuddered.

"Tell your children and your grandchildren," Gweric called into the silence. "That was the mystery of the ilian bond played out on a scale bold enough to be seen. And you have been privileged to see it."

The witnesses burst into cheers again, a few of the bravest coming forward to offer congratulations and well wishes. They were accepted graciously and everyone diverted to the wedding supper set up in the reception halls. Kallista and her ilian made a brief appearance before slipping out with the excuse that the children needed to be put to bed.

Kallista was worried. The demons had left them alone for a whole day. What did it mean? Did they have more time? How much?

Did they dare sleep tonight? Did they dare . . . not sleep? A great deal of sex had been done lately, to the accompaniment of a great lot of magic. The demons could not possibly have missed it. Why hadn't they attacked? Could they still be hoping Kallista might meekly give up and go away? Surely not.

She stole one of the flaky honey-and-nut pastries from the tray brought to her chamber where they'd all gathered, and swore when the honey dripped onto her elaborately trimmed tunic.

"What is it now? Not just the honey." Torchay handed her a plate with more substantial food on it.

"Isn't anyone else wondering what they're waiting for?" She waved Padrey into a chair and took the one beside him.

"Who?" Padrey asked.

"The demons," Aisse whispered to him.

"Vulnerability," Joh said. "Since they didn't—perhaps couldn't—attack before Padrey's mark, I'd wager they're waiting for something to soften us up. To make us an easier target."

"But *what?*" Kallista thought hard while she ate, the others apparently doing the same.

"The kids," Keldrey said after a time. "They're our weak spot. We should've left 'em home."

Kallista shook her head. "We'd have been weaker without them and less able to protect them. With them here, we *know* if they're safe, and I can maintain the protections around them, So we tighten their protection." Kallista touched Padrey's hand as she threw another layer of shielding up, taking delight in the eager response of the magic. "And we act."

"Tonight?" Torchay lifted an eyebrow.

"I said act, not attack—though if we have to . . ." Kallista called magic, shaped it to hunt, gave it teeth and armor and sent it out. "It's late. Tonight, the magic can hunt. Tomorrow is soon enough to follow where it leads. We can rest tonight."

Aisse gave her a wicked grin, sliding into Padrey's lap. "You believe we will get any rest?"

Kallista laughed as Padrey's surprise melted into a cheeky grin. "Eventually. I hope. The bed is awfully small."

"We'll manage. We did before." Fox scooped her off the chair and tossed her onto the bed, then stripped off his tunic. "Everyone playing?"

Not everyone spoke, but everyone agreed.

"Oh dear." A little twinge of nerves, laced heavily with anticipation, slithered through Kallista.

"Oh *good*." Aisse's voice sounded all anticipation and immense satisfaction.

"It is our wedding night after all." Fox squeezed closer to Kallista to make room for Padrey against his back, with Aisse on the other side.

"Do we want magic?" Kallista twisted her *hand* in the links, but didn't call.

"Enough to bind us," Torchay said. "To feel each other."

"Enough to help us wait." Obed kissed Kallista's nape.

"But no more." Viyelle hooked an arm around Joh's neck. "Just . . . enough."

"Done." Kallista called magic as she returned Fox's kiss.

Kallista woke late. Again. But this time, the bed was crowded with naked bodies and someone was knocking at the chamber door. A brisk knocking, not timid, but not a frantic pounding either. Important news, but not desperate.

"Hey." She worked a hand out of the crush and patted some part of someone's body. Ribs, she thought. Male. "Whoever's on top, go answer the door."

"Already done." Keldrey tied off his trousers and slipped out the door to see what was wanted.

Kallista used elbows and hands to clear a space big enough to wriggle through, slapping away Fox's hands when he tried to pull her back. She was belting her houserobe by the time Keldrey returned. She took a second to check her hunting magic. Nothing. Had she hurt the demons so badly?

"What is it?" Kallista didn't like Kel's grim expression.

"Message from the justiciars. Without evidence of wrong-doing, our accusation against Chani's dismissed."

"Without evi—" Kallista stopped her outburst.

Keldrey had more to say. "Apparently, there is no sword."

She frowned. "We sent it. With the complaint."

"Well, they haven't got it. That's what they say, anyroad."

She took in a deep breath, let it out again as her mind laid plans. "So either it didn't reach them, or somebody's lying. And since we sent the sword with Nur im-Nathain, I think we can count on the lie." She flicked a glance at Keldrey. "Send an escort for Nur Truthsayer. Ask him to bring another blade and meet us at the Justice Chambers. That's where we'll begin."

"Begin what?" Joh pulled his hair forward over his shoulder to begin the process of combing and braiding it.

"Our demon hunt." She held her hand out to her new godmarked ilias. "Come, sweeting. Time to hurry. Anyone who's coming with us had better hurry too."

Chapter Twenty-Nine

All nine of the godmarked rode to the Daryathi Chambers of Justice in Mestada, Keldrey once again staying behind to keep guard over the children. Kallista had to admit it eased her mind to know one of their own watched their horde of little ones. She just wished she had better contact with him so she could reassure herself whenever she wanted that all was well.

Nur Truthsayer was already through the gate, escorted by his own local bodyguard-champion rather than the soldiers Kallista had sent. Clever of him. The justiciars would have no chance to cry collusion. Kallista rode into the courtyard at the head of her party and dismounted. Only she and Allanda the lawyer—and Obed as Reinas and bodyguard, and Padrey who couldn't be left behind—joined the truthsayer at the Chambers building entrance, waiting for the justiciars to arrive.

"May I ask?" Kallista edged nearer to Nur, speaking without looking at him. "Why did you leave the temple?"

"Do you know what it is to have magic and not use it?" He replied in the same manner. "It seemed to us better to use the magic in constructive ways, ways that would help others, rather than simply— venting the pressure. When the temple walls fell—"

"Ah." Kallista nodded. "I understand." Then she straightened as the wide double doors opened. She'd have to ask later about the temple walls.

"What is the meaning of this?" The woman who had spoken for the presiding justiciars at the court arena stood in the open doorway, as if she would bar it with her body.

"I bring my response to your communication of this morning." Kallista inclined her head in a slight bow. "Since you claim that you received no weapon to support my complaint of tampering with justice by means of drugs in the arena, I have asked Nur im-Nathain to bring another."

Behind the speaker, Kallista saw shadowy forms gathering in the dimmer light of the buiding's entry hall, at least one of them white-haired. With luck, that might be the head justiciar from the trial. Maathin, Obed had called her.

"I have had possession of this blade since the trial." Nur stepped forward. Lifting the sword in his hands, he pulled an inch or so of steel from its sheath. "It was taken by our own healer nathain from one of the Habadra champions after he fell in the Varyl-Habadra trial. It has not been touched since it came into her possession in the infirmary."

The speaker-for-the-justiciars held out her hand, her face a blank mask. "I will take this weapon for consideration."

Nur lifted it just out of her reach. "As you took the last weapon out of my hands?"

The woman's blank mask cracked and fear showed through. "I—yes. That is—"

Maathin pushed her way through the door. "Did you receive an earlier sword, speaker? I thought you said you did not."

"I—I may have been confused—my memory—when the sword wasn't with the complaint, naturally I assumed I hadn't got it, and I—"

The white-haired woman cut her off with a brusque wave of her hand and gave Nur Truthsayer a questioning look.

"Not truth." His mouth twisted a bit.

"*Did* you receive the sword with the Varyl complaint?" Maathin's voice cut as sharp as the steel.

"Erm—I—" The speaker turned her eyes all round, as if looking for escape. "I suppose I may have, yes."

"Truth," Nur said.

"Where is it now?"

"I'm sure I don't know."

"Truth." Nur sounded surprised.

Kallista wasn't. She knew how literal truth could hide lies. "May I ask a question?" She bowed a bit deeper to the head justiciar. Maathin frowned, but nodded.

"What did you do with the sword when it was given to you?" Kallista asked.

"Why, nothing."

Nur opened his mouth, but Kallista waved him to silence. "You didn't bring it inside and place it with the complaint?"

"Oh. Well, yes, of course I did." The worry began to leave the speaker's face.

"Truth." Nur's expression had soured.

"And then what did you do?" Kallista continued.

"Nothing."

Kallista wanted to smack the smug expression from the woman's face. "Nothing at all?"

"I listed it on the register of complaints and informed the Head." She bowed to the white-haired justiciar.

"Whom you told that no sword had come with it."

"Yes." The speaker blinked, realizing what she'd said. "No! That is, I'm sure I said nothing about the sword at all."

"Lie." Now Nur was looking smug. Funny how it didn't make Kallista want to smack him.

"*Speaker.*" The snap in Maathin's voice made the younger woman jump. "What did you do with the sword?"

"Noth—" She slanted her eyes at Nur and didn't bother finishing the word, falling into sullen silence.

"*Tell me.*"

The speaker cringed. "I hid it behind the file shelves and sent word to Habadra, who sent someone to collect it. I truly do not know where it is now," she cried in desperation, then sank back into sullenness. "Who knew these Adarans had another?"

"The healer collected five of them," Kallista said.

"*Why?*" Maathin's voice held anguish. "Why would you subvert our justice like this?"

355

The speaker flinched, tucking her hands in the folds of her robe. "*They* have no respect for justice. You saw how she behaved after the first day of trial. They are a race of slaves!"

Even Maathin recoiled at that, but Nur shook his head. "That is not all the truth. It is very little of it." He pointed at her hands. "What are you hiding there?"

The speaker glared at him, defiant.

Maathin put out her hand, palm up. "Show me. *Now.*"

Reluctantly, the younger woman brought out her hands from the folds of her white robe. Rings adorned four of her ten fingers, gold rings with glittering stones.

"How much did the Habadra pay you?" Kallista asked quietly.

The speaker turned her defiant glare on Kallista, refusing to answer.

"Whatever it was," the head justiciar said, "it was not enough." Maathin snapped her fingers at the Justice Chamber champions and indicated her be-ringed junior. "Take her away. And bring me paper and ink. I am writing out a warrant for the arrest of Habadra Chani for perversion of justice."

Kallista bowed and backed away, satisfied at achieving her goal. She was still curious though, and watched as Maathin turned to Nur.

"It seems we owe you thanks again, Truthsayer," she said. "Shall I appoint you justiciar?"

The young nathain bowed deeply. "That is not my role, madame. I do not judge, only speak truth."

"Perhaps truthsayer is a new position for Daryathi justice." Obed startled everyone when he spoke. "Edabi held a trial not long ago with a truthsayer. I am sure they would be willing to share their experience. Especially since Edabi Skola will no longer be providing champions for the trial arena, and I am sure the other skolas will soon follow their lead."

"Nine-marked." Maathin gave Obed a deep bow—deeper than the one she'd given Kallista. "We will consider your words."

She turned aside to write on the portable desk held by a junior apprentice. When the ink was dry, she rolled the paper, sealed it and handed it to a six-marked justice champion.

"Thank you, Aila." Kallista bowed again as Nur gave custody of the second sword into the head justiciar's hands. "You give me hope for Daryathi justice."

Maathin's mouth twisted. "I do not like change. Our ways have worked—perhaps not well, but they have worked for a hundred years. Still, if there is a better way . . ."

Kallista's smile flickered into being. "Exactly. Now, if you will excuse us—"

The head justiciar held up an imperious hand. "Do not interfere with this arrest."

Kallista feigned shock. "I wouldn't dream of it. But—if there's trouble your people can't handle, we can help." She gave the old woman a bland smile. "Surely you cannot refuse that."

"Do *not* interfere," Maathin repeated, and with a brusque bow, disappeared inside chambers.

"So." Kallista returned to her godmarked. "At last, we ride against Habadra."

"You heard what the justiciar said," Allanda warned. "Do not interfere."

"I heard." Kallista swung onto her horse. "Three times now. And we won't. I promise. Unless."

"There's always an 'unless'," Torchay said, not helpfully.

"The justiciar's champions can't handle a demon." Kallista led the way back into the street.

"What? Demons?" Allanda scrambled to follow.

"You think Chani harbors the demon?" Obed asked.

"She's one of the few I haven't dared search." Kallista waited to let the escort form around her.

She glanced at Padrey, who sat awkwardly on his horse next to her. He obviously hadn't ridden this much since childhood, if ever. Kallista eased a bit closer. "How are you bearing up?"

He flashed her an ill-at-ease smile. "Fairish. I don't like being in the front of things. It's bad for a thief to be noticed. Or a spy." He paused for another, cockier smile. "But I like hearing everything first hand. I like *knowing*."

Kallista laughed. "That's my spy." She urged her horse ahead as they started toward Habadra House. "Tell me—what do you know about Habadra's slaves?"

Padrey's smile vanished. "She has more than fifty, at least half of them too young for magic—maybe more than half. Of the adults, three of the women and one man have magic—all south. Two bakers, a weaver and a brewer. She bought two of 'em, from smaller Lines. Poorer ones."

"Ah. How are they treated?"

Padrey shrugged. "They're slaves. They're fed, kept alive, but—"

Kallista felt the sadness and anger through his link and sent love and promises back. Then she changed the subject a bit. "Where are they kept?"

"In the back. Behind the kitchens. There's a big room—"

By the time they reached Habadra House, Kallista knew everything Padrey did about Habadra's slaves.

The Adarans hung back, across the broad square fronting the house, as the champions approached and demanded entry.

"Joh? Ride close and watch for me." Kallista sent him off with his escort. Dressed today in working clothes as they all were, he wouldn't be as easily noticed as Kallista, and she could watch through his eyes.

What would Chani do? How would she react to this outrage? And no question, she would consider it an outrage. What if she truly was—as Kallista had come to suspect—demon-ridden?

Kallista held her hand out to Padrey and sidled her horse closer to his. "Come, sit behind me."

"Why?" His look wasn't quite suspicious.

"Because I still have to touch you to reach your magic." She beckoned to hurry him. "If I have to call it quickly, I want to be ready."

He slid from his saddle onto Kallista's horse. He almost fell before settling behind her, his arms round her waist.

"One hand here." She moved his hand from her waist to rest on the bare nape of her neck beneath her queue. Over her mark. It tingled just a bit, as if the mark recognized him. "Skin to skin, remember? This way, my hands are free. Just don't let go."

"I won't." He leaned into her, breathed warm on her neck. "Seems a strange way to go into a fight, though."

Kallista had to smile. "It is. But it works. We've done it before, when Joh was new. Don't let me fall off the horse."

"Are you likely to?" Padrey sounded a bit alarmed.

"Not if you hold on tight." Kallista squeezed the hand still at her waist. "Poor Padrey, so many strange things. I can see through Joh's eyes. But while I'm watching, I tend not to pay attention to what *I'm* doing. I've been known to fall off perfectly still chairs. And since this horse isn't still . . ."

"Right." His grip tightened.

"Hold on." Kallista slid down her link with Joh and blinked her vision into alignment with his.

Joh stood just outside the outer gate, at an angle where he could see the inner gate without being easily seen himself. He'd dismounted and his infantry dun tunic blended nicely with the local shades of dirt. His guard, in red-and-white-trimmed black, was a deal more noticeable.

Through Joh's eyes, Kallista watched the justiciar's champions wait while Habadra Chani was summoned from within the house. As they did, the outer courtyard filled with more and more champions wearing Habadra's purple cranes painted and embroidered on their kilts, until those in justiciar's black-and-white could barely be seen.

I don't like this, Kallista whispered through Joh's thoughts. Aloud, she said, "We need to move closer."

The six justice champions were beginning to look a trifle concerned about the situation as well. Kallista brought her people to stand behind Joh and pulled back into her own vision. She called magic and sent it questing out for fresh demonstink, then called more, piling it up to be ready, in case.

Finally, Habadra Chani sauntered through the inner gate into the outer courtyard of her Line's House.

The six-marked champion in charge of the justiciar's company handed the scroll to Chani who cracked it open and read it. The champion with tattooed hands and feet nodded at his underlings. Two of them moved to take the Habadra by the arms.

The sound of a double score of blades clearing sheaths hissed through the courtyard, but the justiciars held firm. Chani wadded up the warrant and let it fall to the paving.

"I am Head of Habadra Line," she said. "I do not submit to arrest." She shook off those holding her and this time, they allowed it. Naked steel had that effect, even on the bravest.

"Do you defy Daryathi law?" the six-marked asked.

"I see armed Adarans at my gate." Chani sneered at Kallista, waiting in the street. "Is that Daryathi law?"

"This is Daryathi law." The champion pointed at the warrant crumpled on the ground.

"No, *I* am Daryathi law," Chani retorted. "I am Head of Line, of the richest, most powerful line in all Daryath, and I do not submit to the accusations of foreign upstarts."

Kallista had listened to enough. She didn't take offense at Chani's sneering words. Kallista *was* foreign, and she wasn't from a prominent family, which she assumed made her an upstart. How could she take offense at truth? But she'd never had much patience, and she was tired of listening to them argue.

She siphoned off a good-sized chunk of magic and shaped it to hunt. She gave it a nice sharp spear point, and she hurled it at Chani. She *hurled* it, and the magic *flew*.

It didn't ooze or dribble or trudge, it flew fast and hard and straight and true, and it slammed into Chani, cutting off both speech and breath.

Time seemed to freeze as everyone went still, most not understanding what had happened to the Habadra. The rest waited to see what the magic would find.

Chani screamed, the sound slashing through the air to shatter the stillness. "Kill them," she raged. "Kill them all!"

Her champions attacked the justice company, cutting half of them down before they could draw weapons.

"Help them!" Kallista cried.

At the same moment, Chani shouted, "No, *them*—the Adarans. All the Adarans! *Start with the slaves.*"

A party of purple-clad champions split off to dash back into the house. Kallista snatched magic and dropped them, sent them to sleep. She called more and put the rest of them down—all but Chani and the justice champions.

Kallista had intended to leave the justiciar's people awake, but Chani should have gone down with the rest. Kallista scrabbled for her hunter-spell and pulled back a stub.

The demon boiled up out of Chani—Khoriseth who had hidden from Kallista six years ago inside Serysta Reinine's High Steward. Now it had hidden inside Chani during Kallista's searching, Khoriseth, who had *quenched* her magic in Arikon before Leyja's marking as their then-ninth had enabled Kallista to drive it off, if not destroy it.

Kallista grabbed for magic. She wrenched it from her iliasti and still could not demand more than was poured into her. Kallista threw up shields, creating a pen around the demon. It shrieked on a plane not audible to human ears. But the horses heard it, or sensed it, for they panicked.

Padrey shouted as the horse he shared with Kallista went up in the air. He tried to hold on, Kallista tried to hold him, but she didn't dare let go the reins. He fell, hard, the impact shuddering through Kallista still in the saddle. The horse crow-hopped away from him. But the magic didn't break.

She still had hold of that joyous eagerness he brought to the whole. Had the link formed so quickly? How? Did it matter? She slid from the saddle, unable to concentrate on the magic and fight the frightened animal at the same time. Her shields began to buckle under the demon's violent attack.

"Is that a—?" Padrey's horrified whisper reached her as he caught her hand.

"Yes." She didn't have time now to explain about the link forming, so she let him hold on while she called more magic to shore up the weakening shields. One more order to give before she could forget everything but destroying this demon.

"Send a company to the slave quarters," she said to whoever was nearest. "Get all the Adarans out and back to the embassy."

"Yes, my Reinine." Joh answered, gave the order.

Half the escort broke off and trotted on foot through Habadra's gate. Kallista still stood outside in the street, she realized. No matter. She was fighting Khoriseth, not Chani.

Gathering her strength, Kallista wrapped magic around the shields she'd built and began to squeeze, compressing the demon trapped within. It squalled, eating away at the shields like acid on glass, tearing at them with a thousand new-grown demon claws. But the shields had been shaped only to keep it inside. The new magic surrounding the shields was made to destroy.

The demon broke through the shields and shrieked as the magic attacked it, dissolving it from the outside in. It fought, punching at the magic that enveloped it. Kallista wrapped *hands* in the links to her mates and hauled out still more.

It was working. Khoriseth could quench some of the magic, but it could not stop all of it at once. Kallista laughed out loud. *She was winning*.

The demon lunged at a corner of the trap she'd caught it in. The magic gave, bulged out. Before Kallista could slap a patch over the weakness, the demon burst through and escaped.

It skipped across the sleeping champions and flowed through the walls to take up residence on the shoulders of a well-dressed woman in a sedan chair, then left her for a man on horseback, and him for a racing youth.

"Follow!" Kallista cried. "We have to follow it." She looked frantically for her horse. Surely someone had caught the reins. "Where's Gweric?"

"At the embassy." Torchay had the horse. "Watching for attack against the children."

"Oh. Right." Kallista couldn't see the demon any longer, but she could smell the stink it left behind. She furled out a bit of magic and sank it like a fishhook in the demon's side. The demon would destroy the magic before long, but while it lasted, the spell would tell her where the demon went.

"Up you go." Torchay started to boost Padrey onto the horse behind Kallista, but she waved them off.

"The link's formed," she said. "Already. Emergency situation, I suppose. Or I didn't wait too long before the binding, or something."

"Good." Torchay tossed Padrey onto the nearest unoccupied horse just as the six-marked champion came into the street to block Kallista's path.

"Get out of my way." She urged her horse forward.

The champion caught her reins, refusing to back down. "What has happened here? What have you done?"

"Found one of the demons that have been corrupting Daryath. *And it's getting away.*"

"What is getting away? What madness is this?" The man tightened his hold on the horse's head.

"*Truth,* not madness. The One's marks are real. Demons are real. There was a demon in possession of Habadra Chani—can you understand that? It rode her. Twisted her. And now it's left her." Kallista paused as a thought bubbled through her narrow demon-aimed focus. "Is Chani dead? Sometimes when a demon leaves, it leaves the person dead. I didn't kill her."

"No." The champion sounded a bit shaken. "No, not dead. Demons are real?"

"If you had any magic, I would show you. Yes, they are real, and that one is getting away." She stabbed a finger toward Khoriseth's escape route.

"What am I going to tell the Head?" the champion muttered as he released Kallista's horse.

"That you've arrested Habadra Chani." Kallista gathered her mount and her thoughts, and spurred them both after the demon.

Where would it be running? To its master? To the ancient evil Gweric promised was lurking here? Was she ready to face such a foe?

She had to be.

As they raced after the fleeing demon in the bright chill of the autumn morning, their horses slipping now and again on the rounded cobbles, Kallista could sense the demon tearing at the magic hook sunk into its spirit-flesh. Desperate to rid itself of the tell-tale, it tore away bits of itself that floated a moment before merging again with the whole. Kallista formed her hunter-killer magic and sent it to make sure no bits were left behind, even as the hook came free and died.

The demon's path tended generally toward the city's center, toward the temple and the Seat of Government. Who—or what—could it be seeking there?

"Chosen!" The shout came from the lush garden behind the piles of rubble that had been temple walls, piles that shrank as people carried away the stone for their own building projects.

"Chosen of the One!" A cleric stepped out of the shadows.

"Not now," Kallista cried. She didn't have time for anything now but following that damned demon and ripping it into nothingness. They were almost—

She called up a demon-destroying veil, named it and threw it out, hoping she'd come close enough to do the thing some damage. "Khoriseth!"

The demon vanished. Before her magic reached it, without ever touching it, Khoriseth was just . . . gone. Kallista shifted her vision to see the dreamplane as well as the physical, but the demon wasn't there either. She hadn't destroyed it. There hadn't been any screaming or gnashing of metaphysical teeth. It was as if the thing had simply winked out of existence.

Had it hidden itself again?

"Fox, what do you see?" She wheeled her horse in the middle of the broad plaza.

He looked, first with his eyes open, then he closed them and seemed to look through his eyelids from one side of the vast square to the other. He shook his head as he opened his eyes again. "Nothing," he said. "Sometimes I can use that sense you gave me with my eyes open now, but I can sense nothing. No demon-twisted people. I—" He stopped and shook his head again.

"Damn it!" Kallista added several of the choicer oaths from her soldiering days. Her horse picked up her agitation, expressed it by dancing in place.

"Chosen." The cleric had come close enough that the horse threatened to step on her. Other clerics clustered in a knot behind her.

Shock rippled through Kallista as she realized the cleric wore a yellow robe marked with a full compass rose. The High Prelate of Daryath, a South naitan, was standing outside the temple, in a public street.

"Chosen—what was that?" The prelate's face registered shock and horror. "That thing you were chasing?"

"A demon. You saw it?" Kallista swung down to the paving and handed her reins off to whoever was there—Torchay again. "Did you see where it went? What happened to it?"

"I—no, it—it vanished. It just—vanished." The woman's eyes were wide. "That was a demon?"

"One of them." Kallista grimaced. "The small one. Where was it, exactly, when it vanished? Could you tell?"

The high prelate looked out over the plaza. "Exactly? I'm not—" She waved her arm toward the Seat. "That way."

Kallista huffed a little breath, hands propped on her hips. "That's all I could see too. Damn it. Now I'm going to have to go dig it out. Somehow. These things can hide from me."

The prelate looked up at Kallista. "How may we serve you? How can we help fight this demon?"

Kallista blinked in astonishment, then she grinned and startled everyone, including herself, by hugging the prelate. "Can any more of you see the demon?"

She looked at the timid naitani who clustered behind their leader. Several of them lifted their hands.

"Excellent." Kallista clapped her hands together and rubbed them. "If you would try to discover where the demon might have gone, it would be a tremendous help. Any healers among you—demons tend to lash out without concern for who else might be hurt. Farspeakers—perhaps one with the searchers and one at the temple for communication? You shouldn't search unguarded—are there champions who might—"

"I will guard." The justiciar's six-marked champion stepped forward.

"You're here? I thought you took your prisoner back to Chambers."

"I sent a man with her. The other stayed with our injured." He bowed. "Thank you for the care of your medics."

"Prelate, there are injured—" Kallista began.

The high prelate signaled to one of her people who trotted off in that direction. "We have a few champions of our own."

"Then are we set?" Kallista surveyed her forces.

"What are *we* going to do?" Torchay asked.

"Hunt demons."

"Yes, but where?"

Kallista's gaze fell on the Seat of Government. Khoriseth had been hiding inside one of the executive councilors. Would the greater demon ride a lesser-ranked? She'd encountered it at the Seat only two days ago. It could be there now. Besides, the en-Kameral hadn't answered her demand. They might be interested to know she'd already liberated Habadra's fifty-plus slaves.

She glanced over her troop as she mounted. Half the escort was gone, sent back to the embassy with the freed slaves. And they'd brought a smaller than usual number with them, to leave more guarding the children. But her magic was complete. Strong.

"Chosen." The high prelate called Kallista's attention. "Not all the clerics nor all the nathains agreed with my decision to leave the temple. There is a split. The Samerics have stirred up the people. Be careful."

"You as well." Kallista bowed from atop her horse.

"Where *are* we going?" Torchay asked again as he fell in beside her.

"There." She pointed at the Seat.

Torchay sighed. "I was afraid of that."

Chapter Thirty

As they traversed the short distance to the government building, Kallista reinforced the shielding around her people, sharing as much as she could with the searching nathains. They could be exposed to the demons, but her godmarked were the ones going into battle with them.

She left the soldiers in the street with the horses and instructions to call for help if a riot started. And to come at once if Kallista called. Surrounded by her godmarked iliasti, she strode up the steps and into the en-Kameral chamber.

Many of the seats in the multi-tiered room were empty. The Kameri present gathered in small groups to talk. Two members of the executive council stood near the dais, conferring with some of their colleagues. The other councilors were nowhere to be seen. Everyone looked up in surprise when Kallista entered.

"Reinine—" The Head of Tathiwa Line and the elder of the two councilors present took a hesitant step forward. "Did we have an appointment?"

"We did not." Kallista bowed a fraction lower than she would have otherwise, in apology. "But I thought to inquire about your response to my request of Thirdday past."

"*Request?*" One of the Kameri talking with the councilors broke in before Kallista could continue. "That was no request. It was an ultimatum. An insult."

"To my ultimatum, then." Kallista's hand moved instinctively toward her sword hilt. She stopped herself before it arrived. No use stirring up trouble sooner than needful. "You might like to know that

Habadra Chani has been arrested for perversion of justice for poisoning the weapons her champions used in the recent trial. And—"

"Habadra would never submit to arrest," the Tathiwa exclaimed.

"So you agree she is capable of the crime? She did not submit. But she is nonetheless in custody of your justiciars." Kallista scowled. She'd expected demon attacks on her shielding the instant they entered the building—or at least when they entered this chamber. Why didn't it attack? Was it even here?

She called magic, shaped it for hunting and sent it plunging into the nearest Head of Line. The woman stiffened, groaned, but didn't react further—perhaps because she was less stained by demon touch than many. Kallista instructed the magic to keep going, to search every Daryathi in the room. Then she turned her attention back to the councillors.

". . . this is a deliberative body. We do not act foolishly or in haste," the Tathiwa was saying. "We—"

"You might be interested to know," Kallista said. "We have already freed the slaves at Habadra House. I also spoke to your High Prelate in the street just now. Your own naitani—your nathains will no longer cloister themselves in the temple. All your own people who manifest magic will be free to use it outside the temple for the benefit of everyone."

"Blasphemy!" someone cried from a tier near the top.

"Is it blasphemy when your own high prelate has spoken? You shut your own nathains away to 'protect' their magic, but have no trouble enslaving mine so you can still use magic. You cannot have it both ways." The hunter magic had scoured through at least half the Kameri and their bodyguard champions without finding more than stain and it worried Kallista.

"You have no more need of slaves." Kallista's voice filled the chamber. "I want my people back. *I will have them back.*"

If the demon wasn't here, where was it, and more, what was it doing? Kallista spoke quietly over her shoulder to Torchay. "Someone should check on the troop, make sure things are still quiet outside."

He nodded and slipped away. She hadn't meant for him to go himself, but then with only her godmarked present—the lawyer had returned with the freed slaves—he was probably the best choice.

"You do not rule here!" shouted the Head of Line who'd protested first. "We will not let you come in and destroy our society or the traditions handed down to us by our mothers."

"Your traditions have the taint of demons, twisted from older, better ways. Do you truly wish to live by *demon*-birthed ways? Under *demon* law?" Kallista made a supreme effort and put a name to the woman in yellow-green with tall-horned cattle marching round her gold pectoral collar. She was the Nabili, one of the most conservative of the Kameri who'd visited the embassy. She was beginning to annoy Kallista mightily.

"This is Daryath," the Nabili sputtered. "*Our* home. *We* rule here. We do not take orders from insignificant amateurs with delusions of godhood."

"*You dare?*" Kallista lost her grip on her temper and sent the hunter magic slamming back into the Nabili.

This time, the woman screamed—and the magic sputtered and died.

Kallista snatched for more, but it slipped through her fingers, refusing to answer her call. What was going on? The magic had never failed her before. Not like this.

"What are you doing to us?" The Tathiwa's voice held horror. She supported the gasping Nabili.

"Searching for demons." Kallista let her hand rest on her sword. "Your whole misbegotten land is riddled with the stink of demons. Since the time of the battle in the Empty Lands, a demon has hidden here and ruled over this society you are so proud of. I will rid you of them—both demons and traditions."

"Kallista—" Torchay bent close to speak in her ear. "Things are tense outside. Crowds gathering, throwing curses. Next will be rocks. Best we leave, if you've no' found the demon."

Kallista sent her gaze around the chamber, searching the Kameri and their champions with her eyes as she'd searched them with the magic. "One way or the other," she said. "I will have my people back. Better for you if you give them up willingly."

She spun on her heel and stalked away, hoping desperately that no one saw her shaky panic. What had happened to the magic? She reached for it, and hesitated, afraid to try calling for fear it wouldn't answer this time either.

"Where's Padrey?" Torchay took a long stride to catch up with Kallista on the high porch.

"Right th—" She turned to point, but their new ilias wasn't just behind her, where he'd been all morning. She lurched toward the door, to go back inside and look.

Torchay stopped her. "He's no' inside. No' in the meeting room." He looked at the others who'd gathered round at the top of the steps. "Did anyone see him go inside with us?"

"No." Aisse frowned. "How can he not be with us?"

"The link's formed." Kallista bit her lip. "Already."

"Then—where is he?" Viyelle asked. "Can't you sense him through the link?"

Kallista was afraid to look with her magic falling apart like this. Were the links still there? What was going on?

"*Kallista.*" Obed's voice held the same urgency she felt. "Is he out in that?" He pointed.

The streets seethed with activity, their Adaran troop a lone pool of relative stillness. The soldiers stood in a half-circle facing out, the horses behind them, held by a few of the men. They held their carbine pistols pointing up at the sky, a visible threat against the rising hostility of the people in the street being harangued by shaved-bald Samerics.

Fighting back her fears, Kallista *reached*, not for magic but for her links. If the links were there, maybe the magic would be too. Carefully, as if reaching for a skittish animal, Kallista slipped her *fingers* around the links. Relief flooded her as she embraced them, counted them. All eight were here, humming with life. And magic. Would it answer her call?

She would try later. For now—quickly she separated out the link that bound her to Padrey. "There." She pointed at the building they'd just left.

"Inside?" Viyelle shook her head. "But didn't Torchay say—"

"Not inside. Past the building. Somewhere on the other side. We'll have to go round." Kallista shooed them ahead of her down the steps. "Hurry."

"Where's he going, for the One's sake?" Joh asked. "What's he doing?"

"I don't know." Once more, Kallista swung onto her horse. "But whatever it is, he thinks it's important."

"If it's so important, why didn't he tell anyone?" Leyja complained. "Why didn't he ask for help?"

"I don't know." Kallista couldn't keep the temper out of her voice. *Why hadn't he?* How dare he risk himself alone on these streets? Yes, he'd done it a dozen, a thousand times before. He'd *lived* on the streets, his life forfeit if he was recognized. But he hadn't been marked then. He hadn't been married. He hadn't been so desperately needed.

"He's only been married to us for a day," Fox said. "He was alone for years before that. It's hard to learn new ways."

"He needs to learn faster." Kallista wanted to ride faster, but the soldiers had to force a way through the crowds, using the strength of their horses and the threat of their carbines.

"But he wasn't alone, not completely," Aisse said. "He did have his sedil. And her children."

"He was alone protecting them," Fox said. "As much as an escaped slave and a thief could."

"Maybe that's where he went," Joh suggested. "To Penthili House to get her. He'd know it—he escaped from there, didn't he?"

"I don't know," Kallista said yet again. She was getting tired of having to say it. "But if he's gone off on some half-cocked rescue mission without telling us, I'm going to beat him. Or something."

Ahead, Kallista could see the crowd thin out. The Samerics apparently couldn't stir up tempers quickly enough to keep pace, even at the Adaran's forced slow pace. *"Hurry."*

Padrey slipped through the alley behind Penthili House, feeling conspicuous in his sharp-looking rust red tunic and black trousers. He didn't blend into the sand-colored wall any more. He felt more than a twinge of guilt for coming away like this, but close as Penthili House was to the Seat, he could be in and out again with Nanda and her kids before his new iliasti noticed he was gone.

True, his sedil would be freed when all the slaves were freed, but he couldn't wait any longer. He'd waited too long already—since his escape—and the Penthili was just an older version of the new Head of Habadra. She would destroy a thing rather than let someone else have it. If word got out that Kallista had freed Habadra's slaves—No, Padrey couldn't wait.

He found the place where the plaster over the stone wall had been broken and poorly repaired, and the shallow handholds improved upon by a certain thief. Padrey checked to be sure the alley was empty, and swarmed up and over the wall, dropping into the Penthili pigsty to the squeal of disturbed piglets. *Damn*. Maybe the boots weren't quite totally ruined. They should have let him wear the old ones.

Escaping the pen just ahead of angry mama pig, Padrey scraped off the worst of the muck and started for the laundry where his sedil worked in the mending room. There, she could keep her oh-so-valuable children away from the dangers of laundry tubs and kitchen fires.

In his new clothes with his face fresh-shaved, he couldn't duck his head and play "slave on an errand" as he always had before, the few times he'd dared to come visit. He put on an arrogant swagger to walk as if he owned the place. He was—oh Goddess, he was Padrey *Reinas*. He might not own *this* place, but— He would think about that later. After he got Nanda out.

He strode down the corridor to the mending room, ignoring the few people he passed. They were beneath the notice of—whoever he was supposed to be. Bold as a new-marked dedicat, he entered the room, closing the door behind him.

Startled, his sedil cried out, spread her arms, and her flock of children scurried to huddle under them.

"Saints, Nanda." Padrey tried to count. "You're only twenty-five. How'd you get so many kids?"

"Padrey!" She sprang from her chair to hug him. She'd gone plump and soft, her apron mounding over yet another pregnancy. At least the bastards let their slaves wear clothes when they were pregnant. Otherwise, they wore only the short, white kilts.

"They're not all mine," Nanda said when she let him go. "I watch the little ones, from when they're weaned till they're big enough to work. What are you doing here? It's too dangerous for you. You have to leave—but where did you get such fine clothes?"

"I got married." Padrey felt the blush burn his cheeks and didn't know why. It wasn't like he had run out on his marriage. He wouldn't be here long. "I'll tell you everything later. I've come to fetch you." He stopped her protest with a wave. "You and your brats. You know I wouldn't leave 'em."

"Penna's not here—my oldest." Nanda's eyes were wide with beginning panic. "She works in the house, weeding courtyards."

"*Saints.*" Padrey drew his hand down over his mouth, thinking. "All right. I'll get her. You get everything ready here. I'll be right back."

"Padrey—" Nanda's soft voice called him back. "I'm happy for you."

He frowned. What was she talking about?

"Your marriage?" Nanda gave him a shy smile. "I wanted you to know—in case? I'm happy you found someone."

"*Nine* someones, actually," he muttered, then stabbed a finger at her. "There's no 'in case.' I am getting you out. Now, today. Be ready."

She blinked, then her smile widened and she nodded. "All right."

Padrey hadn't been much in the family sections of Penthili House, but he found the courtyards easily enough. He just followed the sound of water. Unfortunately, like all other Houses in Mestada, it had a multitude of courtyards scattered through the maze of the House. The first two were empty. The third held Penthili men gathering with friends for lunch. Padrey gave that one a wide berth. No slaves would be there unless they were serving, and Penna was too little for that.

Just how many courtyards did this House have, and how many would he have to search before he found the child? At least he didn't have to worry about searching the same courtyard twice. Each one had a distinctive fountain or pool.

"Can I be of assistance, sir?"

Padrey spun around to see the person he hated most in the world, the housekeeper who had made his slave's life miserable with her callous cruelty, an echo of her mistress. Now, Zatha-ti stood with head bowed, hands clasped at her waist, the picture of obsequious humility.

Thinking frantically, Padrey drew himself up, copying dignity from Obed Reinas. Wait—hadn't Kall—the Reini—*Kallista* come to a party-thing at Penthili House before the trial? He didn't have to pretend the impossible. He could be Adaran.

"Adara's Reinine sent me. She lost something—a necklace—and thought it might have been lost here. At the party. The guard at the gate said I could come in and look." Would she believe that enormous lie, especially since the guard hadn't come along? Could Padrey get rid of Zatha-ti and find Penna at the same time? "Can someone help me search? Who tends the courtyards?"

The horrid old woman clapped her hands sharply and a flame-haired, kilt-clad slave boy scurried to answer. "Find the weed girl," she said. "Bring her to me."

The boy bowed without speaking and rushed off. Zatha-ti preferred silence from "her" slaves, and enforced that preference viciously. Padrey remembered all too well.

"What sort of necklace is it, sir?" Zatha-ti joined him in the search, fortunately at the next garden bed, so he had some distance from her.

"Gold, with a red stone." Padrey described the necklace he had stolen, reduced in size. "Small. Of more sentimental value to my Reinine than its worth in coin." Goddess, what if Zatha-ti decided one of the slaves had stolen it, decided to punish them till they gave it up? "And she is not certain she lost it here. It might have fallen in the street on the way, or even at the embassy, earlier. But she did ask that I come look."

"Of course, sir." The housekeeper straightened as the slap of bare running feet on pavement neared.

The slave boy bowed. He reached behind him to grab a smaller child's arm—she was seven, Padrey knew—and haul her forward. The boy, who looked a few years older, bowed again and held the position. The girl bowed too. Padrey grimaced, his back aching in sympathy as he recalled how long Zatha-ti could make them stay like that.

"So, girl." Padrey made his voice overly cheerful. "Have you seen a necklace in your cleaning? Small, gold, red stone. Stand up straight. Look at me. Both of you, now."

Zatha-ti clapped once, as if she couldn't allow Padrey to usurp any of the authority she'd claimed. The children straightened. The girl child looked up at him. Her face brightened—*oh hell,* she recognized him.

Padrey frowned, shook his head, tilted it a fraction toward the awful woman and Penna's expression blanked. The boy shifted his eyes from one to the other of them, but kept silent. Of course. Zatha-ti noticed nothing. He hoped.

"Well?" Padrey strode in a circle round the children.

Penna shook her head, staring up at him. As if she trusted him to know what he was doing.

He had no idea. How in blazes was he supposed to take Penna away now Zatha-ti had latched onto him? Could he even get back to Nanda now and get her out?

"Are you sure? Could it have fallen under some plant? Into some spot that didn't need cleaning?"

Penna shrugged, looking a bit worried as she slanted a glance toward the frowning housekeeper.

"Speak up, girl. I can't hear you think." Padrey folded his arms, tried to look fierce.

With another glance at Zatha-ti, Penna said, "Some of the flower beds don't grow many weeds. I don't have to tend them so often. Maybe—"

"Let's go look, shall we?" He took her hand and started to walk away. Another courtyard, away from Zatha-ti, and they might be able to sneak off.

"I know you," the housekeeper muttered. She said it louder. "I *know* you." She pointed a long-nailed finger at him. "You're no envoy. You're a slave. *A runaway.* Guards!"

"Run!" Padrey grabbed the children and flung them ahead of him.

"Champions! Guards! *Help.*" Zatha-ti hiked up her dress and ran after them, shrieking for help, but she couldn't match their panic-driven speed. "Runaways!" she shouted. "Thieves!"

"This way, this way—" Padrey plunged back into the depths of the House. He couldn't leave Nanda behind. He'd promised her. "Don't wait," he told the children. "Run to the pigsty. You can get over the wall in the corner. When you get out, find the Adaran embassy. Tell them Padrey sent you. Tell them you're kin. Understand me?"

The children's eyes were wide with fear as they ran with him, but they nodded.

Padrey could hear the clatter of weapons and nailed boots. The champions were coming. He shoved the children into an empty courtyard. "Go! I'll get your mother. *You go.*"

"My mother too?" the boy paused to ask.

"Yes. Yes, somehow. Now *run.*" Padrey slammed the window-door and dashed across the broad chamber, slowing just enough to let his pursuers see him before darting through the doorway, to be sure they followed *him.*

He stumbled as a vast strangeness rippled through his body. *Magic.* He'd felt it before but not like this. "Kallista—" His lips formed her name.

The magic pulsed, pure pleasure, and he stumbled again, almost fell. A Penthili champion caught him, slammed him against the wall. Padrey's head bounced and he cried out, choked it off as the edge of a blade pressed against his throat.

"Kill him!" Zatha-ti hobbled into the room, breathing hard.

The champion nodded.

Oh shite. Padrey managed one more thought before the blade sliced into his neck. *Kallista, I'm sorry.*

Chapter Thirty-One

"No!"

The scream sounded in both his mind and his ears as the champion crumpled to the ground. Padrey slid down the wall, his hands clutching at his throat, trying to stop the blood. He choked on it, fought it for breath. He was breathing?

"Easy, lad." Torchay's face swam in Padrey's vision. "No, don't lie flat. Here—"

Hands lifted, moved him and Padrey leaned against something firm and warm—no, *someone*. Someone held him, supported him in his arms.

"Oh God, oh God—" Was that Kallista's voice?

Padrey blinked, trying to see. He could breathe, a bit. The blood didn't choke him so bad now. Wasn't he dying?

He could see Kallista bent over him. Her face was wet. And . . . it had blood on it. She swiped at her face with the back of her hand and got more on. Padrey lifted his hand to wipe it away, but his was bloodier. Oh, that's right. They'd killed him.

He coughed, spraying blood everywhere. "Goddess," he croaked, "Sorry. Watch out—guards."

"No, don't talk. Don't—" Kallista put her fingers over his mouth a moment, then laid her hand on his neck again. "You're not healed yet. And the guards are asleep. Everyone in the House is asleep, except Adarans."

Her voice sounded strange too, sounded—

"'R'you crying?" He couldn't believe it. "Why?"

"Stop talking," she scolded. "Let me finish before you try to undo what I've done. Why do you think I'm crying, you idiot?"

He didn't know, but he wasn't about to dare words, not after that. He tried to ask with his expression, a feeble shrug.

"You almost died!" The hushed volume of her words only added to their intensity. "A little deeper, a little faster, and I couldn't have brought you back."

Padrey had to clear his throat. It didn't hurt, or only a little. He brought his hand up to feel. The skin was tender, but it was closed. "Right," he whispered. "You need me."

"Yes. I need you." She sat back on her heels. "If it hurts to talk, don't. I've never had to heal a voice before."

"Am I healed?" Padrey leaned to the side to spit out the blood in his throat, then struggled to sit up. Torchay, who'd been supporting him, helped.

"How do you feel?" Kallista took a handkerchief from Aisse and leaned forward to clean his neck.

Padrey thought about taking it from her—he could wash his own neck— but didn't. He lifted his chin for her instead. "Sore," he said. "Tired."

"That'll be the blood loss," Torchay said.

"But otherwise?" Kallista turned his face the other way, to get at the other side. "It looks good."

"Yeah, other than that, I feel okay." Padrey nodded.

Kallista dropped the bloodstained handkerchief and gave him an open-handed smack on the side of his head. "Then what in the name of all that's holy did you think you were doing coming off here alone? Without telling anyone!"

"You were busy. I didn't want to bother you."

Kallista wanted to tear her hair right out of her head. Or his. His would do. "So instead, you came here alone to get yourself killed and it never occurred to you that *that* might bother me? Never mind that I was *hunting demons* when you left on your solo expedition!"

"Sorry." Padrey hunched in on himself with a sheepish expression. "I just—I didn't think anyone would notice. Not before I'd got Nanda and got back."

"You didn't—" Kallista threw herself to her feet and paced a few steps away, trying to get a grip on her violent emotions. Because she *hadn't* noticed. Not until Torchay had called her attention to his absence.

But she hadn't thought Padrey would do something so colossally idiotic. And she'd been a bit preoccupied by the demons and her amazing, disappearing magic. Thank the One it had answered her call when she truly needed it, in time to save Padrey from his folly. From her negligence.

Kallista wiped away the stupid tears. She returned to kneel beside Padrey where Torchay made him stay to regain his strength. She took the hand of her young ilias and held it in both of hers.

"Forgive me," she said, "for ever making you feel I wouldn't notice if you were gone. I know it's hard, coming to an ilian after being alone so long, joining an ilian that's been together six years without you. But try harder. Please?"

Padrey swallowed hard, past the new-healed scar in his throat, and nodded, his eyes wide.

She couldn't stop there, much as she wanted to. She couldn't be less than honest. She owed him all the truth—and just maybe it would stop him from taking such insane risks. Or at least from taking them alone. "I can't speak for the others, only myself, but please don't ever think I don't care for you."

Kallista paused, trying to block the memory of the terror that had flooded her, but it was impossible. "Goddess, Padrey—when I felt that blade slash through your throat, when I saw—"

She broke off, fighting tears. "I nearly died when we lost Stone. Literally. Maybe you know that. He was the godmarked bound to me for the longest time, so maybe that made a difference. Maybe losing you wouldn't be so bad—but I do not want to find out.

"I didn't want to care, Padrey. I didn't want anyone else to matter like that. But I do care. I can't help it. It's not just the magic. You've made a place for yourself in my heart just as quickly as this link of yours has formed between us."

Kallista took a deep breath and found a smile. "So, next time, when you feel the urgent need to do something insanely dangerous—*tell* us." She grinned, wiping a last tear or two. "More than likely, we'll come with you. We're like that."

"We came this time, didn't we?" Torchay ruffled up their young ilias's hair.

"They're all out." Viyelle leaned in through the doorway. "All the Adarans, heading toward the embassy."

"Is it wise?" Kallista asked. "To send them all in a group, with the streets like they are?"

"You might get the poor on your side—" Padrey flushed at Kallista's pointed look. "On *our* side, I mean, if you promise to take all the slaves back to Adara. It'll open up work for them."

Kallista stood, her knees aching. They couldn't take much kneeling these days. She offered her hand to help Padrey up. "Suggestions on how to spread the word?"

He grunted as she pulled him to his feet. Worried, she sent a thread of magic sliding through him to be sure all the damage was healed. Everything looked normal.

"Just sore," he said. "And tired. All you have to do is send a few of the slaves to pass the news to other slaves out in the city. Word will get around."

Fox came into the room hauling a pair of filthy, kilt-clad children, one with hair as fiery as Torchay's. "Found them trying to climb over the outer wall from the pigsty and making a terrible job of it. They wouldn't believe I'm Adaran till I brought them to our lad here."

"Uncle Padr—" The smaller child, a girl by the delicacy of the face under the muck, stared wide-eyed at their newest Reinas, her mouth beginning to quiver with frightened tears.

Kallista looked at him. Oh Goddess, his tunic was black with all the blood he'd lost. No wonder the child was terrified. Padrey yanked the tunic off with an oath, but the body beneath was worse, the red smears showing clearly.

He swiped at the blood with his wadded-up tunic. "I'm all right, Penna. It was just a scratch. See?" He lifted his chin to show the new pink scar. "It looks scary, but it's not. Really."

Torchay came up behind Padrey holding up a gray overrobe with black crescent moons and stars embroidered on it. "Here. You don't want to be scaring anyone else."

Padrey frowned as he put his arms into the sleeves. "Where'd you get it?"

"Took it off her." Torchay pointed to a woman with gray-streaked hair lying crumpled on the floor nearby.

Padrey's face changed, turned ugly, and he stalked over to the woman.

"Who is she?" Kallista thought for a moment he meant to kick her, but he didn't.

"Zatha Penthili-ti." Padrey bent and yanked the woman's belt loose. "She likes having slaves to command."

"I hate her," the red-haired child said.

"I hate her too." The little girl edged closer.

"Me too." Padrey winked as he pulled a knife from his belt.

"Planning on killing her?" Torchay leaned casually against the wall. "Probably not the best idea."

"I thought about it," Padrey said. "But no. I do think a little humiliation is in order, though." He used the knife to split the hem of her simple white dress, then ripped it up to the neckline. "The kids need something to clean off that muck."

He rolled the woman out of her dress, split it up the back and handed a piece to each child. Giggling, they wiped away the pigsty muck coating them and dropped the cloths on the floor. Padrey picked up the cleanest rag and did their faces again, then he turned them to face Kallista.

"This is my niece, Penna, my sedil Nanda's oldest," he said. "And this is her friend—" He paused to look expectantly at the older child.

"Tommey," the boy said and bowed deeply, Daryathi style. Lovely manners.

"And *this*," Padrey gestured to Kallista, "is the Reinine of all Adara, Kallista."

Viyelle put her head back through the door. "*Are you coming?* The locals are getting a bit restless."

Fox thumped a champion on the head as he tried to rise, knocking the man back to the floor. "They're getting a bit restless in here as well. I think we've used up our welcome."

At the gate, a plump, obviously pregnant young woman stared worriedly through the bars, clutching a toddler in one arm and holding the hand of another small child who held the hand of one a bit older, perhaps Sky's age. When Padrey appeared with his niece, the woman gave a little cry and rushed forward to hug them, children trailing her like ducklings.

"She would not go with the others," Obed said. "I take it this is the missing child?"

Kallista nodded. "And an extra. He may have family."

Padrey's sedil released him, then smacked his head. "Why didn't you tell me you married the *Reinine?*"

"*Ow.* Why does everyone keep doing that? I'm injured. Look." He showed off his new scar, rubbing his head exaggeratedly.

"If you didn't deserve it, we wouldn't do it." Kallista smacked him again, gently, and bowed. "I am Kallista Varyl. I hope our other iliasti have introduced themselves to you." Quickly she introduced those who had been in the House with her.

"N-nanda Suverr," the young woman stammered, hoisting the baby higher so she could bow.

"If I'd told you I married the Reinine," Padrey said, "you wouldn't have believed me."

"I might," Nanda protested.

Kallista looked around the street. Viyelle was right. The locals were getting restless, and most of these were not the poor, angry over losing work to the slaves. Here in the wealthy sector of town, the people owned slaves, or aspired to own them. They wouldn't appreciate losing them.

No one was throwing stones yet, or threatening attack. They merely gathered in clusters, muttering to one another, sending evil looks toward the Adaran troop gathered outside Penthili House. A block or so away, Kallista saw Samerics rounding the corner, coming to whip the crowd into a fury. Padrey had needed the time they had taken, and it hadn't cost them anything to take it. But the situation had changed.

"We should go," she said. "Padrey, are you strong enough to ride alone?"

"Yeah. Fine."

Kallista wasn't sure she believed him, but she let it go as he swung onto the mount they'd brought from where he'd left it.

"Leyja, would you take Nanda up with you? Divide the rest among you and let's go." Kallista mounted. "I'd like to check with the temple nathains, see if they've found anything—but if the streets are too rough, we'll go straight to the embassy."

"If things get too rough, you can put them to sleep like you did in there," Torchay said, the red-haired boy clinging behind his saddle.

"I'd rather not. I won't run out of magic, but I could run out of strength." Kallista watched as the last child, the littlest, was handed up to Aisse, and a pair of soldiers helped Nanda onto the horse in front of Leyja. "Besides, we don't want to terrify *all* of Mestada. It would be nice to have one or two of the locals on our side. Let's avoid trouble if we can."

Besides, who knew if the magic would come the next time she called it? She couldn't let *them* know that, of course. No use worrying them over something that might not happen again. If they stayed away from the riots, everything would be fine.

She signaled the captain and Kargyll led out.

Kallista studied the scowling Daryathi in their knots and clumps as she rode past them. Unease shivered down her spine. Danger prickled her skin. Worried, she reached for magic, and breathed a sigh of relief when it answered. She didn't *see* any demons nearby, but—she spun a thread of magic into a tracker-alarm, to hunt for trouble and warn them if trouble was found. She used the rest to build shields around their troop.

Something was still wrong.

What? Kallista rose in her stirrups to see beyond her bodyguards and the reduced escort. Nothing. Or nothing in particular. Nothing any different than it had been a few ticks past, before she felt this way.

She tried to sort out the *wrongness*. The air tasted off. Sounds echoed oddly. Colors twisted. She counted her links, tested them—maybe someone was ill. Gweric's cold could have spread—but everyone seemed fine. What in heaven could it be?

Another shiver of alarm, almost panic, whispered through her. It felt—she reached for the feeling, nearly caught hold before it faded to nothing. Her magic failing again? Was this how it felt? Was it leaving her completely?

Fighting down the panic, Kallista checked her shielding—standing strong—and her tracker magic. It hummed straight ahead. Had it found something? She couldn't tell. Nothing definite, then. But the magic was working.

She drew out another little thread, feeling a touch of smug triumph when it came skipping into her hands. The magic wasn't the problem. So what was?

Alarm, *warning* shivered along her nerves again and Kallista tossed the magic at it. The magic strengthened the feeling, clarified it, gave it a definite taste of . . . *Keldrey*.

Goddess, oh *Goddess*, if Keldrey was that worried—*the children*— Kallista fumbled for magic to call the farspeaker she'd brought with her entourage. Taylin had been left at the embassy for just such emergencies, to call if help was needed.

Kallista's call slammed into a wall and shattered. A wall of—

"*Ride,*" she shouted. "The embassy's under attack! *Hurry.*"

The wall was demon-built, echoing her shielding, but black with malevolence. The demon couldn't get past the shields she'd built round the embassy—she hoped—but she couldn't get past the wall it had built. Not with her magic. Not at this distance.

"Who's attacking?" Joh asked. "How many?" He'd been an officer in Adara's army like Kallista had, but with the infantry. He had more experience planning actions like this one promised to be. Kallista wished she had something to tell him.

"I don't know. I can't get through to Taylin or anyone." Kallista pushed her horse faster, despite the way it slipped on the cobbles at that speed.

Torchay caught her reins and forced her to slow. "If your horse falls and you break your neck, you won't reach them at all. And if you can't reach Taylin, how do you know they're under attack?"

"Keldrey," she said. "I sensed Keldrey. He's that worried. The demon's built a shield wall around my shielding and it's blocking my magic. But Keldrey's ilias, even if he isn't marked. There's a link. Can't you feel it?"

Torchay shook his head, but he pushed their speed right to the edge of danger, just short of Kallista's recklessness. He obviously felt the same urgency she did, now she'd explained.

Kallista drew magic, needing to do something more than just ride, but when she called it, she didn't know what to do with it. She wanted to be close, right on top of the demon, so the magic would obliterate it with the first blow.

She held the magic, filling it with her anger and determination, with the demons' names, and without warning, she could see it. Zughralithiss. As if she peered through a ship's telescope, the distance between them withered to nothing.

The demon shields shimmered darkly, half-hiding it behind them. She could see her own shields glowing around the embassy, holding the demon and its hordes between the two, in the wide street outside the front wall. The demon hovered, spread thin over the howling mob. The iron-barred gates held, so far.

A little pile of bodies lay crumpled in a semi-circle around the gates, where Adaran musket fire had taken a toll. As if through fog, Kallista could see movement in the outer court, soldiers firing, reloading and firing again. But the bodies created a protective barricade for the Daryathi to bring up their own few musketeers and crossbowmen to fire back.

"Joh." Kallista called him over, described what she saw.

Rioters began to scale the walls, vulnerable because they were too narrow to post guards on top. Troopers picked the climbers off before they got inside, but soon there would be too many to shoot them all and the outer courtyard would have to be abandoned.

The demon flowed from one point to another, seeming to renew the Daryathi's fury wherever it went. It was anchored in one person—tall, white or gray-haired, probably a woman, Kallista couldn't tell more—but the demon seemed able to spread out from that anchor and directly influence everyone it touched. More Mestadans came through the demon shield to join their fellows, stirred up by Sameric fanatics.

Her horse reared and Kallista clutched at it with hands and legs, her attention jerked from the embassy ahead to those riding with her. They'd stopped; Torchay had stopped her horse.

"We're close," he said when she looked at him. "We can't take babies into battle." He gestured and Kallista turned to see the troop escort she'd sent to the embassy from Habadra House and a clutch of kilt-wearing slaves.

"The Adarans from Habadra are inside," the officer in charge of the half-troop reported. "We were coming back to join you and found these."

"They're not all Penthili," Padrey said. "Word's getting out."

"Is it true?" a young man among the slaves shouted. "Are you taking us all home?"

"Yes, it's true." Kallista stood in her stirrups. "I am Kallista Reinine and I tell you so myself. I will take you all home. As soon as I deal with the demon-touched vermin that dare to attack my children."

"Let us fight with you," another man cried.

"You have children of your own to protect." Kallista signaled and the passengers were set down. "And news to share. Spread the word. Gather the rest of our people. Keep them safe. There are those in Mestada who would be happy to see you go. Ask them to help. As soon as I can, I will send soldiers to bring you safely in. Until then—" She looked the group over, trying to think what else she had to do. "Look after each other."

She settled back into the saddle as Kargyll gathered up her reunited troop. Before Kallista sank back into her magic, she murmured to Joh, "Give them their orders. I know you have a plan. Just get me close enough to destroy that demon."

"Yes, my Reinine." Joh gave her a little bow and rode the few paces to confer with the captain.

"Joh—" Kallista called as she realized. "I may have to break though those demon-built shields before we can reach them. Let me ride a little closer and find out."

"We'll all ride a little closer." Torchay hadn't let go of her reins.

Kallista let him do as he wished, sliding deep into the magic. The demon's walls loomed ahead of her, rising halfway to the heavens, spreading outward across the city's streets as the thing fed in the strength it gained from mortal rage and pain, hatred and death. The street where she stood made an inward bulge in the inverted bowl of the demon shield. Soon, if nothing changed, they would be encased—perhaps trapped—in a bubble.

Kallista sidled her horse closer, stretched out both hand and magic to touch it. She couldn't see it with physical eyes, but she felt it, so cold it burned. She jerked her hand away. Her magic slid along it, rain over glass, unable to find purchase or access.

The demon lifted, opened a trio of red glowing eyes, and turned them on her.

Godstruck. The unspoken naming shivered through her. *For too long you have been a thorn in my side.*

You've been a pain in my ass just as long, Zughralithiss. She hesitated. *Khoriseth? Is that Khoriseth with you? In you?*

The demon's blackness rippled, squeezed, thumped. The third eye vanished. And opened up again in a different part of the dark flow.

My offspring does not seem to want to be reintegrated. The demonstuff rippled again. *It is an indigestible lump in my belly—or what passes for a belly among myself. I should never have split them off from me, allowed them independence. But they're all gone now, taken back into myself or destroyed by you. All but this miserable lump. Children are a sad disappointment, don't you agree?*

My children are pure joy.

What lies. They quarrel. They disobey. They whine. Endlessly, they whine.

True. Kallista smiled. *But they are a joy nonetheless. So why don't you let down this wall? I will rid you of your disappointment and return to my joy.*

I think not. The demon billowed high, filling the space inside its shield. *While we have had our chat, my—what is the word? Minion. Yes, my minions have breached your walls. They will carry me inside your shielding and I will destroy your joy and feed on your pain before I crush you into dust.*

"*No!*" Kallista screamed, sending the magic she had been steadily building exploding outward. It crashed into the demon shield, and for a long agonizing moment, the shield held. Then, finally, it shattered.

Not all of it. Only an opening the width of the street where she and her godmarked and the troop could pour through into the riot-filled space in front of the embassy. The demon shield tried to mend itself as they rode. She held open a tiny gap and threw shielding back through, over the huddled slaves, before the demon's wall closed again, locking them inside.

"At a canter," Captain Kargyll called. "Charge!"

The troop leaped ahead, spreading out to fill the street side to side, two ranks deep, facing the demon's forces. The first rank carried their carbines. The second held cavalry sabers, ready to take the lead after the volley was fired, to allow the first rank time to draw their sabers. There would be no time to reload.

Kallista spurred her mount, ready to charge after them, forgetting Torchay still held her reins. Her poor horse tried to obey, circling him, fighting for its head.

"We follow," Torchay shouted at her. "But slower."

"*Form up,*" Joh called.

Kallista fumed at the waste of time as her iliasti moved into positions they'd decided on without her. Obed and Fox took the lead in a wedge formation, with Joh and Leyja behind and outside them, Viyelle and Aisse in a third rank even further out. Kallista rode in the center, directly behind the two leaders, with Padrey and Torchay on either side of her.

"Can we go *now?*" she asked caustically. "Before the demon kills my children?"

"We're already moving," Torchay growled back. "You're no' in this alone, woman, and I'll thank you to remember that."

Blast the man and his attitude. Kallista reached for the magic, cursing when it responded sluggishly. "Padrey, what are you doing?"

"Nothing. Riding." He gave her a bewildered look.

Kallista swore and hauled hard on the magic. She stretched, looking past Obed and Fox as the carbine volley sounded and rioters fell. She regretted the necessity, but she needed to save her magic—her strength—for the demon. She couldn't put them to sleep like she had the others. The magic never ran dry, but her strength was all too finite, and she'd been flinging magic with abandon for hours. The second rank surged ahead and crashed into the mob, breaking it apart, crushing it under flying hooves. The first rank followed, sabers flashing.

The crowd disintegrated, screaming as they fled. The troopers didn't pursue, fighting straight ahead, clearing a path to the wide-open outer gate.

Her magic rushed toward her in a sudden gust and Kallista scrambled to grab it, managing to stay astride only by instinct and years of riding. What was wrong with this stupid magic? She had a demon to fight. She didn't need to fight her magic too.

Chapter Thirty-Two

The wedge of her godmarked hit the remnants of the mob, scattering it further, dealing sharply with those still inclined to fight. Kallista shaped her magic, gifted it with both demon names, and as she plunged through the gate, she let it fly.

The hunter shape of the magic arrowed straight toward the demon where the spiderweb shape she'd made clung, wrapped around it to prevent escape. The dark destroying veil dissolved the demon's substance, eating through it like acid on stone. The demon shrieked, recoiled, sent claws lashing out.

It struck just as Kallista saw the gaping inner gate. Terror for her children blended with the sharp pain of the demon attack, tearing a scream from her throat. *She had to save them.*

She threw herself from her horse and dashed ahead, through the inner gate, across the courtyard into the embassy.

"Kallista, wait!"

Torchay's shout was noted and dismissed. She couldn't wait. Her children needed her.

Darting through wide chambers and down narrow corridors, Kallista drew magic, struggling with its erratic response. She swore as she fought it. Where was this attitude coming from? She did not have time to stop and straighten out her iliasti.

The magic bucked and she slapped it down. She shook it, willing it to behave, to do what she wanted it to do, as she ran blindly ahead. Straight into the arms of Daryathi champions.

Kallista laughed as one of them snatched her up, pinning her arms to her sides. She didn't need hands to use her magic. These men had no idea what she could do. She split off part of the magic and shaped it. Just as she pushed it out to drop them in their tracks, it crumbled. Vaporized into nothingness.

No! Not again.

She heard Torchay bellow her name as her captor bore her off, leaving his comrades to fight. She heard the clash of steel as her men attacked the champions behind her. Obed would be at Torchay's side, fighting with his usual silence. Fox—yes, that was his shout. Kallista tested her links, counted them, shielded them. They were all there. So why wasn't the magic?

She couldn't even reach through the links and touch it inside them. It was there. She could sense it. But she couldn't touch it.

Bouncing over the shoulder of the champion in the unpainted kilt as he carried her deeper into her residence, Kallista called her old magic, the lightning that had come to her when she was leaving childhood. With her hands pinned against her hips this way, she would burn herself as badly as the man who carried her, but she didn't care. She wanted free. She needed to save her babies.

But if she broke free now, she would be alone in the midst of the demon's minions with her magic gone missing. And if she didn't free herself, they would carry her to the leader of this attack—and that person's demonic rider.

And her magic had gone missing.

She wanted to reach the demon. But *with* her magic. Without it, she was as helpless as one of the slaves she'd just freed, as one of her children. *Where had it gone?*

Once more, she reached back down the links with her godmarked, almost dove bodily through them to grab hold of her magic. It slipped through her grasp like minnows in a pond. The sound of fighting grew louder again. She was out of time.

Frantic, Kallista lashed out with her lightning, stifling her cry as it singed along her leg. Her captor dropped like a felled ox with a deep grunt of sound.

The men to either side shouted and grabbed for her. Kallista, on the floor over the fallen man, caught their wrists and fed the lightning directly into their bodies. They collapsed into two twitching, drooling heaps.

A gunshot rang out behind her and Kallista ducked. The fighting behind was catching up. Her iliasti would reach her soon. All she had to do was wait. But her babies were in danger.

All of them were hers, from baby Lissta to just-found Sky to her beautiful, beautiful twins. She had to get her magic back and save them. And while she worked on that, she could creep ahead—careful not to get captured again—and spy things out.

The thought hadn't fully formed before Kallista moved, slipping from the corridor into the maze of rooms that would take her eventually to the fighting near the nursery. She passed quickly through the empty rooms, listening through doors or draperies before inching them open to look, then scurrying across. But finally, the rooms didn't connect any further. She would have to risk the corridor again.

Kallista lay flat on the floor to peer through the gap under the hallway door. A man lay on the floor outside, staring back, tattoos stark on his blood-smeared face. Alarm pounded through her until she recognized the blank stare of the dead.

Booted feet thumped past her view, running toward the nursery, and Kallista slid on her stomach to change her angle, see further in that direction. More feet, more than she could count quickly, pushing, slipping, bracing . . . fighting. The men on those feet were fighting. Which meant Keldrey still held, right?

She felt a tug on one of her links and tugged back, instinctively. *Here. I'm here.*

A wave of worry, approaching terror, surged toward her from all her links. She tried to farspeak them but couldn't catch enough magic even for that. She could only send back the sense that she was safe for now, and a warning to be careful.

Their relief was so strong, it wrapped around her like a blanket and made her smile. Then came a rush of anger from Torchay, capped with an imperiousness that could only mean "Stay there." She had to smother a laugh that dissolved into a sob. What had happened to their ilian, that the magic had dissolved?

The magic was still there. She could feel it. So why couldn't she call it? Why couldn't she . . . ?

Was *she* the problem? Could it be?

Kallista sat up, set her back against the door carefully, so it didn't rattle. If anyone wanted in, she wouldn't be taken by surprise. She had to *think*.

Where was Joh when she needed him?

Again, Kallista's heart froze. The thought had been a joke, an attempt to lighten her heavy-weighted thoughts, but was it really? She'd been captured because she'd left her iliasti behind. Was there more to her abandonment than that? When had the magic first vanished on her?

This morning, when she'd tried to send the magic into the Nabili, the magic had dissipated like fog in a breeze. But earlier, when Khoriseth had punched out of the bubble where she'd trapped it . . . . She'd felt the magic weaken, just before the demon escaped. *Why?* What had been different about that moment? About all the other moments?

She tried to rebuild that instant of time. Her soldiers had been *there*, the justice champions *there,* Chani with Khoriseth between them. Kallista had caught the demon inside shields and wrapped the destruction magic around that. When it worked, she'd felt so—so *triumphant.* And then the demon had escaped.

Was that it? Feeling too much glee over defeating demons? But when the magic actually vanished, she hadn't been gleeful. She'd been . . . Kallista shuddered. She'd been angry. She hadn't sent her magic into the Nabili to search. She'd already searched the woman. She sent it to punish her. For daring to defy Kallista's authority.

Kallista's authority.

Oh *Goddess.* Kallista hid her face in her hands and hunched over the sudden pain in her gut as shame hit her.

"You're not in this alone," Torchay had said.

She had forgotten that. Had got so caught up in what she could do, so wrapped up in being the Reinine, in being the one with all the pretty magic, she had forgotten that none of it was actually *hers.*

All of it—the magic, the title, even her precious family—all had been given to her by the One Ruler of All. *All*, not just Adara or Daryath, but everything. Including life itself. Her very life was a gift from the One, and she had forgotten.

"I'm sorry," she whispered, rocking herself back and forth, weeping in remorse. *Of course* the magic wouldn't come, if she failed to recognize its source. It came *through* her iliasti, the godmarked, but it came *from* the One. And it was not meant to be used for her petty whims or to make her look important. She herself had no power at all.

She'd been able to call the magic to heal Padrey. Maybe because her focus had been on him, not herself. But she hadn't learned from it. Now, again the magic wouldn't answer—perhaps to be sure she did learn—and she didn't know how to fix it.

A whisper of sound brought her head up, her hand swiping across hot, wet eyes when Torchay, Obed and Fox burst quietly into the room. The others followed the instant Fox signaled as he tucked a pistol in his belt. He'd been the one shooting.

Torchay rushed over, sliding the last bit on his knees, sheathing his swords before he reached out to examine her. "Are you hurt? What's happened?"

Obed stood over them, listening at the entrance, peering through the crack between the double doors. The others stayed back a space, behind Fox who stared without seeing at Kallista.

"I'm fine." She swiped at her cheeks again, pressed her fingers against her burning eyes.

"We'll see them safe." Torchay apparently agreed with her assessment. He put an arm around her and squeezed. He must think she wept over the threat to the children.

"Are you sure you're all right?" Fox asked. He blinked, and looked through his new-healed eyes *at* Kallista.

She frowned. "Mostly. Why? What do you see?"

"What do you mean, mostly?" Torchay caught her chin and turned her to face him again, searching for injury.

She pushed his hand away and stood, wincing as the burn down her leg rubbed against her trousers.

"Damn it, what have you done to yourself?" He attacked her laces, to pull the trousers down and see for himself. "I don't see any blood."

"There isn't any. It's a burn, all right? I burned myself with my lightning. It's not that bad." She watched Fox who watched her right back.

"I'll be the judge of what's bad or no'." Torchay hissed as he exposed the burn. "Bad enough. There's blisters."

Kallista ignored him. "What do you see, Fox?"

He shook his head. "I don't know. It's—I haven't seen anything like it before, exactly. I—I can see it both ways, with my eyes and my knowing."

"Can the rest of you see anything?"

Torchay looked up in the middle of covering her burn with a soft bandage. "I don't see anything different."

The others shook their heads, Joh and Obed after them, taking longer to look.

"How did you get the burn?" Joh asked softly. "Why?"

Kallista couldn't meet his eyes for more than an instant before she had to look away. She licked her dry lips, swallowed hard. But she wouldn't lie to them any longer. "Lightning was the only magic I could call."

Torchay's head jerked up. Aisse clapped her hand over her mouth. They all stared at her in horror.

Tears filled her eyes again as Torchay laid his hand on her stomach, under her tunic. "Are you—?"

She shook her head, flinging away tears. "No, I'm not pregnant. Even if I was, it's too soon for that to stop the magic, and it would stop the lightning too. No, this is my fault. My own stupid pride."

"What do you mean?" Obed touched her cheek, his concerned frown making the tears come faster.

Kallista caught his hand, held it and ignored his question. Other things were more important now. "Fox." She held his gaze. "What *exactly* is it you see?"

He cleared his throat. "A . . . shadow. I don't know how else to describe it. There's a shadow round your throat and down your chest. Over your heart. It's very faint, but . . ."

She looked with all her vision and couldn't see it. She wanted to scream with frustration.

"Where is it?" Padrey approached, looking back at Fox. "Here?" He touched the side of her neck.

Kallista shivered, and for an instant, she thought she saw a flicker of—of *something*. "Wait."

She pressed Padrey's hand flat against her neck, but the flicker didn't return. She slid her hand onto Torchay's nape as he finished his task, and she reached toward her mates with her other, still clasped in Obed's hand. "Come. All of you. The links are there. They're stronger when we touch."

They crowded round her. Leyja slid her hand onto the other side of Kallista's neck. Aisse covered her hand where it rested on Torchay. Viyelle set her hand beside Aisse's, sliding it up Kallista's sleeve to clasp her wrist. Joh joined Obed, holding her hand between theirs, and with a cheeky grin and a wink, Fox dropped to one knee and wrapped his hand around her unbandaged thigh, since Torchay hadn't put back her trousers yet.

Kallista opened the links wide, praying for the magic's response, but it didn't seem to hear her. She had only the magic given her so many years before, at her childhood's end. But she'd been able to see magic even then. She peered at herself with her other "eyes" and saw the faintest hint of shadow just where Fox said it was—over her heart, rising toward her throat.

The door slammed into them as someone forced it open, sending them all tumbling.

Obed was the only one who didn't fall. He gained his balance in a graceful whirl and waded into the champions crowding through the door. Fox, who hadn't had far to fall, sprang up and helped him drive them back.

Kallista kicked off the trousers tangled round her ankles. They hurt her burn anyway. She reached for Padrey, Aisse—anyone she could touch. She had to rid herself of that shadow.

Torchay moved to help Obed and Fox, and Kallista called him back. "No, help me here. The door is a choke point. They can hold it for now."

He knelt again and laid a hand on her ankle, but though his magic was the strongest of her mates, his presence didn't seem to make a difference now. Or not enough of one. She still couldn't see the shadow. So she would have to work blind.

"Forgive me my foolishness," she whispered. "Help me now. I can't do this alone."

"O' course we forgive you." Padrey's voice startled her, sent chills down her spine as his words echoed with greater power, deeper meaning. "What can we do?"

Tentatively, Kallista reached for magic, but again it eluded her. She growled in disgust. Without her magic, she couldn't rid herself of the shadow, but she couldn't touch her magic.

"Kallista, let me take Fox's place." Torchay pleaded with her. "He can see it. Perhaps he can see what to do."

"Yes, all right." She had no better ideas.

Torchay joined the defenders at the door and after a moment, Fox edged away. He stepped backward until he reached Kallista. With a glance back at her to be sure of his location, he knelt and laid a hand over her ankle.

"Can no one carry out a simple task?" A voice—female and oddly familiar—carried through the open doorway from beyond. "All you had to do was kill her. She's half dead already."

Kallista gagged as something—the shadow magic—tightened around her throat. *She couldn't breathe.*

"No!" Padrey's cry distracted her men at the door. Not long, but enough for them to be driven back. Fox let go of her and returned to the fight. Kallista thrashed, desperate for air.

"Padrey, can you see it?" Viyelle demanded.

"Maybe. I think." He sounded on the edge of panic.

Kallista was too near panic herself. She needed air. She grabbed his wrist, tried to beg with watering eyes.

Looking almost as frantic as she felt, Padrey scooped his fingers along her neck. She expected him to close his hand on nothing, to play at pulling away air, but when he jerked his hand back, the noose around her neck loosened and she gasped a shallow breath.

"Again!" Viyelle cried.

"I see it," Joh said. "I see it too." His hand brushed her neck as he pulled shadow from her.

Leyja joined their defenders, and Viyelle. The invaders had pushed halfway into the room, far enough to open a space behind them. A woman entered inside their protection. Shakiri Shathina.

The demon entered with her.

Kallista snarled, her strength returning as her iliasti peeled away the shadow sucking at her. "I should have known."

The fighting slowed, stopped as the two women faced each other behind their champions' protection.

"You should have." The demon gloated, speaking with Shathina's voice. "I knew this moment would come. You are weak. Controlled by emotion. *I* sent the assassin's darts to Arikon. I knew your faults would lay you open to me. Attaching the leech was a simple matter. I did not expect you to come *here*, however. Bekaara has spoiled my plans for the last time. The draining has taken longer than I hoped, but it was only a matter of time."

So long ago? No wonder she had behaved the way she had, with the demon's magic draining her all this time. And yet, it was her own fault. She complained about the duties and burdens of rule, but she had loved being Reinine, enjoyed the power it gave. She'd made herself vulnerable to the thing. But the One had still been able to open her eyes to the truth.

Padrey and Joh tore at the demon leech, barely staying ahead of it with the demon near enough to feed the thing power. Now she was aware of it, Kallista could see how the shadow magic had twisted her thinking, had reinforced her errant thoughts and urged her farther along the wrong path, bit by insidious bit. But it had only fed on flaws already there.

With a struggle, and Aisse's help, Kallista rose to her knees. Silently, she cried out to the One. *Forgive me. If I've gone too far wrong, I accept whatever punishment I deserve. But my iliasti are innocent of what I have done. They tried to turn me aside from my wrong, and I would not listen to them, as I would not listen to you. Save them. Save our children.*

"What are you doing?" Zughralithiss-Shathina demanded. "Stop!"

The leech magic tightened around Kallista's throat again, despite all Padrey and Joh could do. She ignored it. *Take me,* she begged. *But save them. Please, save my family.*

Everyone in the room seemed frozen, most of them focused on the silent, nearly invisible, deadly struggle around Kallista. Save for the three clustered around her. Joh clawed at the shadow over her heart while Padrey seemed to wrestle snakes near her neck. Even Aisse had plunged in, though Kallista knew she couldn't see it. Aisse brushed her hand along Kallista's throat. And the magic stirred.

Kallista grabbed it. Loyalty and utter devotion seeped past a tiny crack in the demonspell. With a sob, Kallista wrapped the thread of magic round her fingers and pulled it through.

Torchay flinched at her sob and Kallista sent reassurance through all her links. She caught Joh's hand, found a wisp of clarity and a second thread of magic. She bound it with that from Aisse and *pulled*.

Joh's gasp made Padrey look up. With a flick of his eyes from their clasped hands to Aisse's ecstatic face, he seemed to take in what was happening and slid his hand beneath the shadow onto Kallista's mark. Joy rushed into her and Kallista laughed out loud. She pushed the shadow back and took her first deep breath in too long.

"Kill her!" the demon cried. "Kill them all!"

The warriors' stalemate ended on that shout. The Adarans attacked before the others could react. The Daryathi fell back a step or two, but more of them fed through the door to take the place of the fallen and push Kallista's people back.

She reached through the links to her iliasti defending them too pitifully few but could not grasp their magic. Half-frantic with fear, Kallista squeezed Joh's hand, took a tight grip on his magic and let go.

Yes. The magic stayed, even when they didn't touch. She needed the touch to recover the magic, but once captured, she did not need to maintain the hold. "Joh, take Viyelle's place. Send her to me."

He nodded and slipped away, exchanging smoothly with their prinsipella ilias. Kallista took Viyelle's hand and used it to pull herself to her feet as she caught hold of Vee's magic and creativity. Viyelle laughed as her magic streamed into Kallista and was bound into the web.

Torchay glanced back and almost paid for his inattention. Joh warded off the blow and Viyelle laughed again, coming to take Torchay's place with the defenders.

A clatter had him springing past Kallista toward the other entrance, but he held his blow as Tayo Dai bodyguards crowded into the chamber.

Good thing the big room hadn't been furnished, as many warriors as it held now.

"*Torchay.*" Kallista called him to her, needing the calm strength his magic gave.

The Tayo Dai swept past her to join the fight—only six of them, but gratefully welcomed—while Torchay clasped her outstretched hand. His powerful magic poured into her. The instant Kallista bound it with the rest, the leech magic squalled as it vaporized in a wisp of smoke—as if Torchay's magic had grown so attuned to hers, she didn't have to consciously shape the whole for it to act.

"*No-o-o-ooo!*" The demon shrieked with both Shathina's voice and its own in the dreamplane.

Torchay brought Kallista's hand to his lips for a kiss, his eyes holding hers for an instant before he released her and plunged back into the battle. "Fox, Obed, Leyja—all of you go."

The demon lashed out at the three not yet bound back in. Kallista leaped forward to defend them, and went nowhere, restrained by Aisse and Padrey. She threw magic out to stop it, to shield her three, but without Fox's order—

The magic skidded, almost missed them in its haste, but Padrey's magic was not so wildly impulsive as Stone's. It *listened* better. Or something. The shields were weak, the approach skewed, but it served. Long enough for the three warriors to reach her and clasp her hands.

Magic roared into her—Fox's order, Obed's truth, Leyja's unconditional love. Tears fell through Kallista's laughter and she hugged them to her, hugged their magic tight, then bound it into the web as the demon fought to keep them apart.

I love you, she sent to her godmarked. *Love you all so much. Take care of each other.*

Torchay swung around, leaving the fight to others, his eyes wide. "Kallista, what—"

She smiled at him as she gathered the magic in her hands. She shaped it for sleep. Those not directly involved in the fight with the demon would only get in the way. She didn't have to conserve anything. It wasn't her own strength that fought here. The One would provide whatever was needed. She whispered her instructions to the magic and set it loose.

Everyone in the embassy slowly crumpled to the floor. Daryathi champions, Adaran bodyguards, clerks, servants, even the children slept under her protective shielding. Everyone save Shakiri Shathina, Kallista, and her godmarked iliasti.

"Now," Kallista said. "It is as it should be. You and yours, me and mine."

"Not fair!" the demon whined. "You have more than I do."

"True. The power of the One is so vast, it must be spread out through more of us." She sighed. "It's too bad the One chose to use such a weak vessel as myself. But here we are."

She gathered magic and the demon attacked, tearing at her, at her links. They shuddered, but held. They would hold no matter what. Kallista knew that now. Only death could part her from those she loved, and even that was not final. She would see them again. And Stone was waiting.

Kallista named the magic. *Zughralithiss. Khoriseth.* The smaller demon still existed somewhere inside its parent. She threw the magic out and immediately called more. Khoriseth had been able to—yes, it *quenched* the magic. Put out the fire before it burned much. No matter. She had more demon-killer to send.

Again and again, Kallista called, shaped, sent. Again and again, the demon fought it off, clawing at her, tearing off bits of her self as her magic ate away its substance. Even with the magic pouring into her, shoring her up, bracing her against the awful attacks, she knew it would be a close-run thing.

Yes, she had the infinite, endless power of the One behind her, but she herself was all too mortal. She wasn't meant for so much power. But she would stand. She would endure. She would use what the One had given her to destroy this demon even if it destroyed her in the doing. The One had accepted what she had offered, and what she had offered up was her whole self. All of her heart, her body, her soul. All of her love.

Kallista opened herself and let the magic pour in, arms spread, head back, her beloved iliasti behind her, beside her, holding her up.

The magic filled her until her body felt separated into the tiny bits that formed her, no longer quite real, no longer connected into a whole, because the magic needed the space between all her bits.

She *saw*. Saw the writhing, twisted evil of the demon woven through the twisted, hate-filled heart of Shathina. She saw her willful, loyal Keldrey lying asleep in the corridor at the head of a troop where he had pushed out from the nursery, driving back their attackers. She saw her children, shining with promise and innocence, glowing with the love showered on them. She saw her godmarked, saw their hearts, their true selves, known already through the magic that bound them together.

There, shining in the distance, impossibly far away yet as close as a whisper, she saw the light of the One. Love, joy and righteous anger shivered through her, shuddered in the magic.

"*Zughralithiss*," she whispered. "*Khoriseth*."

The magic exploded from her, leaving all her bits and pieces stranded in their isolation. Kallista *saw* the magic fall on the demon, saw it consume all the darkness remaining before it flashed outward, into Mestada and beyond, in the instant she had left before the isolated bits of herself crumbled into oblivion.

Chapter Thirty-Three

"No! Goddess, *no*." Obed's knees failed. He would have fallen as Kallista's body went limp in their arms, but for the others holding him up. He couldn't lose her now, after all this.

"Obed!" Torchay reached across her, gripped his arm. "We have to go after her. Are you with me, man?"

"Wait, what are you doing?" Leyja caught Torchay's queue and yanked hard for his attention.

"She taught us how," Obed said, frantic to begin. "We won't put ourselves in danger. Look to her."

"Joh, you're in charge," Torchay said. "See if you can get ours awake before Shathina's. Kel first."

"Right." Joh drew away, taking the younger ones with him.

Obed slid to the floor in unison with Torchay, holding Kallista between them.

"She's not breathing," Leyja said, her hand on Kallista's throat. "Her heart's stopped."

"So breathe for her," Torchay said. "You kept me alive. You can do it for her."

"How long?"

"Till we bring her back," Obed snapped, losing patience.

He closed his eyes. For a moment, he thought his fear would prevent him from escaping his body. Then he somehow heard the beating of Torchay's heart beyond Kallista between them. Obed reached out, across Kallista, below Leyja where she worked. He caught Torchay's hand reaching for his, and together they stepped up to the dreamplane.

The gray mist looked just as it had before, splotched with bright glowing wisps of color. Obed turned in a circle, Torchay moving with him. Even here, they held onto each other. Especially here.

"Where is she?" Torchay sounded as desperate as Obed felt. "She's here. I know she is. She's no' gone, no' yet."

Obed fought back despair. Torchay's words felt right, but the demon had been so strong, the fight so terrible— Obed clung to one thing. Kallista said he held truth. He could see the truth, know it. So where was the truth here, in this place?

He turned round again, searching harder. The mists billowed up, and in one place, they thinned. Obed *looked*.

"*Oh Goddess.*" The groan tore from his throat. Jerking Torchay after him, Obed ran.

Kallista lay on the mist, flat and insubstantial, shattered into tiny pieces as if she'd become a mosaic of herself. Was it truly Kallista, or just an image of what they sought? Obed found the truth. This was Kallista.

"*Hurry.*"

At the sound of the familiar voice, Obed whipped around to see Stone, whole and alive, standing on the dreamfog. Illusion? *Truth.*

Stone stopped them before they could leap across the distance to embrace him. "No time for that. You have to save her. She doesn't think she can go back."

"Save her *how?*" Torchay's voice was rough with pain. "She's in pieces. We don't have any magic."

Stone's smile was so beautiful, it made Obed's heart ache. "The only magic you need is love."

"That, we've got." Obed looked down at the broken thing that was Kallista. Could they just . . . sweep her back together?

He let go of Torchay and knelt beside her, afraid to try, afraid not to. What if it didn't work? But he'd rather try and fail than not even try. Carefully, to be sure he didn't miss any, Obed brushed his hands through the fog, pushing the bits of mosaic together. They clung to his fingers, making him shiver like touching her often did. And the bits clung to each other.

"Help me." Obed kept sweeping as he glanced up at Torchay. "It's working. She's going back together. She's not like broken glass. More like clay. She sticks."

Torchay's face held the panic Obed felt. "She looks . . . wrong. Lumpy."

She did. The pieces stuck where he scooped them, misshapen and awkward. "She's *together*." Obed deliberately refused to look any more than necessary. "If we get her back where she belongs, she'll sort it all out."

"What if she doesn't? What if we get her back and she's no' all there?"

"I don't care." Obed shook his head hard enough to send his hair flying, sweeping bits of Kallista back into a whole all the while. "I can't leave her here like this. If she comes back crippled or simple, they can select a new Reinine and I'll take her home to the mountains and take care of her there. I'll feed her, clean her, carry her on my back—whatever I have to do, whether you or anyone else comes with me."

"You know I'll be there." Torchay knelt on the other side of the Kallista bits, working more slowly and carefully than Obed, trying to pat her back into proper shape.

"Stone said to hurry," Obed reminded him.

"That's right, he did." Torchay swept faster, forming the leg bits into a lopsided ball. "That's a good sign, isn't it! That Stone was here?"

"He's gone?" Obed took half an instant to look around.

"Aye. But he came." Torchay worked with Obed to press the pieces of Kallista's head together with extra care.

"Have we got everything?" Obed stirred the streamers of dreamfog, terrified they might leave something vital behind.

"I don't see any more pieces." Torchay frowned. "How do we get her back into herself? We were assuming she'd be conscious if we had to come get her."

"Do you remember how she put you back, the first time you came here?"

"Perhaps."

"We can only try." Obed narrowed his eyes, looking at the dream-Kallista they'd mashed together. Some of the lumps seemed to be smoothing out, the fingers separating from the solid mass he'd pressed them into. "Does she look better to you?"

Torchay took a deep breath and closed his eyes a moment before turning his head to look, as if afraid of what he might see. His eyes widened when he opened them and the tension on his face eased. "Aye. She does." He pointed. "Her legs are almost the same length again."

"So let's put her back where she belongs." Obed clasped Kallista's hand and reached across for Torchay's. "Surely she'll stick there too."

"If she doesn't, we'll hold her down till she does." Torchay sounded grim, but his eyes shone with hope as he met Obed's gaze and took his hand. Torchay wrapped his hand around Kallista's and together, they stepped out of the dreamplane.

Light pierced her eyelids. Kallista expected that. Heaven would be filled with light.

What she hadn't expected was pain. She hurt all over. A groan escaped her before she could bite it back. It was rude to groan in heaven, wasn't it?

"Kallista?" The voice in her ear belonging to the body at her back wasn't the one she expected. For one thing, it was female. Stone wasn't.

"Leyja?" Kallista's voice sounded as rough as she felt. "I thought I was dead."

"So did I." Leyja hugged her, actually weeping, to Kallista's shock. Leyja hated tears more than Kallista. "So did we all, even after Torchay and Obed went to bring you back."

Leyja sat up and Kallista collapsed onto her back. She cracked an eye open and saw Leyja wipe both eyes with the heels of her hands before putting on a work face.

"Can you look at me, sweeting?" Leyja began her medic's examination as Torchay and Obed skidded into the room.

"Blessed be," Obed whispered, staring at her.

"Kallista?" Torchay moved hesitantly toward the bed. "How are you feeling?"

"Terrible." She winced as Leyja probed a tender spot. "Wonderful." Kallista stretched hands out to both of them, smiling as they came. "I didn't think I would get to see our babies grow up."

These tears she didn't mind so much, the happy kind. When the four of them had cried on each other all Kallista could stand, Leyja and Torchay consented to help her sit up. "Where are the others?" she asked. "How are they?"

"All well," Torchay said. "Keldrey took a bad cut across the ribs, but as long as you don't hug him too hard round the middle, he's well enough. They're just outside, anxious to see you, waiting their turn. We didn't want to overwhelm you."

"Overwhelm, overwhelm!" Kallista beckoned with both arms, her aches and exhaustion leaving faster with every moment. "Fox!" she called. "Aisse, Joh—*all of you,* come!"

They burst through the door with a happy babble of sound. Kallista hugged and kissed every one of them. She insisted that Keldrey open his invalid's wrap-front shirt to show her his wound. She called magic, delighting that she could, and healed him enough that she could hug him tight. She kissed Fox's nearsighted eyes and laughed when Aisse and Viyelle climbed onto the bed with her for their hugs. Joh's hair was loose this late in the day, spilling unbound over his shoulders in a silky brown curtain around her as they kissed. Kallista had to grab hold of Padrey and pull him from behind the others to hug him. Would he ever be comfortable with them?

"So," she said, when the tears were dried and her ilian ranged around her, "What's happened? How long has it been?"

"Three endless days," Obed said. "It's Peaceday."

The end of the week that had begun with the trial on Firstday. So much had happened in that short time.

"Shathina is dead?"

Obed nodded. "Bekaara is Head of Line now. She's already arranged to remarry Thalassa's father. All the slaves have been set free. The embassy is packed with freed slaves, and more are at Shakiri House. Bekaara has pledged to help us."

"We've already started sending them downriver to the coast," Viyelle said. "To be transported home. So many are children, we can't send them over the mountains."

"No protests from the en-Kameral?" Kallista was surprised. "What happened to the riots? To the Samerics?"

"Some of them died." Viyelle shifted position, sitting cross-legged on the bed. "But not as many as I would have thought, from the tales of your first demon."

Kallista shifted too, leaning back against—she looked to see—against Fox and Keldrey. "I saw the magic blow out, after it destroyed the demon. It didn't kill half the city?"

"Apparently not." Joh swept his hair forward over a shoulder in a futile attempt to control it. "It—it seems to have broken something loose. Or perhaps bestowed something new."

"What?" Kallista's patience had never been long.

"Magic." Aisse pillowed her head on Kallista's lap and said nothing more. Kallista looked back to Joh for answers.

"People are coming from everywhere," he said, "manifesting magic they swear they never had before, hundreds of them. The High Prelate is frantic, wondering how to train them all." He paused. "She's asked for our help."

"We'll give what help we can, of course." Kallista idly stroked Aisse's hair as she thought. "Hundreds—half the population? A quarter?"

Joh considered. "About a quarter, I'd say. Maybe a little less. About the same as the ratio of naitani in Adara."

"So." Kallista held up her hand and ticked items off on her fingers. "We have our son home with us. The local naitani have pried themselves out of their temple isolation. The justice system is beginning to reform. Magic has been restored in Daryath. The Adaran slaves are freed. The last demon is destroyed. Anything else we've forgotten to do?"

Everyone went still, ticking through their own mental lists, but before anyone could speak, the door opened and Lorynda peered in. The fearful expression on her face was swallowed up by joy as she threw the door wide and ran across the room, leading the children's invasion.

She scrambled onto the bed to hug her mother, then bounced off again to help Niona and Rozite lift the little ones up. Kallista hugged as many of them as she could, together and separately, not bothering to hide her joyous tears.

"See? I *told* you she was awake," Lorynda announced to the nursery servants trailing behind. She climbed back up to claim a place under her mother's arm.

"Let them stay." Kallista lifted Omri onto her lap before putting her arm back around Rozite as the servants discreetly vanished.

"I believe there might be one thing left for us to do," Torchay said, pulling Sky into a rough embrace.

"And what could that possibly be?" Kallista hugged her children tight, worried. *Had* they left something undone?

"It's time we took this mob home and lived happily ever af—well, for however long we can." Torchay cocked a significant eyebrow at Lorynda. "Depending on how many of them decide to manifest their magic early."

Was that how Lorynda—? Kallista eyed her red-haired daughter. Just what had all that magic done when she'd been pregnant with the twins? She exchanged a glance with Torchay and the others.

Their future might not be quite as calm and peaceful as she might have hoped, especially when the children started growing into teenagers. But it would be full of the gifts of the One—family, laughter, and most of all, with the eternal gift—love.

APPENDICES

APPENDIX 1
CAST OF CHARACTERS

The Adaran Royal Family

Kallista Varyl – Reinine of All Adara and Godstruck of the One
Torchay Omvir – ilias, bodyguard & sergeant in Adaran army
Stone Varyl vo'Tsekrish – ilias, former Tibran warrior
Obed im-Shakiri – ilias, nine-marked ex-dedicat from Daryath
Fox Varyl vo'Tsekrish – ilias, former Tibran warrior
Aisse Varyl vo'Haav – ilias, Tibran emigre
Joh Suteny – ilias, retired lieutenant in Adaran infantry
Viyelle Torvyll – ilias, prinsipella of Shaluine in Adara
Merinda Kyndir – ilias, East magic naitan
Leyja Byrek – ilias, bodyguard and ilias of current & former Reinine
Keldrey Borr – ilias, bodyguard and ilias of current & former Reinine

The Children of Royal Family

Rozite – age 6, daughter of Kallista & Stone, twin to Lorynda
Lorynda – age 6, daughter of Kallista & Torchay, twin to Rozite
Niona – age 6, daughter of Aisse & Fox
Tigre – age 5, son of Aisse & Joh
Sky – age 5, son of Merinda & Stone
Vonni – age 4, son of Viyelle & Fox
River – age 3, son of Aisse & Fox
Omri – age 3, son of Kallista & Obed
Sharra – age 2, daughter of Viyelle & Joh
Lissta – age 1, daughter of Aisse & Keldrey

The Adarans

Gweric vo'Tsekrish – West magic naitan & Tibran emigre
Edyne – High Steward in Arikon palace
Namida Chand – Adaran ambassador to Daryath
Allanda Vartain – ilias to Namida, lawyer specializing in Daryathi law

The Adarans (Continued)

Jondi – bodyguard to Reinine
Samri – bodyguard to Reinine
Bay – bodyguard to Reinine
Kerry – bodyguard to Gweric
Genista Fynli – bodyguard to Reinine's children
Sandrey – bodyguard to Reinine's children
Taylin – farspeaker & secretary to Reinine
Fenetta – farspeaker & secretary in Arikon palace
Ronda Kargyll – captain of Adaran army escort
Padrey Emtal – Adaran thief in Daryathi capital, Mestada
Nanda Suverr – Padrey's sedil, also in Mestada
Penna Suverr – Nanda's oldest child
Tommey – servant in household with Nanda & Penna
Serysta Reinine – Adaran ruler previous to Kallista, killed at end of rebellion
Penrith Ko – long-dead legendary member of Tayo Dai, Islander
Hoban Felessan – long-dead legendary member of Tayo Dai, from far north

The Daryathi

Bekaara il-Shakiri – Obed's cousin & heir to Shakiri Line
Thalassu il-Shukiri – Bekaara's daughter
Thiben – Bekaara's ex-husband, father to Thalassa
Shaneen il-Shakiri – Obed's deceased mother, Bekaara's younger sister
Shakiri Shathina – Bekaara's mother, Obed's aunt, Head of Shakiri Line
Habadra Khori – Head of Habadra Line, rivals to Shakiri
Chani il-Habadra – Khori's daughter & heir to Habadra Line
Night Varyl-sa – gift from Habadra Khori to Varyl Line
Nur im-Nathain – West magic "nathain," Truthsayer
Maathin – Head justiciar in Mestada
Murat Konethi-ti – Grandmaster of Edabi Skola
Ruel Dobruk-sa – champion & dedicat-candidate at Edabi Skola
Athen im-Nuredi – dedicat at Edabi Skola
Yanith Nabili-tha – dedicat at Edabi skola

The Daryathi (Continued)

Kassid Penthili-tha – "fuzzhead" at Edabi Skola
Farrin Chosidi-sa – champion at Edabi Skola
Jaget – gatekeeper at Edabi Skola
Cori – Elder of Edabi village
Lutha – Elder of Edabi village
Sothi – Elder of Edabi village
Sadim – metalsmith in Edabi village
Falon One-Eye – Dockside thug in Mestada
Kerik – champion-for-hire in Mestada
Zyan Habadra-sa – housekeeper to Habadra House
Zatha Penthili-ti – housekeeper to Penthili House

The Demons

Khoriseth
Zughralithiss
Tchyrizel (destroyed in Tibre)

APPENDIX 2
ADARAN CALENDAR

The Adaran year has 389 days, divided into forty-three weeks, plus two days for year's end and beginning. The weeks are nine days long—six weekdays, which are numbered (Firstday, Secondday, Thirdday, etc.), and three days for the week's end: Graceday, Hopeday and Peaceday.

There are eleven months in the year. Seven months are 35 days long, four have 36 days—exactly four of the nine-day weeks.

The months are: Donis, Lutis, Terris, Miel, Katenda, Norenda, Vendra, Silba, Orade, Forende, Tyrell.

Miel, Norenda, Orade and Tyrell are the thirty-six-day months. The year being slightly longer, the seasons are slightly longer as well. The year changes at midwinter in Adara with the two-day year's end holiday.

APPENDIX 3
COMPASS MAGIC

The magic is represented by the compass rose symbol. The red rose in the center stands for the One God from whom all things come, including the gifts of magic. About twenty percent of women and ten percent of men have a magic gift. A person is born with magic, or they are not, but whether one is gifted is not generally known until puberty when most magic manifests.

South is represented by a yellow flame. South magic is the magic of hearth and home, and thus the origin of fire magic, as well as more practical magics like those that preserve cloth or food, pest control, brewing and so on. The majority of those with gifts of magic have South magic.

East magic is the next most frequently encountered. East magic has to do with living things, with birth and other beginnings. In the compass rose symbol, it is represented by a green twining vine. East magic is agriculture and animal husbandry, fertility, health and medicine and similar sorts of things.

North magic has to do with non-living things, such as earth, water, wind, electricity and metals. It shows up in the compass rose as a blue lightning bolt. North magicians are relatively rare. They have talents for mining, controlling winds, forging, earth moving and other things of that sort.

West magic is the rarest of the four. It is represented by a black briar, and has to do with death, endings and mysteries. Some West magic, such as far-speaking and far-seeing, was folded into North magic when West magic and naitani were suppressed, because it was too useful. Other types of West magic, such as foreseeing or speaking with ghosts, vanished. West magic is not easily explained and makes most people—even others with magic—uneasy.

• One (1) – Number for the One God. The One is made up of many parts, but is still One.

• Two (2) – Humanity, and by extension, all creation, because of duality of sexes, two arms, two legs, two eyes, ears, etc.

• Three (3) – "Perfection," humankind plus God.

• Four (4) – Family, human community.

• Seven (7) – A "bad" number, indicates imperfection, falling short, flaws. A number for demons and bad omens.

• Eight (8) – Two fours, the number of human completion, human understanding.

• Nine (9) – Three threes, perfection completed.

• Twelve (12) has a faint symbolism, a feeling of family completed—which is perhaps why it's considered the maximum number of adults married into an ilian—but it's not as important as the other numbers.

Numbers have less symbolism than colors. Most Adarans wouldn't necessarily consider having seven in an ilian bad luck, but having three, four, eight or nine of something would be a good omen.